T0328516

NOW
FOLLOWING
YOU

NOW
FOLLOWING
YOU

Fiona Snyckers

Publication © Modjaji Books 2015
Text © Fiona Snyckers 2015

First published in 2015 by Modjaji Books Pty Ltd
info@modjajibooks.co.za
www.modjajibooks.co.za

ISBN 978-1-928215-06-6

Editor: Helen Moffett
Book design and layout: Monique Cleghorn & Liz Gowans
Cover artwork: Danielle Clough
Cover design: Danielle Clough & Liz Gowans
Author photograph: Jeanette Verster

Printed and bound by Mega Digital, Cape Town
Set in Palatino Linotype and Avenir Next Condensed

1

Jamie Burchell flexed her fingers, shifted in her seat, and forced herself to focus on the screen.

Part of her longed to jump up and make another cup of tea, check her Facebook page, let the cats in. To do anything, in short, that didn't involve squeezing words out of the toothpaste tube of her mind and onto the screen. But it was already 9am and she needed to get this instalment posted.

Her eyes slid to the window. The jacaranda trees were starting to take on a faintly purple haze.

Then she frowned.

There was a toddler running around in the road. He seemed perfectly happy – stopping now and then to squat down and examine a tiny stone or whatever took his fancy. But the point was, he was right there in the middle of the road.

Jamie stood up and peered through the glass, sure she would spot whoever was looking after him. Toddlers didn't go for walks all by themselves, not even in this quiet suburb.

A car drove past, close enough for the rush of air to knock the little boy onto his well-padded bottom.

"What...?"

Grabbing the remote for her gate, Jamie slipped on her shoes and rushed out of the house.

"Hey, little guy." She crossed the road and scooped the toddler into her arms. "Hey, buddy. What are you doing out here all on your own?" Her eyes swivelled, looking for an adult who might be in charge of him.

There was no one around. Normally at this time of day, there were gardeners mowing lawns and domestic workers taking their breakfast breaks. Today the street was deserted.

"Where do you live, buddy? Huh? Where's home?" A slight panic fluttered in her as she realised the child was probably too young to answer any of these questions. Jamie was no expert, but he seemed barely to be at the "mama" and "dada" stage. The chances that he was going to start reciting his name, address, and mother's cellphone number seemed remote.

She tried pointing in different directions and saying, "Where's mama? Where's mama?" but he just grinned and bounced in her arms and pointed at whatever she was pointing at.

"Oh, dear."

Jamie pulled herself together. Toddlers didn't appear out of thin air. He must have come from one of the houses along the street. She shifted him onto her hip and walked up and down, looking for an open gate or a door left ajar. There was nothing. Every house was shut up tight.

"What am I going to do with you, little guy?"

He looked up as she spoke. She stared down into his chocolate-drop eyes and her heart stumbled in her chest.

"Dooce," he said, as though he'd been considering her question. "Dzooce."

It took her a moment.

"Juice?" she ventured. "You want some juice?"

From the way his legs kicked against her and the gummy smile that broke out across his face, it seemed she'd translated correctly.

"Well, I can't leave you out here on your own..."

Feeling like a baby-snatcher, Jamie took one last look around and pressed the remote to open her gate.

"Okay, bud. Let's go inside and get you some juice."

She took him into her house and sat him down on one of her kitchen chairs. He promptly lurched sideways. She leapt forward and caught him approximately one second before his head connected with the tiled floor.

"Oh, my goodness! No, don't cry. Don't cry, sweetheart. I'm sorry."

It wasn't his near-miss with the kitchen floor that was making him wail, she realised, but the distress in her voice. So she held him close and did a little jiggly dance around the room, talking soothingly to him all the while.

"Okay, no more chairs for you, big guy." She put him down on the floor once he'd stopped crying. Sweating a little, she turned to the fridge to get out some juice. She'd poured almost a full glass when the image of those blindingly white little teeth came into her mind. Along with the thought that it might not be the best idea to bathe them in the concentrated sugar of fruit juice.

So she poured two-thirds of the juice out and filled the rest up with water. Feeling grown up and responsible, she handed him the glass.

"There," she said. "What do you say to that, sweetie?"

He snatched the glass from her hands, and promptly upended it all over his face and shirt. As the icy-cold liquid hit his skin he started to wail again, flinging the glass onto the floor, where it smashed into pieces.

"Fuck. Oh, fuck! The glass. You'll cut yourself."

She lifted him up in her arms and awkwardly set about cleaning up, wielding a mop one-handed. She hadn't realised parents needed to be ambidextrous. Only once every single shard had been cleared away did she wipe him and set him down again.

"You need a dry T-shirt, sweetie, but that'll have to do for now. Now let's try the juice thing again."

This time she filled a glass and held it to his lips so he could sip from it safely. He almost drained the glass. "You were really thirsty, weren't you, darling? Now let's put you down on this lovely soft carpet where you can't hurt yourself."

"Psss!" he said. "Psss, psss!"

"What's a psss?"

He toddled over to the window to look out into the garden.

"Oh, you're talking about the pussycat, aren't you? Yes, that's Watson. He's my pussycat and he just loves to tease the neighbour's dog."

9

They watched together as Watson picked his way along the branch of a tree that hung over Jamie's wall and stretched into her neighbour's property. The golden retriever next door went hysterical with fury at the sight of his enemy sitting just out of reach. Radiating smugness, Watson stropped his claws on the branch, then settled down to eyeball the furious dog.

Jamie giggled. "He always does that. It drives the poor doggie crazy."

"Doddie," said her new friend. "Pore doddie."

"Yes, poor doggie." She hugged him in delight. "And aren't you just the cleverest little boy in the whole wide world?"

He stretched out his arms longingly to the cat. "Psss!"

"You want to go and cuddle the kitty? Of course you do. I bet he'll love you. And maybe my other kitty will come along and say hello, too. His name is Holmes and he's also super cuddly."

She took his hand and led him towards the patio door. They had hardly gone two steps when the bell at her front gate rang.

"Now, who can that be?"

It rang again. And again, and again. Then the person leaned their thumb on the button so that the bell rang in one long, demented peal.

"Why do people have to be so impatient? Okay, okay, I'm coming. Jeez!"

Jamie peeped out the kitchen window. There was a man standing at her gate. He was hopping from foot to foot and grimacing. As she watched, he took his thumb off her doorbell and shook her gate with both hands. Then he turned back to the bell again. His brown hair was standing up in tufts all over his head.

He looked … unbalanced, Jamie decided.

"I think you'd better stay in here, angel." She put the boy back down on the carpet and handed him a plastic spatula to play with. "I'll go and see what the crazy man wants."

She went out into her driveway, and the noise switched off like magic.

"Oh, thank God!" the man said when he saw her. "I'm looking for my son. Have you seen him? He's eighteen months old and he's wearing blue jeans and a red shirt. And ... and trainers. Have you seen him?"

"Your son?" Jamie asked, puzzled.

"Yes! My son. He might have been on the sidewalk, or even..." He broke off to scrub his hands over his face. "Or even in the road. Have you seen him? His name is Ben."

She was opening her mouth to answer him when he suddenly lost it.

"BEN!" he yelled, so loudly that Jamie jumped. "Ben! Oh my God!"

Jamie whirled around to see that her little friend had toddled out of the door behind her, and was now standing and grinning at the man.

"You found him! Oh thank God!"

Jamie would have been the first to admit that she wasn't doing a superb job of looking after the little boy, but even she knew better than to hand him over to the first random stranger who came to claim him.

"I'm sorry, but I have to be careful. How do I know he's your son?"

"Yes, yes," the man said. "I'm white and he's black. I know that. Big deal. But I can assure you he's still my son. I adopted him at birth. He's mine and I'd like him back. Look," he added when she hesitated. "Ask him who I am. Go ahead."

"Okay..." She bent down to pick the little boy up again, lingering over the action, loving the way his body fitted against hers. "Who's that?" she asked, pointing to the man. "Who's that man?"

He just giggled and turned his face into her arm.

"Who am I, Ben?" the man asked in a cracked voice. He had a slight American accent, Jamie noticed. "Who am I?"

The boy turned a laughing face toward the man and said as clear as a bell, "Dada!" Then in a louder voice, on a rising giggle, "Dada, Dada, Daddeeee!" He wriggled out of Jamie's arms and ran toward the gate on sturdy legs, his arms outstretched. "Dada!"

Jamie pressed her remote to open the gate and the man ran inside to sweep the boy up into his arms and cover him in kisses. "Ben!" he muttered. "My Ben. Oh God, I thought you were gone."

Jamie smiled at the reunion. It was nice to feel she'd done a good deed. She stepped closer to the man, prepared to accept his thanks.

"What the hell did you think you were doing – snatching him like that and taking him into your house? Do you have any idea how worried I've been? He could have been killed by a car," he snarled.

Caught off guard, Jamie found herself apologising. "I'm sorry, but I didn't know where he'd come from."

"Oh, sure. And I suppose you spent ages ringing the doorbells of every house in the street. I live next door to you. Right next door! And you couldn't even be bothered to knock and ask if I might possibly be missing my son."

"Look, he was thirsty. He might have been dehydrated for all I knew, so I just…"

"Thirsty?" the man exploded. "Well, that explains why he's covered in juice and soaked to the skin. You decided to throw the juice all over him, is that it?"

Jamie folded her arms across her chest and glared at him. "You might at least thank me for…"

"Fuck," the little boy interrupted happily. "Oh, fuck."

Cringing, Jamie watched as a tide of red surged into the man's cheeks.

"What did he just say?"

"Look, I'm sorry," she babbled. "I might accidentally have said that word in front of him. You see, he had just spilled the juice all over himself and smashed a glass, and I was still rattled from when he almost fell off the kitchen chair and I…"

"Oh, fantastic. Not only do you grab my son off the street, but you drench him in cold juice, expose him to cut glass, and let him fall off a chair. Oh, and you teach him his first curse word too. And I'm supposed to thank you?"

"You might at least…"

"You might at least have tried to find out who he belonged to. Now, will you let me out of here so I can take him back home?"

Feeling somewhat shaken, Jamie pressed the button again to open the gate and watched as he marched away. The little boy turned in his arms to give her a mile-wide smile. Then he lifted one chubby hand and waved at her.

"Wait!" Jamie said.

The man turned back to her with a sigh. "What now?"

"Can I ... I mean, could you...?"

"Could I what?"

"Could I possibly ... see him again? Ben, I mean. We kind of bonded, and I'd really love to spend some time with him, and..."

The man snorted. "Yeah, right. That's going to happen."

He turned and walked away.

2

. . . .

Jamie Burchell @jamieburchell
I've just met the rudest man in the whole of South Africa.

Jamie Burchell @jamieburchell
I rescued his son from being squished by a car and he screamed at me like it was all my fault.

Amanda Stanislau @stani2
@jamieburchell OMG! He sounds horrible! What happened?

Jamie Burchell @jamieburchell
@stani2 I found his toddler wandering in the street & instead of saying thanks he yelled like I'd kidnapped the kid.

Gugu Motsepeng @gugz
@jamieburchell Dude, he sounds like a psycho.

Jamie Burchell @jamieburchell
@gugz: I know, right?

Cyril Attlee @inthemiddlecyril
@jamieburchell Maybe he was angry with himself for losing the kid and took it out on you?

Jamie Burchell @jamieburchell
@inthemiddlecyril: That's what I'm thinking too…

Jamie felt calmer after pouring out her indignation on Twitter and Facebook. The sympathy of her virtual friends never failed to soothe her. They didn't question her version of events or second-guess her.

It was only her own conscience that pricked her as she remembered how she'd been just about to take Ben to visit the cat instead of trying to find out where he lived.

Obviously, she would have got around to that eventually. And obviously it was important to keep him calm and happy before she went wandering the streets with him. But she had to admit she'd enjoyed his company so much, she'd been in no hurry to find out who he belonged to.

Even now, hours later, she wanted to hold him again. She'd never clicked with a child like that, not ever. At twenty-eight, she was already an aunt and had several friends with babies, but none of them had made her feel like this. None of them had inspired her with a desire to scoop them up and keep them all to herself forever.

She pressed her knuckles to her temples. Maybe she *was* turning into a baby snatcher.

Her ears pricked as she heard a key turning in the lock at her front door.

"Is that you, Faith?" she called out.

"Yes, Jamie. Yes, it is me."

The subtext was, "Of course it's me. Who else would be letting themselves into your house at ten o'clock in the morning?" Faith had a way of cramming a lot of subtext into a few words.

Jamie bounded out to greet the housekeeper.

15

"So, how was your weekend?"

"It was fine, thanks. I went shopping in town on Saturday and then I went to church on Sunday. I had the grandchildren with me all the time, so I am tired this morning."

To illustrate this, she sat down on a kitchen chair and sighed. Then she reached out a hand to flip the kettle on.

"You had the kids the whole weekend? Where were their mothers?"

"My daughters were spending time with their boyfriends." Noticing the tightening of Jamie's lips, Faith added. "They are paying for their children, those fathers. They are good fathers. If my daughters neglect them, they will stop paying. I don't mind having the children for the weekend. It's just that they make me tired. I am too tired to polish the furniture today. I will do it tomorrow."

"That's fine." Jamie's interest in furniture-polishing was minimal. It was information she wanted from Faith, not gleaming wood. "So, listen. You know my next-door neighbour?"

"That side?" Faith pointed towards the west.

"No, not the Greek couple. The other side. The man with the little boy. Do you know anything about him?"

Faith started to heave herself out of the chair, but Jamie gestured for her to relax. "Don't get up. I'll make you tea while you talk."

"Yes, I know that man. The lady who works for him is Vuyiswa. She is my friend. She lives in Honeydew, just a few minutes from my house."

"So what do you know about him? Tell me everything."

Faith stirred sugar into the mug she had been handed while staring into the middle distance. Jamie fought the urge to hurry her along. Faith had her own narrative style, which involved ordering her thoughts in advance. When the story finally came it would be comprehensive and accurate, and that's what counted.

Faith took a long sip of her tea and sighed again, a contented sound this time.

"It was two years ago. No, not so much. Maybe one year and a

16

half. Before you come to live here. This man, this Mr Elliot, is working at home when a lady rings at his door. She is from far away. Far, far away. From up there." She gestured northwards. "She is a *bokufika.*"

"An immigrant," Jamie translated. "A Zimbabwean?"

"No, she is not from Zimbabwe. Her skin is very dark and her eyes are like this." Faith drew circles in the air in front of her face to indicate round eyes. "She is from somewhere else. Not Zimbabwe. Not Nigeria. Somewhere else."

"Okay. Was she looking for work?"

"Yes, she was looking for work. And Mr Elliot, he say to her he already has Vuyiswa to work for him. He has no work for her. But this lady, she can't stand up. She is so sick, she is fainting. And she is carrying a baby on her back. A baby that has just been born. Mr Elliot, he hears it crying and crying, like a baby that has not been fed."

Faith paused to take another sip of tea.

"Then what happened?"

"Mr Elliot, he runs to the front gate and he catches her before she faints. He carries her inside and lays her down on his bed. He picks up the baby, but it cries and cries. The mother, she has no milk for it. So he calls the ambulance and he rides in the ambulance with her to the hospital. And all the time, he is holding the baby like this." Faith mimed clutching a tiny baby to her heart. "The ambulance men, they have no milk for the baby, but they say there will be milk at the hospital. The child, he stops crying and he goes to sleep. Mr Elliot thinks he is dying, but it is not the child that dies, but the mother."

"No!"

"Yes, the mother dies in the ambulance before they get to the hospital."

"That's terrible. Did she have Aids?"

"No." Faith sighed. "Not Aids. It is a fever." She cupped her hands over her lower abdomen. "A very bad fever. Sometimes the mother gets it when she has just had a baby. If she doesn't get medicine very soon, she dies. This mother dies."

"That's awful. And what about the baby?"

"At the hospital, the nurses give Mr Elliot a bottle of milk for the baby. Then the social worker comes and she wants to take the baby, but Mr Elliot won't give it to her. He says it is his baby now and he will look after it. So then the police come and they try to take the baby, but Mr Elliot won't give it to them either. So then they arrest him and take him to jail."

"Good grief." Jamie turned her eyes towards Elliot's house.

"Yes. Mr Elliot, he asks to see a magistrate and he knows what to say to the magistrate because he is a lawyer, that one."

"A lawyer?" Jamie frowned. "Are you sure? What kind of lawyer spends so much time at home?"

Faith shrugged. "This is what Vuyiswa tells me. He talks to the magistrate for a long time and makes him believe it is best for the child to stay with him. Then there are papers and visits from social workers and a case in court, and after many, many months the child is his. That child is his own son now."

"And he's not married?"

"No, he is not married. You know this man, Jamie. You told me. You see him when you go for your run in the morning."

Jamie took a moment to process this. She closed her eyes and imagined adding mirrored sunglasses, a Jeep cap, a running vest and shorts to the crazy man who'd shouted at her that morning.

"No way! He's the hot guy? He's Hot Running Guy? Why didn't you tell me he lived right next door?"

"I thought you know already."

"I had no idea. I thought he just lived in the area. Well, that's one way to get over a crush fast. He's the rudest man I've ever met."

They both jumped as the metal flap on the letter box attached to Jamie's front gate slammed.

"What was that?"

Faith levered herself out of the chair to peer through the kitchen window. "Your neighbour. He has left something for you."

"Really?" Jamie ran to the window, then shrank away as she realised she could be seen. "What could he possibly want? Won't you go and get it for me, Faith? Please?"

This earned her a sideways look from the housekeeper. "I have to start the wash now."

"Please, Faith. I don't want him to see me and think I'm interested in whatever he's left for me. It's probably just an apology or something."

With a sigh, Faith snagged a bunch of keys off the hook and went to the front door.

———————

Jamie read the note again, cackling to herself and rubbing her hands together. If ever fate had handed her the opportunity to crush someone like a bug, it was now.

And another thing – your bloody cat keeps on annoying my dog. It's driving me crazy. I expect you to make it stop immediately!

Tom Elliot

"I expect you to make it stop immediately," Jamie mimicked in a prissy voice. "Immediately!" Laughing like a mad scientist, she started drafting replies.

Dear Tom,

No, that sounded too friendly.

Dear Mr Elliot,

I have had a word with my cat and he informs me that your dog started it.

Dear Mr Elliot,

I will train my cat to stop teasing your dog when you train your dog to stop reacting.

Dear Mr Elliot,
My cat says he will stop teasing your dog when your dog stops calling him names.

Dear Mr Elliot,
What you need is inner peace. I suggest you take up meditating.

Dear Mr Elliot,
Maybe if you spent less time worrying about my cat and more time keeping your own son safe…

No, that was a bit mean. She crumpled that one up and threw it in the bin. Not that he didn't deserve it. Her blood still boiled when she thought of the way he'd shouted at her for being irresponsible – when he was the one who'd let his child out into the road in the first place.

Still, she couldn't bring herself to use that against him.

Dear Dog,
Stop sending me passive-aggressive notes or I'll drop a piano on your head.
Sincerely,
The Cat

Yes! Perfect! That was the zinger. And if he was as fluent in sarcasm as he appeared to be, not a single nuance would be lost on him.

Still chuckling, Jamie folded up the note, threw a handbag onto her shoulder and let herself out of the house, calling goodbye to Faith as she went. She knew the housekeeper would be gone long before she got back from work.

Holmes and Watson had been sunning themselves in the driveway, but now they got to their feet and made a spirited attempt to escape into the street as she opened the gate. Nudging them back with the ease of long practice, Jamie shut the gate and kept an eye out for her neighbour. There was no sign of him.

The thatched house with its pale yellow walls was still and quiet.

He had a letterbox set into a pillar next to his gate, just like Jamie's. She opened it, shoved the note in, and let the flap fall with a clang. Then she walked away briskly.

She had only gone a few steps when something caught her eye and made her turn around.

There was a thick clump of bushes across the road. It grew against the wall of her opposite neighbour's house. Slowing her pace, she stared into the leaves.

Nothing stirred.

What exactly had she seen? Perhaps nothing more than a change in the quality of light out the corner of her eye. Maybe the suggestion of a rustle. As Jamie stared into the bushes, a tiny bird flew out of the leaves and landed on the telephone wire above her head.

Smiling to herself, she walked on.

3

The man watched Jamie walk away. She had a long, ground-eating stride that carried her swiftly to the end of the block and out of sight as she turned left. He wouldn't follow her, he decided. Not this time. What was the point when he knew exactly where she was going?

He was intrigued by the note she had posted into the letterbox, but there was no hurry for that either. He would read it soon enough. What worried him was that she had sensed him somehow. He had been as still as a mouse, as silent as an owl, but something had made her turn and stare at him until it felt as though her dark eyes were penetrating the foliage and looking right into his soul.

It had been both terrifying and exciting.

When he was sure that she wasn't about to turn around and come back home because she'd forgotten something, he eased his way out of the bushes and stood in the road brushing his clothes with his hands.

His heartbeat returned to normal and the sweat on his skin evaporated as a breeze swirled around him. Today was a good day, he reminded himself. The day he got to watch her at work. He only allowed himself to watch her once a week, and never twice in a row on the same day of the week. Nothing would be allowed to spoil that.

An hour later, he tucked his knees under a table in the cosy, fragrant atmosphere of Delucia's Bakery and Coffee Shop. It had been hard to restrain himself for a full hour, but now it was half-past twelve and the lunchtime rush was in full swing. Nobody gave him a second glance among all the other single men glued to their iPads and laptops as they forked food into their mouths.

He propped the menu up in front of his face and allowed himself the pleasure of watching her.

She looked just like her photographs. So many of them didn't. So many of them turned out to be a disappointment. His hands curled into fists at the thought.

They lied in their photographs. They took extreme close-ups of their faces, or posted pictures that were ten years old. They prevaricated and they falsified. Only Jamie had not lied. Her big, dark eyes were real. Her sunstreaked ponytail was real. Her body was real too – long and lean, but still feminine. And that face. It haunted him online and it haunted him now, with its wide, full mouth and strong bones.

Sweat beaded his upper lip. He rubbed a forefinger under his nose and tried to decide what to order.

Jamie dug her fists into the small of her back and stretched. "Busy today."

"It's picking up," Pumla agreed. "We're taking some of the lunchtime trade away from Antonia's, and also from the Earl & Badger. I think people like the fact that the food is fast and fresh."

"They like the fact that they can walk straight out of their offices and into a coffee shop," Jamie said. "No need to get the car out and fight for a parking space, not to mention paying for parking."

"Well, whatever. It's picking up, anyway. We turned over seventeen tables between midday and 2pm. That's up on last Monday. If you can hustle them out of here faster, we'll bring that up to twenty."

"People don't like to feel rushed when they're having their lunch-break."

Pumla shook her head. "They want their bills processed quickly so they can get back to the office. They want speed and efficiency."

"Then they can go to McDonald's."

"We don't want them to go to McDonald's. We want them to come here. Fresh, homemade food with McDonald's efficiency."

"That doesn't mean bringing them the bill before they've even asked for it. What if they want another cup of coffee? Or what if they change their minds about ordering a slice of cake to go with it?"

"You can't compare the price of one slice of cake with turning the whole table over so that someone else can order lunch from scratch."

By now they were standing toe-to-toe and arguing in fierce whispers. They sprang apart as the front door swung open.

Jamie fixed a professional smile on her face and picked up a couple of menus. "And if they feel rushed, they'll never come back again," she hissed, hoping for the last word.

"They'll come back because the food's good," Pumla hissed back, thwarting her.

The routine of welcoming the elderly couple settled Jamie down. They were regulars, so she made a special effort to make them feel at home.

The trouble with going into business with someone you'd known forever was that you kept reverting to old behaviour patterns. Every morning Jamie made a private vow not to fight with Pumla, and every afternoon she gave in to temptation.

They were too similar, that was the problem. At school, they'd competed for the same honours in academics and sport, and they'd hung out with the same crowd. Things got heated when they'd gone after the same boy at the age of seventeen. Then they'd found out that he was also looking for Mr Right, so no blood was spilt.

On the last day of high school, Jamie had honestly believed she would never lay eyes on Pumla Maseko again. The thought had not brought a single tear to her eye. She was going to hotel school to pursue a career in the hospitality industry, while Pumla had been accepted to study business science at the University of Cape Town.

But Jamie's younger sister Ella had stayed in touch with Pumla over the years. Ella had been the one to tell Jamie that Pumla had left her high-flying job in the corporate world to buy up a failing bakery only a block away from their childhood home. And when their grandmother had died and left them each an inheritance, Ella had conveyed the news to Jamie that Pumla was looking for an investor to add a small coffee shop onto the bakery.

Burnt out after nearly ten years of working in hotels and restaurants, Jamie had jumped at the chance. She'd been looking for a way to stay in the business, but to cut back on her hours so she could finally get serious about writing. The fact that the coffee shop was only open on week-days made it perfect. She hadn't thought for a moment that their old rivalry would be a problem.

They were grown-ups now, after all. Women of the world. They would put all that high school nonsense behind them and build a successful business together.

Jamie almost snorted at the memory. It had taken less than a week for the veneer of politeness to rub off and the bickering to start. But Delucia's was doing well, despite the friction between its owners. They'd each invested too much money not to take it seriously. So their squabbles came to nothing, and they kept their eyes on the prize.

"What bug crawled up your butt today?" Pumla asked as Jamie handed over the elderly couple's order. "Apart from the usual, I mean."

Jamie rolled her eyes. "Don't pretend you don't know. You saw my tweets and my Facebook update."

"Oh, yes." Pumla smirked. "Hot Running Guy turns out to be Mr Rude. How could I forget?"

"Do you know him? Has he ever been in here?"

"You know, I think he actually has. He's come in once or twice for breakfast, which is why you've never seen him. He was with a little black boy both times. I just assumed he was taking the maid's kid out for a treat."

"Well, he wasn't. That's his actual son."

"Poor kid. He'll never know his own culture. He'll never feel like he belongs anywhere. He's just a rich man's toy now."

"Yeah. He would have been so much better off if he'd been left with the police. Just think, he could have been raised in an orphanage and shunted around to different foster homes. What a great life he's missing out on."

"It's better than being picked up like a stray puppy."

Jamie arranged two slices of red velvet cake on a tray and added forks and napkins. She shot a sideways glance at her partner. "What's up with you? You're sounding pretty cranky yourself today."

"Nothing. I'm fine." Pumla set one decaf latte and one pot of Earl Grey tea down on the counter with a snap.

Jamie loaded everything onto the tray, added milk and sugar, and took it over to the customers. She fussed over them for a minute, checking that they had everything they wanted, then went back to the counter.

"Try again," she suggested, sliding the empty tray over to Pumla. "I know a snit when I hear one."

Pumla sighed. "It's nothing. Just the usual. My aunt came to visit me last night. I knew my mother had sent her and I was right. It was the same old story. Why don't I have a baby yet? Do I want to die alone? Don't I care that all their friends think I'm barren? Don't I realise that no man will ever want me if I don't prove I can have children first?"

"For goodness' sake, Pumla. You're a successful businesswoman. You've done really well for yourself, and you're only twenty-eight. There's plenty of time to have kids later on."

"Listen, if I fall pregnant right now – today – I'll be thirty-six years old when that child goes into Grade 1. I worked it out last night. I'd be the oldest mom on the playground. People would think I'm the granny coming to fetch it from school."

"Bullshit. Women are having babies later and later these days. Lots of them are waiting until they're over thirty-five before they even try to fall pregnant."

"Ja, well. Not anyone my mother knows." She put on plastic gloves and started rearranging the doughnut display behind the glass counter. "And then I see this man come in with a baby that isn't even his. And I think, that should be me. I should be the one with a toddler running around in here. And I wonder what's wrong with me for not even wanting that."

26

4

Eve couldn't stand the prodding, probing fingers any longer.

"Has the baby turned?" she asked. "Is it facing the right way now?"

The midwife spared her a glance, but continued to probe her abdomen with ungentle fingers. When she finally straightened up, she spoke to Abraham, not to Eve.

"The baby is still breech. It's lying with its head under the ribs and its buttocks on the right side of the pelvis. The knees are tucked up here on the left."

"What are the chances of it turning?" he asked.

"Small, at this stage. It could come any day now. I'll try to turn it during the delivery, but I might not be successful."

"And if you can't?"

The midwife wrinkled her nose. "Breech deliveries are always messy. There is usually tearing, and sometimes we have to use spoons to try to get the baby out. We are not always successful. I must remind you of the regulations governing the safe disposal of human remains. Especially with regards to the types of wood approved for coffins. New-growth pine only. Certainly no oak."

Abraham flushed and shifted his body as though to hide the little side table that the midwife's eyes had flickered towards.

"That's an antique," he told her. "It belongs to my wife's grandmother. She is very old."

Eve heard the clicking sound of her grandmother hobbling into the room with a stick.

"That table is registered and approved," the old lady told the midwife in her papery whisper. "I have the documents if you wish to see them."

"No need." The midwife closed her hemp sack. She stood up to go, but the old lady wasn't finished.

"What about an operation?" she asked.

The midwife turned slowly. "What did you say?"

"An operation to remove the baby from my granddaughter's womb. Otherwise she and the baby will surely die."

"Such things were outlawed many years ago."

"Not on Olympus," the old lady persisted. "There are rumours that they exist to this day. Especially among the families of the Controllers."

Eve exchanged an uneasy glance with her husband. "My grandmother is just joking, aren't you, Grandma?"

Jamie skimmed over that morning's blog post before scrolling down to the comments. The last few days had been her most productive in weeks. Instead of obsessing about her rude neighbour, she had channelled her anger into a flurry of writing. And if she sometimes caught herself longing for his little boy, she simply gathered up that emotion and used it to describe Eve's worry about the baby in her belly.

It was the first time maternal emotion had ever felt real to her, and when things felt real, she wrote them better.

Even her readers had sensed the change. Comments on her blog were up to thirty a day. That was a lot, even for the most successful bloggers – the kind that didn't have to go looking for a book deal, but had it handed to them on a plate.

Allowing herself to daydream, Jamie scrolled through the comments.

Posted by: **Shoobeedoo**
Ha! I knew the granny was going to turn out to be a rebel. Great post, thanks! Can't wait to see what happens next.

Posted by: **Cyril Att**
I can't work Abraham out. Is he a good guy or a bad guy? And I don't really have a handle on his relationship with Eve. Sometimes he seems to care about her and other times he seems quite cold.

Posted by: **Dineo**
Yoh! Dis is 1 messed up wrld uve made. Hw can d Controlers tayk ol d gud stuf n lv nuttin 4 d rest f d ppl?

Posted by: **Gugz**
OMG! Your not going to kill Eve off are you? I will be so pissed. You can't kill her and the baby.

Posted by: **Foully Wooing Won**
Can I call you Jemima?

Posted by: **Ella**
Don't do it, Foully Wooing! She hates being called Jemima. ☺

Posted by: **Ella**
Seriously though, I love the way you're building up the tension. This is better than The Hunger Games.

And so it went on for another twenty-four comments. Yes, four of them were written by her sisters, and another six by her close online friends, but Jamie knew that even friends and family would soon stop commenting if they got bored. The fact that they logged on every day to read what she'd written had to be a good sign.

She looked up as she heard the clank of the letterbox and saw the postman riding away on his bicycle. It reminded her that she'd been meaning to clear the junk mail out of her postbox since Wednesday. Picking up her remote, she went outside to tackle the mildly irritating chore.

The letterbox was in even worse shape than she'd thought. The local community newspaper was still wedged in there from Wednesday morning, along with a property magazine, a catalogue from Game, and another from Checkers. And that was in addition to a blizzard of flyers advertising everything from plumbing to tiling to tree felling.

Using both hands, Jamie started pulling out the mass of paper. It had rained the night before so everything was wet and pulpy. She was concentrating so hard on scraping bits of *papier mâché* out from the depths of the letterbox that she didn't hear the man come up behind her.

"Want some help?"

Snatching her hands free of the letterbox, she scraped her wrists against the metal flap as she spun around.

"Who...?"

It was her neighbour.

"What do you want?" she demanded, still jangling from adrenalin and the pain in her wrists.

"Sorry, I didn't mean to startle you."

"You didn't starrrtle me," Jamie said, mocking his American accent. "You scared the crap out of me. Don't you know better than to sneak up behind a woman like that?"

He shoved his hands into his pockets. "Like I said, I'm sorry. I saw you come out here and I took the gap. I've been wanting to talk to you."

"I think you said more than enough last time." Jamie heard her voice ice over.

"Yeah ... about that. I wanted to apologise. I was out of line and I said a lot of things I shouldn't have. I was so worried about Ben that I took my feelings out on..."

"Fine," she interrupted. "You're sorry. Apology accepted. Now, I've got work to do."

He pushed his hands deeper into his pockets. "Listen, can't I buy you a drink or something to say sorry? I feel like we really got off on the wrong foot here and I'd like to make amends."

"Not necessary."

"But ... we're neighbours and..."

"That's just one of those things. Doesn't mean we have to like each other." Jamie pushed the button to open her gate and stepped briskly through, closing it behind her.

"Well..." He scuffed the ground with his toe. "If you change your mind..."

"I'll know where to find you." Jamie nodded. "Sure. Goodbye now."

"Bye."

`She turned and walked into her house, resisting the urge to look back. Her busy writer's brain could already picture him shuffling back to his house. She knew she was probably imagining him as more disappointed than he really was, but it was good for the ego.

———

Back at her desk, Jamie found herself unable to settle. She fell back on her tried and tested remedy of updating her Facebook status:

Ha! Vengeance is mine, sayeth the Jamie. Obnoxious Neighbour Guy, formerly known as Hot Running Guy, just stopped by to apologise. Says he was out of line. Yes, you damn well were, sir. Then he offers to buy me a drink to "make amends". Needless to say, I declined.

She sat back and waited for the supportive comments to roll in.

Janeesha Jerrald Sounds like he needs to be downgraded to Not-so-bad-after-all Neighbour Guy.

Cyril Attlee Well done on declining. This guy could be a serial killer for all you know.

Amanda Stanislau A cute serial killer who adopts babies? I don't think so. Next time let him buy you a drink at the Earl & Badger. Well-lit public place – what harm could it do?

Zanele Motsoepeng I'm with Janeesha and Amanda. He doesn't sound all that bad. Hope you weren't rude to him! *raps Jamie over knuckles*

Pumla Maseko *beats Jamie with big stick*

Jamie Burchell I wasn't rude!!!!!

Jamie Burchell Okay, maybe I was a bit rude…

Jamie Burchell Dammit, now I feel bad! You guys are supposed to make me feel better about myself.

Zanele Motsoepeng Tough love, babes.

Jamie gave up trying to work. It was a waste of time. She was just staring at the screen, re-reading the same few sentences over and over again.

She'd acted like a bitch. She knew that.

The fact that he'd behaved badly first was no excuse. She'd been ungracious and snotty, with the result that she was now feeling ashamed of herself. She needed to do something to make up for it.

Something short of knocking on his door and saying, "So, how about that drink?" obviously. There were depths to which she would not sink.

But the next time she saw him she would definitely smile and wave. That was the nice, neighbourly thing to do. And she would stop avoiding him during her morning run. All week long, she'd been going to the gym – which she hated – instead of running on the road. So she'd go back to running her normal route at her normal time, and if she happened to pass him, she'd greet him politely.

There, all better now.

With that out of the way, Jamie allowed herself to think about the fact that it was Friday night and she had no plans. By plans, she didn't necessarily mean a date. She could have had a date if she'd wanted one. Of course she could. She wasn't some stay-at-home saddo who needed to beg her friends to set her up with someone.

So it wasn't the lack of a date that was bothering her so much as the lack of any plans whatsoever. And if she was honest with herself, what bothered her most was how unbothered she was about it. Was it normal to be such a hermit? Was she turning into a crazy cat lady whose two-week-old corpse would one day be discovered half-eaten in her home?

The thought had her almost picking up the phone to call one of her sisters. One or both of them must be in town. They were always up for a night out.

But she didn't really feel like going out at all. She had a good bottle of white wine, Netflix subscription, and Mr Delivery's number on speed-dial. To her, that spelled the perfect Friday night. If it weren't for an indefinable fear of missing out, she would be perfectly happy.

Jamie wandered to the kitchen to pour herself a glass of wine. In her mind, she was already composing the blog post she would write on the subject. "Fear of Missing Out", she would call it. "Is the anxiety that someone somewhere is having more fun than you are spoiling your alone time? This uniquely 21st-century phenomenon has its own hashtag on Twitter – #FOMO."

It was perfect women's magazine fodder. Just a few months earlier one of Jamie's blog posts had been picked up by the features editor at *Her*, who had paid her a gratifying sum of money for permission to reprint it in the magazine. Perhaps she would pitch her "Fear of Missing Out" idea to a few of the editors she knew and hope one of them liked it.

She was just about to twist the cap off the wine bottle when her doorbell rang again.

"Probably someone selling something," she told Holmes and Watson, who had appeared in the kitchen in the hope of more supper. Jamie moved the kitchen blind to one side and peered out the window. It was her neighbour again.

She pressed a button on the intercom. "Hello?"

"Uh … hi…" he said. "It's Tom Elliot here. From next door? Could I possibly have another quick word?"

"Just a minute."

Exchanging raised-eyebrow looks with the cats, Jamie let herself out into the driveway. She crossed her arms over her chest when she saw him.

"Hi."

He held up a bottle of wine and a packet of Doritos. "Peace offerings. If you don't feel like sharing them with me, you can just accept them to show that I'm forgiven."

Jamie's arms tightened across her chest. "I said I accepted your apology."

"Your words said acceptance, but your eyes said everlasting hatred." He waggled the bottle of wine from side to side. "Come on. Give me the chance to prove I'm not a total asshole."

She hesitated.

"What do you say?"

"How do I know you're not going to tie me to a table leg or murder me if I let you in?"

He smiled. "Because of my honest face?"

"Hmm."

"Seriously, we could do this at my place if that would make you more comfortable. My domestic worker, Vuyiswa, is babysitting tonight, and she could chaperon us."

Jamie looked at him for a moment. Then she pressed the button to let him in.

"It's okay," she said. "We can do it here. But I'm only letting you in because I feel bad about being horrible to you earlier."

"At this point, I'll take what I can get."

She accepted the wine and bag of chips, and led the way into the house.

"I'll get us some glasses."

Her hand hovered over the cheap wineglasses at the front of the cabinet. But then she reached in further for the good crystal glasses. This wasn't a date – not by any stretch of the imagination – but somehow the fact that it was Friday night and she had a guest made her feel festive.

Deciding to go all out in the gracious-hostess stakes, Jamie selected a silver tray for the glasses, and a hand-painted ceramic bowl for the Doritos. Then she poured some sour cream into a small bowl and spiced it up with a squirt of Worcestershire sauce and a splash of Tobasco.

Next, she picked up a ripe avocado, a sharp knife and a potato masher, and proceeded to make fresh guacamole. Tom watched, apparently fascinated.

"Those are very superior dips for my lowly packet of Doritos. My stomach thanks you in advance, even as my waistline winces."

Jamie glanced at his tight abs, covered only by a thin T-shirt. "I don't think your waistline has much to worry about."

He smiled, leaving her wondering if her comment had been too flirtatious.

"Let's sit on the patio. There's a great view." Balancing the heavy tray along the length of her arm, Jamie scooped up some napkins and the wine bottle, and led the way outside. "Don't you love jacaranda season?"

The slope of the garden framed a view which the blooming trees had turned into a riot of purple.

"Sure. It's one of the best things about living in Joburg. When I moved here two years ago, it was October. It felt like the trees had put on a show just to welcome me."

She poured them each a glass of wine – adding a few blocks of ice to hers and nudging the ice bucket closer to him.

"That's another thing I forgot while I was away." He scooped some spicy cream onto a chip and crunched it up with relish. "South African women and their passion for putting ice into white wine. It's like you can't even taste it unless it's cold enough to freeze your tongue off."

"Hey, you're as South African as I am. I can hear it under that American accent. You make it sound like we're different species."

"Both my parents were American and I was born in northern California, so we are from different continents. But then my mother died and my father married a South African woman. We moved to Cape Town when I was eight years old, and lived there until I was eighteen. I went to the US for college and only came back here a couple of years ago."

Jamie sipped her wine, and felt it rush straight to her head.

"Oops." She fought off a wave of dizziness. "I must have forgotten to eat lunch again. This wine is making me feel funny."

He pushed the Doritos closer to her. "Well eat, for Pete's sake."

"You haven't left me much." She reached for a chip and loaded it with guacamole.

"Yeah, sorry about that. Growing boy here. I'll spring for the pizzas later."

Tom felt a grin trying to crack through his poker face as he watched her searching for a polite way to tell him that there wasn't going to be any "later". She probably had plans to boot him out as soon as the last Dorito crumb was finished. They would see about that.

He watched Jamie nibble on her crisp like a tentative squirrel, then put it down when she took a sip of her wine, and forget to pick it up again. It was no wonder she was so skinny. Fit, yes, and probably healthy as a horse, but a bit on the lean side for his taste.

Still, she made up for it with all that dark blonde hair and those big eyes. All in all, she was a hell of a package. He could kick himself for having freaked out on her like that at their first meeting. Time to correct that unfortunate first impression.

"So why did you come back?" Jamie asked. "I love stories about people who come back to South Africa. Maybe because I've never really left." She thought about that for a while, then added, "Although, I have travelled, of course."

She heard the careful dignity in her tone, and knew she was getting tipsy fast.

Tom hesitated. Then he said, "I came back for my step-mother. She got to a point where she couldn't come out to visit me regularly any more. I'm all she has, you see. She was already over forty when she met my dad, and they never managed to have any kids together. She's only sixty-five now, but she has early-onset Alzheimer's. She can travel when I'm with her, but the days when I could just send her a ticket and meet her at JFK are over."

36

"That's so sad!"

"Yeah, we've had some bad moments. But I'm glad I came back. I was getting into a rut in my old job."

"And now you've given your step-mom a grandson. That's so sweet. She must be so proud of you." Tears pricked at the corners of Jamie's eyes. Oh, yes, she thought. Tipsy, for sure.

Tom looked down into his wine. When he looked up again, he wasn't smiling. "Not really. That's actually one of the things I wanted to talk to you about. I feel I owe you an explanation for my behaviour…"

"You don't have to apologise again. I said I understood, and I do. Really."

"You can't understand without knowing the whole story."

"Okay." She sat up straighter and put down her wineglass.

"The thing is, my step-mother is one of those old-school white South Africans who don't even bother pretending to be glad that apartheid is over. She was horrified when I adopted a black baby. Completely horrified."

"I'm sure that was just the Alzheimer's talking."

"I thought of that. Because that's one of the symptoms of the disease – it can turn you into a caricature of yourself. I hoped that when she got used to Ben, she would mellow towards him. And now that he's walking and starting to talk, he's so bright and funny, I was sure he would win her over."

"Didn't it work?"

"Well, that's the thing. I thought it was working. She hadn't made any unpleasant comments for ages, and she'd been having really good weeks where she was lucid most of the time. When that happens it can almost trick you into thinking she's getting better. So
I had her over for tea on Monday morning – she's always better in the mornings – and Ben was really charming and it seemed he was finally getting through to her." He paused to take a sip of wine.

"Anyway," he went on. "I got a work-related phone call while we were having tea and I thought it was fine to walk into the next room where it wasn't quite so noisy. I mean, Vuyiswa was right there in the kitchen, and she's very vigilant. Then when I went back into the living room a minute later, Ben was gone. I asked my step-mother where he was, and she said he'd gone into the kitchen to ask Vuyiswa for something. Vuyiswa said she hadn't seen him, but then she mentioned that she'd heard the front door opening and closing."

"Oh, no."

"Exactly. I ran out into the street and he was nowhere to be seen. So I ran back into the house and asked my step-mother what she'd done. She hadn't let him out into the road, had she? She just sipped her tea calmly and said, 'It's for the best, dear.' Of course by then I was completely frantic, imagining him kidnapped or hit by a car or whatever. I ran out into the road and started ringing on doors like a maniac."

"You did look a little deranged," Jamie admitted.

"My step-mother had just tried to kill my son. Perfectly calmly, as though she knew exactly what she was doing. I was so angry I was beside myself. And the thought that I should never have left them alone together, that was the worst. Because she's the one who's ill, not me. And that made it more my fault than hers. But I shouldn't have taken it out on you like that. If it hadn't been for you, he might really have been hurt or killed, as I realised when I finally calmed down. "So…" He blew out a breath. "Thank you. Thank you for saving my son."

Jamie looked at him for a long moment. Then she reached for her phone and started scrolling through her contacts.

"What are you doing?" he asked.

"I'm calling Pizza Oven," she told him. "You owe me a pizza, and I think we could both use another glass of wine."

5

. . . .

Jamie Burchell @jamieburchell
Hot Running Guy AKA Rude Neighbour Guy is HERE! In my house!!!

The Tenant @squatter
@jamieburchell Wow! How come?

Gugu Motsepeng @gugz
@jamieburchell Did you let him in??

Jamie Burchell @jamieburchell
@squatter @gugz He invited himself in for a glass of wine. Now he's paying the delivery guy. We're having pizza!

Cyril Attlee @inthemiddlecyril
@jamieburchell Careful! He's a stranger, remember? Send up a flare if you need rescuing. #TwitterSOS

Jamie Burchell @jamieburchell
@inthemiddlecyril Will do. If I don't tweet again in an hour or so, call the cops!

———

Jamie had slipped off to the bathroom to post Twitter updates and to splash water on her face. Her head had finally stopped spinning. Once she had a few slices of pizza on board, she expected to sober up even more.

She wondered if she would regret asking Tom to stay for pizza. Having a meal together added a new dimension to the evening. It had moved beyond polite-apology territory, and was looking more and more like a date.

The thing was, she couldn't kick him out into the cold after that revelation about his step-mother. He'd looked like a lost little boy while he was telling her the sorry story, and her heart had been wrung. The least she could do was keep him company in case he wanted to unload any more.

They were settled cosily in her little kitchen now – elbows on the table, eating slices of pizza with their fingers. There was no way she could match him in consumption, so she didn't even try. He was on his third slice while she was still nibbling at her first.

"So tell me the story of your life, Jamie Burchell." He reached for his fourth slice. "In the interests of full disclosure, I must add that I already got the highlights out of Vuyiswa. Seems she and your housekeeper are besties, so I've got the basic outline."

"Okay, while we're being honest, I got the story of how you adopted Ben from Faith. Who, by the way, is my parents' housekeeper, not mine."

"How does that work?"

"This is their house – my parents'. It's the house I grew up in with my sisters. When my dad took early retirement last year they moved down to Umhlanga Rocks to be at the coast. The property market was going through a dip so they decided not to sell this place, but rather hang onto it and wait for the market to recover. They didn't want to let it out to tenants because that's a fast way to have your house trashed, but they didn't want it to stand vacant either. So they asked me if I'd be prepared to move in."

"And you said yes?"

"I said hell yes. I was living in a pokey, one-room flat in Linden. I jumped at the chance to move into a four-bedroom house in the suburbs with a garden where my kitties can frolic like spring lambs. It suits all of us."

Tom watched as she put her slice of pizza down yet again. She seemed to play with her food rather than actually eating it. He'd had girlfriends who'd monitored every bite they took, and he'd found it very tedious. But in Jamie's case, she genuinely seemed to forget about her food. She liked to wave her arms around as she talked, as though she had to throw her whole body into the act of conversation. Her cats had gathered expectantly next to her chair and were watching her like hawks, hoping that one of her sweeping gestures would dislodge a piece of pepperoni.

It wasn't as though she didn't enjoy food, he decided. The sounds she made when she bit into the pizza were almost orgasmic. She was apparently just absent-minded when it came to finishing meals.

Enjoying her and enjoying finding out more about her, he encouraged her to keep talking about herself.

"Okay, so by day you are part-owner of a very charming bakery, but what about by night? What do you do when darkness falls and you swirl on your superhero cape? Do you have a secret identity?"

Smiling, she leaned towards him. Their knees were touching under the table, but she didn't pull away. "Well ... as a matter of fact ..."

"I knew it!" He grinned. "You do have a secret life."

"I actually kind of do. Part of my reason for wanting to get out of the hotel industry was to have more time to work on my writing."

"Oho. You're a writer? Tell me more."

"Still unpublished, unfortunately. Except for a couple of short stories and an article or two in magazines. But I'm writing a novel and posting it in instalments on my blog. I'm hoping it will get noticed by a publisher and I'll get offered a book deal. It's going really well so far I think. I have a lot of regular readers."

"Okay, so let me get this straight." He tapped on the table with his finger. "You're giving away for free something you hope people will eventually want to pay you for?"

Jamie shook her head and reached for the bottle of wine. If she had to justify her career choices, she needed the assistance of alcohol.

"What you should be doing is sending out three chapters and a synopsis to all the publishers you're hoping to impress," Tom went on. "Most South African publishers will still consider unsolicited manuscripts. But if you're hoping to get published overseas, you'll need an agent."

"I know all that. Don't you think I've tried that? I've sent my novel to every publisher in the country, just about. They all rejected it. And a whole bunch of agents did too. I'm thinking outside the box here, using guerrilla tactics. See, the thing is, I know it's a really good book. It just doesn't fit their mould of what's selling well at the moment. It's not edgy like Lauren Beukes, or fantasy like Cat Hellisen, but when they see how well readers are responding to it, they're going to change their minds." She toasted him with her wineglass. "You wait and see."

He toasted her back. "Then I wish you well, guerrilla novelist of the suburbs. I hope…"

They both jumped as something heavy fell against the kitchen window.

"What was that?" Tom stood up.

"Probably one of the cats."

"How many cats have you got?"

"Two. They like to chase moths near the windows at night."

"There are two cats under the table right now cleaning up the pepperoni you dropped."

Jamie looked under the table and saw that he was right. Holmes and Watson were busily hoovering up spicy sausage, and ignoring her completely. "Well, it must be one of the neighbours' cats, then."

"I don't think so." Tom put down his wineglass and went to the door. "That sounded way too big for a cat. Have you got a gun?"

Jamie stared at him. "Of course I don't have a gun. What do you think this is – the Wild West?"

"Pity. Okay, I'm going to have a look. You stay here.."

"Yeah, like that's going to happen." Jamie was right behind him, picking up her hotel-grade meat cleaver from the knife block. "Just don't scream like a girl if we find something."

Tom's lips twitched, but he said nothing.

"I left the patio door unlocked." Jamie frowned as they ventured out into the dark garden. "I'm usually more careful than that."

"Is this the kitchen window?" Tom leaned across a flower bed and tried to peer back into the house.

"Yes, that's where the noise came from. You can see where we were sitting at the table. There's nothing here. I'm sure it was just a wandering cat."

"I don't think so," he repeated.

Jamie watched as he pulled a key-ring out of his pocket and switched on a powerful maglight torch. Suddenly the three-foot radius around them was as bright as day.

"Good grief. Where did you get that? M15?"

"Close." He knelt down on the grass to inspect the flower bed. "Yes, I thought so. Look here. Footprints. One and a half footprints, to be exact."

Jamie crouched next to him to peer at the soil. "That could be from me."

"Too big."

"Or from my parents' garden service."

"When do they come?"

"On a Wednesday morning."

"That was two days ago. And it rained last night. These are fresh, Jamie. Someone was standing here just a few minutes ago. Look, you can see how he squashed the grass on the edge of the bed. He was probably leaning across to watch us through the window. Then he lost his balance and fell against the glass. See how he took one step into the soil and then dug his toe in to get his balance."

Jamie felt the hair on the back of her neck rising. "Are you saying he's still hiding in the garden somewhere?"

"I highly doubt it. I think he rabbited after he fell. Either through my yard or through your other neighbour's property. Probably the latter. Silver isn't exactly guard-dog of the year, but she would make a lot of noise if someone ran across my yard."

He surprised her again by reaching into his back pocket and pulling out a camera. It was small, but fancy. He proceeded to take photographs of the footprints and of the grass that Jamie could see had been slightly flattened.

———

They walked back into the house, with Jamie taking care to lock the door behind them this time.

"Your dog is called Silver?" she asked. "I would have said she was more gold, myself."

"She's named after the Silver Surfer. You know – from the Fantastic Four? The comic books, not the movies. I was a fan before the movies came out."

Jamie smiled. "You could put that in your Twitter bio."

Tom looked blank. "Twitter? Oh, the social media thing. I don't really go in for that, do you?"

"I do. Social media is the most important weapon in my campaign to get published. And I'm a total addict, so I'd do it for fun anyway."

"I just don't feel comfortable sharing my life with the whole world via the internet. It doesn't feel normal."

"It's the new normal."

They turned back to their neglected pizzas.

"We need to talk about why someone was prowling around your garden at…" Tom glanced at his watch. "Nine o'clock on a Friday night."

Jamie shrugged. "This is Joburg. It was probably just an opportunist looking for an open door or window."

"Yes. Probably. Have you ever had a break-in before?"

"Not for years. The last time was when I was a kid. We didn't even have bars on the windows back then. They walked off with the TV, the DVD-player and a couple of computers. Then my dad had extra security put in and we haven't had a problem since."

"No issues with anyone watching the house or hanging around outside?"

Jamie remembered the weird feeling she'd had that someone had been watching her from the shrubbery across the road. But that had turned out to be a bird. She'd feel an idiot mentioning it.

"No, not that I've been aware of."

Jamie was losing interest in the hypothetical intruder. She picked up her wineglass and waved it at Tom. "Now it's your turn to answer some questions, Mr Bond. Just what line of work are you in, anyway? And why do you carry a torch and camera around with you like a spy? Faith said you're a lawyer, but you seem to spend a lot of time at home. Are you some kind of security consultant?"

He laughed. "You're way off base. Yes, I have a law degree, but I'm an academic. You're looking at one of the Visiting Professors of Criminology at the University of the Witwatersrand's Faculty of Law."

'So you're like an expert on crime?"

"Not exactly. Criminology is the intersection between law, psychology and sociology. It's about seeking explanations for criminal behaviour on a macro or micro level. Some days I feel more like a social worker than a lawyer."

It was a job that was so far outside Jamie's realm of experience she hardly knew what to say about it. All she could think was that if she ever wrote a book with a criminologist in it, she'd know who to go to for material.

They had finished their pizza by now, and the bottle of wine stood empty. This was the part of the evening that could get awkward. If they'd been at his place, she would now be getting to her feet and saying she should really be getting back. But they were in her house, and she was too well brought up to hint that he should leave. Even glancing at her watch went against her code of hospitality.

The real problem, if she was honest, was that she didn't quite trust herself to deflect any moves he might be thinking of making. He was so damn attractive. More Indiana Jones than law professor. And frankly, he had her hormones in a twist. Wild scenarios rushed through her mind. She could almost see herself sweeping the pizza boxes onto the floor, grabbing him by the collar, and pulling him across the table for a kiss.

She blinked the image away. Impulsive physical relationships were not her thing. She needed to remember that.

Relief and disappointment warred in her when he was the one who stood up and glanced at his watch.

"I left Vuyiswa babysitting," he said. "She turns into a pumpkin at ten o'clock, so I'd better go and relieve her. Thanks for letting me make amends. Maybe we can do this again some time."

"I'd like that."

"Walk me out?"

"Of course."

Jamie was smiling as she unlocked the front gate. See, she told herself, it didn't always have to be complicated. It didn't have to be awkward. Sometimes a man and a woman could just spend a pleasant evening together and bring it to a natural conclusion. No pushiness on one side or hurt feelings on the other. Sometimes it actually rocked to be a grown-up.

Even when he turned on the way out to give her a farewell peck on the cheek, she wasn't fazed. So she had no idea what it was that made her shift at the last moment so the kiss landed squarely on her mouth instead of on her cheek. It was a childish move – one that would have annoyed her if she'd been on the receiving end.

He drew back in surprise. Then he reached out and gathered her in.

His hands gripped her hips and pulled her against him. His mouth came down on hers, warm and hard. For a second, she trembled on a precipice of shock and lust. Then he was already stepping back, almost peeling her off him.

Their eyes met for a long moment. He reached up to brush a wisp of hair off her cheek.

"Something to think about."

Then he turned away to let himself into his own house.

6

FROM JAMIE BURCHELL'S FACEBOOK PAGE:

Don't know what got into me. Hot Running Guy was giving me a platonic kiss on the cheek to say goodnight when I turned my head to kiss him right on the lips. Have I lost my marbles?

Ella Burchell Ha! I knew this would happen! Just call me psychic.

Pumla Maseko Then we're psychic too, Ellz. I think we all saw this coming.

Amanda Stanislau So, is he a good kisser? Tell us all, omitting no detail, however slight. ;)

Jamie Burchell "Good" doesn't even begin to cover it, and that's all I'm saying. *zips lips*

Liezel Lamprecht You must be careful of teasing guys like that. They cant always control themselves.

Janeesha Jerrald *rolling my eyes*

Liezel Lamprecht if uve got something to say to me janeesha why dont u say it?

Janeesha Jerrald Okay, then I'll say that the notion that men aren't in control of their sexual urges, and that it's the responsibility of women not to "provoke" them, is a patriarchal myth!!

Liezel Lamprecht Its not about myths its about common sense. If you stir a guy up you have to take the consequences.

Janeesha Jerrald What, like RAPE?

Liezel Lamprecht alot of rapes could be prevented if girls took more precautions

Janeesha Jerrald Oh, for God's sake!

Pumla Maseko Girl fight! *grabs popcorn*

Jamie Burchell ANYWAY! He may have great kissing skillz, but it's his son who's really got my heart. I just can't stop thinking about that little boy. The other night I dreamed I was helping him lace up his sweet little shoes. I woke up almost in tears that it wasn't true. ☹

Tom lifted his son so he could spit toothpaste into the basin.

"Spit, Benny! Spit it all out. And again. Good job. Now, put this water in your mouth and spit again. No drinking, remember. Just spit."

The first gulp of water was swallowed straight down, but Ben remembered to spit out the second. And that, Tom thought, was as good as it was likely to get tonight.

This tooth-brushing routine was still fairly new. It was only recently that Ben had acquired enough teeth to make it worthwhile to brush them. Tom had held out for six teeth, having visions of fluoride poisoning as toothpaste ran down his son's throat in an unending stream.

At least they made special babies' toothpaste these days so it wasn't a disaster even if he did swallow most of it. Maybe mothers had some secret method whereby they managed to stop toddlers from swallowing toothpaste, but Tom hadn't discovered it yet.

"Story time now, Benny."

Tom lifted him up to carry him to his bedroom, but Ben kicked and squirmed until Tom put him down again.

"Oh, so tonight you want to walk, huh? That's cool."

The last five nights he had insisted on being carried, as though the carpeted distance from bathroom to bedroom were a day's hike across the Sahara.

Ben ran into his bedroom and made a beeline for the bookcase. His eyes tracked across the collection of picture books until he spotted the one he wanted. Then he pounced on it and carried it to his father. "Wild!" he demanded. "Want Wild."

Tom ignored him.

"Look, Benny, look!" He picked up the book he'd already laid on the little racing-car bed. "Look at this new book! This book is FUN! Look at all the great pictures in here. See, here's a gorilla. He's all big and hairy. Boy, I bet this book is going to be exciting."

He sat down and opened the book with all the authority he could muster. "*Traditional Fairytales from the Democratic Republic of Congo*. Doesn't that sound awesome?"

He sneaked a look at his son and saw that the little boy's face was set in mutinous lines.

"Want Wild!" he repeated. "Wild! Wild! Wild!"

"Okay, how about I read you Wild and THEN the fairytale book? How about that, Benny?"

"Wild!" Ben enunciated carefully. It didn't take a genius to realise there would be no other books read that night.

Tom put down the Congolese fairytale book and took the copy of *Where the Wild Things Are* that Ben was waving under his nose.

He cursed the day he'd ever bought the damn book. Sure, it was a classic, but who knew the kid would become obsessed with it?

Tom objected to it on several grounds. One – Ben was apt to take the "wild rumpus" part too literally and tear up his room before bedtime. Two – it was a Eurocentric story that added nothing to Ben's knowledge of his own cultural origins. Three – Tom was sick and tired of reading it. He'd enjoyed it the first three million times, but now it was starting to pall. And four – it reminded Ben of the one thing Tom could never give him, which was a mother. The one who "loved him best of all".

"Daddy loves you best of all," he whispered in Ben's ear as the second reading came to an end. "I love you, my Benny."

"Daddeee." Ben pressed his hands against his father's cheeks and scrunched up his face for a kiss.

———

Twenty minutes later, after one request for water, two requests for more light, and yet another request for water ("It's right here next to your bed where you can reach it, Benny, see?") Tom finally settled down in his study to do some work.

At least the requests were for water these days rather than milk or juice. Tom considered that progress, and all the toddler websites agreed with him.

He tried to concentrate on the lecture he was delivering the next morning, but it didn't really need more work. He'd delivered it several times before, and had already adapted it for the South African setting.

"Seeking Legitimacy in the Police Custody Process."

The final-year law students he was delivering it to would be joined by members of the South African Police Service, who had also asked to attend. It would be one of those lectures where everyone was there because they wanted to be there, and that made it Tom's favourite kind. Speaking to a bunch of undergraduates who were only taking Criminology because they didn't know what other elective to choose was not his idea of fun.

As he fiddled with his presentation and triple-checked his statistics, he asked himself why he didn't just pack it in for the night and crack open a beer in front of ESPN. The truth was, he was steeling himself to do something that felt like an invasion of privacy.

Ever since Jamie had told him she was a social media addict, he had been tempted to check her out online. So far, he'd managed to resist. It felt like going through someone's trash to find out more about them.

But she was the one who'd put her personal details online in the first place. If she wanted to keep things private, she shouldn't post them all over the internet, should she? And, yes, he knew he was justifying.

He had the software and the access to do a formal law enforcement run on her. He could call up her credit history, her employment records, and even her medical aid records. But that really would be out of line.

"Okay," he said out loud. "It would be wrong to run her, but a simple google check can't hurt."

Enough stalling.

He entered "Jamie Burchell" into the search engine and watched as the first of over two thousand hits filled his screen.

Strong social media presence didn't begin to cover it. The woman was everywhere.

She was an early adopter of every new application that reared its head. You could trace her evolution as an online creature from MySpace to Facebook, from Flickr to Instagram, from Friends Reunited to Linked In, from Blogger to Posterous to Wordpress. And now Twitter, Pinterest, Keek, Bing and Snapchat had joined the lineup.

Every aspect of her life was public. There was nothing she'd locked or limited in any way. Every word she wrote – every image she posted – was open to the public. It was as if, Tom decided, she had taken that trash bin and shaken its contents out all over the street.

And she wasn't careful with it, either. This wasn't harmless or generic material she was posting. It was all her most personal thoughts, her most private reflections. She seemed to view the internet as her trusted shrink.

Tom hesitated again when he got to her writer's blog. In his experience, unpublished writers were unpublished for a reason. He didn't want to read her work only to confirm his suspicion that she was no good at it.

51

But curiosity got the better of him. He cracked open the beer he'd been thinking about and settled down to read.

Ninety minutes later he was done.

He pushed his chair back, crumpled his beer can, and sent it winging into the nearest bin.

It was a relief to admit that she could write. She had a way of spinning a yarn that sucked you in and kept you reading. The creepy dystopian future she'd created was compelling and believable, and Tom was fairly sure nothing quite like it had been done before.

Organic, homeopathic, tree-hugging vegetarians taking over the world? Wouldn't that be a kick in the pants? Tom had found himself caring to an absurd extent about whether Eve would have her baby safely, whether her grandmother would organise an underground resistance movement, and how the whole lot of them were going to turn out.

He noticed she tended to post early in the mornings. Perhaps tomorrow he'd go online before leaving for work and see what the next episode would bring.

He flipped between her Facebook and Twitter feeds.

It amused him to see himself described as Obnoxious Neighbour Guy in her posts after their first meeting. Fair enough – he'd earned that title. But it was also good to see he'd gone back to being Hot Running Guy.

Then he read her comments about Ben, and that wiped the smile off his face.

It's his son who's really got my heart.

I can't seem to stop thinking about that little boy.

Tom pushed his chair away from the computer and stood up, frowning. If she thought she was going to get her hands on Ben, she was mistaken. Yes, he wanted to see her again, but not if she was interested in Ben.

She would have to learn that Ben was off limits.

7

Another narrow escape.

Even narrower this time. The first time had just been bad luck. It was instinct, nothing more, that'd had her turning towards the bushes where he was crouching as quiet as a mouse. He hadn't done anything wrong. Hadn't made a mistake. And he'd kept his head, kept his cool, as she'd swept the bushes with those big brown eyes that seemed to look right through him.

He'd kept still, and within seconds she'd turned her eyes away and walked on. Then only had the sweat burst out in great beads along his forehead, his upper lip, all the damp and secret parts of him.

But this time he'd made a mistake. Yes, and he was man enough to admit it. He'd been watching them. He'd been leaning across the flower bed and watching them eat pizza in the kitchen. It disappointed him that Jamie would let a man into her house. What did she know about him? One couldn't be too careful.

He hoped Jamie wasn't going to turn out to be a disappointment like the others. She hadn't lied about herself in her photos, and that was a good sign. But had she lied about being a focused young woman who didn't need a man to complete her? Only time would tell.

It wasn't his fault that his foot had slipped in the mud and he'd fallen against the window. Was it?

Yes, yes. He would be honest. He could afford to be. He'd always prided himself on his honesty.

Perhaps falling against the window hadn't been accidental. Perhaps he'd sort of, kind of, *allowed* his foot to slip in the mud. They'd been ignoring him – that was the problem. They'd been unaware of him watching them from the garden. Like he didn't count. They were so wrapped up in each other. Smiling into each other's eyes. Chatting intimately. Like he didn't exist. Wasn't important.

He'd frightened them though, hadn't he? Yes, he had. Alarm. Fear. That's what he'd seen on their faces when they'd heard the crash. For one terrifying moment, he'd thought he was going to shatter the window and fall through the glass. But it hadn't even cracked.

Again, he'd reacted quickly. He'd been across the garden and over the wall almost as soon as they'd stood up. Not into the garden with the dog. No. He hated dogs. Horrible, smelly things with loud voices and snuffling noses.

The other side. The house with no pets and nice, low walls. And only once he was out in the street had the sweat come – pushing through his pores like a live thing.

He needed to rein himself in now. To regroup. No more taking chances. No more narrow escapes. Give it a few weeks. Let her get comfortable again. He should spend more time following her online and less time watching her in real life.

If only the narrow escapes didn't make him feel so wonderfully alive.

———

Jamie read through her blog again, slowly this time. Normally she did two quick read-throughs and a light edit before pressing "post". But the traffic to her site had spiked in the last few days. Someone was paying attention, and that meant it was time for her to pay attention, too. No more typos or sloppy phrasing could be allowed to slip through.

Some women monitored the All Share Index, some kept track of current affairs, some weighed themselves every day. Jamie watched her blog statistics. She monitored them like a hawk, even subscribing to a service that analysed the data for her, breaking her page views down by country of origin, search terms used to find the blog, amount of time spent on her landing page, and repeat visits. And of course she kept track of all pingbacks, trackbacks, social media mentions, and indeed any reference to herself or her work throughout the entire internet.

Something was definitely up.

Someone was watching her online activity, and watching it closely. There was no way this was just a normal increase in traffic caused by growing popularity.

Trying to focus, she read through the last paragraphs of her post again.

Eve felt for eggs. If there was one, she offered up a little prayer of thanks to the hen. Through the door of the henhouse, she could see Abraham carrying a bucket into the cowshed. It was kind of him to take over the milking during her last month of pregnancy.

Possibly her last month of life, she thought with a flash of self-pity.

Pulling herself together, she focused on the thought that human death was nothing to fear, nothing to mourn. Hadn't she been taught that since birth? It was good for the earth when humans died – a cause for celebration, not sorrow. Human beings were a contagion on the face of the planet. They were dirty and greedy and selfish. If too many of them lived, they would once again become a burden upon nature.

In the natural course of things, Eve would have perhaps ten children, of which maybe two would survive. It was wrong for her to be so invested in the well-being of this, her first baby. First babies didn't often survive. The mother was inexperienced and the birth canal tight. If the birth took too long, the midwife would often elect to cut the baby into sections and deliver it piecemeal.

It made no sense for Eve to have fallen so much in love with this parasite that had taken over her body.

Back in the kitchen, she took the dough out of the lower section of the oven where it was proving, and beat it down. Then she shaped it into loaves and returned it to the oven for its second rising. A glance at the slanted sunrays that were creeping into the kitchen told her that it was earlier than usual. She was ahead of schedule. She could afford the time to visit her grandmother.

She knocked on the old lady's door and entered, almost without pausing.

"Grandma, I ... oh, I'm sorry. I didn't mean... what are you doing?"

Ayn had a needle sticking into her arm. It was attached to a clear glass cylinder, with a plunger she appeared to be pressing down. She started when Eve entered, but managed to hold the device still, continuing to press downwards until the small amount of clear liquid in the cylinder was gone.

"I remember!" Eve spoke wonderingly as her grandmother pulled the needle out of her arm. "Oh, how I remember. I saw you doing that when I was a child. You told me I had dreamed it."

Okay, that would do. Jamie forced herself to stop obsessing and pressed "post". There was such a thing as over-editing. One could tinker too much with a post and end up spoiling a perfectly good piece of writing.

She refreshed the page to make sure it had loaded, and then forced herself to shut it down.

Unwilling to step away from her laptop, she opened her email. And goggled in disbelief at the screen as she saw the message she'd been waiting for for so long.

FROM: editor@magnumbooks.com
TO: Jamie Burchell
SUBJECT: Offer to Publish

Dear Ms Burchell,

One of our junior editors brought your blog to my attention, and the good news is that I love your story! I've sent the link to some of our readers and they all love it too. Good work! The publishing industry is such a tough, competitive marketplace that it's really hard to get your work noticed.

The even better news is that we would like to make you an offer to publish your novel. We think it would be a good fit for our Spec Magnum imprint. I see it as a 30,000 word story with a lot of punch and zip. Check out our website at www.specmagnum.com to see some of the awesome cover art we have done for our authors.

We pay in US dollars – a once-off fee of $350 that will be deposited into your nominated bank account on the day of publication.

Congratulations!

I hope to hear from you soon so I can forward you our contract and get our team of professional and experienced editors working on your manuscript.

Kind regards,
Mari-Lee Bax

Jamie skimmed the message quickly and then read it again. Then yet again to confirm that her eyes weren't playing tricks on her.

Her dream had come true. Her tactic had worked. Putting her novel on the internet had got it noticed by the right people, and now she had a genuine, bona fide offer to publish sitting in her inbox. And not just from a local publisher either. This was the real deal. An American publisher. Her work would be read internationally.

"Yes!"

Jamie jumped up and punched the air. Then she did a victory dance around the room. Ha! So much for those doubters who thought she was crazy to give up her job in a hotel chain to chase her dream of becoming a published author. That dream had just become a reality.

She scrabbled for her phone to call her mom and then put it down again when she remembered that her parents were on a scuba-diving course, and wouldn't be back until the afternoon.

Who else could she tell?

Her sister Ella's phone went straight to voicemail. She was probably already in rehearsal for her performance in *The Nutcracker*. Her sister Caroline's phone rang six times, then went to voicemail. She would have it on silent while she was operating.

Jamie glanced at her watch. Not even nine yet. Faith wouldn't be in until ten and, let's face it, wouldn't be all that interested when she did arrive. If it didn't involve her kids, her grandkids or her neighbours, Faith didn't want to know.

Jamie knew she could call Pumla and scream the news over the phone, but it would be more satisfying to tell her in person later. Her fingers itched to update her Whatsapp status, her Facebook status, and her Twitter account with the news, but she knew better. Until the contract was signed, it wasn't a done deal. Lots of things could still go wrong.

For one giddy moment, she thought about dashing next door to share the news with Tom. But that might be weird, especially after that ambush kiss the other night.

She'd go for a run instead, she decided. Today was supposed to be a rest day, but she couldn't sit still.

She ripped off her dressing gown and pulled on lycra shorts, a sports bra and a tank top. She laced her running shoes, tied up her hair, and pulled the ponytail through the back of a cap. Then she let herself out into the street and took off like a greyhound, feeling invincible.

Adrenalin carried her through the first kilometre and halfway through the second. By the 1500m mark, she felt it finally burning off. Her heartbeat settled down to an easy thud and her breathing grew regular. Even her thoughts stopped hopping around like bunnies on speed. She loved to run – loved it like she loved breathing. It was her drug, her pick-me-up and her settle-me-down. There was no problem that didn't look more manageable after a run – no triumph that didn't glitter more brightly.

And look there, she thought as a figure came into focus in the distance. Wasn't that a nice bonus? Another jogger – one of the male variety, if she wasn't mistaken – pushing something in front of him that looked like a pram.

She picked up the pace.

There was no guarantee it was him, she reminded herself. This wasn't his usual running time any more than it was hers, and she'd never seen him pushing a pram before. But something about his stride and the back of his head looked very familiar. And hadn't she seen that New York Marathon T-shirt before?

She lengthened her stride again. Yes, it was him all right. The man ran like a cheetah. She'd never been able to catch up with him before, and the only reason she might manage it now was because the pram was slowing him down.

The thought of that pram and what it contained gave her a boost. She started to close the gap between them.

Hot daddy and charming toddler. How could she resist?

"Morning!" she said on a gasp.

"Good morning." Tom gave her a relaxed smile. "Little late for you to be out, isn't it?"

"You ... too," she puffed.

"Lewis Hamilton here wanted to go racing." He glanced down at the pram and the little boy who was bouncing around in it. "So I rescheduled for after his breakfast. How about you?"

"Supposed ... to be ... a rest day. Running ... to celebrate ... good news."

"No kidding?"

"Nope." She sucked in air gratefully as he slowed his pace. "I've got an offer to publish my book."

"Wow!" He did a fist-pump in the air. "Well done, you! That's fantastic. Who's the publisher?"

"It's ... uh ..." She hesitated as she tried to remember the name. "Magnum books. Yes, that's it. They're an American publisher."

"Excellent! So you'll be celebrating tonight?"

"Yes, I'm really stoked. And the best part is that I was right. Good writing gets noticed. All you have to do is put it out there long enough and eventually someone will pay attention. I knew this would work. I knew it!"

"You deserve it. I read your blog myself the other night, and your story's really good. It hooked me immediately and now I'm a regular reader. I'm going to be kind of bummed if you stop posting every day and I have to wait for the book to come out."

Jamie ran in silence for a moment. "I hadn't thought about that. I should probably speak to the publisher about whether I should take the blog down. That'll be weird. I've got used to writing it every day."

"The main thing is that you've done it. You've got a book deal. That's really awesome news. Settle down, Benny."

Jamie looked down to see Ben twisting around in his seat and holding his arms out to her. "Lady," he was saying. "LADEEEE!"

Tom gave an awkward laugh. "He's taken to referring to you as 'Lady'. Seems he still remembers the day you rescued him."

A huge grin split Jamie's face. "Really? He remembers me? That's great!"

"He'll get over it. Sit still, Ben."

Ben was almost climbing out of his seat by now. Only the harness was preventing him from flinging himself at Jamie.

"Oh, look at that. He wants a cuddle. Can't I hold him for a moment? Please?"

"Sorry," Tom said. "We've got to get on. See you later."

He picked up the pace and left Jamie in his dust. Strange how he'd gone from friendly to distant like that.

Jamie thought she knew why. He remembered what a mess she'd made of looking after Ben that first time. Spilling juice on him, teaching him to swear. Now Tom didn't trust her. Well, that was fair enough. She could understand that kind of protectiveness. She'd just have to show him she knew how to care for a toddler.

If she really won his trust, he might let her babysit Ben sometimes. Vuyiswa would probably be glad to have a few nights off.

Relaxing into the run, Jamie gave herself over to a fantasy in which she and Ben were cuddled in front of the fire watching a Disney movie. The cats were lying next to them and she and Ben were sharing a bowl of popcorn.

Wait. Was popcorn safe for toddlers? She'd have to google it.

Tom Elliot would learn how dependable she could be.

———

When Jamie walked into Delucia's at 11.30am, she could see that now was not the time for her big announcement. Pumla was in the middle of what sounded like a fraught telephone conversation with a supplier, and hadn't even started the set-up for lunch. In a short while they'd all be too busy to chat. She would wait until the lunchtime rush was over.

As expected, Faith had been underwhelmed by the news, but Jamie hoped Pumla's reaction would be more satisfactory. Without exactly saying anything, Pumla had always seemed somewhat amused by Jamie's writing ambitions. "Don't give up your day job" summed up her attitude. Of course, that didn't stop her from visiting Jamie's blog daily, and leaving comments, but she didn't seem to take it seriously.

Jamie raced around the coffee shop scooping up breakfast menus and replacing them with lunch ones. She looked into the kitchen to find out what the soup of the day was and wrote it on the specials board. Then she went to work on the bakery counter display to give it a more lunchtime feel. She pushed fruit tarts, Florentines and lemon meringue pies to the front, and retired muffins, Danishes and scones to the back. Then she opened up the savoury section and started setting out the samoosas, Cornish pasties and homemade pies that did so well as takeaways for office workers.

By the time Pumla got off the phone, Jamie had the lunchtime set-up under control.

"Such a cheek!" Pumla fumed. "He's charging us more for flour, self-raising flour, baking powder and cornstarch. Tells me he's raising his prices across the board. Same deal for all the restaurants he supplies. Meanwhile, I know damn well it's because we've had a good two months. He knows our profits are up and now he's trying to screw us over. Bastard!"

"What did you say to him?"

"I told him to stop being such a pirate or we'd change suppliers."

"And now?"

"He's gone away to think about it. I've given him until four this

61

afternoon. If he doesn't change his mind by then, I'm cancelling our contract with him and phoning The Flour Man."

Jamie winced. "They're even more expensive."

"I know, but they do same-day deliveries. And anyway it's the principle of the thing. He needs to learn he can't mess us around like that. He's going to cave, you'll see."

Jamie would have taken her to task for playing russian roulette with their profits, but the door dinged and the first of their lunch customers came in. Within minutes she was too busy to think about anything except who wanted their Coke with ice and lemon, and who only wanted it with ice.

As she carried glasses of wine through for yet another table, she had to admit Pumla had been right about applying for a liquor licence. Jamie had argued that it was too expensive and that office workers wouldn't drink at lunchtime, but Pumla had pushed ahead with it. Now white wine was one of their biggest sellers and they were doing a good line in champagne breakfasts too, especially on Friday mornings.

It did her heart good to see the credit card slips piling up on the spike next to the till. If October was as good as the projections suggested, she'd be able to buy herself that bikini she'd seen in the window at Azura. And maybe the matching espadrilles, too. If that wasn't a good enough reason to book a beach holiday, she didn't know what was.

"Avo and chicken mayo ciabatta, no bacon. Thai beef tramezzino. Toasted four-cheeses on rye. And the avo and chicken mayo ciabatta with bacon." Jamie recited the order as she put the plates down in front of the customers at table three. "Can I bring you another Miller's, sir?"

As Jamie looked up, her eyes collided with the customer sitting on his own at table one. Every time she looked up, he seemed to be staring at her. She lost her train of thought.

"I beg your pardon, sir. Did you say you would have another Miller's?"

"No, I asked for a Peroni!" the man replied in that eye-rolling tone of voice every waiter gets used to hearing.

"I'll bring it right away."

It occurred to Jamie that the man at table one was probably just trying to attract her attention. He already had everything he'd ordered, but maybe he wanted something else.

"Can I help you with anything, sir?" she smiled.

He shook his head and blushed, burrowing deeper into the newspaper he'd brought with him. She did a quick scan of his table, clearing away a paper napkin he'd shredded, a straw wrapper and an empty glass. His eyes looked familiar, but she was sure she'd never seen that shade of bottle green in real life before. He also had an improbable amount of facial hair. His face was all but hidden behind a bushy brown beard.

As she reached across the table for an empty sugar packet, she glanced at the side of his head, half-expecting to see loops going over his ears, like a kid at a fancy-dress party. But there was nothing. He was wearing a short-sleeved shirt that had half-moon sweat stains creeping all the way down the sides. Her skin crawled. She turned away and went to pour the Peroni.

By 2.45pm, they were in a lull again. The staring guy had left and there were just a few clients lingering over coffee.

"Guess what?" Jamie joined Pumla behind the counter. "I've got a book deal!"

"A book deal?" Pumla's eyebrows twitched upwards. "Really? Are you sure?"

"Of course I'm sure! An American publishing company wants to publish my book."

"Are they going to pay you?"

"Yes, they're going to pay me." Trust Pumla to be sceptical and suspicious. "I'll show you the email if you don't believe me."

She started scrolling through her phone to find the message, but Pumla just waved in the direction of the office. "Forward it to the work address. I'll check it out on the big screen. Fifty bucks says it's a 419 scam."

Almost gnashing her teeth, Jamie said goodbye to the last of the lunch patrons and walked into the office behind Pumla.

"It is *not* a 419 scam! It is perfectly legitimate and above-board. And Magnum Books *does* exist. I googled them."

Pumla made shushing noises as she read through the email. "Okay listen, here's the first thing I don't like. This bit where they say what a tough and competitive marketplace it is, and how lucky you are to be chosen. Like they're doing you a big favour or something."

"Well, it's a difficult industry to break into. They're not lying about that."

"And here where they talk about their 'professional and experienced' editors. I call bullshit on that. If they've got such a hot editorial team they don't need to boast about it."

"But…"

"And are they kidding about this fee? Three-fifty dollars? That's like, what, R3000, R4000? As a once-off payment. What about royalties? Aren't writers supposed to get royalties?"

"Look, as a first-timer…"

"First-timer, nothing. Here's something else. Didn't you tell me your book was going to be 100,000 words long? They're offering to publish it as a 30,000 word story. You'd have to cut it down to the bone. To the bone, *kemo sabe*. Why would you want to do that to your novel?"

Jamie rubbed her hands over her face. "Look, they obviously have their own house rules, and as a first-time writer I wouldn't feel right about making demands. The point is that I'm going to be published at last. My book is finally going to appear in print. That's huge. You have no idea what it means to me."

"In print, you say?" Pumla snorted. "We'll see about that."

"What are you doing?"

"Nothing. Go away. I'm googling. Go and do the teatime set-up. I'll call you when I'm done."

Seething, Jamie went out front to fine-tune the restaurant for teatime. The kitchen staff doubled as runners, and had already cleared and relaid all the tables. All Jamie had to do was take fresh flowers out of the cooler and make sure every table-setting sparkled. Attention to detail had always been her strong point, but it was hard to concentrate while worrying about what Pumla was up to.

"Yo! Burchell!"

The call had her scurrying back to the office.

"What? What have you found?"

"I thought so! This isn't a real publisher at all. It's an e-publisher. Your book will never come out in print. Look here – all they do is create a digital cover for it and put it up on their website, and on Amazon. This is a total scam."

Jamie wasn't ready to let go of the dream.

"Amazon? That's huge, right? My book will be exposed to millions of people."

"Only if they buy it. Which they won't."

"And anyway, e-books are the way of the future. Soon there'll be no paper books left at all. Everything will be in e-format."

Pumla laughed. "Not in our lifetime, darling. This is a totally bogus, second-rate offer. In fact, it's third-rate. Fourth-rate."

"You don't have to sound so pleased about it."

"I'm not pleased. I'm just telling it like it is."

But Jamie's disappointment had coalesced into fury against her partner.

"It would kill you to be happy for me, wouldn't it? You have to be negative about everything I ever do. I came in here all happy and excited about my book deal, and you had to shoot it down from the start."

"Well, I was right, wasn't I?"

"That's not the point! You've never believed in me as a writer. You've never supported me."

"Hey, I'm not your mother. I don't have to believe in you or support you."

"We're supposed to be friends, dammit!"

Jamie's accusation hung in the air. The clattering in the kitchen had gone quiet as the staff strained to catch the next words.

Pumla folded her arms and turned away. "We've never been friends. Not really. We're just people who've known each other a long time. And we're business partners."

Jamie crossed her own arms, gripping her elbows. The rising pressure in her chest warned her she was about to burst into tears. Which would be stupid. Pumla's opinion of women who used tears as a weapon was well known.

"Well, that clears it up, doesn't it?" She turned on her heel and walked out of the room.

"Your book deserves better."

Pumla said it so quietly, Jamie thought she'd misheard.

"Excuse me?"

"You heard me."

Before Jamie could demand an explanation, the front door dinged and Pumla brushed past her to take up her post behind the till. Jamie took a deep breath and went out to welcome their customers.

8

Conundrum. I got an offer to publish my novel today. The upside is that it's a serious offer and they will pay me a once-off fee of $350. The downside is that it's a digital publisher, so my work would only appear on their website and on Kindle. Also, they want to hack it down to 30,000 words. They're called Magnum Books, if you want to google them. I don't know what to do. Would I be mad to turn this down?

Ella Burchell They want to publish your book?!? Wow, that's awesome. Congrats!

Sheryl Witbooi Urgh. A digital publisher. I'm not so sure.

Parvani Naidoo What's wrong with a digital publisher????

Sheryl Witbooi Have you seen the kind of rubbish they publish? It's nearly as bad as self-publishing.

Liezel Lamprecht "Nearly as bad as self-publishing"? I published my self-help book through Icarus Press and i get email's all the time from people telling me how much it has helped them.

Sheryl Witbooi I'm sorry, but if Jamie wants to be taken seriously as a writer she can't go the digital route. Or the self-publishing route.

Parvani Naidoo That's exactly the kind of arrogant attitude I'd expect from you established writers! You think you're better than the rest of us.

Janeesha Jerrald Sheryl IS better than the rest of us – better at writing, that is. That's why she got the big advance and the three-book deal from Random Penguin…

Foully Wooing Won You looked really pretty in that red shirt Jamie.

Parvani Naidoo And you're with Penguin, Janeesha, as I'm sure you're DYING to tell us all. Well, I bet neither of you has ever made as much money as E L James from 50 Shades of Grey. And that started out as Twilight fan fiction that she self-published on the Internet.

Sheryl Witbooi The point about the exceptions like E L James is that they prove the rule. For every self-published or digitally published author who makes it, there are thousands – probably hundreds of thousands – who disappear into obscurity.

Liezel Lamprecht So what? You think that makes you better than us?

Janeesha Jerrald This isn't about you, Liezel. It's about Jamie and the decision she needs to make.

Jamie Burchell The thing that scares me is that this might be the only offer I ever get. Say I turn it down because I'm looking for something bigger or better, and nothing else ever comes along. At least this would be a start. It would be a foot in the door.

Sheryl Witbooi It wouldn't be a foot in the door, it would be a closed door. Because this digital publisher would then own the exclusive rights to publish your book and you wouldn't be allowed to sell it to anyone else.

––––––––

Justine Elliot was meeting her husband at the car so he could take her home after shopping. If only she could remember where he'd parked. She was sure he sometimes moved the car just to annoy her.

She needed to get home quickly to put the ice cream in the freezer. Otherwise it would melt and then freeze again, and become all horrible. And there were people coming for dinner tonight. Friends of her step-son, Tom. He was inconsiderate like that. Always inviting people over at a moment's notice and expecting her to entertain them. Where was Ben – her husband? She'd told him to meet her at ten o'clock and it was already…? Where was her watch? She was sure she'd been wearing it when she left that morning.

"Ben?" she called out. "We need to leave now. Where are you?"

There was a maid walking past holding a toddler by the hand. It seemed to Justine that the woman was going to have the cheek to accost her. She hesitated, but Justine glared at her, and she walked on.

The child she was leading looked just like that dreadful black baby Tom had adopted. She would get Ben to talk to him about taking it back to wherever he'd found it. God knew, he never listened to her, even though she talked herself blue in the face. Maybe he would listen to his father.

But Ben was dead. Of course he was. She was visiting Tom at his house. But where was his house? She'd just gone outside for a moment, and now she was all turned around.

It was all Ben's fault. If he would only leave the car parked in one place she'd be able to find it.

———

Jamie was in her kitchen, waiting for the kettle to boil. She stared out the window, mulling over her dilemma.

There was no one out there today except for an old lady who was tacking up and down the street like a rudderless ship. No sooner had she disappeared from Jamie's view on one side, than she reappeared and made her way across to the other.

And what was she wearing? Some kind of dressing gown. A navy-blue dressing gown that was far too big for her. It looked as though it belonged to a man.

Jamie frowned. The woman was old enough to take care of herself, but she looked just as clueless out there as Ben had. She needed to get out of the road before she wandered in front of a car.

Jamie headed out the door and into the street.

"Excuse me!"

The woman looked back at her with unfocused eyes.

"Can I help you at all? Are you looking for something?"

"Yes dear. I'm looking for the car. My husband parked it somewhere near here. I have to get this chicken into the fridge before it turns nasty."

"Right." The woman was carrying nothing except a balled-up tissue. "Well, did he definitely park it here in Sixteenth street?"

"I don't remember," the woman said. "I just don't remember."

The woman pottered away again, heading for the busy avenue at the end of the block. Jamie watched her go. What was it that Tom had said about his mother – no, his step-mother – suffering from dementia? Could this woman be her?

Jamie caught up with her in a few strides. She took her arm before she could step into the busy road. "I'm sorry," she said. "But do you know anyone by the name of Tom? Tom Elliot?"

The old lady's eyes sharpened and focused, almost as though a mist had been lifted from in front of them.

"Of course I know Tom Elliot, young lady. He's my step-son. I'm visiting him this morning. I just stepped out for a little break."

"Okay. Well, he's probably looking for you. I live right next door, so I'll walk you back."

Jamie steered her toward Tom's house. She gave a silent sigh of relief when the old lady came along without protesting.

"So you're Tom's neighbour," the woman said as they walked slowly back the way they had come. "I don't know how you can stand it."

"Stand what?"

"The noise that child makes. His behaviour is just dreadful. He screams and screams with no regard for my nerves."

"I've never heard him."

"Oh, you must have. Those people have no idea how to raise children. None whatsoever."

"He's being raised by Tom, isn't he? Your step-son."

The woman gripped Jamie's wrist and turned to face her. "It's in the genes. You can expel nature with a pitchfork, you know, but it will always return."

Weird, Jamie thought. One moment she's stumbling around, wondering where her dead husband parked the car, and the next she's quoting Shakespeare.

"Here's the house. We should probably go inside now."

The front door was shut, but it opened when Jamie turned the knob. She stuck her head inside as she knocked on the open door. There was no way she was going to dump the old lady and leave. She'd probably go straight back outside again.

"Hello?" Jamie called. "Anyone home?"

The only answer was the distant roar of the vacuum cleaner. Jamie stood and listened. It seemed to be coming closer. Vuyiswa came into sight, backing down the passage and pulling the vacuum cleaner after her. Ben was strapped to her back with a blanket. He had his cheek pressed against her back and was fast asleep.

As she got to the end of the passage, Vuyiswa shut the vacuum off and turned around. Her eyes widened at the sight of Jamie. "I'm sorry," she said. "I didn't hear the doorbell."

"I didn't ring." Jamie glanced over her shoulder. The old lady had walked into the kitchen where she could be seen switching on the kettle. "I found Tom's step-mother in the road. She looked a bit lost."

"In the road? You mean, outside?" Vuyiswa waved her hand to indicate the great outdoors.

"Yes, in Sixteenth street. She was wearing a man's dressing gown and wandering around. I thought I'd better bring her home."

Vuyiswa shook her head and clicked her tongue. "That's bad. She's never done that before." She peered into the kitchen where Tom's step-mother was getting milk out of the fridge. "That's Tom's dressing gown she's wearing. She must have got it from the bathroom. He's working upstairs. I'd better call him."

Jamie took that as her cue to leave. She didn't need to hang around for whatever was coming next.

71

But then Ben started to stir. Whether it was the sudden silence after the noise of the vacuum cleaner, or the fact that Vuyiswa was now standing still instead of moving around, something had woken him up.

He looked up and rubbed his eyes. Then he pressed his forehead into Vuyiswa's back as though he wanted to go to sleep again. Then he lifted his head again, his eyes much clearer.

"Lady?" he said, looking at Jamie. "Lady?"

He stretched his arms out to Jamie and leaned sideways.

"Can I hold him for a moment?" Jamie asked. "Look! He still remembers me from that time he spent at my house. Please can I give him a little cuddle?"

Vuyiswa reached back with one hand to hold Ben against her back while she untied the blanket with the other. Then she slid him slowly to the floor. As soon as his feet hit the ground, he took off at a run and launched himself at Jamie.

She scooped him up and hugged him hard. "I've missed you, Ben. It's so good to see you again."

"Lady!" Ben grabbed her ponytail and ran it through his fingers. "Lady hair."

"Yes, that's my hair, Ben. Clever boy. Tell me, can you say 'Jamie'? Say 'Jamie', Ben."

"Damie," he managed on his first try.

"Yes, that's nearly right. I'm Jamie. Jamie. That's my name, you see?"

"Jamie?" He shook his head. "Not boy."

She laughed. This kid was so bright it was scary. "That's right, I'm not a boy. But my name is still Jamie. It's short for Jemima, see? Je-mi-ma."

"Mi-ma." He struggled out of her arms and slid to the ground. Then he galloped upstairs. When he came back down again he was carrying a book, which he thrust at Jamie.

"*The Tale of Jemima Puddleduck*," she read. "Yes, you really are spookily bright, aren't you, my darling?"

"Wead!" he ordered. "Wead it."

Delighted, Jamie picked him up and carried him to the sitting room, where a cream leather sofa seemed to invite her to curl up on it.

"Okay, let's see…" She opened the book, surprised by how many words there were on each page. She hadn't seen or thought about Beatrix Potter since her own childhood. She started to read.

"What a funny sight it is to see a brood of ducklings with a hen!"

Ben sat quietly throughout the story. Every now and then he would reach out to touch the duck in the poke bonnet or the fox reading the newspaper.

"Jemima Puddle-Duck was escorted home in tears on account of those eggs," Jamie read, nearing the end of the story. "Jemima was sad," she explained to Ben. "But it's all going to be okay, you'll see.

"She laid some more in June, and she was…"

"What the hell is going on in here?"

Jamie and Ben both jumped. Tom was standing in the doorway wearing jeans and an old T-shirt. His feet were bare and his hair was ruffled.

"Dadda?" said Ben.

Tom's tone softened. "Come here, Benny." He held out his hand. "Come here now."

Ben scrambled off Jamie's lap and ran to his father. Tom picked him up and gave him a kiss on the cheek. Then he put him down again. "Go and find Vuyiswa, Ben. She's in the kitchen. Go and find her."

As Tom turned back to her, Jamie stood up from the sofa. She felt as though she'd been caught out in something disgraceful. Which was absurd. What could be wrong with reading a picture book to a toddler?

Tom's face was tight and angry, but he kept his tone polite. "Did we have an arrangement for today? It must have slipped my mind."

"No," Jamie said. "There was no arrangement. You know there wasn't."

"So why do I come downstairs in the middle of the working day to find you keeping my son up when he's supposed to be having his nap?"

"He's already had his nap. He woke up a few minutes ago. I was just reading to him. He brought me a book and asked me to read it to him. What was I supposed to say? No?"

"Foxes and ducks and archaic language. Eurocentric nonsense. I'm trying to put him in touch with his own culture. How am I supposed to do that when you're filling his head with olde worlde drivel?"

"Hey, if you don't like the book, don't keep it in your house. And don't pretend you've never read it to him before. He knows that book like the back of his hand. He went straight to his room and got it."

Tom decided not to answer this charge. It wasn't the point. Not even remotely.

"The point is – what are you doing in my house at eleven in the morning on this fine Wednesday in October?"

Jamie pushed past him on her way to the front door. "Ask Vuyiswa."

She let herself out into the street, slamming the door behind her.

Tom was on his way to do just that when he heard Jamie's scream rip through the late-morning quiet.

———

Tom rushed outside to see what was happening. Was Jamie being mugged? Hijacked? Vuyiswa followed closely on his heels, but he waved her back into the house.

"No. Stay with Ben and my step-mother. If there's trouble, call the security company."

He found Jamie standing in front of her gate. She didn't seem to be hurt.

"What is it?" he said. "What happened?"

Jamie pointed at the gate. "That … that…"

Tom shaded his eyes against the strong sunlight and stared at the black thing hanging on her gate. When he saw what it was, he recoiled.

"God. Is that...?"

"A rat," Jamie said. "It's still alive..."

The rat had been tied to Jamie's gate with plastic cable ties. Its belly had been slit open from neck to groin so that its entrails hung out in a blood-stained mess. Tom thought Jamie was wrong about it being alive. But as he watched, it squirmed against the restraints.

He took a deep breath. "Okay, we need to get that thing down."

Jamie made an effort to pull herself together. "I know. We have to cut those ties to get it off the gate. I have a pair of scissors in the kitchen, but I'm worried about slicing through its paws. I don't think I could bear it if I did."

"I'll do it with my knife. It's sharper and more precise." He reached into his pocket and took out a long blade. It wasn't a Leatherman or a Swiss army knife. Jamie hadn't seen anything quite like it before.

"Don't you want a pair of gloves?" she asked. "Rats are dirty and it might bite you. I can lend you a pair of rubber gloves."

Tom looked at her. "You're talking about those bright yellow Marigold things, like for washing up?"

"Well, mine are pink, but yes."

Tom decided his masculine *amour propre* couldn't stand the blow. "I'm good, thanks."

He took out his camera and photographed the rat from various angles.

Jamie shuddered as he sliced through the four cable ties holding the rat in place. He lowered it to the ground, where it continued to twitch.

"Shouldn't we ... you know ... put it out of its misery or something?"

Tom tried to imagine chopping the rat's head off with a spade. No. That was exactly why he'd left his old line of work. He couldn't live with the images taking up residence in his brain.

"I'd really rather not. It'll be dead in a minute, anyway."

Jamie went inside to fetch a brush and pan. When she came out again, the rat was indeed dead.

"At least this part is familiar." She scooped the rat up and deposited it into her wheelie bin. "You can't have two cats without clearing up rodent corpses on a regular basis. I don't know why this one bothered me so much. I think it's knowing that a human being did it deliberately. Someone took the time and trouble to catch a rat alive, tie it to my gate, slit its belly open, and leave it there for me to find."

"Can I come in to wash my hands?" Tom asked.

"Yes, of course. Sorry, I should have offered. And let me make you a cup of coffee. I've got twenty minutes before I have to leave for work."

"I never say no to coffee. But I should be making it for you. You've had a shock."

It was only once they were in the house and waiting for the coffee machine to warm up that Jamie remembered she was furious with Tom.

She slid her eyes towards him and decided to let it go. For now.

"Any theories on who might have done it?" he asked.

She shrugged. "I have no idea. Neighbourhood kids, maybe? We'll probably never know."

"Most kids are in school at this time of day. And it doesn't feel like a childish prank to me. I've never actually tried to tie a wriggling rat onto a gate, but I would imagine it's not a simple matter. I'd say you've got yourself an enemy."

"Don't you think it's more likely to be random? They could as easily have chosen your gate to decorate."

"Except that they didn't. And this is your second incident in a couple of weeks, isn't it?"

She frowned. "Oh, you're talking about my night-time visitor? Why would you think they're connected?"

"Why would you think they're not? You've been targeted twice.

To me, that's the beginning of a pattern."

"I hope you're wrong." She handed him his coffee, and took a sip of her own. "I find it hard to believe anyone would target me in particular."

"Attractive young woman living on her own. It happens."

Jamie thrust the thought out of her mind. "Well, we'll see."

"In the meantime, you might think about taking extra precautions. I've noticed you broadcast your movements on Twitter a lot. 'Off to the shops now' or 'Home for the evening'. That kind of thing. You're basically doing the bad guys' work for them. And there's that other thing you do. The 'Jamie Burchell just arrived at Delucia's' thing."

"Checking in."

"That's the one. You might as well take out an ad in the newspaper, 'My house is standing empty right now. Come and help yourself to the TV and stereo.'"

"Now you sound like my mother. Everyone checks in on Facebook."

"I'm just saying it might be an idea to be more circumspect."

Jamie never enjoyed being told to circumscribe her digital life. "I'll think about it," she said stiffly. "But now I've really got to get to work. Thanks for doing the whole knight in shining armour thing. I'd have been a mess if you hadn't been here."

9

. . . .

Jamie Burchell @jamieburchell
My latest blog is out. 'My Edgar Allan Poe Moment'. In which I find a live rat tied
to my gate. Read it for your daily dose of horror: bit.ly.3jdej4.com

Gugu Motsepeng @Gugz
@jamieburchell OMG! That is terrifying! Who would do such a thing?

Jackson Smith @Smithie621
@jamieburchell Sounds like someone with a sick sense of humour.

The Tenant @squatter
@jamieburchell Takes a special kind of psycho to do something like that.

Bronwyn Jones @redhighheels
@jamieburchell Not to freak you out or anything, but if it were me I'd be scared
to go to sleep at night knowing someone like that had been at my gate.

Foully Wooing Won @foullywooingwon
@jamieburchell You have an impressive scream, Jamie. I thought my eardrums
were going to crack.

Jamie Burchell @jamieburchell
@foullywooingwon What makes you think I screamed? I might have just let out
a ladylike squeak. ;)

Cyril Attlee @inthemiddlecyril
I wish you'd take better care of yourself, Jamie. I worry about you living all alone
like that. Couldn't you stay with one of your sisters for a while?

Jamie Burchell @jamieburchell
@inthemiddlecyril I could Cyril, but then there would be murder done. I love my sisters dearly but I couldn't live with them. #noways

Ella Burchell @whiteswan
@jamieburchell @inthemiddlecyril I second that tweet. If Jamie tries to move in here, I'll yell for the cops. ;)

Jamie Burchell @jamieburchell
@whiteswan Haha! Love you too, Ellz. xx

His ribs hurt from laughing so much. Who knew this would be such fun?

Every time he thought about the look on Jamie's face when she saw the rat, little snorts of laughter bubbled up inside him. And when he remembered the way she'd screamed – the high, brilliant sound of it splitting the silence – he felt he could almost die with happiness.

Oh, it was wonderful. How had he lived without this for so long? Every part of him felt tingly and alive.

He hugged himself as he imagined Jamie trying to figure out how he'd done it. She'd never guess. Yes, there'd been failures in the beginning. The first four rats had died from an overdose of the sedative he'd put in their food. They'd simply stopped breathing. And the fifth rat had been far too lively. There was still that puncture wound in his thumb from where it had bitten him.

But the sixth rat was the Goldilocks rat – the one that ate just the right amount of sedative. It had started stirring while he was tying it to the gate. And that was another unexpected thrill. He'd had no idea how it would feel to hold a warm, living thing in his hands and know it was in his power. He'd nearly crushed the life out of it in his exuberance. But that would have meant catching another rat, and time was marching on.

Still, he'd had his reward when it came to slitting the belly open. Blood and viscera had spilled all over his fingers. Along with the excitement of knowing someone could come along and catch him at any moment, it was no wonder he'd sweated right through his shirt.

"Bloody, bloody internet. Why won't you help me?"

Jamie slammed her hand on the desk. The keyboard jumped and Holmes opened one eye. When he saw it was just Jamie throwing a strop, he sighed and laid his chin back down on his paws. Watson didn't even stir.

"Tell me what to do!" she commanded.

The cursor blinked at her.

"Okay, fuck off then."

Jamie got up to pace. The internet was her virtual office and her water cooler. It was the place where all her colleagues lived. If she wanted to know something, she googled it or threw the question out on social media. This system had never failed her before.

But this offer from Magnum Books was different. All Jamie wanted to know was whether she should accept it or turn it down. Google had no clear answers. Facebook and Twitter had plenty of strong opinions, but no clear answers either.

Jamie knew she couldn't string it out much longer. She had to reply to Magnum Books today. They were already sending her passive-aggressive emails about how she would "lose her place" on their list if she didn't accept their offer.

"Where's the harm?" she demanded of Watson, scratching him behind the ears. "Where's the harm in saying yes? This is what I dreamed about. I put my writing out there and somebody noticed. Somebody thought it was good enough, and made me an offer to publish it. I am living my dream."

Watson yawned and rolled over so she could rub his tummy.

"Okay, you're thinking about the word length, aren't you? I will concede that 30,000 words is not very much, but it's not fair to call it a short story either. Let's say it's a novella. A novella is nothing to be ashamed of for your first book."

Holmes noticed his brother hogging all the attention. He head-butted Jamie's hand until she started to stroke him instead.

"No, I haven't forgotten about the rights issue," she said. "I know I'd never be able to use the story again in any form. And no, I'm not sure I'm ready for that."

That was the stumbling block, she realised. She wasn't at a point where she could admit that her story would never be anything more than a straight-to-digital novella that might garner twenty-five downloads, if she was lucky.

Relieved to have found some clarity, she typed a letter of refusal and clicked SEND before she could change her mind.

A twinge of refuser's remorse gripped her, but there was no recall option for emails. At least now she could get on with the business of writing. Flexing her fingers, she made herself look down at the last passage she'd typed.

Eve had never felt any curiosity about what her grandmother had done in the Old Times. It was such a barbaric time, by all accounts, that it was considered impolite to ask people about what their lives had been like in those days. And by now there was hardly anyone left who remembered. Ayn was a great rarity – a woman who had reached her eightieth birthday.

"I was twenty-one when the Rebirth happened," Ayn explained. "I was studying to be a doctor. I had just completed my fourth year."

"A doc-tor?" Eve stumbled over the unfamiliar syllables.

Ayn clicked her tongue. "A Healer, as you would say."

"But Grandma, Healers are born, not made. It is not something you can train for."

Jamie forced herself to type on.

"It was in those days," Ayn said grimly.

No, not 'grimly'. Too adverby.

"It was in those days," Ayn said.

Actually, she didn't need 'Ayn said' at all.

"It was in those days."

At this rate it would take her all morning to write one paragraph. What was going on? What had happened to her speed? A thousand words an hour used to be no problem for her. What if she couldn't take her manuscript seriously anymore? A publisher had read it and rated it as straight-to-digital. Now every word she typed seemed clunky.

She glanced at her watch and cheered up when she saw it was 11.15. Time to get ready for work. For the first time ever, it was a relief to flip her laptop shut and head out for a seven-hour shift of manual labour.

———

Pumla ignored Jamie as if she were a stop sign at rush hour when she walked in the door.

That was par for the course since their fight. Jamie was tempted to go along with it. It would be easy enough to get on with work, speaking to Pumla only when it was unavoidable. But Jamie'd had enough. High school was ten years ago. It was time for them both to stop acting like adolescents.

"A word," she said as she strapped on the purple-and-white-striped apron that all Delucia's employees wore.

"Not now." Pumla nodded at the party of six office workers who'd just come in.

It made sense to do it later, but Jamie was afraid she might lose her nerve.

"Five minutes. Nomsa can cover."

Pumla signalled to the pastry chef to take over waitressing duties. Then she marched to the back office and turned to face Jamie, arms folded across her chest, radiating hostility.

Jamie forced her own arms to relax.

"Listen," she said. "About the other day. I overreacted, and I'm sorry."

"What are you talking about?"

"You were trying to warn me that the publishing deal I'd been offered wasn't as fantastic as I hoped. I didn't want to hear it, so I snapped at you. I'm sorry about that."

Pumla didn't relax her posture. "But you took it anyway, right?"

"No, I didn't. I turned it down. I made the final decision this morning and sent off the email. I feel a bit sick about it, to be honest, but I've done it."

Pumla dropped her arms. "Well, that's something at least. You're not desperate. You don't have to take the first offer that comes along."

"Actually, I am a bit desperate."

"Nonsense. It's a good story. Everyone who's reading it thinks so. It deserves better than to be chopped up and sold off cheaply. That's what I was trying to tell you."

"I get that now. You might have been more diplomatic."

"Diplomacy's not my strong suit. You should know that by now."

Jamie had to laugh. "I should, shouldn't I? So … are we okay?"

Pumla mimed a punch at her arm. "We're okay." Then she hurried out of the office and into the madness of the lunchtime rush.

And that, Jamie thought, as she went out to join her, was as close as the two of them ever got to hugging.

———

The back of Jamie's neck prickled as she noticed the single man sitting in the corner of the restaurant at table five. His face was hidden behind a newspaper, but she had a feeling she'd seen him before. Nomsa must have taken his order because he had a drink and a small basket of bread with dipping sauces at his elbow, and his menu had been cleared away.

She heard the ting of the bell signalling an order ready to be collected and hurried to the serving hatch to pick it up. Aha, she thought. Table five had ordered a Caesar salad with dressing on the side. Perhaps she'd work out where she knew him from when she served it to him.

"Your salad, sir," she said, putting it down in front of him. "And our house dressing." She almost spilled it as he looked up. "Oh, it's you."

Tom put his newspaper down and stretched his legs.

"Thanks," he said. "It looks good. But then the food in here always does."

"We take pride in our presentation."

"Well, that answers that question."

"What are you talking about?" She cleared away an empty glass and the wrapper from his straw.

"I took a bet with myself that your gratitude for my rat-clearing services would fade as the memory of my dickhead behaviour returned. Looks like I won."

"Good for you."

"Look, I'd really like to talk to you. To explain myself, if that's possible."

"I'm working."

"Sure, I know you're busy. But if I stick around until lunch is over, perhaps we could have a word then? You must quieten down some time, right?"

"Not before half past two, usually. You'll finish your salad long before then. You should go home, Tom. You don't owe me any explanations."

"I really do. So I'll sit here with my paper and my iPad until you're free to talk. You can't duck me forever, Jamie. I know where

84

you live, remember."

"That's actually kind of creepy."

"Sorry." He held up his hands. "It wasn't meant to be. My failed attempt at humour. Five minutes is all I ask. Then I'll get out of your way."

"Fine. Five minutes."

Jamie stalked back to the bar to pick up a tray of drinks for table four. Once she'd delivered them and was standing scoping out the room, she felt Pumla come up behind her.

"That's him, isn't it?" Pumla said. "Hot Running Guy? Where's his kid today?"

"I have no idea. At home, I presume."

"What does he want – aside from lunch?"

"He wants to talk to me, and he's going to hang around here until we quieten down to do so."

Pumla wiggled her eyebrows. "Dedicated! I like that."

"More like bipolar. The way he flips from friendly to angry and back again – I can't keep up. Who needs that kind of drama anyway?"

"Looks like he's in a friendly mood today. He can't keep his eyes off you."

Jamie forced herself not to turn around. "Really?"

"Really. He's looking at you like a kid eyeing an éclair. If you decide you don't want him, send him my way. He looks just fine. Perhaps I'll let him be the father of my child."

Jamie grinned. Of all the dirty tricks she and Pumla had played on each other, boyfriend stealing had never been one of them. Then her brain clicked into gear.

"Wait a minute. What do you mean, the father of your child? What child?"

"The child I've decided to have. Table three is calling you, by the way."

Jamie dashed over to table three. Then the bell rang to pick up an order, and then another one. Soon she was so busy she didn't have time to wonder about Pumla or Tom, or anyone else who didn't want food or drink from her.

By half-past two there was just one table besides Tom's still occupied, the customers lingering over coffee.

"What child?" Jamie hissed in Pumla's ear.

Pumla smiled. "Go and talk to your guy, before I poach him out from under your nose. Go on, he's been waiting long enough."

So Jamie picked up the plate of penne primavera that the kitchen staff had made for her, and went to sit at Tom's table.

He put down his iPad and smiled at her. "I need to apologise, again. And to thank you, again. This is becoming a habit."

"If you wouldn't keep flying off the handle, you wouldn't need to keep apologising to people."

"True. You probably won't believe me, but I'm a pretty even-tempered guy most of the time."

Jamie swallowed a mouthful of courgette and shook her head. "You're right. I don't believe you."

"Well, it's true. I just have a short fuse when it comes to Ben. But that's not the point. The point is, you very kindly came to my step-mother's rescue and brought her home. I should have been thanking you, not making you feel like an intruder."

"Look, I get it. It can't be easy, looking after someone who's liable to wander off at any moment."

"The wandering-off thing is new. She used to be quite happy to spend the day at my place, puttering around in the yard and dusting things. She gets bored at the retirement centre, and it does her good to have a change of scene. But lately she's become more unpredictable. I'm arranging for a carer to keep an eye on her when she's with me. Vuyiswa and I can't handle her alone any more. We both have our own work as well as Ben to look after."

"That sounds like a good idea."

"I'm just glad you found her when you did, and persuaded her to come back to the house. She could have been hit by a car, or gotten hopelessly lost."

There was a silence. Jamie wanted to leave it at that, but the pique she'd been carrying around was too strong. She had to say something. "Why did you shout at me like that?" she blurted. "You say you're sensitive where Ben is concerned, and I get that, but I wasn't doing him any harm. He asked me to read him a story and I did, that's all." Tom looked down at the table. "Yes … I know."

"I was telling him that my name is short for Jemima and…"

"And he ran straight upstairs to get *Jemima Puddleduck*, right?"

"Right."

Tom's face was a picture of pride mixed with frustration. "He's such a bright little guy. I just wish he didn't love those old-timey English stories so much. I'm trying to interest him in his own culture, but he's all about the Beatrix Potter and the Dr Seuss. And *Where the Goddam Wild Things Are*."

"What is his own culture?"

"Uh…" Tom looked sheepish. "I don't exactly know. I've been trying to trace his mother's origins for months with the help of a private detective. Nobody knows where she came from, except that it wasn't Zimbabwe, Malawi, Mozambique, Zambia or Nigeria. All I've got to go on is that it was somewhere further north. We're pretty sure his biological father is South African."

"How on earth do you know that?"

"A DNA test. It cost a fortune, but it's gotten us closer to figuring out his origins than anything else. Now we're waiting for the results of the mitochondrial DNA test, which will tell us more about his mother's people."

"Okay, but still." Jamie dragged the conversation back to her original grievance. "None of that explains why you were so rude to me. I was reading him a story, not corrupting him. What did I do wrong?"

There was a pause, during which Jamie managed to get nearly halfway through her pasta.

"It's my issue, not yours," Tom said at last.

"You made it my issue by yelling at me, and now you owe me an explanation."

"Okay." He leaned forward across the table, then leaned back, then leaned forward again. "It seems presumptuous to say this, because we haven't really got anywhere yet."

"We as in 'you and me'?"

"Yes. We've spoken a few times and we've shared a pizza, but that's it. I was kind of hoping to take it up a notch. Maybe ask you out to dinner some time. I haven't dated much since Ben came into my life. It's practically impossible with a tiny baby. And it's not all that easy now that he's a toddler either. The few women I've dated had no interest in Ben. Oh, they thought the story of how I adopted him was adorable and everything, but they had zero interest in him as a child."

Jamie opened her mouth to say that she wasn't like that, but Tom carried on.

"And to be perfectly honest, I prefer it that way."

"You prefer women who have zero interest in your son?"

"Yes, exactly. It keeps things simple. You see, I was raised by a single dad. I remember the procession of women he let into our lives, and how entangled I would get with them. And how painful it was when they were ready to disentangle themselves, and I wasn't."

"But then he married your step-mother," Jamie pointed out. "And she's still in your life. She's the one who stuck, isn't she?"

"Yes ... she's the one who stuck."

Jamie tried to read the expression on his face, but found it unfathomable.

"I don't want that for Ben," he said. "I don't want any surrogate mother figures in his life. I'm his dad. I'm his permanence. And I don't want to be responsible for causing him heartache. He's had enough loss in his life already."

A dozen counter-arguments rose to Jamie's lips, but she didn't voice them. Who was she to tell this man how to raise his son? Or to insist on being allowed into his life? Could she guarantee that this ... whatever it was ... between her and Tom was going to last? No, of course she couldn't – it had barely started. Any more than she could guarantee Ben wouldn't be hurt when it was over.

"Okay," she said. "I think I understand. So when you came in the other day to find me reading Ben a story, it must have felt … weird."

He nodded. "Exactly. But that's no excuse for the way I behaved. I was rude to you and I'm sorry for that."

"Apology accepted."

He dredged up a smile. "This whole conversation is moot if you don't want to go out with me again. So what do you say? Any night this week that suits you. The Earl & Badger – or somewhere else if you prefer."

Jamie hesitated. This man had baggage. Baggage with a capital B. And the part she wanted to share with him most was the part he was most prickly about – his son. Going out with him would be the emotional equivalent of gambling. It wasn't smart. It wasn't sensible. And Jamie was known for being both.

"The Earl & Badger sounds great," she said. "How about Thursday night?"

10

So I've decided to have a baby, Facebook peeps. Ke nako – it is time. Starting auditions for a baby daddy tomorrow.

Sizwe Dhlomo Ooh, ooh! Me! Me! Pick me!

Pumla Maseko Sizwe, I totally would, babe. Like a shot, you know that. But you're gay, and I really don't want to involve any turkey basters in this exercise.

Jamie Burchell Are you Out. Of. Your. Mind?

Victoria Mooki That's very judgemental, Jamie. Why shouldn't she have a baby if she wants one?

Jamie Burchell She DOESN'T want one. That's the whole point.

Pumla Maseko Maybe I've changed my mind.

Jamie Burchell And maybe you're just caving to pressure.

Victoria Mooki It's still her business, not ours.

Jamie Burchell Hey, if you put it up as your Facebook status, it becomes everyone's business.

Victoria Mooki I happen to think Pumla will make an awesome mom.

Pumla Maseko Thanks Vix.

Jamie Burchell Remember those sugar babies we had to carry around in Grade 7? Those bags of sugar with faces drawn on them? We had to carry them around with us 24 hours a day – feed them, burp them, dress them, keep them warm. They were supposed to teach us about the responsibilities of parenting. Remember how many sugar babies you killed? Five! You still hold the record for bursting the most bags of sugar over a two-week period.

Pumla Maseko I was THIRTEEN! That was, like, FIFTEEN years ago. I like to think I've grown up since then.

Sizwe Dhlomo Of course you have.

Pumla Maseko And anyway, I'm tired of people looking at me with that subtle pity in their eyes. Like there must be something wrong with me. I'm going to do this before I end up the oldest mom on the playground.

———

Jamie thought she was doing a good job of not obsessing over what to wear for her Thursday night date.

She'd only tried on and rejected five outfits before settling on one. And instead of leaving all the discarded clothes in a heap on the bed to sort out later, she'd hung them up and put them all away. Her super neat sister Caroline would have been proud of her.

The thought sneaked into her brain that by tidying her bedroom she was leaving open the possibility of bringing Tom back to it later. She shook her head. This was only their first date. Well, their second if you counted the pizza night.

And while Jamie considered herself a feminist, and refused to judge herself or other women by their sexual choices, she still liked to know exactly whom she was letting into her bed. There were too many unknowns with Tom Elliot – too many closed doors. In some ways he felt familiar, as though she'd known him her whole life, but in others, he was a complete mystery.

91

Jamie didn't go to bed with complete mysteries.

She stood in front of the mirror and brushed out her hair. Black trousers, a sparkly sleeveless top, and some good jewellery completed the look. She swiped on mascara and lip gloss, and considered the job done. As she slid her feet into a pair of wedge-heeled sandals, she took a moment to be grateful that Tom was tall enough to make the wearing of heels no problem.

She took a quick photo of herself in the mirror and posted it to Facebook and Twitter, inviting outfit-feedback. It was getting too late to change anything, so she did it as much for reassurance as for advice. The responses came almost immediately: the Twitter community was nothing if not quick off the mark.

Jamie Burchell @jamieburchell
My outfit for date with neighbour. Hot or not? #selfie http://instagram.com/p/ePSLKFHKDH/

Bronwyn Jones @redhighheels
Love the silvery earrings! Pretty, but understated. #hot

Amanda Stanislau @stani2
I like it! Go get 'em, tiger! #hot

The Tenant @squatter
Sexxeee! ☺

Cyril Attlee @inthemiddlecyril
Maybe a jacket or a wrap? I know it's October but the nights can be quite chilly.

Making a firm resolution not to check her phone during dinner, Jamie dashed off replies to her Twitter friends. She pressed send on the last one as her doorbell rang.

"I thought we'd walk to the restaurant so we can both have wine," Tom said as he leaned down to brush his lips against her cheek. He smelled of pine forests. Quite delicious. It relaxed her to know he'd also taken some trouble over his appearance. He'd shaved, showered and put on a blue linen shirt.

"Did Ben go to sleep all right?" she asked.

"All right is a relative term." He pulled a harassed face. "But as bedtimes go, it was it wasn't too bad. In the top thirty per cent, let's say."

"A B-minus. That's pretty good." Jamie looked up at his house as they walked past. Tom had asked if he could call for her at eight to give himself time to put Ben down. Jamie would have loved to be there for his bedtime. She imagined herself bathing Ben, rubbing him dry with a huge, soft towel, pulling his pyjamas over his head, and reading him a story until he got sleepy. If she closed her eyes, the tactile memories of his warm weight pressing into her lap and his hair tickling her chin were as vivid as ever.

The Earl & Badger was less than a block from Delucia's. An English-style pub, it offered sport on the big screen, several draught beers on tap, and reliable if unimaginative food during the day. At night, the dining room opened, and the menu choices became more interesting.

Jamie greeted the owners by name. They were brothers – sons of the Greek greengrocer who had a fruit and vegetable shop further up the road. She had gone to school with them, although they were a few years older.

Delucia's business overlapped somewhat with the Earl & Badger's, especially at lunchtime. But there were more than enough customers to go around. So the Nikolaides brothers popped into Delucia's most mornings for their coffee-and-doughnut fix, while Jamie and Pumla often had sundowners at the Earl after closing up at six in the evening.

The man watched Tom and Jamie turn into the little parade of shops where the Earl & Badger was the main tenant. Tom walked just behind Jamie, with one arm extended – not quite touching her, but ready to if necessary. Pompous prick.

Jamie didn't seem to be enjoying herself, which was a small consolation. She'd looked thoughtful on the short walk to the pub. Probably wondering how soon she could ditch the loser and get back home.

As usual, she looked even more beautiful in person than she had in the photograph she'd shared on Twitter. That was very pleasing. However good she looked on the screen, she always looked better in the flesh. How many women could honestly say that in this age of Photoshop and crop-and-save?

It was rare to find someone as honest as Jamie Burchell. She was perfect in every way. Almost. If Jamie had a fault, it was that she tended to ignore him. He'd addressed several remarks to her online now, and so far she'd only responded to one. That wasn't nice. It wasn't polite. She'd paid attention to the rat, though. If she was going to make a habit of going out to dinner with strange men, she might need another lesson in manners.

He'd already searched for Tom Elliot on the internet, and hadn't been impressed with what he'd found. His social media presence was almost zero. He was a nobody – unworthy of Jamie's attention. Some sort of lame academic, a bleeding heart criminologist, preaching about how people were bad because they were poor and desperate. Criminals couldn't help themselves. It wasn't their fault. Boo hoo.

What bullshit.He didn't understand how Jamie could fall for that crap. She was an intelligent young woman. Surely she could see through the rubbish this man churned out?

It was time to give them something else to think about. Tom Elliot had a dog. A big yellow dog. The trouble with dogs was that they didn't take kindly to strangers hiding in gardens. Dealing with the dog would kill two birds with one stone.

Two birds with one stone. He snickered to himself at the thought.

"I never get this table." Tom indicated the corner two-seater they'd been ushered to. "This is the best table in the house."

"Professional courtesy." Jamie smiled and slid into her seat. "Our waitress used to work at Delucia's. She left because we couldn't offer her as many hours as she wanted."

The waitress came back with menus.

"Thanks, Mpho. Is there anything we should stay away from tonight?"

The waitress leaned in closer. "Don't order the scampi. It gets delivered fresh every Friday morning, so the stuff they're serving tonight is nearly a week old. Also the porcini special has been coming back to the kitchen uneaten all week. I think Pietro is using too much cumin in the recipe."

She straightened up and put a smile on her face.

"Our specials today include fresh asparagus, lightly steamed, wrapped in thinly sliced Parma ham and served with a wasabi Béarnaise sauce. Then for the main course we have linguine served with fresh porcini mushrooms in a creamy white wine *jus*, spiced with a hint of cumin. Our line fish of the day is yellowtail, filleted, pan-fried and served with a trio of sauces – lemon butter, tartare and our trademark dill-and-basil mayonnaise."

She left them poring over their menus with a basket of bread and the drinks they'd ordered.

"What the hell is cumin again?" Tom asked.

"It's a spice used in Indian cooking. One of my favourites, but I'd never use it on mushrooms. It would overwhelm them and leave them tasting curried."

"I guess the restaurant trade is like any other. When you get too close to it, it strips away the glamour and you find out things you'd rather not know about – like week-old scampi."

"Hey, when it comes to elderly seafood, ignorance is most definitely not bliss."

"So what should I order? I normally have a steak in here, but if I wanted to branch out?"

Jamie considered the menu. "All the Greek dishes are good because they're Mama Nikolaides' recipes, and she's an outstanding cook. I'm saving room for baklava afterwards. I know it's good because I got the recipe out of Pietro one night when he'd had a few beers. Now we use it at Delucia's."

"So the lamb kleftiko, maybe?"

"Excellent choice. And I'll have the lamb chops."

They put down their menus and looked at each other. Candlelight suited Jamie, Tom decided. Her face didn't need the flattery of low-lighting, but it was fun to watch the shadows play over her features. Her dark eyes seemed almost black in here.

He took in the details of what she was wearing. Earlier, when she'd answered the door, he'd seen only her. The long, lean length of her, the warmth of her smile, and the sun-streaked hair that made him want to reach out and touch. But now he noticed that her top was glittery and sleeveless, accenting slim arms. And that the pendant she wore glowed in the candlelight.

Jamie laughed. "You look like you're committing me to memory so you can do a reconstruction with a police artist later."

"Sorry. I'm told I can get a little intense."

She took a sip of her wine. "Tell me something about Tom Elliot – something I don't know. Like what do you do when you're not being a mild-mannered academic? I especially want to know why you carry crime scene paraphernalia around with you like you're on *CSI*."

He smiled. "I don't think a torch and a digital camera count as crime scene paraphernalia exactly, but I admit some of the stuff I carry is a little unusual."

"Okay. Why?"

"I worked in Afghanistan and Iraq for a while before I came back to South Africa. I guess I got used to being prepared for all kinds of situations."

"Afghanistan and Iraq?" Jamie's eyebrows shot up. "Were you in the military?"

"No. I worked for an NGO that consulted to the US government on how to improve community relations in the Gulf. The idea was that civilians should start seeing American soldiers as friends rather than enemies. As a criminologist, my role was to analyse what drove civilians to commit acts of violence against the US military."

"Well, let's see. The US invaded Afghanistan and Iraq and killed lots of civilians. I'd be a bit peeved myself if I were an Iraqi."

"That was a stumbling block, yes."

"So why did you leave?"

"I realised it was a situation I couldn't win so I cut my losses and got out of there. It was taking a huge psychological toll on me. If I could only have felt I was making the tiniest bit of difference, I might have stuck it out longer, but I wasn't."

Jamie wanted to know more, but decided not to push it. You didn't quiz a man about his involvement in a very ugly war over dinner. Besides, their food had arrived.

"So will you be sending Ben to nursery school next year?" she asked, picking up her knife and fork.

"No!" He looked quite shocked. "He'll only be two in April. That's not nearly old enough for school."

"Parents seem to be sending their kids to playgroups younger these days. It's a definite trend."

"I don't believe in judging other parents, because God knows I'm not perfect, but I'm not quite ready to feed Ben to the system yet. He's only just learning to talk, so he wouldn't even be able to tell anyone if something was bothering him."

"You know," Jamie leaned forward, "that child of yours is amazingly intelligent. His understanding is huge, and the way he makes connections between things is just incredible. I'm no expert, but he really impressed me."

The smile on Tom's face could only be described as a beam. "The other day he saw the moon in the sky during the daytime, and he pointed at it and said, 'Moon'. Then he frowned at me and said, 'Not night?' So I launched into a long explanation about why the moon is also visible during the day. He got bored and ran away. I'm not an expert either, but I do think he's pretty smart."

"He called my cat a 'Pssss' and wanted to go outside and stroke it."

"Oh, he's crazy about animals. Crazy. He and Silver are best buds. Maybe I could bring him to your place sometime so he could make friends with the cats. He'd love that."

"I'd love that too!"

At the sight of Jamie's glowing face, something in Tom retreated.

"Well … it's kind of an imposition. But perhaps we can set that up some time."

Jamie wanted to insist, but the look in his eyes warned her to leave it alone.

He reapplied himself to his lamb. It was excellent, as promised. Jamie announced that her cutlets were good too, although she hadn't made much progress with them. He wondered if her habit of picking at her food would start to irritate him after a while.

Probably not as much as her habit of slipping under his guard. What was he thinking, chatting about Ben like that, as though they were a couple of besotted parents discussing their son?

How could he have known how seductive it would be to talk to someone who was as interested in Ben as he was? Or who seemed to be. He'd thought he was alone in his fascination with every aspect of his son's development.

Yes, Vuyiswa was fond of Ben, but she had a son of her own and, naturally enough, was focused on him. Some of Tom's colleagues had children and would listen to his stories about what Ben had done or said. But their own families came first. Even the leader of the toddler group Tom and Ben attended once a week had eight other parents dying to chat about the brilliance of their offspring.

It was natural that Jamie's interest in Ben would catch him off guard and lure him into talking about his favourite subject. But he couldn't risk her interest waning if Ben became a daily burden rather than a weekly novelty. No one knew that better than Tom. It was a pain he was determined to spare his son.

"That much deep thought deserves dessert," Jamie said, watching him brood. "Dessert makes everything better."

Tom pulled himself out of the past. "Dessert it is then. How about I order the baklava and we get two spoons? I don't think I could stand watching you send half of it back."

Jamie laughed. "It's a terrible habit, isn't it? And you'd think I'd know better, working in a restaurant. Nothing is more irritating than seeing food you've spent ages preparing coming back half-eaten. That's why I always ask for a doggy bag. At least that way I get to eat according to my appetite without offending the chef. And as a bonus, I take something delicious home with me."

The baklava, when it came, was a ringing testimonial to Mama Nikolaides' skill. A perfect symphony of butter, nuts, honey and phyllo pastry, it was squishy in some parts, and crunchy in others. Jamie made Tom laugh by telling him that Mrs Nikolaides would go to her grave before she would admit it, but her baklava was actually based on a very old Turkish recipe. She told him that the Greeks and the Turks were in perpetual dispute over who had first invented the delightful dessert.

"What about your partner?" Tom asked. "Is she involved in the baking side of things?"

"Pumla? No way. She can't stand cooking and baking. She's a brilliant entrepreneur, though. She turned Delucia's around from a greasy little bakery that was about to close its doors into a successful business. Pumla's always had big ideas. I wonder if she'll put them on the back-burner when the baby comes?"

"Oh, is she pregnant? I didn't notice."

"Not yet, but she's hoping to be soon."

"So she and her partner are trying for a baby?"

Jamie snorted. "I wish! There is no partner. She just wants a baby. Or, I should say, she's giving in to pressure to have a baby. Crazy woman."

Tom lifted his hands. "I don't think you should be telling me all this. I hardly know her. I'm sure she wouldn't want me knowing her private business."

Jamie waved this away. "Oh, please. She's even created a Facebook group for it. It's called 'Pumla's Baby-Daddy Search'. We're all supposed to nominate guys that we think have awesome enough genes for her to breed with. This is hardly a secret."

Tom blinked at her. "You know, Jamie, I'm thirty-one years old. That's only – what? – about four years older than you and Pumla?"

"Three years."

"Okay, so why do I feel like a doddery seventy-year-old when I talk to you? Who creates a Facebook group for their baby-daddy search? It's insane. What happened to boundaries? Doesn't anyone have boundaries anymore?"

"Sure they do," Jamie said. "They're just more porous than they used to be."

"More like non-existent."

"Nonsense. There's nothing wrong with crowd-sourcing your personal decisions. In fact, it makes sense to get a range of opinions before you make a choice."

Tom shrugged and ushered her out of the restaurant.

The air had cooled a little, making the moonlit walk back pleasant. A breeze stirred the air. It was gusty enough to make the Joburg-born Jamie wonder if a thunderstorm would enliven the small hours of the morning.

As they turned into Sixteenth street, the pale wash of moonlight took on a yellowish glow from the streetlights. It was Jamie who saw it first.

"What's that on my gate? It looks like a bird or something. No, two birds. What are they doing? It looks like they're trying to get through the bars. That's so weird."

Tom followed the direction of her pointing finger. "I think ... I think they're stuck."

"Oh, God!" Jamie's voice was full of distress. "It's happened again." She broke into a run.

"Hey, wait a minute!" Tom had to run too, to catch up with her long strides. He got to the gate half a second before she did.

"Oh, no! Oh, no!" She clutched at her hair. "They've been tied to the gate, just like the rat. Oh, the poor things. Have they been hurt, do you think?"

Tom looked at the sticky wetness that coated the feathers of each pigeon and nodded. The streetlights leached the colour out of everything, but he knew blood when he saw it. "I'm afraid so. No, don't touch them. They'll peck you."

"I want to help them."

"Me too, but we need to see what's going on first. Why don't you go inside and get those rubber gloves you offered me last time?"

While she was gone, Tom switched on the LED torch attached to his key-ring and shuddered at what it revealed. The pigeons had been severely battered. They were tied by their feet to the bars of the gate, where they fluttered feebly. And what was that?

Tom peered at some kind of lump that had been sellotaped to the gate next to the pigeons. He'd take it down for a closer look when he had the gloves on. Right now, he needed to photograph the scene in its undisturbed state.

When Jamie came back with the gloves, he used his knife to cut the pigeons down. He laid them gently on the tray she'd brought.

"Same cable ties as last time," he commented. "You can get them at any hardware store."

The lump under the sellotape turned out to be a large and blood-stained stone. Tom and Jamie carried everything into the house, including the pigeons.

"They won't make it, will they?" Jamie looked with pity at the mangled birds still stirring fitfully on the tray.

"No, they're badly injured."

"What's going on here, Tom? This isn't kids playing a prank, is it?"

"No. Not unless they're deeply disturbed. I think it's an adult. I don't know if a kid would have come up with this message he's left for you."

"You mean two birds with one stone? Yes, I thought of that, but what does it mean?"

"Hell if I know."

One of the pigeons had stopped moving, its claws contracted in the rictus of death. The other was still twitching. As with the rat, Jamie couldn't bring herself to finish off the perpetrator's work. Birds don't have very complex nervous systems, she told herself. They don't feel pain like we do. But still she felt for the suffering creature, and a new fury bloomed in her chest against the human who had done this.

"Has anything like this ever happened to you before?" Tom asked. "Or to anyone you know?"

She shook her head. This was so completely out of her realm of experience, she could hardly order her thoughts.

"Can't you think of anyone who might want to upset you in this way?" he persisted. "Maybe someone you've had a neighbourhood dispute with? Or that your parents have, seeing as they own this house?"

"Minor stuff," she said. "Minor, trivial stuff. Like the guy who used to live in your house was convinced that his rat problem was coming from our compost heap. So my parents cleared it away, and then I came to live here with my cats, and, hey presto, no more rat problem."

Tom continued to look at her with raised eyebrows, so she sighed. "Okay, what else? There was a motion to enclose the suburb a couple of years ago. You know the kind of thing. They wanted to block off some of the roads and put up guarded booms. My parents voted against it, which didn't go down well in certain quarters. And every time it's come up since, I've voted against it, too. I'm sure we're a little unpopular with some people, but I can't see anyone going to these lengths. It's hard to imagine anyone having a rational motive for this kind of behaviour."

"Okay, let's move onto the irrational motives, then. What about your online life? Any stalkers, trolls, assorted nuts there?"

Jamie shook her head. "That's such a cliché. Why do people always think the internet is populated by nutcases? My followers are nice, normal people."

"You know them *all* personally, do you? All two thousand of them, or whatever it is?"

"It's two thousand, one hundred and fifty-six. And, no, obviously I don't know them all personally, but I have met a lot of them at tweet-ups."

"At … what was that again?"

"Tweet-ups. That's what it's called when you meet up with people you know from Twitter. Anyway, the point is, I've always found them to be perfectly normal folk who are pretty much as you'd expect from their online profiles."

"Hmm. Well, if anything strikes you as weird, you should pay attention to it."

Jamie made coffee for them both with hands that weren't quite steady. Decaf, as she didn't think her system needed any more hyping. The second pigeon had finally stilled, the panicked pulsing of its chest slowing and stopping. There was something unsettling about watching the life force slip out of another creature in front of your eyes.

"Do you think I should go to the police?" she asked, handing Tom his coffee. Then she laughed and rubbed her hands over her face. "I don't know why I keep asking you for advice. You're an academic, aren't you? Not some kind of private detective. It's just that one always thinks of criminologists as being somehow experts on crime."

"In some ways, we are. I specialise in the social conditions that cause crime to proliferate, but I know a bit about criminal procedure too. The thing is, this guy hasn't broken any laws. It's not against the law to kill rats or pigeons, or even to decorate someone's gate with them. If he accelerates, it could be a different story. Like if he went after your cats, for example."

A chill curled down Jamie's spine. "You're trying to scare me."

"If you're scared, you'll be more careful."

"Well, then. Mission accomplished."

He rubbed a hand up and down her arm. "I hope you'll be able to sleep tonight. Maybe you should put some brandy in that coffee."

Jamie shook her head. "I'm going to blog about it. That's my version of a double brandy. Blogging about things helps me to sort them out in my head."

"You do realise that if this person is someone who follows you online, he's going to be encouraged by the attention you're giving him?"

"I'm not going to shut up to suit him. Women have been doing that for long enough."

11

The Baby Daddy Search is narrowing. I've got it down to three candidates. There's Luso, the bad boy. He won't interfere with how I raise the kid and he played a year of professional soccer so the child will get great sport genes. There's Chester who already has three kids by three different baby mamas so he's super fertile. And there's Dumisani who is kind of boring and stable but he likes me. What do you say, peeps?

Nonna Mzambo Girl, you make me laugh. Choosing the father of your child on Facebook. LOL! You nuts.

Victoria Mooki Go for the football player. Your kid will thank you some day. It's nice for a boy to be good at sport, you'll see. Or even a girl.

Pumla Maseko Good point, Vix. Thanks.

Jamie Burchell I'm going to vote for the underdog. I like the sound of Dumisani. Boring and stable are not bad qualities in a baby daddy. And he likes you! Bonus points for him.

Michael Blackthorn Excuse me butting in. I don't know you very well, but I have to ask. Are you planning on telling the guy about this or are you just going to trap him?

Pumla Maseko Michael, I'm planning on having consensual, unprotected sex where he knows I'm not on the pill. That's not entrapment. He knows what the risks are just as well as I do.

Zanele Motsoepeng Steer clear of Chester. You don't want all that baby-mama drama in your life. Believe me, I know what I'm talking about. ☹

Pumla Maseko Yeah, good point.

So Pumla was going ahead with the baby thing. Jamie tried to imagine her as a mother and found it wasn't hard. She would probably make a success of motherhood, just as she made a success of everything else she did. Her days as a rampant killer of sugar-sack babies were far behind her.

And maybe she did have hidden maternal longings. Maybe it wasn't just a matter of conforming to expectations. Jamie decided to give her the benefit of the doubt and be more supportive.

In the meantime, it was taking her too long to respond to all the comments on her blog. By now she should already have been working on the next day's instalment of her novel. But something about the pigeon story had captured the imagination of her readers. The post had gone viral, attracting record numbers of shares on Facebook and Twitter and nearly a hundred comments. Speculation was running rampant about who her mystery stalker could be, and what the meaning behind his gruesome tokens was.

Jamie could hardly keep track of the theories. He was in love with her. He hated her. He was obsessed with her. He was someone who'd met her in the bakery. He was someone who'd found her online. He was an old boyfriend. He wanted to be a new boyfriend. He wasn't a he at all, but a she riddled with bunny-boiler jealousy. There was even a school of thought that he was Tom. Several commenters found it significant that Tom had been with her on both occasions when she had discovered the half-dead animals. On all three occasions, if they counted the time she'd found footprints in her garden. The fact that he'd been sitting next to her when they'd heard the thump on the window didn't seem to matter.

The phone rang and Jamie reached for it automatically, forgetting to check caller ID.

"Hello?"

"Hello, Jamie. This is your stalker speaking."

She hesitated for a fraction of a second and then laughed.

"Ha bloody ha, Ella."

"I thought it was quite amusing," her sister said.

"You would. What's up?"

"I actually *am* phoning about your stalker. To check whether you're okay and so forth. You can't post stuff like that on your blog and expect your family not to worry."

Jamie thought about this for a moment. "So are you phoning on your own behalf, or did Mom put you up to this? She's only rung me twice already this week to nag me about security."

"I haven't been appointed family spokesperson if that's what you're worried about. Mom may have suggested that I drop her an SMS to let her know you're okay, but it was my idea to call."

"Okay…"

"So, how are you really?"

"I'm fine. It's all good fodder for the blog. You wouldn't believe the page views I'm getting."

"Aren't you scared, though?"

"Not really." As she said it, Jamie realised this was almost true. "I was worried about the cats for a bit, but then I remembered they never go out of the garden anyway. And Dad is sending a company to install electric fencing all the way around the property. So this guy, whoever he is, won't be able to get in again."

"Well, that's something. Listen, we were thinking, Caroline and I, that we should come and see you. Like a girls' night kind of thing."

"You mean to check up on me?"

"No. For heaven's sake, Jamie, don't be so prickly. We haven't hung out in ages. We want to hear all about this Tom guy. Maybe even meet him."

Jamie pulled a face at Watson, who had wandered in to rub against her leg. "We're not really at the meeting-each-other's-family stage of the relationship. In fact, it's a bit of a stretch to call it a relationship at all. Every time we start making progress there's some kind of crisis to keep us apart."

"Hey, maybe that's what the stalker wants. Maybe he's trying to keep you and Tom apart."

"Yeah, well..." Jamie grumbled. "He's doing a good job of it."

"Anyway, we don't have to meet Tom. We can just discuss him in great detail. Over wine and snacks."

"When were you thinking of?"

"I don't have rehearsals until tomorrow afternoon, so I thought maybe tonight. I can let my hair down a bit. Maybe even have a second glass of wine."

"You rebel. And what about our dear sister? Won't she need forty-eight hours written notice of this social occasion?"

"I told her about it yesterday. She's not on call tonight. It's in her diary, cross-referenced to her iPhone, iPad and iMac."

"Spontaneity is her middle name. Listen, come at about six o'clock. Tom often takes his little boy for a walk in the pram about then. You can catch a glimpse of him and give me the thumbs-up. Or down, as the case may be, although frankly you'd have to be blind. If I'm not back from Delucia's, just let yourselves in and wait."

Tom got his son in a headlock and gave his face a thorough wiping with a damp facecloth.

Ben's supper was always a stressful time in the Elliot household. The high chair was liberally smeared with chicken casserole (*Cooking for the Single Mom: 21 Easy Meals for You and Your Toddler*), and so were the table and the kitchen counter. Also the light fitting, Tom noticed with resignation as he reached up to give it a wipe.

Ben was at an in-between stage with his eating. He resisted being spoon-fed, but didn't have the co-ordination to spoon-feed himself with any reliability. The books and magazines all said he should be helping himself to finger food. Baby-led weaning, it was called. But his son regarded food the same way Babe Ruth regarded baseballs –

as something to be swatted as far and hard as possible.

Tom had discovered that if Ben was distracted by an absorbing toy, something that required fine-motor co-ordination, he would allow his father to shovel the last few spoonfuls of food into his mouth. So every night they went through the charade of letting Ben play with his food, before Tom got serious and started feeding it to him.

Tonight's toy had been a small cardboard box with a slit cut into it, into which Ben had been posting little plastic discs. Also peas and bits of carrot. It looked ready for a steriliser. No, make that an incinerator.

Tom pulled a thin sweater over his son's head and got out the pram. As soon as he saw it, Ben started bobbing up and down and clapping his hands. He loved these late evening walks as much as his father did.

"Pwam!" He flung himself at it like a miniature prop-forward. "Mine pwam."

"That's yours all right." Tom lifted him into it and fastened the five-point harness with the ease of long habit. "That's your pram and nobody else's."

"Run, Dada!" Ben ordered, kicking his legs. "Run."

"No running today, my love. Just a civilised walk. But maybe we'll see the kitties next door." If Ben sat very quietly, Holmes and Watson could sometimes be coaxed up to the gate to say hello.

As Tom let himself out into the street, he was surprised to see two women and a man standing at Jamie's gate, ringing the bell. She hardly ever got visitors.

"She might not be back from work yet." He gave them a smile, but his eyes were watchful. None of them seemed to be carrying any half-dead wildlife, but you never knew.

The smaller of the two women – a skinny blonde – shrugged her shoulders. "We'll go in and wait then. She won't be long."

She produced a small remote from her handbag and made as if to go inside.

Keeping his pleasant expression firmly in place, Tom stepped forward.

"I'm sorry, but would you mind if I asked who you are? One can't be too careful. I'm sure you understand."

The taller woman looked at him approvingly. She was wearing a dove-grey suit with something lacy underneath. Tom looked at her face, blinked, and looked again. Yes, she was still the most beautiful creature he'd ever seen.

"We're her sisters," said the vision. "I'm Caroline and this is Ella. We have keys to get in because this is the house we grew up in. You must be her neighbour, Tom. I'm glad to see she has someone looking out for her."

"And this must be Ben!" The skinny blonde leaned forward. "Isn't he gorgeous? Oh, you are just the most handsome little guy on earth, aren't you, Ben? Aren't you handsome?"

Ben grinned at her, lapping up the attention.

"Yes, I'm Tom." Tom held his hand out to the man who was with them. "And you are...?"

"Oh, that's Peter," Ella said over her shoulder. "He's my manager. And my boyfriend."

The two women were crouched down on the pavement, cooing over Ben. They stroked his hair and pinched his cheeks and kissed his forehead. They dangled the long, twisty pram snake for him to catch hold of. And Ben, who usually got impatient when people fussed over him, was playing to his audience like a seasoned pro.

None of this fitted with Tom's plan to keep his Ben-world and his Jamie-world separate and apart. These people were clearly not vermin-torturing psychopaths, so it was time to move on.

"We'd better get on with our walk, Ben," he said. "Say goodbye to the nice ladies now."

"Bye bye, ladies!" Ben waved his chubby hand. "Bye, ladies! Bye!"

Then he broke into heartrending sobs as Tom said his own goodbyes and wheeled him down the road.

"Bit abrupt, wasn't he?" Caroline commented. "We weren't doing any harm. He could have let us play with that cutie-pie a bit longer."

"We're the enemy, remember?" Ella said. "We're part of the plot to have Jamie worm her way into Ben's affections and then break his heart when she moves on."

"Of course." Caroline rolled her eyes. "How could I forget?"

Peter snorted as they let themselves into the house. "I don't know what she sees in him. The man has no manners."

"I can't imagine, Peter," Caroline said. "Tall, good-looking single father of an adorable toddler. It's a mystery all right." She ignored the dirty look her sister gave her.

"Let's see what Jamie has in the fridge for us." Ella flung the fridge door wide. "One bottle of wine! That's not going to get us very far, is it?"

"You shouldn't be drinking at all, darling," Peter said. "You know that."

"Why, is she pregnant?"

"Of course she's not pregnant. But she's auditioning for a very important role next month. She has to be in peak condition."

"I don't think a glass of wine tonight will affect her performance in a month's time."

They heard a key in the front door and turned to greet Jamie. To Ella's relief, she was carrying a shopping bag full of clinking bottles and a covered caterer's tray that promised elaborate snacks.

"Hi, Ellz! Hi Caro!" Jamie kissed her sisters. "And Peter too! What a surprise." They brushed cheeks. "Won't you take some of this stuff out to the patio? I'll come through in a minute. Give me a hand, Caro?"

"Sure."

As Ella and Peter went outside, Caroline lifted her eyebrows. "What?" she asked.

"What's he doing here?" Jamie hissed. "I don't remember inviting him to our girls' night. I thought the whole point of a girls' night was that no men were allowed."

"He's being his usual control-freaky self, what did you expect?

Ella's not allowed to go anywhere without him. Not even to visit her family, apparently."

"That's ridiculous! I bet he's here to make sure she doesn't put one more calorie into her mouth than necessary."

"He's already started on that. Just before you came in, he was going on at her about how she shouldn't be drinking wine because she's in training for some role or other."

Jamie started to cut warmed pita bread into triangles with jerky movements. "Why does she not just ditch him? I cannot understand it."

"He's her manager as well as her boyfriend. He's been good for her career. She's been dancing more important roles since he took her on."

"It can't be worth it."

"Look, I think he does care about her in his own weird way. He's always holding her hand and hanging on every word she says."

"In a creepy way, not a good way. I can't stand how he plays with her fingers all the time. Fiddle, fiddle, fiddle. It would drive me mad."

They took the wineglasses and the last plate of snacks out to the patio where Ella and Peter were snuggled on a sofa. Peter was indeed playing with Ella's fingers as though he were learning to count on an abacus. Apparently, she didn't mind because she was smiling and leaning against him.

Jamie dived straight into the gossip. "So I saw Tom out pushing the pram as I was walking home. Did you guys run into him?"

Ella grinned. "Yes we did! It worked perfectly. He came out of his door just as we were ringing your doorbell. And he was all like, 'Who are you and what are you doing here?' He was totally macho and protective. It was kind of delicious, actually." She looked to Caroline for confirmation.

"Delicious is the word," Caroline nodded. "He's very aware of who's coming and going at your place. And not just in a neighbourly way. I'd say he's smitten with you. Lucky girl."

"He is nice, isn't he?" Jamie beamed. "You should see him in a vest and running shorts."

Ella patted her chest. "I don't know if my heart could take it."

"Sometimes when he runs, his vest sort of rides up and you get these tantalising glimpses of a six-pack and those muscles that run down the sides that some men have…"

"Shag lines," Ella confirmed.

Caroline slid sideways in her chair. "Smelling salts!" she said in a faint voice.

The sisters broke into giggles.

Peter stood up. "You're being very silly this evening. Silly and sophomoric. Caroline, I thought you were the sensible one."

"Sorry, Peter, but this is what happens on girls' nights." Caroline emphasised the word *girls*. "We drink wine and talk about men."

"If this were a group of men talking about women and objectifying their bodies like that, you'd all be screaming sexism."

Ella was contrite. "You're right, Peter. I'm sorry. That wasn't very sensitive of us. Why don't you go inside and make some calls and work on your iPad for a while? You'll just get bored if you stay out here."

Jamie held her breath as Peter considered this. For a moment it looked as though he was going to stay on the patio. Or, even worse, insist that he and Ella should go home at once. But then his frown disappeared and he smiled.

"Of course. You girls stay out here and have a good old natter. I'll just take a glass of wine and a plate of snacks with me, if that's okay. Jamie, do you mind if I set myself up in your sitting room? I do have quite a bit of work to get through."

Jamie waved at the house. "Make yourself at home, Peter."

He loaded some snacks onto a plate and topped up his wineglass. "Go easy on the sausage rolls," he told Ella. "And remember that protein is always a better choice of snack than carbs."

They waited until he was in the house before conversation resumed.

"How can you let him boss you around like that?" Caroline demanded. "Why don't you tell him to take his protein snacks and shove them where the sun doesn't shine?"

"Shhh!" Ella said.

"Don't shush me. I'm serious."

"Look, there's no point in taking it personally. It's got nothing to do with the way he likes me to look or anything like that. The fact is, I'm a ballet dancer. My body is the tool of my profession. You have to keep your tools in good shape or you can't work with them anymore. Look at it this way – if I were a surgeon and he were always on at me to keep my scalpels clean and sharp, you wouldn't mind, would you? You wouldn't keep saying, how can he be so controlling?"

Caroline shrugged, reluctant to concede the point.

"But because it's my body, you see it as some kind of personal insult. Like he's trying to take away my freedom as a woman. It's got nothing to do with that. Peter is my manager. He has to make sure I keep my body as strong and flexible as possible. And yes, okay, as light as possible too, because when the guys lift us they feel every extra pound, and if we're too heavy it makes the whole action look clumsy."

"Sure," Caroline said. "I understand." But Ella wasn't done.

"So I'd really appreciate it if the two of you would stop moaning about Peter behind my back and rolling your eyes every time he says something."

"Deal," said Jamie. "We didn't realise it was upsetting you."

"Great. Then let's talk about your stalker instead."

Jamie groaned. "Must we? I feel like I've been talking about nothing else all week."

"When are you going to stop posting your every move on Facebook?" Ella demanded. "You're basically doing this guy's work for him. Any time he wants to know where you are or what you're doing, he just has to log on to one of your completely public profiles."

"I don't see why I should have to change my behaviour to please

114

some psycho. I'm not the one doing something wrong, he is!"

"It's not a question of right or wrong, Jamie, it's a question of protecting yourself," Caroline chimed in.

"That's what they always say to women, isn't it? *It's not that you're not allowed to wear a mini-skirt, but is it sensible? Aren't you asking for trouble walking around like that?* How about we stop telling women what to wear or how to behave online and start telling men not to be inappropriate idiots?"

Caroline and Ella looked at each other and shrugged. As feminists, they couldn't deny the validity of what their sister was saying, but at the same time they just wanted to lock her up in a room and keep her safe forever.

Jamie sighed. She knew their concern stemmed from love, but being told what to do made her feel cross and prickly. It was time to change the subject back to Tom's shag-lines.

12

It took Jamie a while to settle back into a routine after the events of the past few weeks. As much as she loved writing, it wasn't easy spending so much time alone. She was grateful for the bakery, for having a day job that forced her to leave the house and see people.

Part of her feeling of flatness had to do with disappointment. She'd been convinced that the offer to publish from Magnum Books was just the tip of an iceberg. More attractive offers were supposed to come pouring in afterwards. Surely she was owed some kind of reward for her strong-mindedness in turning down the Magnum offer?

But there'd been nothing. A howling silence had descended on her inbox. Her secret fear was coming true. The Magnum deal was the best and only offer she'd ever have.

Yes, her blog posts about the rats and pigeons had attracted a lot of readers, but as the days slipped into weeks and nothing more happened, those readers went away. Even Jamie had stopped worrying about what her stalker might do next. She no longer approached her front gate with trepidation when she got back from work.

A security company had duly arrived and installed an electrified fence all the way around her house and garden. At first it had felt like living in a prison. The fence was the first thing Jamie noticed when she looked outside. But soon she stopped seeing it at all.

Someone else who had dropped out of sight was Tom. Jamie had hardly laid eyes on him in weeks. On the day the electric fence was being installed, he'd shown up to express his approval. Jamie had started to ask him how he was, but the job foreman had claimed her attention. When she'd turned back to Tom, he had disappeared. And he'd stayed that way ever since.

In the absence of anything exciting going on in her own life, it was good to have Pumla's drama to concentrate on.

"Today is D-day," Pumla announced as Jamie arrived for her shift one morning.

"You said that last week." Jamie tied her apron into place.

"No, but today really is. We're going out to dinner – a small place close to where he stays so it's easy to get back late at night."

"Again, this sounds remarkably like last week."

Pumla shrugged. "I don't know what was wrong with him last week. I practically threw myself at him and he was all, 'Let's not rush into things. I really like you. Let's take it one step at a time.' Maybe he's just not attracted to me."

Jamie found this unlikely. Men were always attracted to Pumla. She was curvy, with a tiny waist and long legs. And she had huge, brown Bambi eyes set in a pretty, pixie face.

"Which one is this again?"

"Dumisani."

"Oh, yes. My pick. Well, listen. Unless Dumisani is blind or gay, he is definitely attracted to you, so it's just a matter of time. Maybe he's a decent guy who respects you as a human being and wants to get to know you better before he jumps into bed with you."

Pumla snorted. "Yeah, right. He'd probably had too much to drink and wasn't sure he could perform. I should have chosen Chester the Supersperm."

"Always pick the nice guy. That's my motto in life. Nothing beats niceness in a guy."

"Hmmm. We'll see how nice he is once he's had his way with me. That'll be his cue never to call me again. In fact, I'm counting on it. I don't want him interfering with how I raise the baby."

"What if he wants to stick around and be involved? What if he decides he's in love with you?"

Pumla smiled. "I'll shake him off, don't worry. Remember Kate Hudson in *How to Lose a Guy in 10 Days*?"

"Uh huh."

"My role model. Dumisani will be thanking his lucky stars to be

117

rid of me. But it won't come to that. I'll just be all needy and clingy after we've had sex, and watch him start calling me a taxi."

"You are ruthless." Jamie couldn't help admiring her single-mindedness. "You are utterly lacking in ruth."

"Damn right I am. Now, what do you think? Should I put the lamingtons in front of the Florentines or vice versa? This gloomy weather should draw them in like flies today. I want them to see something yummy the second they walk in the door."

"Pile the lamingtons in front and then arrange the Florentines like wagon wheels behind them. I'll bring the doughnuts through from the kitchen."

They arranged pastries in silence, trying to get the optimum blend of style and temptation. Back in Jamie's days in the hotel industry, they'd called this "food porn" – making food look so delicious that customers would reach for their wallets regardless of diets and good intentions.

The lunch crowd would be coming in at any moment, but Jamie couldn't get her mind off Pumla's baby mission.

"You realise you're probably going to have to sleep with him more than once," she said as they washed their hands and retied their aprons.

"No, why? What for?"

"To get pregnant. What are the chances of it happening on the first time?"

Pumla gave her flat tummy a rub. "It'll happen, don't worry. I got one of those ovulation tests from the chemist. I'm as fertile as a bunny rabbit this week."

"Yes, but still. You shouldn't be over-confident. You should prepare yourself for disappointment."

"Why?"

The bald question annoyed Jamie. Pumla was always so sure of herself. Anything she wanted just fell into her lap. Infertility was something that happened to other people.

"Most couples try for months before they fall pregnant."

"I'm not most couples. And what's this nonsense about couples anyway? Men don't fall pregnant – women do. That's another advantage of having a baby on my own. I don't have to go around saying 'We're pregnant.' *We* won't be pregnant. I will."

"It's like going to the roulette table and expecting to win big on your first spin. You have to budget for failure. Or at least expect that it might take a while. I realise that's not in your plan, but you need to think about it."

"Listen, both my sisters fell pregnant quickly and my mom has three kids. Infertility doesn't run in our family."

"There's always a first time."

Pumla turned to face her. "Listen to yourself, Jamie. Can you hear what you're saying? It's like you're deliberately wishing failure on me."

"That's not what I'm doing."

"Well, that's what it sounds like."

While they were bickering, a customer had come into the bakery and was standing staring at the display. He was already inside before the discreet chime of the door penetrated their consciousness.

They pulled apart and snapped to attention.

"I'm going to finish the set-up," Jamie said, as Pumla moved into place behind the counter.

She wiped the snarl off her face and walked to the back of the restaurant to open a linen cupboard. As she counted out overlays with one hand, she slipped her phone into her other hand and logged onto Twitter.

Jamie Burchell @jamieburchell
Confidence is one thing, but arrogance is unattractive.

Bronwyn Jones @redhighheels
@jamieburchell Agreed. Who has got under your skin today?

119

Jamie Burchell @jamieburchell
@redhighheels I just think that infertility can happen to anyone. No one is exempt. And it doesn't have to run in families.

Tumi Boapi @tumiboapi
@jamieburchell Ha! If it did those families would soon die out, right? @redhighheels

Jamie Burchell @jamieburchell
@tumiboapi Right! ☺ @redhighheels

Foully Wooing Won @foullywooingwon
@jamieburchell Your friend thinks she is special. Just because her mother had 3 kids doesn't mean she will have any.

Jamie Burchell @jamieburchell
@foullywooingwon I think you shouldn't jump to conclusions.

Jamie raised her eyes from her phone and looked around. Pumla was still waiting for the customer to make up his mind. She'd left her phone on the table near Jamie's elbow and was clearly not posting any tweets. So how did the tweeter know about her mother having had three kids?

Jamie shook her head. The tweeter was probably just taking a shot in the dark. Or maybe it was someone who knew Pumla.

Jamie glanced at the customer, willing him to make up his mind. But the man was in no hurry. He stared at the doughnut display, raising his eyes every now and then to flick glances between Jamie and Pumla.

"The jam doughnuts are good today," she said as she carried the overlays to the front. "Or if you're more of an iced doughnut fan, I can recommend the chocolate-and-vanilla swirls. That way you get the best of both worlds."

His eyes jumped away from hers.

"And of course, we're doing a special on cinnamon buns today. You get a bun and a large cappuccino for the normal price of one medium cappuccino."

She was giving him too many choices, she decided. The sweat was beading on his forehead. He was going to start dripping on the floor if he didn't mop his face soon. The stains under his arms were growing before her eyes.

Jamie looked up as the door chimed again. It was a party of three people looking for a table. She left Pumla attending to the sweaty man while she seated the customers. She prided herself on her ability to set customers at ease, but it hadn't worked with him. As she took drinks orders from the lunchers and welcomed in two more tables, she saw the man accepting the cinnamon-bun-and-cappuccino combination from Pumla.

When she turned away, she could feel his gaze on her, like spiders on the back of her neck. He looked familiar, but she couldn't quite place him.

When she looked up again, he was gone.

"I love the bread in here," a customer said, smiling up at her.

"That's great!" Jamie smiled back, and the sweaty man went out of her head. "I'm so glad you're enjoying it."

"I keep coming back to Delucia's just for the bread. I think I could make a whole meal out of it."

"If that's what you're in the mood for, you should try our Ploughman's lunch. You get a miniature loaf of each variety of bread with a selection of cheeses and dipping sauces, including the onion marmalade."

"What are these breads?" another customer at the same table asked. "We were trying to figure it out earlier."

Jamie gestured to the bread basket. "Well, over here we have a tomato ciabatta. And this one here is a herbed sourdough. And that one is a salt-encrusted focaccia. They're all available in full-sized loaves or rounds from our bakery section. Perfect for dinner parties, or just a casual family supper of soup and bread."

"And the dips?"

"Well, these two actually go together. You see, you dip the bread in the olive oil here and then straight into the crushed sesame seeds. This one is your standard olive tapenade. And the last one is a creamy peri-peri dip."

"Absolutely divine!"

And that, Jamie thought, proved her right and Pumla wrong. Pumla had said it was an unnecessary expense to serve such fancy breads and dips with the meals. But Jamie was adamant that it would bring repeat business back to the restaurant. It was also excellent advertising for their bakery section.

If she was honest with herself, Pumla was rarely wrong, but that didn't stop Jamie from feeling compelled to argue with her. She was already regretting their earlier fight. And she was especially regretting having ranted about it on Twitter.

Tweeter's remorse. You couldn't be a regular on Twitter without knowing what that felt like.

————

As Jamie chatted to the customers about bread, the man stood outside Delucia's and watched her through the window.

Two contacts in one day. One in real life and one on the internet. How thrilling it all was. He'd needed this boost. The day of the pigeons had kept him going for weeks. But then the delicious feeling had faded. He needed more.

Every face-to-face contact was a risk. Even though he changed his appearance for each encounter, it was still a risk. Jamie wasn't stupid. She would start to recognise him soon. If only today hadn't left him feeling so dissatisfied. Yes, she'd looked at him. Yes, she'd acknowledged him, but in such a dismissive way. She'd handed him over to her colleague the minute someone more interesting came along. That was poor service. There was no other word for it. She should have finished with him first.

And the way she'd spoken to him on Twitter was no better. Who was she to tell him not to jump to conclusions? It made him wonder whether she was as intelligent as he'd hoped. Her tone on Twitter was abrupt and disrespectful. The only thing worse than being ignored was being disrespected. That was something Jamie would need to learn.

13

Dear Cat,

I know we haven't spoken in a while, but thanks for not dropping that piano on my head. My human Ben has begged many times to be allowed to come and play with you. I can't understand why my company isn't good enough for him, but hey. So how about it, Cat? Can my humans, Ben and Tom, come around to make kootchi-koo noises at you?

Sincerely,
The Dog

Dear Dog,

I have spoken with my colleague, The Other Cat, and we would be delighted to host your humans on any morning of your choice. Would Tuesday work?

Sincerely,
The Cat

Dear Cat,

Unfortunately Tuesday is the day Tom takes Ben to the regrettably named toddler group "Moms & Tots". Wednesdays are better, as those are the days Tom strips off his pantyhose and heels and takes a break from impersonating a mom.

Sincerely,
The Dog

Dear Dog,

Wednesday would be perfect. Shall we say 10am?

Sincerely,
The Cat

....

Dear Cat,

Looking forward to it. See you over the garden fence...

Auf wiedersehen,
Der Hund

———

Jamie knew she was fussing, but couldn't seem to stop.

Tom and Ben were coming in less than an hour. She'd been up since five o'clock trying to fit in a run, her blog updates, and 500 words of the novel. Then she'd cleaned the house from top to bottom. When Faith came in at nine, she had declared, with an unconvincing show of grumpiness, that everything was already done and she might as well go back home.

Jamie had set her to polishing the silver.

Now Jamie was whipping up some snacks. She'd baked a dozen finger biscuits from a recipe she'd found on a mommy blog recommended by one of her Twitter friends. Apparently they were hard enough for a toddler to suck on them without large bits breaking off in his mouth.

Jamie had coated half of them in carob and left the other half plain. Was Ben a latent chocaholic, or was he more of a straight vanilla man? She couldn't wait to find out.

For Tom, she'd made a quiche Lorraine filled with crispy bacon bits. And if he felt like something sweet, there were the mini-doughnuts she'd baked using Delucia's recipe. She could, of course, simply have helped herself to some straight from the bakery, but that would have felt like cheating.

She changed into a pair of rolled-up boyfriend jeans and a stretchy T-shirt, then rushed back into the kitchen to dip doughnuts into the three types of icing she'd prepared.

Then she rushed back to her room to change into leggings and a loose T-shirt. As she jogged past Faith on her way into the kitchen, the housekeeper stopped her with an explosive click of the tongue.

"What?" Jamie demanded.

"He doesn't care what you are wearing," Faith informed her. "All he cares is that you are not going to make his son love you."

Jamie's shoulders sagged. "Did Vuyiswa tell you that?"

"Yes, she told me. He is worried, that one, that you want to be a mother for his son."

"I don't want to be a mother to him, but if someone is a guest in your home, you have to make an effort. It's only polite."

Faith cast an ironic glance at the homemade finger biscuits. "They sell those at Pick 'n Pay. If you buy them in a shop, you are being polite. If you bake your own, it is too much. He will run away from you."

Jamie gritted her teeth. "I'll tell him I bought them, okay? But he's just going to have to live with the rest of it. He knows I'm a baker. If it makes him want to run, tough."

Faith had already lost interest. A rerun of *Kasi Stories* was about to start on TV. She turned her attention back to the screen, and the little silver sugar bowl she was polishing.

Jamie stood dithering for a moment. Then the doorbell rang, and she dashed into the kitchen to scoop the finger biscuits off the baking tray and into an anonymous Tupperware. Did they look too homemade? Probably. But he was a man, right? What were the chances he would even notice?

The doorbell rang again.

Tom led Ben down Jamie's drive with a sense of trepidation.

He wouldn't even be here if the kid hadn't nagged him day and night for weeks. He could swear the bloody cats were in on the conspiracy because whenever Tom took Ben for a walk in his pram, they were lounging around in Jamie's driveway like a pair of odalisques.

As soon as they heard the pram, they would start rubbing their silky bodies against the palisade fence. But the moment Tom and Ben got closer, they would retreat out of arm's reach. It was as though they were saying, 'You can look but you cannot touch. If you want to touch, you'll have to come inside. Make it happen, dude, or your son's going to hate you forever.' It was worse than a goddamn striptease.

Eventually, he'd cracked and set up this meeting. Or this cat-playdate. Whatever the hell you wanted to call it. He would have loved to suggest that they visit the cats some afternoon when Jamie was at work. Faith could have let them in. Wouldn't that have been brilliant? Rude, yes, but brilliant.

It wasn't that he didn't want to see Jamie. The need to see Jamie had been building in him like hunger. But the combination of Jamie and Ben was one that made his guts churn.

Then Jamie emerged from the house, and every other thought went clean out of his head. Her hair was caught up in a kind of messy bun. It left her neck and shoulders exposed in a way that made him want to take a bite. She was wearing those really tight black pants that women wore for gym sometimes. What were they called? They made her legs look like they went all the way up to her ears.

With her feet bare and an oversized T-shirt slipping off one shoulder, she was a distraction, to put it mildly. With a massive exercise of will, Tom managed to wrench his mind back to the normal courtesies of life.

"Thanks so much for letting us come over," he said. "If you only knew how Ben has been begging."

Tom loosened his grip on Ben's hand. The kid immediately tore free and rushed up to Jamie to fling his arms around her legs. Tom winced, expecting her to sweep him into a hug.

But she just smiled at Ben and bent down to pat him on the shoulder."Welcome, gentlemen," she said, including them both. "Come inside and let's round up some cats."

"Psss!" Ben said, jumping up and down. "Psss! Pssss!"

"The pussycats are out in the garden. If you sit quietly on the grass, they'll come to you, and maybe even sit on your lap."

As Jamie led them through the house towards the patio, Tom felt himself relax. He said hello to Faith in passing, and was pleased to see that she also gave Ben no more than a restrained greeting. Perhaps this was going to work out better than he'd hoped.

As they walked into the bright November sunshine, Jamie saw Tom produce a cap for Ben from the rucksack on his shoulder and fit it over his head. Then he rooted around in the rucksack and came up with a cup of juice. The cup had a drinking spout fitted to the top. Jamie was glad she hadn't brought out the almost identical sippy cup she'd purchased yesterday.

Tom noticed Jamie looking at the sippy cup and said, "I know it looks like juice, but it's really just baby rooibos tea. It won't harm his teeth at all."

Jamie laughed. "That's fine. I'm not the juice police."

"Sorry. I spend so much time explaining myself to the uber-mommies in our toddler group that I sometimes forget not everyone is judging me."

"That sounds tough."

Jamie longed to bombard him with sympathy and enquiries about the uber-mommies, but managed to restrain herself. She led them onto the lawn. There wasn't a cat in sight, but she knew how to rectify that.

"Let's all sit down on the grass," she said. "Yes, like that. Now keep your hands very still and sit quietly, Ben. Just like that. Good!" Jamie didn't know much about twenty-month-old babies, but Ben seemed to understand every word she said.

When they were all settled on the grass, Jamie began to call the cats. "Holmes! Watson! Kitty, kitty, kitty. Come here, boys!"

"I thought cats never come when they're called," Tom said.

"They come when they feel like it. And they nearly always feel like it when we're in the garden. See … here they come now."

There was a rustling in the bushes and two cats emerged from the undergrowth. They trotted across the lawn – the handsome grey and the fluffy ginger that Tom remembered from previous visits. Ben squeaked and lunged towards them, but subsided when Jamie reminded him to sit still.

"Good boys," Jamie said, rubbing ears and scratching chins. "Yes, you're good boys, aren't you?"

Tom held his breath as the cats broke away from Jamie to circle him and Ben. Their postures were wary, but they didn't seem inclined to bolt. He held out the back of his hand to the grey one, just as he would to a strange dog. The cat gave his hand a cursory sniff and allowed him to stroke its head.

Then Jamie took Ben's hand and showed him how to extend it in an unthreatening way to pet the cat. The look of delight on Ben's face was reward enough for Tom. His eyes were glowing.

"They feel a bit like Silver, don't they, Benny?" Tom said. "But they're softer."

"Thoft!" Ben agreed, nodding. "Thoft."

Soon both cats came to make friends with the little boy. The ginger sprawled out on the grass next to him. Tom wondered, as he had many times before, where the animal-loving streak in Ben came from. Was it nature or nurture? Did his birth-mother come from a long line of animal lovers? Or his biological father perhaps?

He would probably never know. Ben's birth-mother had been a refugee from the north. The tears she shed would have been for her family and friends left behind.

And Ben's blood father – a labourer on the mines, as far as Tom's private detective had been able to find out – was no doubt a hard, practical man. But Ben had been nuts about animals from birth. As soon as his eyes could focus, he had been fascinated by Silver. The moment he could reach out, he had reached for the sweet-natured Golden Retriever.

Now he was in his element, running his fingers through the cats' fur, pulling gently at their ears, and tickling their tummies. The usually boisterous toddler was as careful as an altar-boy when it came to animals.

Jamie got to her feet, and Tom followed her example.

"Well, he looks happy enough," she said. "How about something to drink? Tea? Coffee? Or would you prefer a cold drink?"

"Coffee would be great, thanks. But won't the cats follow you if you go into the house?"

"Normally, yes, but they've really taken to Ben. They'll sit there as long as he does."

Jamie went into the house while Tom settled himself in an armchair on the patio. It had taken an effort of will for her to tear herself away from Ben. Just as it had been an effort not to squeeze the breath out of him when he'd run up to hug her legs earlier. She could have sat there watching him enjoy the cats all morning. But it was worth playing it cool to see the strain around Tom's eyes melt away.

She switched the coffee machine on, and filled the kettle to make some tea for herself. Then she took advantage of the lull to update her Facebook status.

Hot Running Guy and Cute Kid are IN DA HOUSE! Am I a lucky girl or what? ☺

Within seconds the first comments had come in.

Ella Burchell Yay! Good luck.

Cyril Attlee Not that guy again? Every time he shows up something creepy happens to you. What do you really know about him? For all you know, he could be the nutter who's leaving half-dead animals on your gate.

Jamie Burchell For the millionth time, it's not him, Cyril! He has always been WITH me when stuff happens. He can't possibly be responsible for it.

Cyril Attlee Well maybe he's getting someone to do his dirty work for him.

Jamie Burchell For what possible reason?

Cyril Attlee Who knows why these nutcases do the things they do? Because they can? You're too trusting, Jamie. This guy came into your life out of nowhere. You know nothing about him.

Pumla Maseko That's not actually true. He's a guest lecturer at Wits. He has been living in the suburb for nearly two years. He looks after his batty old step-mom and his kid. Honestly, you couldn't find a more harmless guy.

Ella Burchell Norman Bates was very fond of his dear old mum too, wasn't he?

Jamie Burchell Oh, stop it, you guys! I'm not listening to any more of this. Tom is a perfectly nice guy. Now I'm going to set a tray and take some coffee and snacks out to him…

Jamie carried the tray to the patio. Ben was tugging his father's hand, trying to persuade him to come for a walk around the garden.

"Look, Bennie," Tom said. "Jamie's got those biscuits you like."

Ben grabbed the biscuit Jamie held out to him, mumbling "fanks" when Tom reminded him of his manners. Then he perched on the edge of the patio with a biscuit in one hand and his sippy cup in the other.

"He loves those," Tom told Jamie, helping himself to a slice of quiche. "How did you know?"

"Oh … someone told me they were suitable for toddlers."

"I buy them from Dischem, but yours look chunkier somehow – almost homemade."

"It's amazing what you can pick up from the home industry these days."

There was no way she was telling this prickly, defensive man that she'd stayed up half the night making finger food for his son.

"I worry sometimes that Ben doesn't get enough home-baked goods," Tom said. "The moms at our toddler group always seem to be baking cupcakes with their kids, when they're not whipping up their own homemade pasta for lasagne, of course."

Jamie laughed. "I find that hard to believe. They can't all be domestic goddesses, right? What about the ones who work? Where would they find the time?"

"I suppose."

"Look, I've never had a kid so I can't really say, but I imagine it's tempting to think everyone is doing a better job of it than you. And also that they find it easier. But everyone struggles – especially parents."

"I just worry that looking after small kids comes more easily to women. That's why they call it mothering, isn't it?"

"That's the kind of thinking that keeps the pharmaceutical industry in business. Society keeps telling women that mothering should come easily and naturally to them. And when it doesn't, they feel depressed and inadequate. I bet the women in your toddler group struggle just as much as you do. You should talk to them about it."

Tom demolished a mini-doughnut and accepted a refill of coffee. "I've tried. I've really made an effort to join in on their conversations, but they treat me like a foreign species. They get all weird and self-conscious around me. The conversation comes to a halt the moment I arrive."

Jamie tried to keep a straight face, but failed.

Tom scowled. "What? What's so funny?"

"Sorry. I can't help picturing it. You being all earnest and wanting advice about, I don't know, teething or potty-training or whatever, and the moms getting into a flutter and wanting to flirt with you."

"Hilarious."

"It is, actually. You need to see it from where I'm sitting."

"Some of them are ten years older than I am. And married!"

The indignant note in his voice made Jamie laugh even more. "You could try growing a paunch maybe … and letting your hairline recede. Oh, and maybe cultivate a creepy little moustache. That should do the trick."

Tom's mouth twisted into a grin. "A paunch? Really?"

"Sure. It would be a shame, though."

"Oh, yeah? And why is that?"

"Well, you've got that really … quite adequate body. It would be a pity to ruin it."

Jamie's eyes drifted across Tom's washboard stomach and broad chest. Then skimmed across his mouth and travelled upwards until her gaze locked with his.

"Is that so?"

"Yes," she said. "A great pity."

The air was suddenly thick with a tension that hadn't been there a moment before. All at once, it didn't seem a bad idea to fling herself across the coffee table, knock the cup from his hand, and straddle him.

Jamie had to blink hard to dislodge the image from her mind.

Tom's thoughts were moving along similar lines. She could see it in the rapid dilation of his pupils, and the way he seemed to have stopped breathing. They stared at each other for a charged moment.

Then Tom moved, as though reaching for her. But before Jamie could react, the air was split by a blood-freezing wail. They both swung around to see that Ben, who had apparently tripped over his own feet, had fallen forward and hit his head on the edge of the coffee table.

Tom was out of his chair in an instant, scooping Ben up and soothing him while trying to take a look at the damage. Jamie's heart squeezed as she saw the tears pouring down his little cheeks. But worst of all was the dark welt blooming on his perfect skin in front of her eyes.

"I'm so sorry! I'm so sorry!" she wailed. "I should never have put that table there. I didn't think. Is he going to need an X-ray?"

Tom raised his eyebrows. "An X-ray?"

"To see if his skull is cracked."

"Listen, it would take more than that to dent this kid's head. If I took him for an X-ray every time he bumped his head, we'd practically live at the ER."

He saw the real distress on Jamie's face and dropped the teasing tone. "Look, don't worry, Jamie. These little bumps happen all the time. Honestly. Several times a day. Ever since he learned to walk, he's been a mobile disaster area. I often say he could find something to crash into if we were in the middle of the Gobi Desert. And he always goes head-first into everything. It's a wonder he's got any brains left in there at all."

"But look at that mark. He's going to have a terrible bruise!"

"He'll be fine," Tom said. "Look, he's already forgetting about it." He handed the sippy cup and a new biscuit to Ben. The old one was a sticky, disintegrating stub on the lawn. Ben took them and perched on his father's lap, hiccupping now and then as his sobs subsided.

Jamie let out a long breath. This toddler-raising business was not for sissies.

14

The man didn't like dogs. He'd never liked them. And they didn't like him either.

They were so snappy and aggressive. They had big teeth and made intimidating noises deep in their chests. Noises that rumbled until they exploded in an ear-splitting bark. You never knew where you were with dogs. If you looked them in the eye, they bristled and became hostile. But if you didn't look at them, you didn't know where they were or what they were doing.

Thank goodness Jamie didn't own a dog. It was bad enough that she had cats. He didn't mind cats quite so much, though. They were just like rats or pigeons. He hadn't minded those either. But dogs were another story. Such suspicious animals. So aggressive towards anyone who was just going about his business.

The big yellow dog that lived next to Jamie was one of the worst. It not only barked when the man went near its gate, but when he went near Jamie's. The stupid animal had no discrimination. It was going to be a positive pleasure to get rid of it.

The man took pride in his work, but this job was going to be extra special. It was fortunate that the dog was allowed out in the street so much. That made his part much easier. Most people kept their dogs locked up behind gates and high walls. It was unusual to find one that was allowed to roam the streets. Probably an American affectation on the part of the neighbour.

Boo hoo. Poor dog. Can't keep it locked up all day. Must give it some freedom.

Today the American would find out what the price of that freedom was.

He watched the dog trotting up and down the street, sniffing at this and that, and setting all the other dogs in the neighbourhood to hysterical barking. He had the food inside his bag. It was just a matter of time before the dog smelled it and came over to investigate.

Shielded by his favourite clump of bushes, the man opened the bag he was carrying and began to make preparations. There would be no time to practise as he had with the rats. He had to get it right first time. God bless the internet. You could ask it any question at all. Like, how much Dormicum you needed to knock out a fifty kilogram dog. There was your answer at the click of a button. Wonderful.

It was stressful, though. He worried about the dog turning vicious went it woke up. What if it bit him? He shivered. Dogs were horrible to touch at the best of times. They made his flesh crawl. One of his earliest memories was of his mother gripping his hand and forcing him to touch a dog, puzzled by his reluctance.

Whose dog would it have been? Certainly not theirs. They'd never had a dog. It was thought to be a bad idea after what had happened to the white mice. He doubled over as a sudden convulsion of mirth gripped him. Oh, those mice. That had been fun. He took out the extra-strong, extra-long cable ties he'd bought with him, and laid them next to his knife. This would be his first time working with a ceramic knife. They were supposed to be extremely sharp.

He'd mixed the powdered Dormicum carefully into the dogfood, confident that he'd calculated exactly the right amount of food to guarantee that the dog ate it all up.

There was no one around as usual. Another giggle shook him. Talk about hiding in plain sight. If you wanted to do anything in secret, all you had to do was pick a quiet suburban street.

He made clucking noises at the dog as he'd heard other people do. It trotted over to him, looking at him through milky eyes. Then he put the food down and watched as the dog began to eat.

Pumla was in an excellent mood.

As Jamie came through the door, Pumla grabbed her by the hands and led her into a dance that was either Zorba the Greek or the traditional Swazi reed dance.

"We did it!" she crowed. "We did it at last!"

Jamie stumbled and almost fell. "Who? Who did what?"

"It! We! Us! Dumisani and me. We went out again last night, remember?"

"This must be the fifth time you've gone out on a date with…" Then the penny dropped and her eyes widened. "Ohhh! It! You and Dumisani. You mean you've done it at last."

Pumla nodded until her long earrings jangled.

"Well, thank goodness for that," said Jamie. "I was starting to think there was something wrong with the guy. They normally fall all over themselves to get at you. So … how was it?"

She tied on an apron while waiting for her partner to spill the beans. Normally Pumla gave new meaning to the term "too much information". But this time she smiled a cat-like smile.

"Let's just say I've got no complaints. I won't be writing to the manufacturer asking for a refund, if you get my drift."

"I get it, I get it. But what about Dumisani? Now that you've finally done it, has he stopped calling like you predicted?"

Pumla's lips tightened. "No. That's the only downside. He's just as keen as ever. I don't think he got the memo about how guys are supposed to go off you once they've slept with you. He's been calling and texting all morning."

"What a bastard!"

Pumla let the sarcasm wash over her. "I know, right? We're supposed to be the clingy ones. You'd think he'd know that. Anyway, I'll still be able to shake him off."

"Maybe you should wait a bit. You know, in case you need to do it again."

"Do what again?"

"Have sex, genius. What if it didn't work this time? What if you're not pregnant? You might need to go back for another round. You shouldn't burn your bridges with him until you're sure."

"But I am sure."

"Oh, really?" Jamie didn't know why Pumla's confidence irritated her so much, but it did. "Are you telling me you felt the little spark of life magically ignite in your womb? Or have they invented pregnancy tests that can predict the future already?"

"Oh, no." Pumla smiled. "But I just know. We did it four times last night. One of those must have worked. I'm still in my fertile cycle. It'll be fine, you'll see."

Jamie told herself it wasn't worth starting another fight over. And she wasn't going to vent about it on social media either. She just smiled and nodded. They'd see who was right in a few weeks' time.

Seven hours later, Jamie walked home yawning. It had been a long day and she hadn't got nearly as much writing done in the morning as she'd hoped.

She longed to take off her shoes, open a bottle of wine, and watch the sun go down from her patio. But a glass of wine in the evening always sounded the death knell for her chances of getting any work done at night. So she would put together a little meal and drink it with something cold instead. That way the only effort involved would be peeling the lid off the container of chicken and avocado salad she'd taken home from Delucia's.

Then she would settle down to write, and only once she had met her word quota for the day would she allow herself that glass of wine. It would be pitch dark by then, so the wine would accompany something trashy on the TV rather than a gorgeous sunset.

Feeling slightly more energetic, she rounded the corner into Sixteenth street.

A group of people were standing clustered in front of her house. They were pointing at something. Jamie could hear loud exclamations. She could see arms waving about.

She quickened her footsteps. Could something be wrong with

Faith? No, Faith would have left hours ago. A break-in, maybe? But what could have brought a group of people to a halt like this?

Then she realised that it wasn't her house they were looking at, it was her gate. And she started to run.

Not the cats, she prayed as she ran. Please not the cats. Anything but the cats. Some small animal like a rat or a pigeon. Something that would evoke pity and revulsion, but not actual grief. Please, not the cats.

When she got close enough to see the size of the animal tied to her gate, her heart sank into her shoes. She knew that golden fur. She knew those soft ears and that wedge-shaped head, now slumped forward. It was Silver. Tom and Ben's beloved pet.

The group of pedestrians turned around as she came running up. Their eyes were full of shock.

"This is your dog?" a man asked. "Is it yours?"

"No, no!" The words choked Jamie as they fought with tears to escape her throat. "Not mine. His." She pointed at Tom's house. "It's my neighbour's dog."

"Who did this?" another man asked. "Who killed this dog and tied him here? Did you do this?" The others looked from the dog to Jamie and back again.

"No!" she cried. "Of course not. It's some maniac. I need to tell my neighbour his dog is dead."

"Is it dead? For sure?" The first man touched the dog lightly on the flank.

Jamie tried to pull herself together. Silver had been cut open from chin to tail and her insides hung out in a grotesque mess. But the other animals hadn't been dead, she reminded herself. There was a chance Silver could still be alive. They could rush her to the vet and save her life.

Gritting her teeth, she lifted the dog's head and looked at it closely. Then she let it fall again. The half-open eyes with their sightless, milky-pale irises told their own tale.

"She's dead."

Seeing her distress, one of the women touched Jamie on her arm. "Can we help you?"

"Did you see anything?" Jamie asked. "Anything at all? Was there anyone running away when you arrived – or driving away?"

They shook their heads. There was no one. They had seen nothing. It wasn't surprising.

"Do you want us to walk into the house with you?" asked the first man. "In case someone is still inside?"

Jamie shook her head. "That's very kind of you, but no thanks. I can't go home yet. I need to see my neighbour first." To tell him that the dog he and Ben had loved so much was dead because of its connection to her.

"Take my cell number," said the man, pulling a pencil and a crumpled receipt out of his pocket. "I am Solomon Ndlovu. If you need to speak to me, you can phone."

He handed her the paper with his name and number written on it. Jamie thanked him in a daze. The pedestrians muttered words of comfort and then moved on, looking behind them once or twice at the bizarre scene they had just left.

Jamie forced herself to ring Tom's bell. She waited a moment, and then rang it again. And again. Panic wanted to rise at the thought that he might not be there. That she would have to carry the weight of this news on her own for longer.

But after a moment the front door clicked open, and she rushed inside. Even if only Vuyiswa were home, at least she would be able to tell someone – share this terrible burden.

But it was Tom standing in front of her. Whatever he saw on Jamie's face had him hurrying towards her. "What is it? What's happened?"

"Oh, Tom. Thank God you're home. It's happened again. On my gate."

"On your gate? Another animal? You haven't touched anything, have you?"

"No, no!" She shook her head. "Tom, I'm so, so sorry. It's Silver

140

this time. He got Silver. She's … she's dead."

Jamie watched Tom's face, waiting for the shock and grief to take over.

There was shock certainly, but also puzzlement.

"Jamie…" he said. "Silver's fine."

Oh no, she thought. Let him not go into denial. She couldn't cope with having to batter down a wall of disbelief.

"Tom, Silver's not fine. She's dead. I'm so sorry, but it's true." Her voice broke on the last word and she lifted her hands to her face.

Tom took her by the shoulders and led her into the house. "Look, Jamie. Look over there. Silver's fine. There she is. And she's fine."

Jamie stared across the sitting room to where Ben was throwing a plastic ball across the carpet for Silver to chase. The big, golden dog – vibrantly alive – bounded after the ball and brought it back to lay at Ben's slippered feet.

Jamie's knees began to tremble and Tom led her to an armchair.

"Thank God!" she gasped. "Oh, thank God. That poor, poor dog. But thank God it's not Silver."

Tom knelt down on the floor and looked into her face. "Okay, let's rewind here. There's something on your gate? Your front gate. Like those other two times?"

"Yes, it's a dog. I thought it was Silver. It looks exactly like her."

"I need to see it. Can you stand up?"

Jamie brushed his hand aside and stood up. She swayed for a second, but managed to steady herself.

Then she led the way out into the street.

———

If Jamie's gate had attracted attention before, it had now gathered a minor mob. Three separate cars had stopped to stare at the gruesome sight, along with a straggling knot of pedestrians.

Jamie felt their stares as she and Tom pushed their way towards the gate. *What kind of sicko lives here?* they were probably thinking. It made her want to put up a sign stating that none of this was her doing.

Jamie and Tom were bombarded by questions as they stepped up to examine the dog. Closing her mind to the noise, Jamie tried to concentrate. Now that she was thinking clearly, she could see details she had missed earlier. This was a much older dog than Silver. It was gaunt where Silver was sleek, and its fur was rougher. Even the whiteness of its eyes spoke of cataracts rather than death, as she'd assumed earlier.

Tom was going around the little crowd of people and talking quietly to them. She hoped he was persuading them to move on.

Sure enough, they started to move away. Car engines were turned on and bags were hoisted onto shoulders. Jamie was dismayed to see a number of flashes as people used their cellphone cameras to record the grisly sight. Now it would be all over the local press and radio stations by morning.

Tom went into his house and came out with a pair of surgical gloves, some large bin bags, and a wire cutter. When everyone had moved away, he took his own photos of the scene and then set about dismantling it.

"I recognise this dog now," Jamie said as she helped him put the body into a bag. "It lived in a house down the road. The people who used to stay there moved overseas about six months ago and left their gardener in charge of the house and the dog. It spent a lot of time wandering around in the street. Why would anyone want to hurt a harmless old animal like this?"

"Because it looks a lot like my dog?" Tom gathered up the cable ties and slipped them into a smaller bag.

Jamie thought about this. "I'm going to have to go to the police, aren't I? This isn't just a malicious prank. I don't know what you'd call it, but it's not a joke anymore."

"I don't think it ever was."

"Can you put all that stuff in my car? I'll probably have to show it to the police before they take me seriously."

"I'd like to come with you," Tom said. "I'm pretty sure my dog was supposed to be the target of this attack. And I know the station commander at Morningside South Police Station. I gave a lecture there a few weeks ago. Let's go in my car." Before she could protest, he added, "We'll have to take Ben, so we'll need the car seat."

15

Jamie's only experiences with the Morningside South Police Station had been two occasions when she'd had to report motor vehicle accidents. The memory of those two fender benders did not encourage her to hope that this would be a quick exercise.

But either the station had improved its efficiency, or having Tom along was speeding things up. She suspected a bit of both. One big improvement was that you were now allowed to write your own incident report. The last time, she'd had to tell her story to an officer of the law, who wrote it down at the snail speed for which bureaucrats everywhere are known. Now she was handed a four-page form with plenty of space to write out her own statement.

Writing the story down made Jamie wonder why she had waited so long to report the incidents, while still fearing she was wasting police time. Then she thought about the old dog she used to see sniffing around in the street, and knew he hadn't deserved such a cruel end.

Tom sat with Ben while Jamie spoke to one of the officers. When she was finished with the paperwork, he stood up and announced that he was going to see the station commander.

"Come, Ben," he said, bending down to pick him up.

"Wait!" Jamie said. "Why don't you leave him here with me? It won't be much fun for him in there, and you'll get on faster without him. I won't take my eye off him for a second, I promise."

Tom hesitated. Then Ben started wriggling in his arms, trying to squirm his way back down to ground level. Tom closed his eyes as he considered his son's unendearing habit of pulling papers and files off desks when he was feeling ignored. Ben started to whine, a niggly, persistent sound that quickly climbed in volume.

"Thanks," he said, putting Ben back down. The whining stopped at once. "Please watch him carefully. He can move like lightning when he feels like it. I'll be about fifteen minutes."

Ben watched his father walk away without a murmur. When Tom turned out of sight, he swung around and enveloped Jamie's legs in a hug. "Lady!" he said happily. "Mima."

Looking down into his chocolate-drop eyes, Jamie felt the first gleam of light break through in this whole horrible day. She scooped him onto her lap and hugged him hard. At last she could do what she'd been longing to do. With Tom's wary eye removed, she could cuddle Ben all she liked.

The little boy erupted into giggles as her squeezing turned into tickling, while she pretended to make snarling, chomping noises at the back of his neck. As his giggles subsided, she pulled him against her chest and breathed in deeply to inhale the baby-shampoo smell of his head. A gush of love welled up inside her.

Before she could get too comfortable, he slid off her lap and onto the floor. Jamie watched as he walked up and down the row of unoccupied chairs next to her, tapping each one with his hand. If he got rowdy, she'd control him, she told herself. She couldn't bear parents who let their children run wild in a public place. She would never let a child under her care behave like that.

A beeping noise in her handbag told Jamie she had an incoming text. She looked around for her bag, momentarily confused about where she'd left it. Oh, there it was, behind her chair. She reached into her bag and pulled out her phone. When she looked up again, Ben was gone.

For a second, she stared at the empty waiting area in disbelief. Then her heart started banging, and she leapt to her feet.

Where was he? She'd taken her eyes off him for two seconds, no more. Where the hell was he?

An icy fist clutched at her as she imagined him being snatched. Or running out into the busy road outside and being hit by a car. No, the door leading out of the station was too big and heavy for Ben to pull open on his own. Wherever he was, he hadn't gone outside.

"Where did he go?" she demanded of the bored clerk sitting behind a desk. "The little boy who was sitting here with me just a second ago. Did you see where he went?" The clerk just shrugged and shook his head.

Swallowing her panic, Jamie dashed across the room and looked down the corridor where Tom had gone.

"Ben!" she hissed. "Ben! Where are you?"

Her knees went weak with relief as a dark little head peered at her around one of the doorways.

"There you are!" She darted forward to pick him up. "You mustn't run off like that, Bennie. You nearly gave me a heart attack. Were you looking for your dad?"

"Dada!" Ben said, injecting maximum longing into his voice. "Want Dada!" You'd swear the kid had been separated from his father for five years instead of five minutes.

Nerves jangling, Jamie carried him back to the waiting area, wondering if she would survive until Tom came back. Fifteen minutes, he'd said. And that was five minutes ago. Only ten minutes to go. He'd better not be one second late.

A quarter of an hour later, Jamie felt as though she'd aged several years. In the time they'd been waiting, Ben had managed to hit his head jumping from the chairs onto the floor. His wails on that occasion had plaster practically falling from the ceiling. Then he'd discovered the water cooler, which entertained him for approximately thirty seconds before he'd tugged the hot water switch and burned his hand. More wails, more plaster falling from the ceiling.

Jamie poured him some water in a plastic cup, which delighted him for all of twenty seconds until he realised it was more fun to throw the water on the floor and demand a refill than to drink it. He then proceeded to slip in the puddle he'd made and land hard on his bottom. This precipitated still more tears and wailing.

She had just managed to calm him down for the third time when Tom appeared. The look she cast him was so filled with gratitude he couldn't help smiling.

"You look like someone who's just spent twenty minutes alone with a toddler."

She managed to grin. "You weren't kidding about how fast he can move. Oh, by the way, he's got a bump on his forehead and a tiny burn on his wrist. The desk clerk gave me some burn cream and a plaster."

"That's fine. Sounds like an average day in the Elliot household. Thanks for looking after him."

Tom expected her to shove Ben at him like a politician passing the buck, but she just lifted him onto her hip and slung her bag over her shoulder. As they walked to the car, the little boy's head drooped, and he fell asleep against her neck.

Back at Tom's place, Jamie waited downstairs while Tom changed Ben's nappy, wrestled him into his pyjamas, and put him to bed. The exhausted little boy barely woke up, even for the token tooth-brushing.

Jamie used the time to update her Facebook status and to tweet some details about the latest development in her stalker saga. She would write a proper blog post tomorrow if she could get her thoughts in order. Few things had shaken her as much as the sight of that dog tied to her gate. Tomorrow would bring the unpleasant task of going to tell the gardener across the road that the dog he'd been looking after was dead.

"What are you doing?" Tom asked once he was finished putting Ben to bed.

"I'm tweeting and Facebooking."

"About tonight?"

"Yes, about tonight. I always write about what's going on in my life, and right now, this is it."

"You know that this guy is almost certainly using social media to track you?"

"Then we can use it to track him. Social media is a two-way street. If he's on Facebook or Twitter, he must be using an identity."

"Not necessarily. He could be doing that thing where you just watch and observe but don't participate. You social media types have a word for it."

"Lurking?"

"Yes, that."

Jamie thought about it. "He could, I suppose, but that strikes me as a little low-key for his ego. This guy wants to be noticed. I don't see him as a shrinking violet."

"You could be right. Let's have something to eat and then go through your followers to see if we can identify him. Unfortunately, the chicken stew Ben had for supper has completely dried out. I left it on low to keep warm, but it's stuck to the bottom of the pan by now. How do you feel about pizza?"

Jamie consulted her stomach. "Not fondly," she decided. "Why don't I take a look in the kitchen and see what I can throw together?"

"You can look, but I don't think you'll find anything. I was going to order groceries tonight. We're low on just about everything. If you can find enough to make an actual meal, I'll be surprised."

"A challenge!" Jamie perked up. "I like the sound of that. Give me half an hour and if I haven't come up with something edible by then, the pizza is on me."

"Done."

Jamie opened Tom's fridge and stared at its unpromising contents. She refused to be daunted. The kitchen was her happy place and always had been. Even though she spent more time serving food than preparing it these days, she could still be soothed and comforted by the rhythm of meal preparation. It was easier to block the memory of the eviscerated corpse hanging from her gate when her mind was calculating cooking times and methods.

She found a pack of frozen chicken breasts practically glued to the side of the freezer. She hacked them free with a bread knife and checked the packaging. Only a month old. That was fortunate. Giving herself and Tom salmonella poisoning wasn't part of her plan.

A bag of frozen mixed vegetables was also excavated from the ice. What else, what else? She struck gold in the pantry in the form of two-minute noodles. There would be no need to eat either her words or a pizza tonight.

Working quickly, Jamie simmered the chicken breasts in a deep pan filled with wine, water, half a stock cube, some pepper corns and a bay leaf. She would have preferred to bake them in the oven, but she only had half an hour standing between her and a takeaway dinner. The instant noodles were set to soak in a jug of boiling water.

While the chicken breasts poached, Jamie set the wooden kitchen table with some plates she found in a drawer. There were placemats and napkins she recognised from the flea market at the annual Grahamstown Arts Festival. The cutlery was bone-handled and clearly vintage. Tom had either picked it up at a craft market, or it had been in his family for generations.

The glasses were of the cheap-and-cheerful supermarket variety. Jamie guessed that having a toddler in the house made one less choosy about what one drank out of.

When the chicken breasts were almost done, she scooped them out of the pan and sliced them into thin strips. She heated some oil in a fresh pan, and flash-fried the chicken strips together with the frozen vegetables. Ideally she would have preferred to do them in an electric wok, with its pinpoint heat control, but Tom's kitchen didn't run to such things.

She drained the instant noodles and added them to the mixture, drizzling sesame oil and soy sauce over everything. Then she transferred the food to two warmed plates and shouted for Tom. She had exactly thirty-five seconds to spare.

"Very impressive," he said, sitting down and shaking out a napkin. "I can't pretend I wasn't secretly hoping for pizza, but this smells good enough to change my mind."

"Pizza is the food of the gods. This is a well-known fact. But there are times one wants something more vitaminy."

"A vegetarian pizza is vitaminy."

"Maybe, but this is better for you. Taste it before you decide."

Tom did, and had to concede that Jamie hadn't wasted the years she'd spent at hotel school. The stir fry was as good as anything you'd get in a restaurant, minus the MSG aftertaste of the Chinese takeaway he usually patronised.

Afterwards they took their coffee to the living room. Instead of sitting down, Jamie wandered around the room looking at photographs.

"This must be your father," she said, pointing to a man in bathing trunks standing on a beach. "You're very like him."

"Yes, that's the original Ben Elliot."

"Oh, you named Ben after him? How lovely. He looks so happy in this picture."

"He was. That was taken in Orange County. My mother was still alive then."

Jamie looked at a series of black and white pictures, all featuring the same woman. Her eyes seemed almost too large for her thin face, and her skin was very dark, although that could just have been a trick of the light.

Jamie looked a little closer. "Is this ... Ben's mother?"

"Yes, that's her."

"Where did you get these? I thought she died straight after you met her."

"She did. I got them by sheer luck. It turns out the guy across the road from us has a security camera facing the street."

"The house with the blue wall?"

"Yes."

"He's a security nut. He has cameras all over his property."

"Never thought I'd have cause to be grateful for a neighbour's paranoia, but this time it came in handy. When Ben's mother came to my gate that day, his camera caught her on tape. I've kept a copy of it for him to watch one day. He will see himself as a tiny baby tied to her back. I hope he'll know how much she loved him."

"She must have been desperate, going from door to door like that when she was so ill."

"Yes. She had advanced puerperal fever. She was minutes away from death."

"So these pictures are stills from the tape rather than photographs?"

Yes, I had them made so he will grow up always knowing her face."

Jamie shook her head. "I thought adoptive parents were supposed to feel threatened by their kid's biological parents."

"Maybe some of them are, but I know what it's like to long for your biological roots. It can become an obsession in adolescence. When I was a teenager, I missed the memory of my mother, but I also wanted to connect with her heritage. I used to spend hours staring at photos of her, trying to figure out whether I had her nose or her chin or whatever. I only got to know her family when I moved back to the States as an adult, but it was very satisfying to meet them at last."

Jamie stared at Ben's mother for another moment. Then she sat down and picked up her coffee cup.

"I've been thinking about what happened tonight."

"Me too," he said. "And I'd like to trawl through your social media accounts."

"Trawl away. All my stuff is public."

"No, I mean I'd like full access to your accounts – like you have. In other words, I need your passwords to log onto them as a user, not just a viewer."

Jamie pursed her lips. "Because?"

"If you're right about social media being a two-way street and this guy needing attention – and I think you are – it might be possible to figure out what screen names he's using. This isn't exactly my field, but it's close enough for me to have a decent shot at it."

Jamie hesitated. She'd never given away her password before. Not since she was a kid on the old Friendster site. But what did she have to hide? She'd never posted anything she wasn't comfortable sharing with the whole world. If Tom wanted to tunnel around in her online world, he was welcome.

"Fine. What do you need?"

"Everything."

It took a while. Jamie kept remembering things like the second Instagram account she'd created and forgotten to close, the Pinterest account she'd opened for her novel before she'd decided to use her personal account for all pinned images, and the Facebook fan page she'd started for her novel before realising nobody was going to join it.

But once Tom had everything he needed and started trawling through her accounts, it took him less than an hour to hit the jackpot.

"This is him," he said, jabbing his finger at the screen. "He calls himself Foully Wooing Won. He might have other identities too, but this is definitely one of them."

"That guy?" Jamie bent down to frown at the screen. "The name rings a bell. I think I might have interacted with him once or twice."

"He follows you on Twitter and Facebook, and leaves comments on your blog."

"Okay. Why do you think it's him?"

"Every time there's been an incident at your gate, he's referred to it as though he were there, as though he were watching you. Look, he says that you screamed when you found the rat. And he talks about a conversation you had with Pumla as though he was right there listening to it. This is definitely him."

"It's such a strange name, though. Foully Wooing Won. What does it mean? He hasn't tried to 'woo' me. Why would he choose such a weird screen name? Especially if he wants to keep a low profile."

"It's an anagram."

Jamie blinked at the screen, trying to rearrange the letters in her head. "It is? I'm hopeless at those. I can never figure them out. What's it an anagram of?"

"Now Following You."

All the hair on Jamie's arms stood up. "That's a Twitter term.

When you get new followers, Twitter sends you an email to say that so-and-so is 'now following you'."

"It's also an appropriate name for a stalker. I think you should block him."

Jamie thought about this. "I've blocked trolls before, but all they do is change their user names or IP addresses. I'd rather be able to keep an eye on him."

Tom turned his head and saw the distress on her face. He stood and put his hands on her shoulders. "Hey, it's okay. Don't get upset. Honestly, this is a good thing. The more we know about him, the better."

"It's just … I keep seeing that poor dog tied to my gate with his head drooping and his body stiff. He was such a harmless old thing. He loved pottering around in the street, sniffing things and greeting everyone who passed. I used to give him a pat whenever I saw him. What kind of evil bastard kills a dog like that just because he can? And what have I done to make this happen?"

Her voice broke and a tear rolled down her cheek.

Tom put his arms around her and pulled her against him. "It wasn't your fault. None of this is your fault."

"I'm sorry," she sniffed. "I never cry. I hate crying."

"You're entitled."

So Jamie allowed herself to relax against him as she sobbed for the dog that had somehow been killed because of her. Soon the shudders left her body, along with the tension she'd been carrying around all evening.

Tom drew back and smiled at her. "Better?"

"Yeah. Thanks." She scrabbled in her bag for a tissue to dry her eyes. Then she looked up at him again. "Just … come back here a minute, I want to check something."

Puzzled, Tom took a step towards her.

Jamie wound her arms around his neck and pulled his head down to kiss him. His response was immediate and enthusiastic. The horror and sorrow of the day flowed out to be replaced by the heat of his body, warming her to the bone. Everything about his kiss was new and stimulating, but somehow also familiar, as though she were remembering something she'd once had a long time ago.

Excitement leapt in him as she plastered her long body against him. You'd never know to look at her that she would be so soft to touch. As the kiss deepened, he allowed his hands to travel over the swell of her bottom and into the hollow of her waist. Desire strained at him. He struggled to control it, to remember the circumstances.

Jamie longed to give herself over to the moment, to allow them to take each other on the spot, or perhaps stagger as far as the sofa. The horror of what they'd been through demanded this exorcism.

His hands flashed up to cup her breasts, so firm and perfectly rounded. But as his system went into overdrive, the image of her face, pale and haunted just a minute ago, came into his mind. Yes, sex would be one way to drive out the demons, but not now. Not this first time.

He managed to disentangle himself, almost pushing her away from him until there was a safe gap between them. Her eyes met his. "What is it?" she asked. "What's wrong?"

He dragged a hand through his hair. "This isn't a good idea."

"Why not? It seems like a fine idea from where I'm standing."

"You're too vulnerable. I'd be taking advantage."

Her eyebrows snapped together. "What kind of patronising bull-shit is that? Why wouldn't I be taking advantage of you?"

"If I'd been through a traumatic experience today and you jumped me, it would also be taking advantage. Sex isn't easy and uncomplicated. Well, not for me."

Jamie let her breath out in a long sigh. "You're right, dammit. I hate that."

"We'd never know if we went into it because we wanted to or because we needed something to make the day go away."

"Right again. I still don't feel any better about it."

The phone in her pocket beeped loudly, making them both jump. Tutting with frustration, she pulled it out and read the text.

Nomsa's at the clinic looking after her mom – appendicitis. She can't do her shift tomorrow. We need a head baker. You're up.

Good old Pumla. You could always count on her to be succinct.

"What's up?" Tom asked as Jamie indulged in some creative swearing.

"I have to take over the head baker's shift tomorrow. Her mom's in hospital with appendicitis."

"Okay. So what's the problem? I thought you loved baking?"

"I do love baking. It's just the baker's hours I'm not so keen on. This means I have to be at work at four-thirty tomorrow morning. Four-thirty! In the morning."

He gave her ponytail a gentle tug. "Good thing we restrained ourselves then. You'd have been a wreck tomorrow."

16

Jamie did love baking, but it took her a bleary half-hour of going through the motions before she remembered how much she enjoyed it.

By five she was into the rhythm, making puff pastry with the automatic motions of long habit. The muscles in her arms bunched and relaxed as she rolled the pastry out as thin as paper. Then she brushed melted butter over the surface with long, sweeping gestures, gathered it up and rolled it out again.

This dough would be used for chicken pies and quiches, but also for sweet croissants, pains au chocolat and fruit tarts. When this was done, she would get started on the choux pastry for the profiteroles, éclairs and crullers, and when that was finished, she would make phyllo pastry for her strudels and Greek confections.

The rest of the team were working on bread dough for the sweet and savoury breads and buns Delucia's offered, forming the dough into loaves and rolls and preparing to put them back for their second rising. The bakery was warm and muggy and smelled like heaven, but like the rest of the staff, Jamie had long since stopped being able to appreciate it.

By six, they were busy shaping the pastries into their final forms. Jamie was quick to notice when shortcuts were taken. She handed over the almond croissants she was making to one of the staff, and went from station to station guiding and correcting.

She was the one who had trained this team in the first place, and it pained her if she saw them taking liberties with her methods. Eighteen months ago she had worked long hours to transform them from unimaginative bakers, accustomed to churning out commercial-grade stodge, into sensitive pastry cooks who would not be out of place at a patisserie in Paris. Nomsa had shown particular flair for the process, which got her promoted to head baker. She not only understood dough, but delighted in it.

"That crust looks like it's been nibbled on by rats, not shaped," Jamie told one of the bakers, pointing to a Cape gooseberry tart in the making. "Fluting takes time, you can't hurry it. Slow down and use the flower-shaping tool."

"There are new moulds on the market," he told her. "I saw them on the Probaking website. They do the fluting for you, which saves time and creates a more uniform effect."

Jamie reached across him to grab a pen. There was no paper in sight, so she made a note on the back of her hand. "I'll look into it. If I like what I see, I'll order some. It's time we took this operation more high-tech."

She moved on, armed with a handful of tasting spoons. She dipped them into the various fillings bubbling away on the burners, and offered criticism and advice that she knew might be resented, but would be taken on board in the end.

"More kirsch in the Black Forest torte," she told one baker. "It's expensive but worth it. If Pumla's been telling you to cut costs, just leave her to me. I'll sort her out." She moved on. "There's too much cornflour in this beef stew. The Cornish pasties and the pepper steak pies should be rich but not sticky."

As she moved on to the next station, she forced herself to face facts. This early-morning stint in the bakery couldn't be a one-off thing. She would have to spend at least one day a month in here to keep an eye on standards. The Delucia's team was first class, and Nomsa was a talented pastry chef, but only an owner had the necessary eye for detail and investment in perfection.

By seven, the kitchen had been cleared, with all stations washed down in preparation for the first breakfast orders. Jamie knew that Pumla had arrived from the way fresh pastries kept disappearing from their wire baskets. She had to fight the urge to go and help with the front-of-house set-up.

There was always a lull after the bakery opened its doors. Most of the early customers wanted their coffee and pastries to go, which Pumla could handle on her own. The kitchen staff took advantage of the quiet spell to grab some breakfast or to pop outside for a smoke. Jamie used it to tie on a serving apron and nip out to check on the set-up.

She had to admit the place looked every bit as fresh and welcoming as she could have made it herself.

"Checking up on me?" Pumla asked by way of greeting.

"It's a compulsion. I can't help myself."

"I don't know how you think I manage this on my own every morning."

"If the place always looks this pretty, it's no wonder business is good."

Pumla waited for the catch, but for once there didn't seem to be one. Jamie leaned against the counter, apparently willing to chat.

"So, what's up with you?" she asked.

"My period is due tomorrow." Pumla lowered her voice even though they were the only people in the room.

"Okay. Well, look, don't get too excited if it doesn't start. You're not as regular as clockwork, are you? You never used to be."

"No, but I'm not usually more than three days out either way. But that's not why I'm excited. I did a pregnancy test."

Jamie frowned. "You're not supposed to do them that early. I thought the most sensitive ones could only pick up something from the first day of your missed period. You're not even there yet."

"Yes, but there's no harm in trying, is there? It almost feels like I could make it happen by taking lots and lots of pregnancy tests."

"Lots and lots of pregnancy tests," Jamie repeated. "How many are we talking about here?"

"Well, I started three days ago with one test, and it was negative. So the next day I bought two tests, but they were also negative. Then yesterday I bought three – also negative. And today I've got three more to try."

Jamie gaped at her. "Are you crazy? This must be costing you a fortune. And you don't even want a baby. You're just doing this to keep your mom happy."

Pumla seized a cloth and wiped up a spill next to the coffee machine with fast strokes. "Yes, I do. You don't know what's going on inside my head, so don't pretend you do. I might have started out trying to conform to expectations, but now I really want this for myself."

"You mean your competitive streak has been activated and now you have to be the fastest person to fall pregnant in the history of the world. You want to have a positive pregnancy test before it's even possible."

"Oh, really?" Pumla flung the cloth down and dug into the pocket of her jeans. "Then what do you call this?"

Jamie reached for the plastic stick Pumla was shoving in her face, then saw what it was. "Eeuw! That's a pregnancy test. You peed on that. Take it away, I'm not touching it."

"Oh, don't be silly. The tip is closed. Look, there's a plastic cap covering it. You won't get a single drop of pee on you. Just take a look at the two little windows. That's where you read the result."

Intrigued now, Jamie took the stick back from her and looked hard at the windows. One had a thick blue line running down the middle of it, and the other was completely blank.

"Okay…" she said slowly. "I'm no expert, but I'm pretty sure there's meant to be a line in both windows. This is a negative test."

"No, no. Hold it up to the light. If you tilt it at a certain angle and look at it really, really closely, you can just about see a very faint little line."

Jamie walked to the window and held the stick in full sunlight. Then she tilted it this way and that, and peered at it. "Hmmm. I guess I can sort of see something. It's more like a shadow than an actual line."

"Exactly! And the instructions say that any line, however faint, indicates a positive pregnancy test."

"The instructions also say the results should not be read more than fifteen minutes after taking the test," Jamie said, pointing to a line of writing on the side of the stick.

"But it looked like that after five minutes," Pumla insisted. "I swear it did. It hasn't changed."

Jamie shrugged. "I still say this isn't a definite result. It's not even probable yet."

"And I say I'm pregnant. In fact, I know I am. I even felt a bit nauseous this morning."

"You're nuts, that's what you are. You need to stop obsessing about this. Just wait and see what happens in the next few days."

———

FROM JAMIE BURCHELL'S PERSONAL BLOG:

The worst part – the very worst part – was having to go over to the house with the bad news.

There's only an elderly gardener living there now. He tells me the owners of the house emigrated months ago. They left him in charge of the house and the family pet so that they would have something to come back to in case things didn't work out in Perth. I guess things are working out because they're not coming back.

I don't understand people who can just up and leave their pets behind like that. Owning a pet is a lifelong commitment – the pet's life, not yours. Yes, if you're fleeing persecution or an earthquake or a genocide, you can leave your pets behind, but swanning off to Perth in search of a "better life" just doesn't make the grade. If you can afford to relocate to Australia, you can afford the quarantine fees to take your pets with you.

If that dog had been put in quarantine, he would have been living in his new home for five months by now. Instead he's dead because he was allowed to wander the streets.

Yes, I know the person who's really responsible for his death is the psycho who killed him, but I just had to get that pet-neglect rant off my chest.

And yes, I also know that I'm displacing my anger because the person who is doing this to me is just a shadow so far. I'm angry and I'm frightened, and I don't like feeling either.

The morning passed in a blur of breakfast orders. By ten, the breakfast rush was over. A few people were still trickling in for coffee and cake, but Jamie could afford to set up her laptop in the back office and log on to her blog to see how many comments she had attracted. She'd finished it the night before, knowing she would be occupied all the next morning.

It didn't surprise her to see more than forty comments already. She helped herself to a cappuccino and read through them carefully. It was the ones at the end that were the most interesting.

Posted by: **Orange Prize**
I hope the police are taking this seriously.

Posted by: **Milatsi**
This isn't police business. You should call the SPCA or something.

Posted by: **Dineo**
Yes the polis must investig8 crimez against humans not dogs

Posted by: **Cyril Att**
He's accelerating, Jamie. Next time he's going to come after you. And I have to point out that, once again, your neighbour was involved. Why is he on the spot every time an incident like this happens? You're too trusting, that's your problem.

Posted by: **Gugz**
Yes, it's not the dog I'm worried about – it's you. All of this has been directly targeted at you. And he is definitely accelerating. Going after bigger prey all the time.

Posted by: **Foully Wooing Won**
Animals are dirty and disgusting. They are full of fleas and lice and they bite.

Posted by: **Shoobeedoo**
Oh, for goodness' sake. That doesn't mean they deserve to be KILLED.

That was the last post, submitted just four minutes earlier.

Jamie held her breath as she read the second-last post. It was him. Foully Wooing Won. He was back, and he wanted her to know it.

She reminded herself that he had no way of knowing that she knew who he was. He couldn't possibly be aware that Tom had trawled through her posts to identify him. Tom had not clicked on his screen name in case he had a system in place to notify him if anyone viewed his profile.

This was just one of his fishing expeditions. She had responded to him before, but always in an offhand manner. His posts had never triggered warning bells. Probably, she admitted, because she was used to the trolls who tried to engage her when she went online. It took a very special crazy to stand out from the rest.

What did he want from her? Did he like the feeling of hiding in plain sight? Did it make him feel clever to flaunt himself under her nose? If that was the case, it was best if she continued to seem unaware of him.

But he was trying to draw her out, wasn't he? His posts were always provocative, as though he were looking for a reaction. Maybe it was time to give him one.

She started to type, reminding herself she could always delete it before posting.

Posted by: **Jamie Burchell**

@ Cyril – don't stress. Tom isn't the one behind this, I promise you.

@ Foully Wooing Won – whatever you may think of animals, this dog was someone's personal property.

@ Gugz – I'm worried too.

She read the post over and over. There was no harm in it that she could see. She wasn't singling him out. She was simply replying to several posts at once, as she often did. There was nothing aggressive in what she'd written – nothing to indicate she was baiting him. The odd thing to do would be to ignore him. He would think she was doing it on purpose.

Jamie hit "post" before she could change her mind.

17

FROM JAMIE BURCHELL'S EMAIL INBOX:

Hi Jamie,

Thanks so much for your article on #FOMO. We all loved it, including, most importantly, our editor, Marilyn. We would like to publish it in our February issue, which will hit newsstands on 16 January.

Our rate for freelancers is R3 per word. Please submit your invoice within 10 days of publication. You can email it to me and I will forward it to the accounts department.

Many thanks for a fun contribution!

Warm regards,
Eliza Rainers
Content Editor
Her Magazine

Hi my love,

I'm sorry things got a bit heated on the phone today. You can't expect your father and me to sit idly by while some maniac threatens our daughter. But I do understand you can't be expected to put your life on hold for this either.

So, we're coming up to Joburg this weekend. We won't stay more than a couple of nights. We just want to see with our own eyes that you really are fine. Dad wants to take a look at the security at the house and see if there's anything more that can be done to upgrade it. We're both very glad you had that electric fence put in.

Why don't we have a braai on Sunday and invite your sisters? And Peter too, I suppose. Caroline isn't seeing anyone at the moment, is she? Actually,

I think she might be. Anyway, the five of us haven't been together since our 30th anniversary in June, so it'll be fun. Don't prepare anything yet, darling. We'll go shopping together on Saturday.

Can't wait to see you!

Lots of love,
Mom

Dear Jamie Burchell,

Congratulations! Your blog is now trending on Thinkblog. Follow this link to see your latest blog stats:

www.mythinkblogstats.com

Regards,
The Admin Team
Thinkblog

Hi Jamie,

We've been following your blog via Twitter and we'd love to have you on the show to take part in a discussion panel about stalking.

Our other guests will include a lady who went through the stalking experience years ago, as well as Dr Erik, our resident psychologist. The show is scheduled for next Thursday at 9.30am. If you could be at the studio in Maude Street by 9am that would be perfect.

Really hope you can make it! We're very excited about having you on the show.

Kind regards,
Jenna Pappadopoulos

Assistant Producer
The Thandi Thandeka Show
Jozi Talks Radio

———————

Jamie's pleasant, predictable life seemed to have taken on the qualities of a freight train. A parental invasion. A radio appearance. An article sold. Her blog going viral.

She still managed to post an instalment of her novel every day, but only just. And the posts were much shorter than usual. Her personal blog was taking up more and more of her time. And with her parents coming for the weekend, she wasn't likely to get anything else done.

A braai.

She needed to think about that. It was all very well for her mother to say "don't prepare anything" but she wasn't the hostess, was she? It wasn't in Jamie's nature to entertain without putting some thought into it. She could be spontaneous if she had to, but she preferred planning.

Gazpacho for the starter, maybe? She got up and wandered into the kitchen to feed the cats. Or an icy vichyssoise rather? Ella and Peter would probably prefer the gazpacho because it had fewer calories. Maybe she'd make both and serve them in tiny ramekins so that people could choose which one they liked. Or was that too dinky?

Hotel training died hard. She had to remind herself that not everything had to be presented in adorable doll-sized portions.

Jamie found she was pacing the kitchen. The cats cast irritated glances at her as they tried to eat in peace. She had so much restless energy at the moment. She'd run fifteen kilometres that morning, hoping to wear herself out and settle down for the day's work. It hadn't worked, but then she hadn't really expected it to.

She knew what ailed her, and it wasn't existential angst.

Her system had been revving ever since that kiss she and Tom had shared. It had accelerated out of control very quickly. She'd been ready to take that swan dive into the unknown, but Tom had pulled back. He was worried about her fragile emotional state, about whether this was what she really wanted.

She didn't feel in the least bit fragile. She also knew that sex with Tom was exactly what she wanted. The little taster she'd had made it clear that the main course would be stupendous.

She'd been attracted to him from the start, and getting to know him had deepened that attraction into respect and affection. He was a good guy. She had no doubt of that. He made her feel safe, as though intimacy with him were something she could risk.

The very fact that he'd stepped back from the brink the other night reflected well on him. But that didn't mean she wasn't frustrated. Very frustrated.

So. Sex with Tom. It was definitely going to happen. The only question was when and where.

The fact that he was a single father complicated things. It took away the spontaneity. But that was all right. All Jamie asked for at this point was Tom Elliot, naked and horizontal in her bed for twenty uninterrupted minutes. Okay, thirty minutes. In fact, call it an hour to be safe. Now, how to set it up?

She reached for a pen, tore a piece of computer paper in half, and started to write.

Dear Dog,

I have been observing my human closely and note that she shows no signs of mental perturbation, post-traumatic stress disorder, anxiety or poor judgement. She does, however, seem to feel that she has some unfinished business with your human. What are we going to do about that?

Regards,
The Cat

Jamie walked quickly to the postbox next door, dropped it in, and walked away again.

She was trying very hard not to think about what she'd just done. Nice girls didn't invite boys over for sex. She had just invited Tom over for sex. Therefore she was not a nice girl. Yes, she had long since rejected that kind of thinking, but early socialisation was a bitch. And now she had to wait for a reply. Which would no doubt take hours.

Her postbox clanged shut, startling her. She ran to the window just in time to see Tom retreating to his own house.

Dear Cat,

I tried to pass the message on to my human, but he was just a blur of motion heading towards your human's house. I have managed to persuade him that 7pm is a more civilised time to make social calls...

Regards,
The Dog

––––––––

When the doorbell rang just after seven o'clock, Jamie was glad there was no one around to see her jump. Her legs felt rubbery as she went to open the door. What exactly did Tom expect, she wondered. Would he jump her straight away? Would he expect her to lead him straight to the bedroom?

Even worse, was there any way he could have misinterpreted that exchange of letters and think this was just a casual visit?

Jamie tortured herself with a brief image of Tom pulling away from her in puzzled disgust as she made a move on him. It was such a hideous thought she felt her cheeks getting hot.

Then she told herself to stop it and let him in.

"You're nervous," he said as he stepped into the light of the entrance hall and took a long look at her. "It takes one to know one.

168

I'm nervous too."

"You don't look nervous," Jamie accused. He looked, as usual, composed in jeans and a crisp shirt. Then he dug his hands into his pockets and she saw that he was indeed not entirely at ease.

"Let's take the pressure off." She led the way to the kitchen and flipped on the kettle. "Let's pretend you've come over for a regular visit. We'll have a stress-free chat and see where we go from there."

His shoulders relaxed. "That's fine. A stress-free chat. I can do that." They exchanged their first real smile of the evening.

"I'll make us some coffee, shall I?"

"Sure," he said, leaning against the counter.

But when she turned to get the mugs out, she found him in her way. Not just in her way, but so close she bumped into him. She put out a hand to steady herself against the cupboard, and found that his was already there. Her heart beat a little faster as she felt the heat radiating from his body and caught the piney scent of him.

She stared at the second button of his shirt. "You're in the way."

"Uh huh."

"I can't seem to reach the cupboard."

"Nope."

"It's a problem. What are we going to do about it?"

His hand drifted up to brush the ends of her hair. "Well, what I was thinking, seeing as we're both so relaxed now, was that we should say a proper hello to each other."

"You mean before we get on with the coffee-drinking and stress-free-chat portion of the evening?"

"That's exactly what I mean."

She tore her eyes away from his shirt and glanced up at him, but the look on his face did nothing to soothe her.

"Just a quick hello?" she repeated. "Before coffee?"

"Yeah."

It was amazing, Tom thought, how calming it could be to realise that the other person was nervous, too. In the hours that had passed since Jamie's note arrived, she had somehow evolved in his head from the sexy girl next door into a hard-edged sophisticate who would expect him to bring his own props and toys to their assignation.

But the moment he saw her face, he realised she'd spent the afternoon in exactly the same agony as he had. That was when everything smoothed out for him.

Now he wasn't aware of anything except how close she was. He could hear the rush of breath from between her lips and feel the unsteadiness of her hand as it rested on his. He closed the gap between them by leaning down to brush her mouth with his.

"Was that it?" she whispered as he pulled back. "Was that the hello?"

"Not quite."

Gripping her waist with his hands, he clasped her against him and brought his mouth onto hers. Her arms lifted to his shoulders, her body pressing against his. He felt scalded by the flash-and-burn urgency of her response.

When Jamie's knees started to buckle, she grabbed a handful of his shirt.

"Bed," she said. "My bed. Now."

He didn't argue, but stumbled after her down the passage, stopping every few feet to drag her back for another kiss. Freed from the control he'd imposed on them, his hands went everywhere, roaming all over her body. When they closed over her breasts and his thumbs brushed across her nipples, she thought she might die.

"Now, now, now," she chanted as her own hands pulled at his shirt. "Too many buttons. Too many clothes."

"Tell me about it," he muttered, fighting with her shirt. He gave up on the buttons, tugged the whole thing over her head, and hurled it away. He smiled when he saw that she wasn't wearing a bra, just a light support tank. In two seconds that had gone the same way as the shirt.

"Hurry, hurry!" She plucked at his belt. She didn't want hands or tongue. Not this first time. She needed to be filled by him, to take him inside her and ride the wave with him.

Understanding the need that raged in her, he scooped her up and tossed her onto the bed. Locking eyes with her, he made short work of his belt buckle and jeans, fumbling the condom from his pocket. Her eyes were almost black in this light, he saw. The urgency in them whipped his need to an unbearable level.

Then he was on her and, with a quick tilt of the hips, in her. She started coming almost at once. Her muscles closed around him like a fist as she gasped. He tried to hold on, but it was too much for him and he let himself fall after her.

Jamie lay spread-eagled on the bed, trying to catch her breath. Every drop of tension had run out of her body. She slid her hand up and down Tom's back, enjoying the ridges of muscle and bone under her fingertips, and the feeling of being pressed against the mattress by his weight.

Yes, she would probably need to breathe again sometime in the future, but until then, she was enjoying the sensation of his heaviness and the thunder of his heart against her chest.

He grunted something into the pillow. It sounded like, "hurry".

"Mmmm?" she said.

He lifted himself up onto his arms and smiled down at her. "I said I'm sorry."

"Sorry for what?" Jamie couldn't imagine being sorry about anything ever again.

"That it was all a little quick. I usually have more finesse than that."

She smiled back at him, loving the way his eyes held hers steadily, without a trace of post-coital awkwardness. "Since I was at least fifty per cent responsible for the rush, I can't bring myself to be sorry back. Besides, it really worked for me – speed and all."

"Yeah, me too." He dropped a kiss on her forehead and rolled over onto his back, pulling her with him so that she now lay on top of him. "Still, I must remember to show you some of my smoother moves sometime."

Jamie laughed. "I'll hold you to that."

"Boy, I've been thinking about that for a long time."

"Thinking about what – sex?"

"Thinking about having sex. With you."

"Re-ally?" She smiled against his chest.

"Oh, yes. Since the day I first saw you, actually. I was so mad at you that day … and so mad at myself for noticing how sexy you were while I was trying to sustain the mad. Plus there was the awareness that I had no right to be mad at all, when I actually owed you big time. That wasn't my finest hour. No wonder it's taken me this long to get you into bed."

A silent laugh shook Jamie. "You didn't get me into bed. I got you into bed. Who sent the note that precipitated all this?"

"You did, you nymphomaniac."

"Stop making me laugh," she begged.

He pulled her closer. "I like it when you laugh. You kind of jiggle against me, in a way that makes me think maybe I should show you some of those moves I was talking about."

"Now who's the nympho?"

"That's a very shaky grip on Greek mythology you've got there, Chef. I'll be the satyr and you can be the nymph."

His hands were busy again, stroking the dip of her back, making their way down to the curves of her bottom.

"What are all these big words you keep using?" she said. "Maybe you should tell me again."

Tom grinned at her before he pulled her mouth down onto his. "Show, not tell."

It was some considerable time later before either of them had the energy to talk again.

"I wish you could stay over," Jamie said. "But I know it's not possible."

"I wish I could stay over too, but as it is, I'll have to be going quite soon." Tom rolled over to take a look at his watch on the nightstand. "Nearly nine o'clock. Vuyiswa likes to leave by ten at the latest on week nights. Which is fair enough, considering that both of us have to work the next day."

"Have you eaten?"

"Now that you mention it, no. I was too nervous earlier, what with having to enter the den of the man-eater..."

"Ha! And I was too nervous because I had Svengali coming over. I fully expected you to be twirling your waxed moustache when you arrived."

Tom stroked his chin. "I could grow a moustache if you like. And invest in a little tin of beeswax."

"Oh, please, no. You'd look like a member of Special Branch." She opened her mouth to explain this, but he shook his head.

"I get the reference. I went to school here, remember?"

"So you did. Sometimes you sound so American I forget that you actually grew up here."

"Ours is one of the hardest accents to lose."

Jamie swung her legs out of bed. "I'll go and put something together for supper."

Since Tom had first-hand experience of her "putting something together", he had no fault to find with this programme. He took a quick shower, got dressed, and wandered through to the kitchen to see if he could help. His jaw dropped when he saw she was already putting warmed plates of lamb tagine on the table.

"I don't care if you are Superchef," he said. "There's no way you whipped that up in ten minutes flat."

She smiled. "Of course not. I made it yesterday. It's all part of my plan to soften you up for the favour I need to ask you."

"Oh, so that's what this was all about." He nodded towards the bedroom. "You softening me up."

"Did it work?"

"Like a charm. So what am I being softened up for?"

They sat at the kitchen table and lifted their forks to dig into the tagine.

"Well, it's like this," Jamie said. "My parents are coming up for the weekend because they're worried about me."

"Okay. And where will they be staying?"

"Right here. This is their house, after all. And on Sunday they've invited my two sisters, my niece, and my sisters' boyfriends for a braai – a term I don't need to translate because you grew up here, right?"

"Correct. In fact, I can honestly say there is no South African tradition I'm fonder of than the Sunday afternoon braai."

"That's good, because I really need you to come to this one."

"Me? But why? Won't your parents want to have you to themselves?"

"They'll have had two days of me by that stage. And here's the thing." She took a deep breath. "I'm worried my parents are thinking of moving back here permanently to keep an eye on me. Or, if not permanently, then at least until this stalker thing has been resolved. And who knows how long that'll take. Reading between the lines, that's what this weekend is all about. They want to see for themselves how much danger I'm really in, and whether they need to move back to protect me. Which would really cramp my style. I haven't lived under the same roof as my parents since I left school. Something tells me it wouldn't be a good idea to start now."

Tom frowned. "Sure, I can see that. But I don't understand where I come in. How will my presence help you with that?"

"If my parents think I've got a big, strong neighbour looking out for me, they'll be happier about going back to Umhlanga and leaving me in peace. It's no good trying to convince them I can take care of myself. Not when there's a dog-murdering psycho on the loose. But if they think you're here and keeping an eye open, it will relieve their anxiety."

"Okay," he said after a moment. "In that case I'd be happy to come. I'll have to check with Vuyiswa first, though, to see if she can look after Ben on Sunday."

"Oh, Ben is invited too, of course. My family don't mind kids. And he'll probably be happy to see the cats again." She forced herself not to say any more, but waited as he turned the idea over in his mind.

"Sure," he said at last. "Yeah, sure. Why not?"

18

"Okay, Ben, how does this look?" Tom waved a bowl under his son's nose. "She's a cook, remember? A trained chef. It's no good buying a ready-made salad and hoping to fob her off with that. This has to be homemade, and it has to be good. So what do you think, huh?"

Ben stared with deep suspicion at the concoction his father appeared to be offering him. It contained nothing he recognised – not even tomatoes, which he had once munched on like apples before deciding one day that they were "yucky". There were green things in it, and there were brown things. And there were greeny-brown things. And then there were brown things that had green things growing out of them. Ben thought they looked exactly like worms.

"Yuck!" he pronounced. "Yucky, ucky, pucky!" He made retching noises to drive the point home.

"Hmm. Coming from you, that's practically five Michelin stars. Now where did I put the dressing?" He scratched around the kitchen for it, before remembering that it was still in the fridge. "Aha! There you are, you little bast- ... dickens. If you don't do the trick, nothing will. Extra-virgin olive oil," he told the wide-eyed Ben. "White balsamic vinegar. Berry-infused vinegar. And a squirt of fresh lemon juice. Does that sound awesome, or what?"

"Aah-sm," Ben repeated solemnly.

"Now you're talking. Let's get you dressed, Bennie-boy."

Ben's bottom lip started to jut. "Am dwessed."

Tom felt a sigh coming up from the soles of his shoes. "Yes, I know you're dressed, but you must put on different clothes to go to Jamie's house. Nice, going-out clothes."

"Want spidey-suit. Want it!" His voice was starting to rise.

"Well, let's go and see what else you've got in your closet." Tom picked him up and started up the stairs with him. He was about halfway up when he had to make a very sudden grab to stop his son from pitching backwards over the banister. Ben had developed an alarming habit of hurling himself backward by kicking out his legs and stiffening every muscle in his body. Tom had almost dropped him more than once.

"Jeez, Ben. My heart. Don't do that, dude."

Tom took deep breaths, and they managed to get up the rest of the stairs without incident.

"Okay! Let's see what's in here!" Tom flung the cupboard open with all the forced joviality of a circus ringmaster, but Ben was having none of it.

"Want spidey-suit," he muttered.

"How about these cool denim shorts with this awesome camo T-shirt, Ben? Just think how handsome you'll look. Jamie will love this outfit, I bet."

"Mima?" Ben asked.

"Yes, Mima. You want Mima to think you look handsome, don't you?"

Ben thought about that for a moment. Then his face cleared. "Mima want spidey suit. Mine spidey suit."

Tom eyed the spidey suit. It wasn't that he had any objection to dressing his son in superhero outfits. It was just this particular superhero outfit he didn't like. It was much too small, for one thing. The tag at the back of the neck declared it to be suitable for babies between the ages of six months and one year. Ben was twenty months old, and on the ninety-seventh percentile for both height and weight.

The nylon Spiderman outfit was literally groaning under the strain of fitting his sturdy little body. The seams had already split in several places, and it was worn so sheer in the rear that you could read the logo of Ben's nappy through the fabric. The pants, which were supposed to be full length, barely covered Ben's knees, and the sleeves were extravagantly ripped in several places.

Ben looked ridiculous in it, but had insisted on wearing it every day for the last two weeks. The only mercy was that he didn't actually sleep in it, so it could be washed at night. Tom had considered slipping Vuyiswa R50 to pretend that the washing machine had shredded it, but couldn't bring himself to face the fallout.

However. There was no way he was going to introduce Ben to Jamie's family in the appalling "spidey suit". Ben would just have to deal with it.

Twenty minutes later, Tom's ears were ringing from the shrieks of his son in the throes of a full-blown tantrum. He had been kicked and punched – accidentally – by the thrashing toddler. And the worst part was that as fast as Tom got Ben into his shorts and T-shirt, Ben ripped them off again. Yes, he'd chosen this moment to demonstrate his new-found undressing skills.

Tom, sweating lightly, closed his eyes and counted to ten. Resisting the urge to scream as well, he dug for the last vestiges of patience. *Pick your battles,* he remembered reading on a parenting website. *Don't sweat the small stuff.*

Okay, so maybe this wasn't the most important battle in the world. Maybe it didn't really matter what a toddler wore to a backyard barbeque. But it galled him to reward bad behaviour by giving in to his son's tyranny. He glanced at his watch. They were already late. The way he saw it, he had a choice. He could either let Ben go out in the stupid spidey suit, or he could watch him run around naked the whole afternoon.

A few minutes later, Ben was magically restored to good humour as he strutted out the house in the spidey suit. Tom's mind was churning with a familiar mixture of guilt and resentment. He felt like a total failure as a parent. Only the suspicion that other parents regularly felt this way helped. Feeling a little sorry for himself, he rang the bell at Jamie's gate.

———

One beer and a few of Jamie's goat's cheese and pesto bruschettas later, Tom felt much better. No eyebrows had been raised at the sight of Ben in his Spiderman outfit. Jamie's mother seemed to grasp the situation at once.

"That's an outfit that only comes off to be washed, isn't it?" she said as Ben ran around the garden, peering under bushes. He seemed to be hunting for Jamie's cats.

Tom couldn't stop a sigh from escaping. "Yup."

"Oh, that takes me back. My youngest daughter Ella had a frilly ballet tutu she wouldn't even take off at night. She wore it all day and slept in it all night. I used to rip it off her body once a week to be washed, while she screamed for two solid hours. Eventually it turned a horrible greyish-pink. I used to hate going to the supermarket. I thought everyone was judging me for being a bad mother."

Pam laughed at the memory, and some of Tom's tension went out of him.

The sprout salad he'd brought seemed to delight Jamie. She cooed over the freshness of the ingredients he'd used, and the tartness of his salad dressing, as she put it on the table with the other cold dishes.

Then Jamie's father William shoved a second beer into his hand, and his relaxation was complete. Helping himself to a handful of nachos, he settled back in his chair and surveyed the scene.

At first glance, Jamie and her sisters had nothing in common. You'd barely think they were related. But if you took a longer look, you started to notice the similarities. And if you paid attention to the parents, you could see how the combination of genes had come about. Jamie and her older sister Caroline were both tall like their father. At six foot two, William Burchell was barely an inch shorter than Tom. But they both had their mother's olive skin-tone and dark eyebrows. Jamie's niece – a quiet eleven-year-old who spent virtually the whole afternoon on her phone – was dark too, and threatening to grow into a beauty like her mother, Caroline.

The younger sister Ella, on the other hand, had her father's sunny blonde hair and milky-white skin, but her mother's tiny build. She was all bones, like an undernourished bird. Pretty, yes, but too delicate-looking. Tom took another pull at his beer and decided that all in all, they were the best-looking family he'd seen in a while.

First prize had to go to Caroline. She had the kind of beauty that made you stare. You kept sneaking glances at her face to check that she was real. It wasn't as though he'd never seen a truly beautiful woman before – just not one so completely flawless. Some women looked better in profile than face-to-face. Some had flat chests or bony hands or thick ankles, or stringy hair. Some had a weird laugh or a funny smile, or something – some attribute – that rescued them from absolute perfection.

With Caroline Burchell, there was nothing. She was flawless from every angle, and in every light. It was a little spooky.

No wonder the poor schmuck she'd brought with her looked like a rabbit caught in headlights. She'd introduced him as "Darryl, my friend from the hospital". But Tom knew he was desperate to escape the friend zone to which he'd been assigned.

"Hey, Tom!" Jamie's father called from the fire he was tending. "Come over here and settle a bet for us."

Tom went over to the fire, nodding to the man who was standing with William. His name was Peter – a suave impresario type, who seemed to be Ella Burchell's manager as well as her boyfriend.

"What's up?"

"You Americans say 'barbeque' for 'braai', correct?" William asked.

"Correct. We do."

"But you also talk about 'eating barbecue', which is a whole different thing, am I right?"

"It's the same thing," Peter insisted.

"No, it isn't, and Tom is going to tell us why."

"You're both kind of right," Tom said. "In the south, barbecue means pork. They roast a whole pig over coals in an open pit. Then the meat is pulled apart and served with a special type of spicy sauce. You go to a place like South Carolina, and that's what they mean by barbecue. What we're doing here – which is cooking meat or chicken over an outdoor fire – they would call grilling. And even then, it's not the same as your South African braai, because they usually grill hamburgers and hot dogs, not steaks and chops like you guys. And definitely not boerwors."

"Can't have a braai without boerewors."

Tom clinked beer bottles with William. "That's the truth."

"Would you excuse us a moment, Peter?" William said. "I have something of a private nature to say to our neighbour."

"Okay. I'll get another beer." Peter wandered over to where Ella was sitting with Ben on her lap. Tom sipped his beer, rocked back on his heels, and awaited developments.

"You and Jamie have become quite close, haven't you?" William said at last, concentrating hard on the lamb chops.

"You could say so, yes," Tom agreed. Sensing that this wasn't a 'what are your intentions toward my daughter?' speech, he decided to answer more fully. "It's still early days, but we have gotten close. Close enough for me to care what happens to her."

This was the opening William was looking for. "In that case, would you mind telling me what the *fuck* is going on with this psycho who's stalking her, excuse my French?"

He looked up from the fire and met Tom's gaze. In those bright blue eyes, so like those of his youngest daughter, Tom saw all the worry and impotent fury that was making the big man look drawn. He knew he wouldn't be able to lie to him. To be fair, Jamie hadn't asked him to. She just wanted him to be reassuring.

"I wish I knew," Tom said. "All I can tell you is that you're right to be worried because it looks like an escalating situation. This is someone who is going to do more to get her attention, both online and in real life."

"Aren't you some kind of a profiler?" William asked. "Can't you figure out who he is?"

Tom laughed. "I'm not a profiler. I'm a glorified academic – more interested in the social conditions that give rise to crime than in catching criminals." He saw the disappointment on William's face so he went on. "Profiling isn't an exact science. It works better in the movies than in real life. If I were a profiler, I'd say we're looking for a single white male, between the ages of twenty-five and forty, who lives alone. There's probably a female figure in his life who didn't give him enough attention, and Jamie reminds him of her. For all the good that does us."

"I see what you mean. It doesn't help us to find him."

Tom decided that more honesty couldn't hurt. "Jamie thinks you and your wife are going to move in here with her until he's caught."

It was William's turn to laugh. "We talked about it. Trouble is, Jamie and her mother can't live under the same roof for long. They're too similar – they both have to be queen of the kitchen. They'd drive each other nuts. More important – they'd drive me nuts, too." He paused to brush some sauce over the chicken kebabs. "We'd do it, though, if we thought it was necessary. We'd do anything to keep her safe, including hauling her down to the coast with us."

Tom watched as Ella handed Ben over to Caroline. The taller woman took his hand and led him toward the kitchen with promises of "helping with the salad". Tom hoped she knew what she was letting herself in for. He turned back to William.

"Would it make you feel better to know that I'm looking out for her?"

"It would if I thought you knew what you were doing."

Tom grinned. "Well," he began, "I might not be much of a profiler, but I am combat-trained, and I've been in several situations where I've had to..."

———

"What does that look like to you?"

"What does what look like?" Jamie paused in the act of setting the table and followed the direction of her mother's gaze. "Oh, that. You mean the big, strong men sorting out our lives so we don't have to worry our pretty heads about my nasty stalker?"

"Exactly." Pamela Burchell put her hands on her hips.

"Dad can't help it, Mom. Don't be too hard on him. He's a fixer. When he sees a problem, he has to fix it. And you know he likes to feel he can keep us all safe."

"Because we're women."

"Because he loves us. And Tom's the same way when he cares about someone. If it makes Dad feel better to talk to him, I'm all for it."

Pam put a loaf of garlic bread next to the potatoes Jamie had prepared. Then she wiped her hands on a damp cloth, and smiled at her middle daughter. "You're hoping Tom will persuade us to go back to Umhlanga and leave you in peace, aren't you?"

"Well..."

"Oh, I don't blame you. I'd be exactly the same in your position. And I admit it does make me feel better to know he's here. He's good at looking out for people."

This was exactly what Jamie wanted her mother to think, but it still bothered her. "How do you know that? You can't possibly decide that after knowing him for one whole hour."

"I'm a mother, my darling. I can tell these things. That man has been keeping an eye on his son since the moment he got here. He always knows exactly where Ben is, even while he's talking to someone else. Right now, he knows Caro has got him in the kitchen helping out, and he's worrying about what chaos he might be causing. Any minute now, he's going to make some excuse to your father and go inside to see for himself."

As she said this, William turned back to the braai to make some adjustments to the chops, and Tom came striding across the lawn toward the patio.

"Just going to check on Ben..." he said.

"It's a little scary how you know these things," Jamie murmured.

Pam smiled. "Like I said – I'm a mother."

They watched as Tom went into the kitchen where Ben was ripping up bits of lettuce under Caroline's supervision. They were presumably not intended for human consumption, given that most of them were ending up on the floor.

"Then riddle me this, mother," Jamie said, as Tom bent down to pick up his son. "Why is that man so protective of his kid? He won't let me near him. I have to pretend not to care before he'll even let me talk to Ben. If I get too close, he shuts me out."

Pam shrugged. "I can't begin to guess. It probably goes back to something from his own childhood. How we raise our kids has a lot to do with how we were raised as kids. Just be patient with him."

Heartrending wails from the kitchen told them Ben wasn't happy about being snatched away from his lettuce-shredding duties. Tom held out for five seconds before putting him back on the floor and letting him carry on with ripping. The noise switched off at once.

"He's not bothering me, if that's what you're worried about," Caroline told Tom. "It's been ages since I had a toddler to look after. I kind of miss it. And I've got the dustpan lined up for when he's finished. He might even enjoy helping me clean up."

"Sure," Tom said. "I just thought … you know … maybe he was being a nuisance."

"Not at all, I promise."

"Okay, then."

He beat a retreat. Telling lies always made him twitchy.

The truth was, it made him uncomfortable to see Ben so happy in this extended-family setting. It forced him to wonder what Ben's life would have been like if he'd had a raft of doting grandparents and aunties to make a fuss of him over weekends. He was a sociable child, comfortable with adults and children alike. His latest thing was to ask Tom repeatedly when he could get a baby brother or sister. He loved the feeling of being in the thick of things. A big family would have suited him down to the ground.

But it wasn't a big, happy family he'd taken Ben away from, Tom reminded himself. It was a lifetime of foster care. Of being shunted around from one carer to another.

Still, it bothered him to see the Burchells accepting and absorbing

Ben like this. They were treating him like a second grandchild, a beloved nephew, and he was lapping it all up. It made Tom's heart hurt to know he couldn't give Ben this all the time. But patchwork families didn't work. Tom knew that better than anyone. After a few years, they always started splitting apart at the seams.

———

By half-past four, Ben was out cold in his pram. A few minutes earlier, he had begun to niggle in a fretful, overtired way. Tom was about to make his excuses and leave when Jamie's dad William offered to take him for a walk in the pram.

"Around the garden?" Tom asked. "Won't that be a little bumpy?"

"No, on the brick pavers around the swimming pool," William said with a wink. "It works like a charm. Trust me, I know what I'm doing. It's not all that long ago that I was walking my granddaughter around this very same pool. I knew we were right not to take the pool fence down. I always said it would come in handy when we had a new generation of toddlers visiting the house."

Sure enough, after about three laps, Ben's eyes started to droop and his restless kicking stopped. By the fifth lap, he was sound asleep. William parked him in the shade and rejoined his family for coffee.

Ben was still sleeping in his pram at five o'clock when Jamie walked Tom out.

"It was a great afternoon, really. Thanks so much."

"It's a pleasure," she said. "Thank you for reassuring my father. He seems much calmer about going back to the coast and leaving me here. Whatever you said to him really worked."

"I didn't try to bullshit him. I think that's the part he appreciated most."

Jamie ran her fingers up Toms's chest and joined them behind his neck. "I wish you could stay."

He looped his hands around her and folded her into a hug. "I wish I could stay, too. But not with your parents here."

She couldn't argue with that. "You'll just have to give me something to think about until tomorrow then..."

Rising to the challenge, he bent to give her lower lip a tiny bite. Then, as her eyelids closed, he sank into the kiss. To torture them both, he ran his hands slowly up and down her body, grazing the sides of her breasts.

When they finally broke apart, they were both breathing fast.

"You'd better go," Jamie said, opening the gate. "Before I decide to hell with my parents and drag you back to my bedroom."

Tom's smile was crooked as he took a grip on the handle of the pram and wheeled his son back to his house.

19

"Check it out!" Pumla slapped a piece of paper on the desk in front of Jamie.

Jamie had been in since early that morning dealing with the paperwork involved in the monthly payroll. It wasn't her favourite job in the world, and now the lunchtime rush was about to start. Having bits of paper shoved under her nose was not about to improve her mood.

"What?" She snatched at the page and stared at it. It said "Lancet" at the top. Was that a catering-supply company? No. Her mind clicked into gear. It was a lab. She was looking at the results of a blood test. But what blood test?

"What the heck is this?" she asked. "What am I looking at?"

"That, my friend, is the result of my pregnancy test." Pumla did a little shimmy around the office. "Human pregnancy hormone and progesterone levels both sky-high. The doctor says he hardly ever sees such high levels in an early pregnancy. I always was an over-achiever."

Jamie's brain struggled to catch up. "You mean you're pregnant? You're actually pregnant? Really and truly?"

Pumla nodded, a huge grin bisecting her face from ear to ear.

"Oh, my God!" Jamie leaped up and flung her arms around Pumla in a rare hug. "Congratulations!"

"Thanks."

They did a little dance around the office, uttering supersonic squeaks of glee.

Then they stopped and grinned at each other.

Jamie's gaze travelled down Pumla's body to rest on her flat tummy. "There's a baby in there," she said. "There's an actual, honest-to-goodness human being inside there."

"I know. Isn't it amazing? I think I'm just starting to show, don't you?" Pumla pushed her stomach out as far as it would go.

"Um … sure," Jamie agreed. "So, how are you feeling?"

"Fabulous!" Pumla beamed. "I feel absolutely great. A bit tired, though. In fact, very *very* tired. At odd times of the day too. Like yesterday, I got home from work at six and just sat down for a minute in front of the TV. When I woke up it was nine. And all I could do was stagger upstairs to bed and sleep for another eight hours. But no nausea. Absolutely none. I have no idea what people are even talking about when they say the words 'morning sickness'."

"Well, that's great. It looks like you're going to have an easy pregnancy."

"I know! Isn't it brilliant?"

"So have you told Dumisani yet? How did he take it?"

Pumla's smile dimmed. She shrugged.

"You did tell him about the baby, didn't you?" Jamie said.

"Yes, of course I told him."

"And…?"

"He's not co-operating at all. He's being a total asshole about the whole thing."

Before Jamie could ask what she meant, the door chime sounded and a rush of early lunch customers came in. There was a table of eight, a table of four, and a table of two. Getting them settled and happy took all Jamie's time and attention. And no sooner did they all have menus and drinks than more lunchers flooded in, leaving her with no room for anything in her brain besides who wanted their dressing on the side, and who wanted rye instead of wholewheat bread.

Pumla was equally busy manning the takeaway counter. Ciabattas and baguettes were flying out the door, and there was a brisk trade in sweet pastries too. Jamie found her eyes being drawn to Pumla again and again. It was as though she were seeing her in a whole new light. No longer just Jamie's business partner and slightly irritating friend – what they used to call a 'frenemy' back in high school – Pumla was now an expectant mother. She was fulfilling her biological destiny. She was gravid. The strange, Latin-sounding word popped into Jamie's head out of nowhere.

She looked at Pumla again. No, she wasn't showing yet, whatever she might think, but wasn't there something subtly different about her? She was paler, for one thing. Instead of its usual healthy colour, her face had a greyish tinge. She looked a bit clammy too.

Her writer's brain stored away these details for later use. This was a great opportunity to observe a pregnant woman up close. Google could only take you so far. Jamie thought she'd done a reasonable job of conveying Eve's pregnancy in her novel up until now, but there were always little touches you could only add as a result of personal observation.

Swallowed up in the lunch rush, she dashed from table to kitchen and back again, sometimes stopping to replate a meal that hadn't been laid out to her specifications.

The crowds were starting to thin out before she had a chance to look over at Pumla again. No, she definitely wasn't looking herself. She was even paler, if that were possible, and her face seemed almost haggard. Something was not right. Jamie carried some plates through to the kitchen and emerged at her friend's side.

"Hey," she whispered. "Are you feeling all right? You look like hell."

Pumla frowned. "That's because I feel like…"

And she slid quietly down to the floor.

"Shit!"

Jamie felt panic rush all over her like a heat rash. A glance at the kitchen told her no one was looking their way. In fact, no one in the restaurant seemed to have noticed anything. Pumla had just disappeared from view and was now lying unnoticed behind the counter.

Jamie remembered once hearing a doctor say that fainting was nature's way of forcing the body horizontal so blood could get back into the head. Ella had been a great fainter as a child – skinny as a stick and constantly overdoing the ballet thing. Some of the routine

189

came back to Jamie. She dropped to the floor and lifted Pumla's legs higher than her head to encourage her blood pressure to equalise.

As the greyish hue of her face receded, Jamie rolled her onto her left side, into the recovery position. Somewhere nearby, she could hear a voice saying, "Wake up, wake up, wake up, dammit!" It took her a moment to realise it was her own.

Several lifetimes seemed to pass before Pumla's eyelids fluttered and opened.

"Ow! My head hurts. Why...?"

"You must have bumped it when you fainted." Jamie ran her fingers over the back of Pumla's head and felt a definite lump. "Yes, there it is."

"Ow!" Pumla said again.

"Sorry. I'll get you some ice for it. How are you feeling now?"

Pumla struggled into a sitting position. "I feel ... I can feel..." She lifted her eyes to Jamie's face. "I can feel something between my legs. I think it's blood."

All the relief Jamie had been feeling ebbed away, leaving her as cold as ice. "It's not blood. It can't be blood. It must be something else."

Pumla's hand clenched on Jamie's arm. "I think I'm having a miscarriage."

"No ... no. You can't be. You just fainted. It was just a faint." If she said it often enough, maybe it would become true.

"What's going on?"

Jamie and Pumla started at the sound of a male voice. Jamie looked up to see a completely strange man peering over the counter at them. She got to her feet and smoothed her apron.

"I'm sorry, sir. There's been a slight accident. I'll get someone to come to your table in just a moment."

"I'm not a customer."

Jamie blinked at him. Then she looked around the restaurant and saw that the kitchen staff had realised something was wrong. Nomsa and Chiwetel were wearing their front-of-house aprons and moving between the tables, clearing plates and bringing coffee orders through. None of the patrons had noticed anything amiss.

She turned back to the man. There was something familiar about him. She'd seen his face somewhere before. Then she got it. She'd seen him online.

"You're Dumisani! I recognise you from Facebook."

"Yes. And you're Jamie. What the hell is going on? What is Pumla doing on the floor?"

"Go away," Pumla moaned, flapping a hand at him.

He stepped behind the counter to crouch down next to her. "I'm not going anywhere. What's wrong?"

"I'm having a miscarriage, okay? So in a few minutes there won't be a baby for you to worry about. Just leave me alone." Her eyes were closed and tears leaked from the corners.

Dumisani turned to Jamie, a desperate question in his eyes.

"She fainted," Jamie said. "She'd been on her feet for hours, and she just went down like a sack of coals. Now she thinks she's bleeding. We should take her to a doctor."

"Fuck that." Dumisani pulled a phone out of his pocket. "I'm calling an ambulance."

———

Jamie Burchell Has a doctor seen you yet? xx

Pumla Maseko Not yet. Still waiting. Probably going for scan first.

Victoria Mooki Sending you good thoughts and healing white light, my darling.

Nala Ahmed All the best!

Jamie Burchell Hey! It's been hours of total radio silence. Your phone is off. How about sending us an update?

Foully Wooing Won I'm sorry to report that Pumla Maseko passed away peacefully at the Morningside Fem-Clinic this afternoon.

Victoria Mooki Oh my God. It can't be true.

Michael Blackthorn I don't believe it.

Nala Ahmed I am weeping now. Just sitting here and sobbing. Please tell me this isn't true.

Foully Wooing Won It's true.

Jamie's fingers trembled. She threw her phone onto the counter next to the till. It wasn't true. It couldn't be true.

She tried to think over the buzzing in her ears. This was the twenty-first century. People didn't die of miscarriages anymore. Not so early in the pregnancy. And not in a high-tech specialist hospital, like the Fem-Clinic.

But why wasn't Pumla answering her phone? Why had she posted nothing on Facebook or Twitter since 3.21 that afternoon? It was nearly six. Delucia's had closed its doors and the staff were cleaning up. Jamie had cashed up for the day. She knew she'd have to double-check her calculations. The only thing she could think about was

Pumla.

How had the stalker hacked into Pumla's Facebook account? Jamie had specifically warned her not to accept friend invitations from anyone called Foully Wooing Won, or any variation of that name. Pumla was no fool and never forgot a thing. She wouldn't have been so careless. It wasn't possible.

And that thing about Pumla being dead. That had to be a scare tactic, didn't it? He was just trying to wind everybody up, that was all. To get a reaction. It couldn't possibly be true.

Could it?

She looked up and almost collapsed. Pumla and Dumisani were on the other side of the glass door, Pumla searching for her key. As they trooped in, some of Jamie's relief evaporated. Pumla's eyes were wide and dazed – she was clearly in shock. Dumisani didn't look much better. Jamie remembered that for them, there was more than just Pumla's well-being at stake.

Forcing down dread, Jamie brought Pumla a chair and waved her into it.

"Sit down. You shouldn't be standing. Do you want to come back to the office and lie down? I thought for sure they'd keep you overnight. Can I get you some water? Juice? Anything?"

"I'm fine. I don't need anything." But Pumla sat anyway.

"Are you all right?" Jamie asked. "What did they say?"

"I … they…" Pumla couldn't seem to get the words out.

Jamie turned to Dumisani, but he was no better. He looked like Wile E. Coyote after the Road Runner had dropped a boulder on his head.

Pumla took a sheet of paper out of her bag and handed it to Jamie.

It took Jamie no more than a few seconds to realise what she was looking at. She was an aunt after all, and had seen her fair share of foetal sonograms. She had friends who posted them on their Facebook pages every month.

She caught her breath. "Does this mean the baby's okay?"

Pumla just pointed at the sonogram.

"Okay. What am I looking at here? Gestational age, seven weeks and two days. That's older than you thought, isn't it? Why are there two black sacs here with little white lights in them? There should only be one. Is this one a shadow of that one? Like an echo effect? Or…?"

The truth struck her with blinding force.

"Oh, my God. It's not twins, is it? You're having twins?"

Pumla nodded her head, her face still dazed.

Jamie felt a bit dazed herself. "I can't believe it! How did this happen? You don't even have twins in your family."

"I do," Dumisani said. "My mother is one of twins, and my father had twin sisters. I also have cousins that are twins. There's absolutely no shortage of twins in my family. As I could have told your friend here if she'd bothered to mention that she was auditioning for a baby daddy."

He glared at Pumla, and she glared right back at him.

"And they're both fine?" Jamie asked. "They're okay? But what about the bleeding and the fainting?"

"The fainting can happen in early pregnancy, apparently," Pumla said. "It's not uncommon. And the bleeding is what they call breakthrough bleeding – not a threatened miscarriage. They gave me some progesterone for it. It's already stopped. They spent ages checking me out. Ages. The babies are both well implanted and their heartbeats are strong. And I'm fine too, if you don't count the fact that I've gone in one day from feeling absolutely great to sick as a dog."

She pressed a hand to her mouth and closed her eyes. The greyish tinge was back in her face.

Dumisani hauled her to her feet and marched her toward the ladies' room.

"Excuse us please, Jamie," he said. "The mother of my children needs to puke."

20

Jamie's heart was beating so hard and so fast she could feel it in her throat. Her hands were shaking, and she had to squeeze her lips firmly together so they didn't start shaking too. She took a deep breath. It sounded like a quavery sigh.

Live radio.

She'd thought it would be easy. It wouldn't be like talking in front of a big audience because you couldn't see who you were speaking to. It would be like sitting in a small room and chatting to a couple of people. Or so she'd thought.

The reality was different. Once her headphones were in place and the "on air" light was blinking, she was struck by a vision of all the thousands of people out there listening to her. There they all were, driving around in their cars, sitting in dentist's waiting rooms, working in their kitchens – all with their radios turned on. Waiting for her to fluff her lines or dry up completely.

If only she hadn't told every single person she knew, including everyone on Facebook and Twitter, that she was going to be on the radio today. How could she have been so stupid?

Pumla would have the radio on in the kitchen at Delucia's, assuming she wasn't throwing up at the time. Tom had said he would livestream the broadcast on his laptop at the university. Jamie's parents had promised to listen in, and so had her sisters.

Her throat was dry and her tongue felt thick. The host of the show, Thandi Thandeka, seemed to realise this, because she gestured to a carafe of water and some glasses. Jamie soothed her throat with little sips of water, and darted a glance at her fellow guests.

The radio psychologist, Dr Erik, looked relaxed. As well he might, since he'd been doing this for a long time. He had a regular Monday slot on the show where he took questions from listeners about their psychological problems. This would be a piece of cake for him.

Next to him sat a woman known only as Seena. She was South Africa's most famous victim of stalking and had often appeared on radio and television. She had been stalked by an ex-boyfriend for several years before she shot him dead on the night he broke into her home and tried to rape her. The trial had gone on for months, and had turned into a full-blown media circus before she'd been acquitted on the grounds of self-defence.

The other guest was called Margie. At first sight, she looked like a classic victim, with her hangdog expression and shrinking demeanour. Jamie was shocked to hear she had several restraining orders against her, all issued by men. She'd been invited onto the show to give the stalker's side of the story.

Margie was the most nervous of them all, constantly taking a balled-up tissue out of her cardigan sleeve and dabbing at her nose with it before tucking it away again.

To Jamie's great relief, she felt herself relax once the discussion began. Thandi Thandeka and Dr Erik took the lead, talking about stalking as a social phenomenon that had only recently been taken seriously by the authorities. Then Seena was invited to tell her story, which she did with the ease of long practice. Much of it was familiar to Jamie. It had dominated news headlines only a few years ago.

Margie was less poised, but very willing to talk about herself and her various neuroses. Dr Erik gave her advice about conquering her compulsion to stalk men, which she accepted with an unconvincing show of humility and a promise to do better in the future. Jamie had a feeling none of the men she stalked would be rushing to cancel their restraining orders.

"Our fourth guest on the show is Jamie Burchell," Thandi said, smiling across the console at her. "She is a restaurant owner and would-be writer who uses social media to publicise her work. It was social media that got you into this fix in the first place, wasn't it, Jamie?"

"Well, Thandi, you're right in the sense that my stalker seems to have found me via social media. That's how he became obsessed with

196

me, and how he continues to track me today."

"Do you still leave a trail for him to track? If it were me, I'd delete all my accounts until the stalker lost interest."

"It's not that simple. Taking a break from social media now would mean giving up all the progress I've made in the last year. I've never been closer to getting my novel published. I actually turned down an offer to publish it digitally just a few weeks ago because I felt it wouldn't do justice to the story."

"Interesting. So what exactly is your novel about, Jamie? Can you tell us a bit of the plot?"

Jamie smiled. The one condition she'd made before going on the show was that she would be allowed to talk about her novel on air. The producer hadn't been thrilled, but she'd agreed.

"It's a dystopian fantasy about a world in which the environmentalists and vegetarians and natural health freaks have taken over everything. The earth has been driven backwards into a pre-industrial age. People can only earn their living through farming and are forced to worship nature. Animals can be kept for milk and eggs, but are not allowed to be slaughtered."

"Sounds perfect!" said Thandi, a well-known vegan and health-food fanatic.

"Not really, Thandi. You see everything is run by these people called the Controllers, who keep all the good stuff for themselves, like modern medicine, antibiotics, electricity, clean running water and so forth. Women die in childbirth and children die of preventable diseases, even though the technology exists to save them. The story is really about a cell of resistance against the Controllers that starts to form in one of the poorest districts."

"Sounds similar to that Ben Elton novel," Dr Erik put in. "What was it called again? *Faith, or* something like that."

Jamie winced. "*Blind Faith*, and no, it's not that similar. Elton's novel was about evangelists and vaccine denialists taking over the world. Nothing about a pre-industrial age."

This was a sore point. She'd only read Elton's novel after she'd started writing her own, and had been dismayed her to find how close the two concepts were. She'd comforted herself with the reflection that no one else was likely to notice. Except now apparently they had.

"To go back to our stalking topic, it's more than just that, isn't it Jamie?" Thandi put on a solemn voice to move the discussion along. "This man has committed some frightening acts. Can you tell us more about that?"

"Well, he climbed over the wall of my property once and watched me through the window. Then he took a rat and slit its belly open so that its insides hung out, and tied it to my gate for me to find. Then he caught two pigeons, battered them with a rock until they were half dead, and tied them to my gate. A few weeks after that, he poisoned one of the neighbourhood dogs, sliced its belly open, and left it dead on my gate as well. So, no, it's not just a simple case of stalking."

When the exclamations of horror had died down, Thandi asked again why Jamie didn't just cut herself off from social media for a while. Dr Erik added his persuasions to hers.

"I can't," Jamie explained. "In a way, this whole stalking experience has been good for me in terms of exposure. My Twitter following has more than doubled. My personal blog has been trending worldwide. Worldwide! That's an incredible number of people reading my writing. I can't give that up just because some crazy person has become obsessed with me."

"But do you have to give him so much ammunition?" Dr Erik asked. "I've looked at your Facebook page. It's completely open to the public. And your Twitter feed is too. Every time you go somewhere, you check in on Facebook. You post pictures of your home and your place of work all the time. Anyone who follows you on Twitter knows your every move."

"But there's nothing unusual about that. Thousands of people do it every day. Sharing your life on social media is the new normal. I've got friends who Instagram every meal they eat. I know people who run parenting blogs and post pictures of their children all the time, along with their real names and which schools they go to. The whole internet is a stalker's paradise. But most of the time nothing happens."

"But this time, it has," Thandi said.

"Yes, but that doesn't mean we must start victim-blaming. Women get told all the time to change the way they act for their own safety. The onus isn't on me to change my behaviour. I'm not the one doing anything wrong. The onus is on him to stop stalking me. Stalking has been around a lot longer than social media, you know. California was one of the first places in the world to introduce an anti-stalking law. That was in 1990 after the murder of the actress Rebecca Schaeffer. That was at least fifteen years before Facebook. This guy – whoever he is – would be stalking someone else if he hadn't happened to find me online. Social media doesn't create the pathology."

"But it does facilitate it," said Thandi. "We're going to take some calls now. Who do you have on the line for us this morning, Jenna?"

There was a pause as the producer sent Thandi a worried look from inside her soundproof booth. "Thandi, we have someone on the line who claims to be Jamie's stalker. Do you want to take the call?"

Thandi's eyes widened, but she recovered quickly. "Thanks, Jenna. We'll take a quick commercial break now while we run that past Jamie. Don't go away, listeners. We're talking stalking today on the Thandi Thandeka Show. You're listening to Jozi Talks radio. I'm Thandi Thandeka and I'll be back in a moment."

Thandi pulled off her earphones. "What do you want to do?" she asked Jamie.

Jamie just gaped at her. "Do you think it's really him?"

"I have no idea. Possibly not. We get crank calls all the time."

"But do you think…? Can the police…? Is there some way we can trace the call?"

Thandi sighed. "We can try phoning the police, but we'll probably spend all our time on hold. There's no way we can trace the call if it's blocked…?" She raised her eyebrows at Jenna in the producer's booth.

"Number withheld," Jenna confirmed through the speaker.

"We won't take the call if you don't feel comfortable about it,"

Thandi said. "If it were me, I don't think I could."

Jamie tried to think. This was live radio. The more people who listened in, the more people might remember her name and google her blog. Besides, it wasn't as though this man were sitting right next to her in the studio. He couldn't hurt her over the phone.

"Fine. I'll do it. I'll talk to him."

Thandi grinned. "Awesome!"

"Ten seconds to airtime," warned the controller. He counted the last three seconds down on his fingers.

"We're back with a very unusual caller. One of our guests in the studio today is Jamie Burchell, who claims she's being stalked by a man who leaves dead and dying animals on her gate. On the line is someone who claims to be that stalker. He goes by the name Foully Wooing Won. Where are you calling from, sir?"

Jamie's skin prickled. It really was him.

"I'm calling from a little place I like to call Metnal." His voice was low and raspy, an obvious attempt at disguise. "You won't have heard of it. I want to speak to Jamie."

"I'm right here." She couldn't make her voice sound nonchalant, so she tried for neutral instead. "Metnal is the Mayan word for hell. You're not the only one who can use Wikipedia, you know." There was a pause, so she continued. "So you're in hell, are you?"

"Yes, I'm in hell," the voice rasped. "And soon you're going to join me there."

This shook Jamie more than she cared to admit, but she kept her voice even.

"Why did you pick me? Why not someone else?"

"You're not like the others. You don't lie in your photographs. When I saw you, I knew you were telling the truth."

"That doesn't make sense. You're punishing me for my honesty?"

"No, no!" His voice got louder and higher. "You don't get it. Even you don't get it."

"What don't I get?"

"I saw something in you, Jamie. You were special. I thought we

200

were on the same wavelength."

"So why didn't you just make contact with me on Twitter like other people do?"

"I'm not like other people."

"Right. I've got that."

"You think I don't hear the sarcasm in your voice, but I do. You're just like all the others. You don't understand."

"Why don't you explain it to me?"

There was silence. Jamie realised she was talking to dead air.

"He's gone," Jenna said from the producer's box.

"Well, that was very interesting." Thandi stepped into the gap. "What I heard him saying was that there was a kind of justification for his actions. Wouldn't you agree, Dr Erik?"

"Oh, definitely, Thandi. This is a classic example of someone who fixates on women who are outspoken and put themselves out there. He feels a need to pull Jamie down because she is in the public eye. He sees her as getting uppity and above herself, so he tries to correct this by making her feel unsafe in her public and private life."

As the psycho-babble washed over her, Jamie sat back and let her breath out in a rush.

———

When she got home from the studio, her hands were still not quite steady. She kept replaying the conversation in her head, wondering if she'd handled it properly. Wondering if she'd done the right thing by talking to him in the first place.

He'd hung up on her, so she had probably blundered in some way. Maybe scared him off. He'd realised that her invitation to "explain" himself to her was an effort to keep him talking – to keep him on the line. Jamie didn't know why she'd said it, except that it seemed to be the kind of thing people said on TV. Only this wasn't TV, and there'd been no one trying to trace his call.

But it felt good to have done something, instead of sitting around waiting for him to make the next move. It felt constructive. She almost wished she could engage with him again. If it came down to a battle of words, Jamie was confident of winning. He'd sounded almost confused, certainly inarticulate, while words were Jamie's bread and butter.

Tom disagreed. He thought she'd made a big mistake by talking to him. He had come around to her place after work especially to tell her so.

"Look, I don't know much about stalkers," he said in a low voice as Ben ran between Holmes and Watson on Jamie's patio, giving them strokes on the head. "But even I know that you never engage with them. All you've done is stir him up."

"Well, what was I supposed to do? We were live on the radio and everyone really wanted me to speak to him. It was very hard to say no."

"Of course you could have said no. Now you've fuelled his fantasy that he knows you – that he has a special connection to you."

"At least I was doing something! Do you know how hard it is to wake up wondering if this will be the day that he kills one of my cats? Or me, for that matter."

"All I'm saying is…" Tom's phone rang loudly on the table between them. He glanced at the display. "It's from the university. I'd better take it."

Jamie shrugged. "Sure."

Tom picked up the phone and paced up and down the garden with it, never straying too far from Ben. Jamie sat back on the sofa and tried to pretend she wasn't listening. She heard him saying, "What? Why not?" and "But how could he?" Then, "That's the most irresponsible thing I've ever heard."

She pulled a face at Ben, who giggled in response, plunging his fist deeper into Watson's fur. Thank goodness her cats were so tolerant, because he seemed determined to love them to death.

"I'm telling you, I can't." Tom sounded even more harassed. "My domestic worker is away for the evening and I have to look after my son. No, I can't bring him with me. He's not even two yet. No, there isn't anyone else."

Jamie pricked up her ears.

"No, I can't ask my mother. For one thing, I only have a step-mother who lives in a home; and for another, I wouldn't ask her even if I could."

Jamie stood up and waved her hands in Tom's face.

"Just hang on a moment." He stopped pacing and covered the phone with his hand. "*What?*"

"I'll watch Ben for you."

"You?"

"Yes, me. You know he likes me and likes spending time here. Or I'll take care of him at your place – whichever you prefer. He'll be fine. We'll both be fine. What is it you need to do?"

"It's a public lecture on the systemic causes of urban violence. They're expecting five hundred people. The guest lecturer who was scheduled to do it has just phoned to say he can't make it. They want me to take his place. I'm explaining why it's impossible."

"Could you do a lecture at such short notice?"

"Yes, I could. I have all the notes I need, and the visuals too. But that's not the point. Vuyiswa has gone home for the evening and I've never left Ben with anyone else before."

"You could leave him with me. I'd take good care of him. You know I would, Tom."

But still Tom hesitated. "I'm not sure…"

"Look, sometimes you have to accept help when it's offered. No one raises a child in a vacuum, Tom. Not even you."

"Yes, but…"

"Listen, the offer's there if you want it."

Jamie turned away and focused on clearing the coffee cups. If Tom thought this wasn't a big deal to her, he'd be more likely to say yes.

She heard him sigh. Then he lifted the phone to his ear.

"Hello, Bongi? Okay, I'll do it. I've sorted out my childcare issues. Yes, I'll be there at 6.15 to set up." He laughed. "Sure, sure … you say that now. Okay, I'll see you later."

He disconnected. "Now Bongi wants to marry me and have my children."

Jamie smiled. "Well, you've helped her out of a big hole. Five hundred people coming to a public lecture, and the lecturer bails? Total nightmare."

"Listen, are you sure you'll be okay with Ben? This is a busy time of day for him. It's all go from now on. Suppertime, bathtime, storytime, bedtime. They don't call it suicide hour for nothing."

"We'll be fine, don't worry."

21

....

Jamie Burchell @jamieburchell
Happiness is – taking care of the world's sweetest 20-month-old! ☺

Elsje Steenkamp @newbiemama
@jamieburchell Ha! I take care of a 22mo every single day and he drives me completely up the wall. #noveltyvalueover

Jamie Burchell @jamieburchell
@newbiemama I know! It's way harder than I expected. But still … I'm so, so happy!!☺

Elsje Steenkamp @newbiemama
@jamieburchell Hmmph! I bet he's been on his best behaviour for you.

Jamie Burchell @jamieburchell
@newbiemama Well, let's see what he's done so far, shall we? Refused to eat his veggies. Chucked food on the floor… (contd)

Jamie Burchell @jamieburchell
@newbiemama …flooded bathroom floor during bathtime and pulled towel into water. Insisted on being carried for a solid hour – screamed if I put him down… (contd)

Jamie Burchell @jamieburchell
@newbiemama …screamed when I tried to read the book his father picked out. Insisted on Room on the Broom – 4x over. I know that book by heart now.

Elsje Steenkamp @newbiemama
@jamieburchell LOL! Sounds like an average Thursday night at our place.☺

Jamie Burchell @jamieburchell
@newbiemama I'm exhausted. Don't know how you mums do it every day.

Bronwyn Jones @redhighheels
@jamieburchell @newbiemama Try doing it all on zero hours sleep a night. My toddler STILL doesn't sleep through.

Jamie Burchell @jamieburchell
@redhighheels @newbiemama That would be a challenge all right. ☹

Nomsa Mahlape @nomnom
@jamieburchell @redhighheels Hah! You think that's bad? Try a toddler who doesn't sleep through at night AND a new baby. #goingcrazyhere

Jamie put her phone down. If you spent long enough on Twitter, you'd always find someone worse off than you were. She couldn't imagine – literally couldn't comprehend – doing everything she'd just done for Ben while also being responsible for a new baby and knowing she wasn't going to get much sleep that night. It was a recipe for madness.

But her happy glow remained. She'd done it. She'd taken care of Ben's evening routine all on her own, and he'd been quiet for nearly an hour now.

"I didn't do too badly, did I?" she asked the dog sprawled at her feet.

Silver sighed and settled as Jamie nudged her with a toe. Jamie sighed too. Then reached into her pocket as an incoming text sounded on her phone.

———

Tom let himself quietly into the house. Closing the door behind him, he stood and listened, alert for telltale sounds of misery from his son. There wasn't a peep. Jamie had texted him updates throughout the evening so he knew Ben was fed, cleaned, pyjama'd, bedtime-storied, and allegedly in bed. He also knew that Ben had a habit of getting out of bed long after he was supposed to be asleep.

Bypassing the living room where he could see Silver sprawled out on the rug, Jamie's sock-clad feet resting on her furry haunch, Tom climbed the stairs to his son's bedroom. The door was ajar and the nightlight was on. Ben was sprawled sideways across the racing car bed he'd recently graduated to. His head was touching the wall and his feet were resting on the side safety rail. Tom's hands itched to rearrange him and pull the duvet over him, but that would be playing with fire. A Ben woken up at night was a Ben who was very difficult to get back to sleep.

Exhaling, Tom backed out of the room.

He could get used to this, he realised as he went back down the stairs. He could get used to coming home at night to find that someone else had taken over the evening chores for him. Cooked dinner too, judging from the smells that were coming from the kitchen. Just the knowledge that he wasn't solely responsible for Ben's welfare was somehow comforting.

And because part of him wanted to embrace that comfort – wanted to share the responsibility and accept the help offered – he hardened his heart. Nothing lasted forever, he knew, and step-parent relationships were especially brittle. This was strictly a once-off event. If Jamie thought this would become a regular thing, he needed to set her straight.

But Jamie wasn't thinking about Ben at all. The text she'd just received had pushed everything else out of her mind.

As he walked into the living room, she turned a beaming face towards him. "Hey, how was your lecture?"

"It went off very well, thanks."

"That's great! I'm so glad you could do it. Everything's okay here.

Ben's fine. He ate well – after I managed to convince him the vegetables weren't actually poisoned. We had fun. He's been asleep since half past seven."

"Yes ... well ... actually, I wanted to talk to you about…"

"Guess what just happened?"

Tom frowned. "I have no idea."

"I've been invited to be on television!"

"Television?" Tom rubbed a hand over his face, trying to switch gears. "Okay, television. That sounds like fun. Why have you been invited to be on television? Hey, is this about your book?"

Jamie smiled at his enthusiasm, but shook her head. "No, not my book. It's about the stalker. The producer of the Kathy Kelly Show just texted me. She caught my interview on the radio. She wants to do a show about stalking, and she wants me to be on it. It'll be some time after Christmas. I'm going to be on live TV!"

"Wow, really?" Tom wasn't sure which part of this disturbed him the most, so he zeroed in on a detail. "How did she get your cellphone number?"

"From my website, of course."

"You put your private cellphone number on your website?" He just shook his head when she nodded. "You must get an unbelievable amount of spam."

"I suppose I do, but I'm used to it by now."

"It's actually kind of surprising you've only managed to pick up one measly stalker in your life so far. I'd have thought you'd have a whole bunch by now."

"Ha ha. Very amusing."

"I was being serious. Kind of."

"But how cool is that? The Kathy Kelly Show! She's like South Africa's answer to Oprah. She's…"

"I know who she is, Jamie. She has a reputation for manufacturing drama on her show, and then milking it for the ratings. I'm not sure this is a good idea."

"It's a brilliant idea. When I was on the radio, only people in

Gauteng got to hear the show. But this is the SABC we're talking about. The whole country will be able to hear me. This is the biggest opportunity I've ever had. I'd be insane not to take it."

"Just think about the danger for a moment. Kathy Kelly loves to stir up controversy. By the end of the show, your stalker will probably feel personally challenged to make another move."

Jamie kept her face still. "That's a chance I have to take. I owe it to my career to grab this opportunity."

Tom held out a hand to her. When she took it, he pulled her off her chair and settled her on the sofa next to him. He stroked her hair, then took her hands and met her eyes.

"What about me?" he asked. "Don't I get a say?"

She frowned. "What do you mean?"

"It's hard to watch someone you care about throwing herself into the line of fire."

Jamie looked down at their joined hands. She was used to passion from Tom – the heat between them had a way of flaring up whenever they were together. But this tenderness was something new. She wasn't sure what to do with it.

"I'm sorry it makes you worry," she said. "It makes me worry too, to be honest. But I can't not do it. And let's face it, whatever he's got in mind for me, he's not likely to change it just because I happen to go on TV."

"First you blog about him, then you discuss him on the radio, and then you build a whole TV show around him. This guy started out as your common-or-garden, small-time stalker, and you're turning him into a celebrity."

22

So that was Christmas! Hope you all had a merry old time.

I'm back from Umhlanga now, and the good news is there were no surprises attached to my gate when I got back. I swung by the kennels on the way home to pick up two deliriously happy felines. You'd think I'd been gone for five months instead of five days. They're looking fat and well cared for, but did their best to convince me they'd been thoroughly starved and maltreated in my absence.

I'll see Tom tonight. Looking forward to that. We stayed in touch via Skype and SMS, but it's not the same, is it?

I hope he and Ben had a happy Christmas with his step-mother. It must be strange celebrating with someone who is sometimes lucid and sometimes not. You never know which version of the person you're going to get. It makes me appreciate my own family more. It was lovely to spend time with my sisters just lolling around the house stuffing our faces with Quality Street and chatting like in the old days. My niece is getting big enough now that she can even join in our girl time. We watched hours and hours of box-set series on my dad's new flat-screen, and generally vegged out for days.

It's funny how when Christmas is over, things that seemed very far away before the 25th now seem to be a lot closer. My appearance on the Kathy Kelly Show was something that would be happening "next year", in other words in the far distant future. Now it's happening next week. That's too close for comfort. I keep hearing Tom's voice warning me that this is a bad idea.

So to distract myself, I've been working on my list of New Year's Resolutions. Here's what I've got so far.

1) Stop fighting with Pumla every day. Every other day is quite adequate.

2) Stop neglecting the novel. Try to keep posting every morning.

3) Cook more at home, instead of pinching food from work all the time.

4) Enter at least four 10k runs this year. This is perfectly do-able. We're not talking the Comrades Marathon here.

5) Finish the food on my plate. There are children starving in India.

6) Two words – flaxseed oil.

How about you? What New Year's resolutions are you drawing up?

COMMENTS:

Posted by: **Orange Prize**

Merry Christmas and Happy New Year! I missed your posts while you were on holiday. Glad you got to relax completely. See my latest post on how I spent the festive season here: http://www.orangeprize.com

Posted by: **Good Witch Glinda**

Hey! Nice to have you back! I thought you might be spending Christmas with Hot Running Guy and Cute Kid?

Posted by: **Jamie Burchell**

Hey, Glinda! ☺ Nah. We didn't even discuss the possibility. We've only been seeing each other for a couple of months. We're not at the spending-Christmas-together stage yet.

Posted by: **Good Witch Glinda**

Hmmm. Did you exchange gifts? Tell Auntie Glinda.☺

Posted by: **Jamie Burchell**

We did. I scored a bottle of *parfum* and he got a runners' wrist GPS.

Posted by: **Gugz**

Lol! Nice, safe, neutral gifts.

Posted by: **Jamie Burchell**

I know, right? But then I went into Toys R Us and nearly lost the plot completely. I just wanted to dive face-first into a heap of Ben 10 action figures. Ben 10 for Ben, get it? I managed to restrain myself to one smallish gift, but it wasn't easy I can tell you.

A sound technician handed Jamie a tiny microphone attached to a wire. He showed her how to pass the mike under her top and clip it to her collar. Then he tested her for sound and handed her over to the producer. It was all so new and exciting, she had no time to worry whether she was doing the right thing or not. From the moment she sat in the makeup chair and closed her eyes, she knew this was going to be an adventure.

Yes, the makeup artist had made her up to look like Lady Gaga, but everyone assured her she'd look perfectly normal on camera.

Now she was meeting her fellow panellists. There was Kathy Kelly herself, an undersized waif of a human being with a doll-like waist and improbably large breasts. She'd greeted Jamie warmly, but was now in intense conversation with Dr Banda – the life coach who appeared so often on her show he had become a de facto co-host. The tabloids claimed they were sleeping together.

Then there was Seena, her fellow guest from the radio show, the one who had shot and killed her stalker ex-boyfriend. Jamie wished she could feel as relaxed as Seena looked. She tried not to think about the fact that her face would soon be broadcast all over the country. Or how her voice might squeak. Or how she might go blank and stare mutely at the camera.

But just like on the radio show, Jamie's nerves settled down once things got underway. She forced herself not to glance at the cameras that circled them, and looked only at the person she was speaking to. That made it easier to believe she was having a conversation with a small group of people.

Kathy Kelly was a dynamic and charismatic host, but it was Dr Banda who really stole the show. He had an avuncular manner and a hypnotic way of speaking. If Kathy Kelly was South Africa's answer to Oprah, then Dr Banda was Dr Phil. Within minutes, he had Jamie confiding more about how the stalking affected her than she ever had before.

"It's a feeling of powerlessness, isn't it?" he said, fixing her with his compelling eyes. "A loss of agency in your own destiny?"

"That's the problem," Jamie said. "No one wants me to stay in control of my life. They keep telling me to change the way I do things. Plus, I've had to take extra security measures at home. I hate that. It's a kind of violation."

"Violation – that's an excellent word for it. You need to take back your agency, Jamie. You need to take back the power."

"But how can I do that when everyone keeps saying, 'You have to keep yourself safe, Jamie. You can't be so open about your life when you're online. You must do things differently now, Jamie.' I hate the way people expect me to make all these changes instead of him – the stalker."

Kathy Kelly leaned forward. "Men pick on women they see as weak or passive, don't they? We did a show about that last year. We had a self-defence expert showing us how to carry ourselves more confidently and how to walk in an assertive way. A lot of women wrote in to say how empowering they found it. This sounds like the same kind of advice – how not to be a victim online." She smiled at Jamie and Dr Banda in turn.

Banda nodded in agreement, but Jamie couldn't bring herself to. She knew victim-blaming when she heard it. It was your fault if a man attacked you – because you were so weak and passive. You should take responsibility for being less of a victim so men would kindly refrain from assaulting you.

"That's like saying women shouldn't wear miniskirts if they don't want to get raped," Jamie blurted. "I didn't cause this situation by participating in social media. I'm not responsible for it. The world needs to stop telling women how to behave online and start telling men not to stalk us."

It came out sounding harsher than she intended, but she couldn't bring herself to care. Anyone who wanted to start policing her tone would get the sharp edge of her tongue.

There was a beat of silence as Jamie's words reverberated around the studio. Then Kathy turned to face the camera. "We're getting a lot of tweets from our viewers on the subject of stalking. Let's take a look at a few of them now."

Jamie followed the direction of her gaze and saw the teleprompter screen she was reading from.

"Marius Ehlers from Carnavon wants to know why Jamie's stalker isn't being pursued by the police's cyber crimes unit. I asked Jamie that exact question before the show started and the answer is because he hasn't committed a serious crime as yet – just malicious damage to property and a possible breach of the Animal Protection Act. Unfortunately, we as humans just don't take crimes against animals seriously enough. And you can't arrest someone for following you on Twitter," she added with a laugh. "Because that's kind of the whole point of it."

She moved on to the next tweet.

"Daneel Februarie from Eldorado Park asks why Jamie doesn't just delete all her social media accounts if she's feeling threatened online. Good question, Daneel! What do you say to that, Jamie?"

Jamie was ready for this. She'd practised her answer in the car on the way to the studio. "I'm a writer, journalist and blogger, Kathy," she explained. "I use social media on a daily basis in the course of my work. Deleting all my accounts would be a serious career setback for me."

"But your life might be at stake here." Kathy Kelly frowned a botoxed non-frown – her trademark 'concerned' look. "Surely it's worth cutting yourself off from social media temporarily to ensure your physical safety?"

"I'm afraid that horse has already bolted. This man knows where I live and work. He doesn't need social media to keep following me. All he needs is determination."

"A scary thought! Going back to the tweets – Indigo Verelst from Cape Town says that Jamie should take a screenshot every time her stalker contacts her so she has proof to show the police. That's not a bad idea at all, Indigo! Someone called 'Foully Wooing Won' – no real name or location given – has sent a tweet to say that Jamie's stalker sounds like a highly intelligent and organised individual. Would you agree with that, Jamie? Jamie?"

The camera, panning to Jamie's face, caught the shock in her eyes. Yes, she'd considered the possibility that he might try to contact her here, as he had at the radio station, but that didn't lessen the impact.

"That's him," she said. "That's his Twitter name. He's watching the show. He's watching us right now."

———

The man hugged himself as he watched the screen. There was his tweet – on television. The tweet he'd sent in just a minute ago had just flashed up on live, national television. Thousands of people were watching it right now. And just a few weeks ago, his voice had been on the radio.

Never in his wildest dreams had he imagined he would succeed like this. He grabbed the remote to play back the moment when Jamie realised it was his tweet she was looking at. The camera had caught it perfectly. Yes, the radio show had been a thrill. It had been delightful to hear the wobble in her voice over the radio when she'd realised she was talking to him. But it couldn't compare to this.

Look at her face. Just look at it. That moment of stunned surprise in her eyes. For that second, she was totally focused on him. Nothing else in the world mattered. He had every scrap of her attention.

He knew he'd been right to choose her. She was perfect for him in so many ways. Not only was she beautiful, she was as hungry for attention as he was. She would do anything for publicity, even risk her life. He would ride her coat-tails into the full glare of the public spotlight. She was his passport out of anonymity.

After a brief kerfuffle, they'd gone to a commercial break. He could just imagine them running around in circles and wringing their hands. *Oh, what should we do? What should we do? There's a real live stalker on our Twitter feed! Can we trace him? Is there any way we can find out who he really is? But, oh, how fabulous all this is for our ratings!*

And now they were back, looking just a little flustered.

A giggle rose in his throat as that TV shrink, Dr Banda, started saying that Jamie's stalker probably had a distant or domineering mother as a child. Most stalkers, according to the good doctor, were working through unresolved mother issues from their childhood. They were either looking for attention from the mother-figures in their lives, or trying to take back some of the control that had been wrested from them by women in their formative years.

Little breathy chuckles escaped from his mouth as he thought about his own mother tucked away in her retirement village in Jukskei Park. She had been neither distant nor domineering. She had been ordinary. It wasn't her fault she had a son destined for greatness.

Now that stupid woman known as "Seena" was giving her two-cent's-worth. It had been ridiculously easy to find out that her real name was Vishna. He had toyed with the idea of following her around for a while, just to teach her not to be so smug about her "triumph" over stalking. But she was old and shop-worn now – almost forty. There was no point wasting time on her when the thrill of following Jamie still burned so bright.

22

Human beings can get used to anything.

This was one of Jamie's mother's favourite sayings. Jamie hadn't given it much thought before, but the truth of it struck her now. She had got used to having a stalker. It no longer kept her awake at night, or had her glancing over her shoulder every time she left the house. She had stopped second-guessing herself online. She shared everything she wanted to share without worrying about who might be reading.

The TV interview had rattled her, coming so soon after hearing his voice on the radio. She'd wondered if she'd ever be able to spend a night alone in her own house again. But that hadn't lasted. Just a few weeks later, she had to concentrate hard to recapture that sense of dread. The fact that there'd been no contact from her stalker since had helped.

She was even getting used to being in a relationship. She and Tom saw each other almost every day. They had got into a routine of eating dinner together at his place. Either Jamie cooked or Tom picked up a takeaway. On his nights, they had stir-fry, sushi, pizza or fish and chips. On her nights, she used his kitchen to try out new recipes. Their evenings consisted of food, conversation and sex. They did not consist of sleeping in the same bed.

They'd come close a few times when they'd both fallen asleep by mistake. But so far, Tom had always woken up in time to hustle Jamie into her clothes and out the front door, watching her let herself into her own house before rushing back up the stairs to Ben.

Which was fair enough, Jamie decided. He'd laid down the ground rules from the beginning. It would be "too confusing" for Ben to wake up and find Jamie in his father's bed. Or in the house at all. So she left, and didn't make a fuss about it.

It was fine. In fact, she approved of the policy. Single fathers who let their kids wake up to a different woman every morning were irresponsible. It was good that Tom wasn't like that.

The fact that it made her feel like a call-girl sneaking out the house every night was her own problem. Tom was just being a good father. She couldn't fault him for that.

She just wished their evening routine could have included Ben. But Tom made sure Ben was always fed, bathed and put to bed before she arrived. The babysitting incident had not been repeated. Jamie got the impression Tom wished it had never happened.

The other thing Jamie was adjusting to was Pumla's pregnancy. Every time she looked at her friend, it gave her a shock to see her swelling belly. She was only four months along, but looked more like six months, given that she was carrying twins. On her petite frame, there was nowhere for the bump to go but outwards. Being pregnant seemed to have swept her away into a world of grownups that Jamie had no passport for.

When the door to Delucia's burst open one afternoon and Ben came bombing into the restaurant, Jamie could only stare. Tom followed at a more moderate pace.

"Mima!" Ben squealed and flung himself at Jamie's legs.

She crouched down to scoop him up, ignoring his father's gaze.

"Hi, Ben! Hi! It's so good to see you. I've missed you so much. You're getting bigger every time I see you. Are you eating your veggies every night?"

Ben pulled an icky face at the word "veggies", and wriggled to get free. As soon as his feet touched the ground, he was off again, dashing to say hello to Pumla and then launching himself into a chair at his favourite table.

"Chino!" he ordered his father, swinging his legs backwards and forwards.

"What's the magic word, dude?"

"Pweez!"

"That's better. We'll have a cappuccino and a baby chino, thanks, Pumla."

As Pumla went off to fill the order, Jamie wandered over, keeping her voice casual.

"This is a surprise. You don't usually come in so late in the afternoon. What's up?"

"Not much. We were picking up some stuff at Spar when Ben begged to come in here. This is one of his favourite places on earth."

Jamie knew from Pumla that Tom and Ben were regulars for breakfast on Friday mornings, but Tom was careful never to come in when Jamie might be there. She decided not to overthink it. The universe had given her a lovely surprise, and she was going to enjoy it.

The coffee shop was quiet. The teatime crowd had moved off and there were only a couple of tables with patrons relaxing over sundowners. The serious happy-hour crowd went across the road to the Earl & Badger. The last half hour of the day was usually spent in cashing up, cleaning the work stations and getting ready for the next morning.

"One cappuccino," said Pumla. "And one baby chino. Enjoy!" She put the mug of frothed milk with chocolate sprinkles onto the table in front of Ben. Then she signalled to Jamie to follow her to the bakery counter.

"This is a good sign, right?" she said. "He never brings the kid in when he knows you're going to be here."

"I don't know. He says Ben begged him to come. Maybe he just didn't feel like saying no."

"That man isn't some kind of wuss who can't say no to his own kid. If he hadn't wanted to come in here, he wouldn't be in here. I'm telling you, it's a sign."

"Of what?"

"That he's starting to mellow. That he's willing to let you into the kid's life."

Jamie pulled a face. "That's a lot to read into one restaurant visit."

"I'm telling you, he's cracked the door open. Now all you need to do is step through. Look how chilled he looks today."

They both turned to stare at Tom. He did seem relaxed. He was building a game for Ben using the salt and pepper shakers and the little sweetener packets that had come with his coffee. As they watched, he and Ben burst out laughing.

Pumla reached behind the counter and pulled out something red and plastic. "Now you go on over there and give that child this colouring-in set and some dough from the kitchen to play with. You'll be his favourite auntie in no time."

Jamie looked at the line-drawing of Donald Duck and the plastic bucket full of short, stubby crayons. "When did you get this? I thought you refused to keep colouring-in stuff for kids. You said it would only encourage their parents to bring them in here more often."

"Yes, well. Let's just say your boyfriend isn't the only one who's had a change of heart. It's come to my attention that these two," she rubbed a hand over her tummy, "will probably need to be entertained in here one day, so I might as well get used to it. I just printed a few pictures off the internet and bought some crayons. No biggie."

"And you used to be such a hard-ass."

"I'm still a hard-ass. Ask Dumisani."

"How *is* the prospective father anyway? I haven't seen him in a while." Jamie held up a finger as Pumla opened her mouth to answer. "No, wait. Save it until I come back. Let me go and do the favourite-auntie thing."

She went to the kitchen to grab a clump of the dough Nomsa was prepping for the next day. "It's for a good cause," she said as the pastry chef gave her a dirty look.

"Hey, Ben!" Jamie held up the crayons and dough as she got to Tom's table. "Look what I've got for you!"

"Awesome!" Tom smiled at her. "I thought you guys didn't do this."

"We didn't, but there's been a change of policy."

"Now I'm never going to be able to walk past here without coming in. What do you say to Jamie, Ben?"

"Fanks!" Ben plunged his fingers into the squishy dough, grinning from ear to ear.

"It's a pleasure, darling. You boys call me if you need anything."

She hurried back to Pumla. "Done. Now tell me your baby-daddy news."

"He still hasn't got it into his head that he's just the sperm donor in this equation, not the co-parent. He's so stubborn I could scream."

Jamie accepted a bundle of till receipts from Pumla and put them into a little plastic bag. "I don't get this at all. You're having twins. Won't it be nice having someone to help out? Someone who cares as much about them as you do?"

"But for how long? How long will he care? Until he meets someone new? Until he finds something better to do with his time? I can't do that to myself or to the kids. What if he waits until they've learned to love him before he decides he's had enough? I won't let them get hurt that way."

"Why are you so sure he's going to hurt them? What if he turns out to be the guy who sticks around for the long haul?"

"I've seen it happen over and over again. It happened to my own mother. Three times! She had three kids with three different dads, and we get to see them maybe once a year at funerals and weddings. If men don't want us to judge them as assholes, they shouldn't behave like assholes."

Jamie couldn't disagree. She'd watched the same thing happen to friends of hers. She knew fathers who apparently thought that divorcing their wives meant divorcing their kids as well. But then she thought of her own father. There was no doubt that some men were loyal, loving parents.

She changed tack. "So what's up with you guys at the moment? Are you totally refusing to see him? Surely you can find a way to stay friends up until the birth?"

There was silence. Jamie turned her head to see Pumla, face averted, cleaning the coffee machine with a spray bottle and cloth.

"Pumla?"

The cleaning continued at a slightly faster pace.

Jamie finished refilling the toothpicks and went over to the coffee machine. "Why are you wearing your guilty face? What have you been up to?"

Pumla flung her cloth onto the counter. "Okay, okay! I'll talk. Put down your rubber hose. We're still having sex, all right? Not that it's any of your business."

Jamie gaped at her. "You're still sleeping with him? But why? I thought you ended that side of things when you got pregnant. I thought getting pregnant was the whole point."

"I know, I know. It's these damn second-trimester hormones. You have no idea what they're like. I'm so horny I could die. It's like I've been turned into a nineteen-year-old guy. I think about sex all the time. I was fine in the first trimester when I was puking all over the place. Dumisani used to hang around sympathetically and bring me ginger ale and Marie biscuits."

"The scoundrel."

"Haha. But as soon as I clicked over to fourteen weeks, all the pukey hormones went away and the horny hormones took their place. Suddenly he stopped looking like Nurse Dumisani and started looking like Dumisani the Sex God. I haven't been able to keep my hands off him."

Jamie let her breath out in a loud puff. "This complicates things."

"Tell me about it. It's hard to convince a guy you don't want him in your life when you keep dragging him off to bed every five minutes."

"So you're using him for sex."

"Listen, he can scream for help at any time."

Jamie sighed. "Don't you have any self-control?"

"No."

They were still giggling when Tom spoke.

"As interesting as this conversation sounds, and I mean that sincerely, hadn't I better pay my bill before you finish cashing up?"

"Uh … right, yes. Let me do that for you." Her face hot, Pumla took the cash from Tom and hurried over to the till to make change.

"I guess we weren't exactly keeping our voices down," Jamie said.

"I guess you weren't."

"Listen, you and Ben probably want to head off now. I'll still be here for a while. Should I come by after seven as usual?"

There was a pause while Tom considered his reply, rubbing his chin. It wasn't like him to be hesitant.

"Why don't Ben and I hang out here until you close, and then go home with you?"

Jamie frowned. "This isn't some 'save Jamie from her stalker' thing, is it? Because I've got my car right here. I haven't walked to work in weeks. Not since we decided I should stop."

"No, it isn't that. I just thought ... if you don't mind hanging around while I feed and bath Ben, we could go back to my place now instead of you coming over later." He looked at her astonished face and shook his head. "Look, forget it. It was a silly idea. Yes, seven will be fine."

"No, wait! You took me by surprise, that's all. I'd love to come over while you bath Ben. I mean, I don't mind waiting while you put him down. I'll find something to do – no problem."

"Great! That's settled, then."

And he completed an afternoon of surprises by bending down and kissing her on the mouth.

The shock on Jamie's face as he'd kissed her made Tom feel guilty every time he thought about it. Something was wrong if the woman you were dating nearly fell off her chair when you kissed her in public. Of course, it wasn't the public part that was the problem. It was Ben. Tom had steered clear of showing any affection for Jamie in front of Ben.

He still thought his motives were sound. It would be confusing for Ben to see his father hugging and kissing a woman who might be out of their lives by this time next month.

And so far, it had all worked well. Jamie never tried to push the boundaries. She agreed to all the stipulations Tom set down, and never questioned them. What he hadn't bargained for was how they would make *him* feel. He hadn't known how much he would miss her after she left his bed in the middle of the night. How he would long for her in the evenings before she arrived. It wasn't as though he needed any help with Ben. Of course he didn't. It would just be nice to know she was there.

Like now. Jamie was in the kitchen warming up a tray of lasagne, and Tom was bathing Ben. It made him feel more settled knowing she was there.

Whatever crush Jamie seemed to have on Ben in the beginning was gone. The novelty had worn off, and she was normal around him. So it was fine to relax the rules a little. Whatever tiny disappointment he felt that her original delight in his son had evaporated was thrust to the back of his mind.

To test himself, he carried Ben downstairs once his teeth were brushed and he was in his pyjamas.

"Hey, would you mind reading this guy his bedtime story? I'd do it myself, but I have an urgent email to reply to. Would you mind?"

He thought she was going to say no, it took her so long to look up from the cheese she was grating. When she did, her face was blank. "Read to him? Oh, sure. No problem. Any book in particular?"

"Depends what he's in the mood for. If you take him up to his room, he'll choose. Don't let him con you into reading more than three books. You don't want to be stuck there all night."

"Don't worry, I won't. Let me just put this in the oven and I'll be right there."

"Mima!" Ben said, stretching his arms out to her.

Tom had to remind himself that the boy wasn't actually trying to say "Mama". "Mama" was a word he hardly knew, except from hearing other kids say it at the toddler group they attended.

If Jamie noticed the similarity, she gave no sign of it.

Tom transferred Ben into her arms and she took him upstairs.

Jamie closed Ben's bedroom door behind her and shut her eyes.

Then she did a happy-dance around the room that had Ben giggling madly in her arms.

"Your daddy's coming around," she whispered in his ear. "He's finally coming around. Soon you're going to be *my* Ben, just like you're *his* Ben. You'll like that, won't you?"

"Mima." Ben wriggled around to return the hug she was giving him.

"Of course you will. I know it. Now what book do you want me to read, Ben? Choose some books, Ben. Choose."

He scrambled out of her arms and attacked his bookcase, pulling books out of it, apparently at random. When he was finished, he dumped the spoils on his bed.

"Now pick three, Benny. Daddy said three only, remember. One, two, three!" She counted the numbers off on his edible little fingers. "Okay, close enough." He'd picked four from the heap. Using her best sleight-of-hand abilities, she slid the fourth back into the pile and replaced them in the bookcase. Then she settled on the bed with him on her lap and looked at what he'd chosen.

It didn't surprise her to see *The Tale of Jemima Puddleduck* at the very top. He'd chosen it on the night she'd babysat him as well.

Dropping her voice to a soothing tone, she began, "What a funny sight it is to see a brood of ducklings with a hen…"

23

Once the stories were over, Jamie resisted the urge to try putting Ben down to sleep herself. Instead, she stood at the top of the stairs holding his hand, and called Tom. He appeared so quickly she was sure he'd been listening.

"Thanks!" he said, taking Ben from her. "I managed to clear my inbox. This should take about ten minutes or so, but I'll be down soon."

"No hurry. The lasagne still has a while to go."

———

FROM JAMIE BURCHELL'S TWITTER FEED:

Jamie Burchell @jamieburchell
Bedtime stories are supposed to calm kids down to sleep. Mine just managed to psych him up. Am I doing it wrong?

Melissa Goldberg @stressedmom38
@jamieburchell Lol! I know what you mean. I think they're making stories too exciting these days. My kids are bouncing off the walls by bedtime.

Jamie Burchell @jamieburchell
@stressedmom38 This was Beatrix Potter. It nearly put ME to sleep! But the kid was totally into it.

Steve Pelser @WhiteZulu
@jamieburchell He is probably ADHD. @stressedmom38

Jamie Burchell @jamieburchell
He's not ADHD! His concentration is amazing. He always knows if you leave

a word out of the story. And he's not even 2 yet.

Melissa Goldberg @stressedmom38
@WhiteZulu I'm sure he's not ADHD. What a dumb thing to say about a kid you don't even know! @jamieburchell

Steve Pelser @White Zulu
@Stressedmom38 @JamieBurchell It was just a suggestion. Take a chill pill.

Cyril Attlee @inthemiddlecyril
@JamieBurchell @stressedmom38 There was no such thing as ADHD when I was growing up. It's one of these phony, new-fangled syndromes.

Jamie Burchell @JamieBurchell
@inthemiddlecyril Yeah. They all just need a good smack, isn't that right, Cyril? ;)

Cyril Attlee @inthemiddlecyril
@JamieBurchell Absolutely right. Without the winky face.

Jamie put her phone down. Discussions on social media skidded off course so fast. Depending on her mood, this either cheered her up or annoyed the crap out of her. Today was one of those "annoyed the crap out of her" days.

She was checking on the lasagne when Tom came down the stairs.

"How did you manage to put him down so quickly?" she asked. "That was the most wide-awake kid I've ever seen."

"At this age they can go from wide-awake to passed out cold in seconds. It's one of the blessings of sticking to a routine. I've trained him like Pavlov's dog. He goes to bed at exactly the same time every night. So even if he wakes up half a dozen times in the night, at least he's always asleep by seven."

They sat down at the kitchen table, and Jamie served the lasagne with a salad.

"This is awesome." Tom scooped up another forkful. "Did you

make it?"

"I didn't, no. But it's from a recipe I introduced to Delucia's. And I trained the kitchen staff to make it."

"It tastes like the lasagne I ate in Milan when I was on assignment there."

"On assignment there. That sounds so James Bond. I don't suppose you can tell me what assignment that was?"

"I don't suppose I can."

"If you told me you'd have to kill me – is that right?"

He grinned at her. "You got it."

"Then I'll tell you something. This recipe comes straight out of Italy. I picked it up when I was doing a cooking course in Florence. The hotel chain I was working for used to send us on these awesome short courses to learn the local cuisine."

"That's great." Tom polished off the lasagne. "You have a real gift for this cooking stuff. It's kind of weird, though – you're a chef who doesn't like to eat."

"What do you mean, I don't like to eat? I love eating! It's one of my passions in life."

Tom just cocked an eyebrow at the slab of lasagne on her plate. There was a bit missing from the side of it, as though it had been nibbled on by hamsters.

"I'm still busy eating. Give me a chance. Just because you gobble your food down in record time."

He pointed his fork at her. "You'll toy with it for a few more minutes, but basically you're done. And that's how you eat every meal that gets put in front of you. You *are* the chef who doesn't like to eat."

Jamie shrugged. "Okay, you've got me. I like the *idea* of eating. I like the *concept* of it. I even love the taste of it for the first couple of bites. But after that I tend to lose interest. It used to drive my mother crazy when I was growing up. On the one hand, she had Ella who liked food, but forced herself not to eat, and on the other hand she had me – who didn't like eating all that much, but was always in the kitchen concocting some dish or other. At least Caro was reasonably normal."

"Do you ever see yourself going back into restaurants or hotels full time?"

She shook her head, stroking the lasagne with the prongs of her fork. "I want to write. I really just want to write."

After dinner, he loaded the dishwasher and cleaned up the kitchen. Vuyiswa would do most of the work when she came in the next morning, but he liked to leave a tidy kitchen for her.

When Jamie picked up a cloth and started wiping down surfaces, Tom came up behind her and plucked it out of her hand.

"Hey!" she protested. "That wouldn't have taken me long."

He tugged at the band holding her braid together and started pulling her hair loose. He loved the honey-coloured lights in it. It was a look no salon could create.

"The way I'm feeling right now, two minutes would be too long." He had succeeded in fanning her hair out, and was now running his fingers through it, enjoying the slight kink that the braiding had left.

Jamie turned and looked at him. "Oh, really? Is there something you need to do urgently?"

"You could say that." His hands abandoned her hair and started stroking her neck and the sides of her jaw – a light, feathery touch that made her nerve-endings tingle and her entire body come to life. He leaned closer and replaced his fingers with his lips, keeping up that barely there contact that whispered along her skin like a promise.

Jamie took his face in her hands and pulled his mouth down onto hers. His lips were firm and soft – so familiar by now, but so exciting. Her body was already clamouring for the pleasure it knew he could bring her. Their tongues met and danced.

They needed to get upstairs to the bedroom, and fast. Or she'd be tearing the clothes off him and lying back on the kitchen table. Not an option with a toddler in the house.

"Upstairs, quick," she said.

"Wait." His fingers tugged at her top. "Just let me." His hands skimmed under her T-shirt, yanked aside the support tank she was wearing, and closed over her breasts. The sensation rocketed straight to her core.

"Upstairs," she gasped. "Now."

They pulled and pushed each other up the stairs, stopping twice to kiss. When they reached the door to Tom's bedroom, Jamie pushed him backwards through it, one hand on his belt buckle. His heel caught the edge of a rug and they both fell over in a heap.

"Sshhh!" Tom hissed. Then they giggled like teenagers afraid to wake sleeping parents. Jamie got onto her hands and knees and crawled toward the bed. "You stay there." She waved her hand at him. "I'm getting onto this bed and starting without you."

He beat her to the bed by a nano-second. "Interesting as that sounds, and definitely something we should explore at a later date, I want to be part of this."

"Then why do you still have your pants on?"

Clothes went flying as they ripped them off with a minimum of finesse.

"That's better." Jamie flung herself down on the bed and pulled him on top of her, desperate for the feeling of his body on hers. Her hand found him rock-hard and ready, and she wrapped herself around him gratefully.

They both let their breath out in a whoosh of relief. But then the sensations started to build, and for a while neither of them were capable of saying anything.

"I don't know why sex with you wrecks me like this." Jamie lay back on the bed sucking in air like a pearl diver and listening to her heart thunder in her chest. "I feel like I've been through a tornado or something."

Tom turned his head to grin at her. "Tornadoes would be a lot more popular in the Midwest if they all ended like this."

"Seriously. I'm too wrecked to hold a conversation." Her eyes opened wide in the dark. "I'm even too tired to tweet!"

Tom rolled her onto her side and pulled her so that her back fit snugly against his chest. "Don't talk then." He draped his arm over her. "Or even tweet. Just sleep."

So she did.

She had no idea what time it was when she woke up, except that it was still pitch dark. Something had woken her. Her sleepy brain held the vestiges of a memory of something…

She lifted her head off the pillow, frowning into the dark room. Perhaps she had imagined it. No. There it was again. A faint, high-pitched wail.

Ben.

Jamie turned her head to look at Tom. This had happened before. Ben only slept through the night about half the time at the moment. She was usually gone when he woke up, but there had been a few occasions in the past when she'd still been here. Tom had always hustled her out of the house at top speed.

She sighed. Time to start looking for her clothes in the dark again.

But why wasn't Tom budging? He was sleeping like a dead man.

"Hey!" she whispered. "Ben's crying."

He grunted and snuggled deeper into his pillow.

She prodded him in the ribs. "Wake up! Ben's crying."

Tom groaned but didn't move.

"Do you want me to go to him?"

No answer.

She jabbed him again. "I said, do you want me to go to Ben?"

He sighed and rolled over. "Uhhh … 'kay."

Fully awake now, Jamie swung her feet out of bed and sat up. Ben cried again, sounding crankier. Jamie got up and groped against the bedroom door for Tom's dressing gown. It wrapped around her like a shroud and hung almost to the floor, but it was better than walking around naked.

She slipped along the passage to Ben's room. He was lying diagonally across his low bed and making bad-tempered little moans. Something told her not to talk to him as she picked him up. A sleeping toddler was what she was aiming for here, not a toddler wide awake and stimulated by conversation.

Now if she could just figure out what he wanted, perhaps she could still get back to sleep sometime before dawn. She ran her hand over his pyjama'd bottom. The nappy underneath felt crisp and dry. So it wasn't a change he needed. She remembered Tom saying he had recently stopped giving Ben milk at night, and how he was sleeping better as a result. So no bottle either. Tom wouldn't thank her for setting his night-time routine back by months.

Jamie noticed a sippy cup sitting next to the bed. She picked it up and sniffed it. Water. Well, that should be all right, shouldn't it? Lots of people woke up for a drink in the night sometimes. She did so herself.

Ben stirred in her arms. "Mima?"

"Sshhh! Yes, darling, it's Mima. I'm going to give you some water now, and then we'll sit in the chair."

She held the spout up to his mouth and he drank almost half the water. She walked around the room jiggling him until she felt him go limp in her arms. Then she sat down in the big rocking chair, with its high arms, and settled Ben against her chest. She nearly stood up again when he lifted his head and arched his back. But within seconds, he relaxed against her chest. His cheek rested against the dressing gown and his body seemed to mould itself to hers.

Jamie decided to give him a few minutes to fall asleep properly. Then she'd put him into his bed and go back to Tom. In the meantime, she'd just rest her head against the back of the chair and close her eyes for a minute.

———

Tom woke up when a beam of sunlight fell across his face. One moment he was asleep, and the next he was sitting bolt upright, blinking in confusion. Something was wrong. Something was very wrong.

He glanced at the bed next to him. Jamie was gone. But she was always gone by this time of the morning. So why couldn't he remember letting her out last night? For a panicky moment, he wondered if the stalker had done something to her.

No. It was something else. What had they talked about last night? She'd asked him a question. Something to do with Ben.

Ben.

Tom got out of bed and pulled on a pair of sweatpants. He walked out of his room and into Ben's room. What he saw there made his heart sink.

Jamie was lying in the rocking chair fast asleep. Her arms were wrapped around Ben who was sprawled, face-down against her chest, also fast asleep. It should have been a sweet scene. Heart-warming, even. Instead it filled Tom with dread. He wanted to rip his son out of her arms.

My child. Mine. Not yours.

But nearly two years of being a parent had imprinted on him the importance of never waking a sleeping toddler. He tiptoed over to Jamie and reached out a hand to touch her. She opened her eyes and smiled at him.

"Hi!" she whispered. "Did you have a good sleep?"

"Put Ben in his bed. We need to talk."

Jamie tightened her arms around Ben and stood up in slow motion. Then she laid him down on the bed and pulled the duvet over him.

"Unbelievable," she whispered when he didn't stir. "I kept trying that last night and he kept waking up. He must be in a really deep sleep now."

Ben sighed and shifted in his sleep. They both froze and watched him. Then Tom beckoned Jamie to follow him out the room.

"Did you sleep well last night?" Jamie asked. "You were

completely out of it when Ben cried."

Tom just tightened his lips. Once they reached the kitchen, he closed the door and flipped the baby monitor on.

"What's going on here?" he said, turning to her. "I wake up to find you gone from the bedroom. Where could she be, I wonder to myself. Oh, look! There she is, sleeping in my son's chair and holding him against her chest."

Jamie frowned at his tone. "So? What's wrong with that? What would you have expected me to do? Leave him to scream?"

"Do you have any idea how dangerous it is to fall asleep holding a baby on your lap like that? What if he'd wriggled? What if you'd relaxed your hold? He could have fallen onto the floor and been killed."

"Oh, please. It's not dangerous. I know lots of mothers who hold their babies like that. And they fall asleep like that, too."

"I think the crucial difference is that they are mothers. And they're holding their own babies. Not someone else's baby."

She gave him a baffled look. "I don't know why you're so upset. That chair has really high arms. There was no possibility of either Ben or me rolling out of it."

"That's not the point."

"Then why don't you tell me what the point is?"

"You can't just go and help yourself to my son in the middle of the night."

"What? I didn't just go and help myself to him. I asked you!" She could hear her voice rising. "Look, I woke up because Ben was crying. I was going to put my clothes on and leave, but you were still asleep. I tried to wake you, but you wouldn't wake up properly. So I asked if you wanted me to go to him, and you said okay. You. Said. Okay." She punctuated her words by stabbing the air with her finger. "You gave me express permission."

"You knew I wasn't properly awake. You knew I wasn't thinking straight. But instead of taking that into account, you took the gap and used the opportunity to get your hands on my child."

Jamie gasped. "What the hell else did you expect me to do? Throw cold water over you? I tried three times to wake you. Three times! Should I have just let Ben scream himself into a fit?"

Tom crossed his arms. "I would have heard him eventually. I always do."

"Yes, by the time he's cried himself into a complete state. That's why it takes you so long to put him back to sleep. You told me once it can take you up to an hour. Well, it only took me a few minutes. A few minutes, and he was fast asleep again."

"Yes, because you let him fall asleep in your arms. If it's all the same to you, I'd rather not spend the rest of my life sleeping in an armchair with Ben on my chest. I'm trying to train him to sleep in his own bed."

"The point is that women are designed by evolution to respond quickly to the high-pitched sound of a baby crying. Men are not. You should be grateful I was there to go to him, instead of acting like I'm some kind of baby-snatcher…"

She stopped dead when the baby monitor crackled into life.

It was Ben. He wasn't crying. He was making the chatty, gurgling noises of a toddler who has woken up naturally and is ready to face the day.

Tom turned to Jamie. "Ben's awake. If you'll excuse me, I have to go to him."

"Be my guest." Jamie turned on her heel and stalked out of the kitchen to get dressed.

24

Jamie had never censored herself online before, and she wasn't about to start now. She did, however, feel too raw after her fight with Tom to blog about it straight away.

When she got back to her own house, all she wanted was coffee and paracetamol to chase away the headache pressing against her temples.

She knew a morning run would work better than painkillers, but she couldn't face it. Instead she changed into comfortable clothes and switched on the coffee machine. While it bubbled and spat, she fed Holmes and Watson, taking comfort in their furry presence.

Then she settled herself in front of the computer and started scrolling through her Facebook and Twitter feeds, and the various blogs she followed. As the lines of text flicked by, she argued with herself about the ethics of blogging.

She should blog about the fight. Now. While it was fresh in her mind.

No, she shouldn't. She was still too angry. She wouldn't present it fairly. There were two sides to every story, and she would only be able to show one.

So what? It was her blog, wasn't it? If Tom wanted to put his opinion out there, he could start his own blog.

But that was the whole point. Tom didn't want to put his opinion out there. He liked his privacy. He hadn't signed up for having his personal life blabbed all over the internet by his girlfriend.

Ex-girlfriend. After this morning, ex-girlfriend was almost certainly the correct description.

Whichever. He was entitled to his privacy.

Everyone was entitled to their privacy, but that didn't mean she was only allowed to write about herself. No one wanted to read a blog about just one person. The friends and family of writers had to get used to being used for material. That's how it was.

No. It was a passive-aggressive stunt to write an angry blog about the fight they'd just had. It would be more honest to say whatever she wanted to say to his face. She knew he read her blog occasionally. It wouldn't be right to blindside him like that.

Jamie stopped scrolling and pressed her hands over her eyes. This wasn't helping her headache at all.

She would compromise, she decided. She would wait a few days to let her passions cool, and then she would write a balanced blog about it. And she would try to be sensitive to Tom's privacy.

There. Decided.

————

FROM JAMIE BURCHELL'S PERSONAL BLOG:
....

... so I've been forced to ask myself if he was right. Did I "take the gap", knowing he hadn't really agreed? Was I so desperate to take care of the baby that I rushed in and ignored a little voice in my head warning me it wasn't the right thing to do?

The truth is, I don't know. I was very tired. I'd just woken up out of a deep sleep. There might have been a part of me that was eager to jump at the chance of caring for Ben.

What I should have done was wake Tom up properly and ask him if it really was okay for me to go to his child. I didn't do that. Part of me probably knew he'd say no. So I take responsibility for that.

COMMENTS:
....

Posted by: **Gugz**
Biggest storm in a teacup ever. Where I come from, it takes a village to raise a child. Literally, because I come from a little village in KZN. If you see a child being naughty, you smack him. If you see a child fall down, you pick her up and put on a Band Aid. If you hear a child crying, you ask what's wrong. You don't first go and

find the parents to ask permission. I swear to God, I have NEVER!

Posted by: **Amanda Stan**
Touchy situation. My feeling is that since he'd asked you to read the kid a bedtime story that same evening, and since you've babysat before, you were justified in thinking it was okay to go to him in the night. But you've obviously trampled all over a sore spot, so basically I just think you need to talk to him.

Posted by: **Dineo**
Srsly, like Gugz said, in owa culcha no parent wd eva fault u 4 wat u did. Totes justified IMO. Dis 1 tym when I wuz a kid I wuz cryin in da street nd no 1 came. My mom she went to all da neighbiz aftawards nd she wuz lyk WHY U IGNORE MY KID? Lol!

Posted by: **Cyril Att**
I don't know why you put up with this guy and his stupid tantrums. He is totally unreasonable. He's always finding fault with you. He should be grateful that you're willing to help him at all. A single father, burdened with someone else's child. He's not in a position to pick and choose.

Posted by: **Jamie Burchell**
Dear Cyril. I know you mean well, but he is not "burdened with someone else's child". That's his own son he's raising. His own child – legally, morally, and on every level. He has the right to decide what kind of contact outsiders are allowed.

Posted by: **Shoobeedoo**
Judging by your earlier posts on this subject, I think you were subconsciously motivated by the desire to get closer to the kid. In which case, you owe his dad an apology.

Posted by: **Foully Wooing Won**
How can you bear to touch that half-breed infant? Doesn't it make your skin crawl?

Jamie dropped her phone face-down on the counter.

He was back.

She wasn't sure if the shudder that ran along her spine was caused by his name or by the repulsiveness of the comment he'd just posted. A half-breed? He was calling Ben a half-breed? What kind of disgusting, right-wing lunatic was he anyway?

In a sudden, violent segue from fear to anger, Jamie snatched up her phone. She wasn't going to stand for this. Jabbing at the keyboard, she began to type a reply.

Posted by: **Jamie Burchell**
How can you say that about an innocent child? You're the one who makes my skin crawl. Keep your disgusting observations to yourself.

She was breathing heavily through her nose when another comment notification flickered onto the screen.

Posted by: **Shoobeedoo**
Don't feed the trolls, babe. That's Internet 101. You should know better.

Jamie bit her lip. She did know better. She never responded to trolls. Everyone knew they thrived on attention. The only reason they posted their shocking or outrageous statements was to generate indignation. They thrived on abuse from other commenters.

She was just thinking about deleting her comment when another notification flashed. She refreshed the feed.

Posted by: **Foully Wooing Won**
I'm calling a spade a spade. Don't complain because I speak the truth that you don't want to hear. A half-breed is a half-breed. They violate the laws of God and nature.

Posted by: **Gugz**
I don't think you've been paying attention to this blog, Foully Wooing. The child is a black boy who has been adopted by a white father. Explain to me how that

makes him a "half-breed"?

Posted by: **Amanda Stan**
Jamie, you seriously need to moderate your comments. Why don't you just delete filth like this? It's dragging down the standard of your comment threads.

Posted by: **Jamie Burchell**
I hear you, Amanda, but I've always had a policy of not deleting comments. I don't want to turn into a blogger who only allows those comments that support me.

Posted by: **Foully Wooing Won**
That baby is a cuckoo in the nest. It should be with its own kind. No good will come from raising it white. The Bible has shown us this again and again.

Posted by: **Jamie Burchell**
You are a sick and disgusting individual. Get off my blog or I WILL delete you.

Jamie put her phone down with trembling hands. Now she knew where the expression "seeing red" came from. A bloody mist had descended and she seemed to be seeing her screen through its haze.

She forced herself to step away from the phone. Pumla had been coping alone with the influx of teatime customers and was starting to give Jamie meaningful looks. Jamie forced a hospitable expression onto her face and went to the door as a party arrived.

"Good afternoon!" She had been clenching her jaw so hard it hurt to smile. "Table for three?"

————

Driving home from work always made Jamie feel silly. It felt like a waste of petrol, an insult to the environment, and a jab in the eye to those pedestrians who had to walk much further to work each day. But she'd promised Tom she would.

It wasn't easy to break that promise, even though their

relationship seemed to be over. They hadn't officially broken up, but in Jamie's book a huge, bitter fight followed by no contact for three days constituted a break-up. She was sure most people would agree.

As she drove past Tom's house, she slowed to a crawl. As usual, there was no sign of life. If he still went running with Silver in the mornings or took Ben for walks in the afternoons, she never saw him.

A small part of her believed this was just a temporary tiff. One of these days he'd phone her, or text her, or ring her doorbell, and admit he'd overreacted. They'd talk the whole thing through, and everything would be back on track. This fantasy wore a little thinner with each day that passed.

Jamie made herself look away from Tom's house. She turned into her own driveway and reached for the remote. Then she froze.

There was something attached to her gate.

The engine stalled as her feet forgot what to do with the pedals. She was halfway out the car before she realised it would be better to get safely inside first. He could still be nearby. He could be watching her right now, waiting for her to panic and do something stupid.

She slid back into the driver's seat and started the car again. It took three tries before she managed to open the gate with the remote. Her car lurched down the driveway and into the garage, only stopping when her bumper hit the wall.

The front gate slid shut behind her. Jamie got out the car and approached the gate on legs that seemed to be boneless. Whatever had been tied there was attached with plastic cable ties, just like the other times. Nothing was moving, thank God. Whatever it was didn't appear to be alive.

"Scissors … I need scissors."

She let herself into the house and grabbed a pair of kitchen scissors. She went back to the gate and cut the ties without looking directly at the object. Only once it was loose, did she pull it through the bars and examine it properly.

It was a small, plastic doll, about the size of a Barbie. It seemed to be the kind of anatomically correct model that was used to teach children about childbirth. The doll had a swollen belly that swung open on a hinge mechanism to reveal the baby inside. No, Jamie thought, looking more closely, two babies. The doll was pregnant with twins.

Just before she dropped it, Jamie noticed two other things about the doll – its skin was dark, and it had a knife sticking out of its belly.

Jamie ran into the house and scrabbled for her cellphone. She needed to call Tom. Yes, they were fighting. Yes, they weren't on speaking terms. But none of that mattered now. It had all been obliterated by this new threat.

"Please answer. Please answer." Jamie pressed the first number for Tom that came up on her phone, which happened to be his home line. "Please be there. Please be there," she chanted as the phone began to ring.

"Hello."

"Tom!" Her voice was unsteady. "Tom. Please come. It's Pumla. The stalker. He … he…"

"Where are you?"

"Home. I'm at home. Please come."

"I'm coming. Is Pumla with you? Do I need to call an ambulance?"

"No! No!" Jamie squeezed her eyes shut. "She's okay. Just come."

"I'm on my way."

The doll lay in a clear plastic bag on Jamie's kitchen counter. She sat at the table sipping sweet tea and trying not to look at it. Tom paced the floor, apparently thinking.

"I'm not overreacting, am I?" Jamie said. "This is a clear threat against Pumla?"

He stopped pacing and nodded. "Oh yes. Very clear."

"Should I tell her? I think I have to tell her."

"Yes. She needs to know about this, and so does Dumisani."

"But she's pregnant. What if the shock brings on a miscarriage or something?"

"We can't keep it from her. You'll just have to tell her carefully. Make sure she's sitting down and that sort of thing."

Jamie pressed the heels of her hands into her eyes. "I don't think I should show her that horrible doll. Just telling her about it will be enough, surely?"

Tom thought about this. "Yes, okay. Showing her the doll would be unnecessarily upsetting. Just tell her about it. But if she doesn't take it seriously, you might need to rethink that."

"I couldn't bear it if anything happened to her or the babies." Jamie tried to get a grip as emotion threatened to overwhelm her.

"It's hard, I know."

Tom's tone was stilted. The air between them bristled with awkwardness. Jamie wondered why her first impulse had been to call him when their relationship had broken down so thoroughly.

And he had come to her. He'd come without question.

But he had no comfort to offer her. His body language was stiff, and his arms remained at his side. He used to touch her all the time when they were alone together, just because he could. Now he held himself aloof.

"We need to know what happened to switch his focus to Pumla." Tom tapped the doll through the clear plastic bag. "He's been quiet for so long now, I think we were both wondering if he'd given up. Something must have happened to set him off again. Do you have any idea what?"

Jamie drained her teacup and took it to the sink. "Yes, I do. It was me. I stirred him up again."

"What do you mean?"

"I got into a fight with him online."

"Jamie! I thought you agreed you weren't going to engage with him anymore."

"I know, I know. I wasn't thinking straight. He made me so angry I flew off the handle."

"What did he say to annoy you so much? Surely you could have ignored it?"

"He called Ben a half-breed and a crime against the Bible."

"*What?*"

Holmes and Watson slunk away as Tom's voice rattled the windowpanes.

"Not so easy to ignore, is it?"

"But what the hell...?"

Jamie picked up her phone and called up the link to her blog. "You'd better read the whole thing from the beginning. I wrote a blog about the fight we had and he commented on it. I don't know what came over me, but I literally saw red and started replying to him without thinking."

Tom took her phone and read her post, stony-faced.

"Bastard," he said when he got to the bottom of the comments thread.

"Yes. And he caught me at a bad time. I think you need to be in a good head space to deal with trolling, and I just wasn't."

Tom sat down for the first time since entering Jamie's house. "This man is watching you, Jamie – both online and in real life. And now he's escalating because he's annoyed. He was pleased with you when you were getting him coverage on radio and TV, but that's all gone away. And instead of being nice to him, you publicly insulted him. He's looking to make his own thrills now."

"If I thought it would keep Pumla safe, I'd delete all my social media accounts right now. But I don't think that's the right thing to do."

"I agree. It might trigger him even more. If he can't make contact with you online, his only option will be to contact you in person."

25

Grocery shopping was never the highlight of Jamie's week. She dealt with it by putting herself on automatic pilot, powering up and down the aisles with her trolley and grabbing things off the shelves according to her list.

Sometimes when she got home she could hardly remember being in the shop at all.

But today, the knowledge that a maniac with a severe personality disorder could be following her around was ruining her concentration. She loaded three boxes of automatic washing powder into her trolley before remembering that she'd stocked up the week before. She took them out again, cursing under her breath. Then she had to go back down the same aisle to pick up the furniture polish she'd forgotten.

This was getting ridiculous.

She needed a Twitter break to clear her head. Pushing her shopping out of the way of other shoppers, she reached into her bag for her phone.

Jamie Burchell @jamieburchell
My nerves are shot. It's taking me twice as long as normal to do the weekly shop. I'm seeing stalkers behind every bush now.

Jamie Burchell @jamieburchell
Doesn't matter that I'm in a safe, public, well-lit space in the middle of the day. Just can't get rid of the feeling I'm being watched. #stalker

She leaned against her trolley, already feeling calmer for having shared her worries. As the notification light on her phone began to flash, she relaxed even more. Twitter was her sanctuary. It always made her feel less alone.

The Tenant @squatter
@jamieburchell It's normal to feel that way after everything you've been through. Just be sensible and stay away from dangerous situations.

Tumi Boapi @tumiboapi
@jamieburchell Maybe you should shop online until this is all over? At least that way you won't have to leave the house.

Jamie Burchell @jamieburchell
@tumiboapi Online shopping too expensive. Can't justify extra expense. And realistically, nothing's going to happen to me in the grocery store.

Elsje Steenkamp @newbiemama
@jamieburchell @tumiboapi Friend of mine was being stalked by ex-boyfriend. He tried to stab her in Pick 'n Pay once. Security guard stopped him.

Jamie Burchell @jamieburchell
@newbiemama That's very comforting, thanks! ;)

Elsje Steenkamp @newbiemama
@JamieBurchell Just don't want you getting a false sense of security!

———

The man pressed back against a display of dried fruit. Why wasn't she moving? Why had she stopped like that and taken out her phone?

It was very annoying of her. It was easy for him to stay unnoticed as long as she kept moving, because then he could keep moving too. A man walking up and down the aisles with a basket on his arm attracted no attention, but a man standing still would soon be noticed.

Frustration shook him. What was wrong with her lately? First she attacked him online, and now she stopped to dither in the middle of her grocery run. Was she trying to irritate him? She'd be sorry if she was.

He turned and stared at the display of chips and popcorn.

Okay, sometimes people couldn't make up their minds. Sometimes it took them minutes to decide what brand of salted snack they wanted. He wasn't one of them, but he could pretend to be. He could blend in with the idiots.

He counted to thirty-two and then shuffled sideways to look at Jamie again. She was still standing, typing on her phone. What could she be texting that was so urgent?

No, wait. He knew that smile. She wasn't texting, she was tweeting.

He took out his phone and opened Jamie's Twitter stream.

"I can't get rid of this feeling that I'm being watched," he read.

Panic crowded into his chest. She'd seen him. She'd noticed him. She was calling the police. He would be arrested.

He ran for the door, dropping his basket as he went.

"Excuse me, sir."

He looked up, ready to kill anyone who got in his way.

It was a shelf-packer.

"You dropped your basket." The packer pointed at the scattering of items on the floor. "Do you still want those things?"

He took a rasping breath. "Yes … okay. I still want them. Excuse me. I'll pick everything up."

He bent down and picked up the items he'd dropped into his basket at random. This didn't have to be a disaster. He didn't have to abort his mission.

Jamie wasn't calling the police. Of course, she wasn't. She was jumpy because of him. He was the one. He had the power to make her feel afraid – to rip aside her illusion of security and leave her vulnerable.

The pleasure of this awareness blended with the adrenaline still coursing through his body. This was what he lived for. This feeling of fear and triumph combined. It was better than anything. It made him feel alive.

He looked at his phone again. Jamie had stopped tweeting. She was on the move again.

Jamie Burchell @jamieburchell
I can't live my life in fear. I will finish this shopping trip and go home. If I stop now because of him, he wins. I won't let him win.

Jamie set off down the aisle, shopping list in hand. She had just made the turn into the dairy section when she became aware of a man walking a few steps behind her. As she glanced at him, he dropped his eyes and stopped walking. When she walked a few more steps towards the yoghurt, he followed.

She stopped again to test him, and he stopped too.

Her heart began to knock against her ribs. Was she being paranoid, or was this person following her?

She glanced at him again. He was about the same age as her. His hair was mousy brown, and his features unremarkable except for a slightly receding chin. He kept his eyes cast down so she couldn't form an impression of them. He was a little taller than she was, and his build was slight.

She made mental notes of what he looked like, pleased that she was keeping her head like this. Grey flannel shirt, faded jeans, high-tops.

She jumped about a mile when he spoke to her.

"Sorry … um … have you got … can you help…?"

She stared at him, too frightened to move. There was nothing he could do to her, she reminded herself. They were in a public supermarket in broad daylight. There were people all around them.

Just then a man pushed past them with a muttered apology. Jamie almost seized his arm to make him stay as the brown-haired guy continued to fumble for words.

"I just wanted … I wanted to ask if you could help me with bus fare to East London. My wife is in labour and I need to get to her."

Pale. His face was very pale, she registered. Then she shook her head. "No, I'm sorry." And she hurried away with her trolley.

Jamie Burchell @jamieburchell
He was at the grocery store. He spoke to me. I was right to be suspicious. #stalker

Bronwyn Jones @redhighheels
@jamieburchell OMG! What did he say?

Jamie Burchell @jamieburchell
He asked for bus fare to East London. Said his wife was in labour.

Bronwyn Jones @redhighheels
Are you sure that was your stalker? He sounds like a beggar. Someone stopped me in the supermarket with that exact story the other day.

Jamie Burchell @jamieburchell
No, he was definitely following me around. I knew there was something suspicious about him as soon as I saw him.

Foully Wooing Won @foullywooingwon
@jamieburchell What about the man who bumped into you while you were speaking to the druggie beggar? Did he also set off your radar?

Jamie Burchell @jamieburchell
@foullywooingwon What are you talking about?

Foully Wooing Won @foullywooingwon
You shouldn't let strange men press up against you like that, Jamie. They might get ideas.

Jamie Burchell @jamieburchell
Can't do this anymore. Logging off for now. #stalker

Jamie bundled her groceries into the car, and jumped into the driver's seat. Instead of driving home, she went straight to Tom's house.

Vuyiswa answered the door.

"Uh, hi," Jamie said. "Is Tom home?"

Vuyiswa glanced at her watch. "In a few minutes. You want to come in and wait?"

"Just a few minutes? Okay, I'll come in then, thanks. Is Ben here?"

"No, Ben is out with his father. You must come in so I can keep the door locked."

Vuyiswa showed Jamie into the sitting room, where Silver was sprawled on the rug. She made for the dog at once, wanting the comfort of her big, solid body.

"Hi, Silver! Hi, girl. I've missed you. Yes, you're a good girl, aren't you?"

Silver rolled onto her back for a tummy rub, which Jamie provided with enthusiasm.

"Oh, my word. Look at this gorgeous figure! He's still running with you, isn't he? He's just picked a new time and a new route to avoid me, am I right? Yes, I know I'm right."

"That dog shouldn't be allowed in the house."

Jamie whirled around. She pressed a hand to her chest as she recognised Tom's step-mother. "Sorry. I'm a bundle of nerves. I didn't know anyone else was here. Hello, Mrs Elliot."

No wonder Vuyiswa was so keen to keep the front door locked.

"Hello, dear. Do sit down. The girl will bring the tea in a moment."

Jamie could make no sense of this. Then she realised the woman was referring to Vuyiswa, and had to resist pulling a face.

"I'll just check if the tea is ready." She went into the kitchen and switched on the kettle. Then she began to set a tray. Luckily she knew where everything was because she had a feeling Tom's stepmother wouldn't be content with tea in a mug.

"Why didn't you tell me Tom's mother was here?" she asked Vuyiswa, who was ironing in the scullery. "Now I have to drink tea with her."

"You sit with her. Otherwise she comes in here and tells me how to iron and how to polish the silver."

Jamie groaned. "What am I supposed to say to her?"

"You don't have to talk. Just listen while she talks."

"Okay."

She set the tray with a lace cloth and took out the 1930s Art Deco tea set that she had long coveted. Scooping sugar into the bowl and pouring milk into the jug, she was aware that these everyday tasks were calming her down. She added a plate of shortbread fingers that she'd baked herself last week and given to Tom.

"Here's the tea." Jamie carried the tray into the sitting room, trying to inject cheer into her voice.

Tom's stepmother was sitting bolt upright in an armchair. She wore a peach-coloured twinset and pearls, and looked every inch the lady, except for her lipstick, which seemed to have been applied in the dark. Jamie was struck by how unlike Tom she was. Obviously one wouldn't expect them to look alike, but there was nothing at all to suggest she had raised him.

Ben already had a way of shaking his head and saying, "Nooooo," that made him look exactly like his father. But Tom's step-mother had failed to leave her mark on him.

"Shall I pour?" Jamie lifted her eyebrows and the teapot at the same time.

Mrs Elliot nodded. "That's a lovely tea set, dear. I used to have one very like it. Mine was by Susie Cooper and it was made in 1934. The pattern was Reverie. It said so right on the bottom. Brown pansies – I remember it so well." She turned one of the saucers over and stared at the writing, a frown gathering on her face.

"But this is mine. This is my tea set. Where did you get it? You stole it, didn't you, you wicked girl!"

Oh, dear.

Jamie summoned up a smile. "No one stole it, Mrs Elliot. You gave it to your son Tom to keep for you, don't you remember? So you could enjoy it every time you visited him?"

"Whose house is this?"

"This is Tom's house. You're spending the day here. He went to fetch you in his car."

Suspicion faded from the old woman's eyes, but she persisted. "Then why isn't he here?"

"He'll be back soon. He had to go out for a while."

Jamie was pleased to see Mrs Elliot's anger subside as she started to sip her tea. When she'd nibbled her way through one of the shortbread fingers, a reminiscent smile lit her face.

"It's funny you should mention the name Tom. I knew a little boy by that name once."

"Did you?"

"Yes, he was my husband's child. Such a nuisance, that boy. He couldn't sit still for a minute, and he kept breaking things. One time he broke a plate from this very tea set. It was part of our wedding china. Fortunately we had nine of everything, so I could still host a tea for eight people."

Jamie smiled and nodded, wishing Tom would get back.

"My husband said I would learn to love the boy for his sake, but I was never able to. I didn't see the point in pretending either. But still, I did my best by him. He never went cold or hungry."

Jamie thought there were different kinds of coldness. Her smiling and nodding were going unnoticed, so she gave up and listened.

"I was never able to have a child of my own." Tom's stepmother helped herself to another piece of shortbread. "Perhaps things would have been different if I had. We didn't have all these test-tube babies that you young people have today. If God didn't give you a child, you simply accepted it. The thing I don't understand is how he could have expected me to love a little black boy – such an unattractive baby too. I thought it was the maid's child when I first saw it. He asked me if I wanted to hold it. Can you imagine?"

She gave a ladylike laugh.

Jamie was gripping the handle of the teacup so hard it was about to come off in her hand. She loosened her hold. It wasn't the teacup's fault. Don't blame the vintage, Art Deco, hand-painted, fine bone china circa 1934. She took a breath and tried to force down the anger that wanted to snarl and bite.

Mrs Elliot's eyes had drifted out of focus and she was swaying in her seat.

Jamie looked up when she heard a key in the front door. Tom. At last.

There were voices in the doorway. Then she heard Tom asking Vuyiswa to keep Ben with her in the kitchen. She couldn't blame him for wanting to keep his son and his stepmother as far away from each other as possible.

When Tom came through to the sitting room, he showed no surprise at seeing Jamie. Instead he crossed over to his step-mother and smiled at her.

"If you've finished your tea, I'll run you home, Mum. You don't want to miss dinner. They're having your favourite tonight – lamb chops."

"Oh, that does sound good," she replied. Then she stood up and went with him.

"I'll be back in fifteen minutes," Tom said over his shoulder to Jamie. "Maybe a little more if the traffic is bad. Don't go away before I get back."

. . . .

26

Surreal day. First a face-to-face encounter with my stalker in the yoghurt aisle. Then a long chat with someone suffering from Alzheimer's. On the bright side, I'm a lot closer to understanding why Tom has so many issues with step-families. Why did no one tell us that growing up would be so damn complicated? Please can I go back to a world where my biggest problem was algebra homework?

Ella Burchell All I got from that was "blah blah face-to-face encounter with stalker blah blah". For goodness' sake, are you okay? Don't force me to call Mom to check up on you!

Jamie Burchell I'm okay! (DON'T call Mom). Obviously I'm okay – I'm posting on Facebook, aren't I? Or did you think I was updating my status from my place of captivity??

Sheryl Witbooi And still she doesn't tell us what happened with the stalker…

Pumla Maseko Yes, tell us about the stalker. We promise to start caring about Tom's family issues afterwards.

Jamie Burchell Okay, but it wasn't really that big a deal. I was in the Spar doing my weekly shop, and I kept getting this creepy feeling that someone was watching me. So naturally I started tweeting about it.

Zanele Motsoepeng Naturally…

Ella Burchell As you do…

Jamie Burchell Then I noticed that this skinny guy WAS actually following me, so

I started getting really freaked out. I was just thinking about leaving my trolley and making a run for it when he spoke to me.

Pumla Maseko What? What did he say?

Jamie Burchell He wanted me to give him money for bus fare to East London. And just then another guy pushed past me. I didn't notice much about him except how sweaty he smelled.

Sheryl Witbooi Annnnnd? Stop keeping us in suspense. This isn't a story you're serialising on your blog, for pity's sake.

Jamie Burchell Then I got a tweet from the stalker (screen name – @ foullywooingwon) and he told me he was the sweaty guy who pushed past, not the other guy at all! And then I left the grocery store. End of scary story.

Sheryl Witbooi Hmmm. Okay. Good enough. Now tell us about Tom's family issues.

Jamie Burchell That's not my story to tell. Let's just say he has some really good reasons for mistrusting the step-parent relationship.

Sheryl Witbooi It's hard to put down the baggage from your past, especially when you're carrying a 16-piece matched set with personalised monogramming. But we can't let the past make our decisions for us. Sometimes you have to trust that things will work out okay. You have to take that leap of faith, and not ask to see the no-escape-clause guarantee.

Liezel Lamprecht Wow. That was a lot of metaphors for one comment, Sheryl. You dont want to get them all mixed now.

Sheryl Witbooi Oh, piss off, Liezel.

Jamie put down her phone, grinning, as Tom arrived back at the house.

He took Silver out and fed her first. Then he walked into the living room and sank into the armchair recently vacated by his step-mother. He sighed and rubbed his eyes.

"Something happened. It's all over your face. What was it?"

Jamie told him.

He listened the way he always listened, with total concentration, his eyes fixed on her face. When she was finished, he took a moment to process the story.

"Okay," he said. "Can you really not remember anything about the sweaty guy?"

"Not a single thing."

"That can't be true, Jamie. You must have formed some impression of his height, for example. I mean, the guy passed so close he actually touched you. Was he much taller than you? About the same size? A bit shorter?"

When he put it like that, she realised she did remember a few things. "I'd say he was about the same height as me. And he was definitely Caucasian."

"Good. Was he bald? Did he have a full head of hair? Or was he wearing a cap, perhaps?"

"I think his hair was ... sort of wispy, maybe. Male-pattern baldness. Not much left on the top, you know. And fair, I think. Definitely not dark."

"Extremely fat? Extremely thin? Or medium?"

"Medium. And sort of soft around the middle. I got the impression he was going to seed a bit. Early middle age, perhaps."

"So late-thirties, early-forties?"

"Maybe even mid-thirties, but definitely paunchy."

"Excellent. You're doing great."

Jamie huffed with frustration. "Tom, I've just described half the white male population of Johannesburg."

"When you think of that moment when he touched you, what's the one thing you remember most clearly?"

"My own fear. My fear of the other guy who I thought was him."

Tom reached out to touch her arm.

"Besides your own fear," he said. "Close your eyes and think back to that moment of contact – that instant when he brushed past you. What is the one thing you remember most clearly?"

Jamie closed her eyes and put herself back in the supermarket. She could taste her own anxiety, her conviction that the man who had accosted her was her stalker. Then the unexpected bump from behind. The sudden incursion of a new stranger into her life. The muttered apology as he forced his way between them.

Her eyes opened. "His smell."

"Yes, you said he was sweating."

Jamie nodded. "But he didn't have the kind of smell that comes from poor hygiene. It was recent sweat. I immediately thought of the gym when I smelled it. It was the smell of men who've been exercising a lot and sweating."

"Right."

"And the thing is … I've smelled him before. I've just realised that. Twice before. Once when he came into the restaurant for lunch and I served him. And another time when he was getting a takeaway. I don't exactly remember how long ago, but it was definitely him."

"Because of the smell?"

"Not just the smell. He was wet with sweat. I'm talking big wet patches under both arms, a shiny, damp face, and practically a lake in the small of his back." Jamie closed her eyes again. "He keeps changing his appearance. Little details that make him look like a different person – coloured contact lenses, a wig, a beard. That kind of thing. But it's definitely him."

"You're sure?"

"Yes. Yes, I'm sure."

"In that case he might have some kind of disorder. A hyper-sweating disorder. We could probably google it."

"All right, but…"

As Jamie was about to speak, two things happened. Vuyiswa brought Ben into the room to tell Tom she was going off for the day.

257

And Tom's phone started to ring.

"Dammit." He glanced at the screen. "It's the conference call I've been waiting for all day."

"You want me to stay?" Vuyiswa sounded obliging but not enthusiastic.

"No, no. You go." Tom touched her shoulder. "I know you want to do homework with Thato before suppertime."

"I'll watch Ben," Jamie said.

Tom weighed up his options. Conduct an overseas conference call with a toddler attached to his leg, or hand said toddler over to Jamie.

"Thanks," he said. "I owe you." And he caught the phone on its sixth ring. "Maxwell! Good to hear from you. Yes, I'm all set."

As Tom went into his study, Ben let out a loud wail and tried to run after him.

"Dadaaaaaaa!" Anyone would think Tom were being dragged off to the guillotine.

"Dada's just talking on the phone right now, Bennie," Jamie explained, bending down to give him a hug. "But I'm here to visit you! Isn't that cool? Mima's here. Shall we read a story?"

"No story!" Ben yelled. "Want Dada."

He slipped out of Jamie's grasp and made for the study door with amazing speed. Jamie caught up with him just as he was about to plough into the middle of Tom's conference call.

As she bore him off to the kitchen, he began to shriek – an angry, ear-splitting sound that rattled Jamie to her very core. Trying to think through that noise was impossible. What did he want? What did he need? A bottle? No, Tom was trying to get him off bottles. Supper? It was only half-past four. A bath? Tom liked to bath him after supper. What the heck did you do with a furious, over-tired toddler when it was too late for a nap, but too early for bedtime? Too late for a snack, but too early for suppertime?

Maybe it was his nappy? No, that felt fine. *What did the child want?*

Okay, time for some distraction. She'd watched *Supernanny*. She'd picked up enough to get by.

So what would Supernanny do? Recommend a timeout, probably. Yeah, right. Good luck getting a furious, screaming, way-beyond-reason toddler to sit on a step for two minutes.

Then Jamie remembered something her mother used to do for her and her sisters when they were very young. Holding Ben's kicking and screaming little body against her side, she opened the cupboard under the kitchen sink and took out a bottle of washing-up liquid. She squirted a liberal amount into the sink and added some water. Then she plunged her hand into the soapy mixture, and pulled it out with her forefinger and thumb curled and touching to form an O shape.

She blew on the thin skin of soap mixture suspended in the O. A wobbly bubble formed and floated down to the floor, where it popped.

Jamie put her hand back in the sink and repeated the procedure. The volume of Ben's screams seemed to decrease as he watched the second bubble float through the air. By the third bubble, the screams had stopped and he was watching intently.

"Do you want to catch the bubbles, Ben?" she said. "Do you want to pop them in your hands?"

Ben nodded and kicked to get down. She blew him another bubble and he toddled after it, laughing when he managed to pop it before it touched the ground. Then they were off, Jamie blowing bubbles, Ben popping them as fast as he could, and both of them laughing their heads off.

When Ben got bored with the game, Jamie offered to play blocks with him. He agreed at once. She got down his bucket of Lego and started fitting them together on the rug in the sitting room. He sat beside her and copied her. In a moment, Silver had joined them on the floor.

As Ben found his rhythm, Jamie's hands stilled. It scared her how completely she'd fallen in love with this child. It was like having all your defences ripped away, leaving you naked and vulnerable to the world. You wore your heart on the outside of your body.

He wasn't hers to love. She had no right to feel like this. He was somebody else's son. But he didn't feel like somebody else's. He felt like hers. And the thought of losing him made her want to panic.

Love at first sight was a real thing, she knew that now. She'd fallen in love with Ben the moment she'd laid eyes on him. With his father it had taken a little longer, but she'd got there in the end. She could admit to herself that she was in love with Tom. It wasn't a good feeling. She'd thought it would feel great to fall in love. Instead, it was terrifying. If this didn't work out, she didn't think she'd find so much rightness with anyone else.

No wonder she felt queasy every time she thought about the Elliots, father and son. It was almost a relief having a stalker to worry about.

A movement behind her made her look up. Tom was standing in the doorway watching them. She smiled at him. "Is your call over?"

"Yes, it didn't take long. What did you do to head off the tantrum? I could hear him through two closed doors. I'm pretty sure they could hear him in the States."

"I distracted him by blowing some bubbles."

"Nice work! Thanks."

"Sure."

Tom sat down on the rug and hauled Ben onto his lap, where he continued to play with his blocks. "So … uh … you and my step-mother, huh?"

"Yes. We had quite a conversation. She doesn't have much of a filter any more, does she?"

Tom pulled a face. "Not much, no. Did she talk about what a pest I was as a child, and how awful the short guy here is?" He gave Ben a squeeze.

"Pretty much, yes." She chose her words carefully. "It must be hard to listen to that now, and even harder when you were a little boy growing up."

Tom handed Ben another block. "Yeah, well. I'm sure I was a trial to her too. I wasn't easy to live with those first few months when she moved in with us."

"You were missing your mom."

"I sure was."

"Step-families are hard," Jamie said. "I understand that. I really do."

"I'm sorry, but with respect, I don't see how you can. You've got a fantastic nuclear family that loves and accepts you. They aren't going to get bored with you or make you feel like an interloper."

"I don't think it always has to be like that."

"Nightmare step-families are a cultural archetype. Look at Cinderella. Look at Hansel and Gretel."

Jamie watched Ben jump off his father's lap and dash across the room to pick up a yellow block that had rolled away. Then he hurled himself back into Tom's lap.

"Those stories often feature a weak or absent father figure," she said. "He lets the evil step-mother do what she likes for the sake of peace. Would you be that spineless father, Tom?"

"No, of course not, but..."

Jamie steamrollered on. "And what about your own father? Was he a bit lacking in the spine department?"

"No, of course he...." Tom broke off and frowned. "Okay ... maybe a little."

She hadn't expected him to agree. "In what way?"

"He knew my step-mother didn't love me. He even knew that she resented me. But he closed his eyes to it because he was so relieved to have a woman running the house again. My dad wasn't wired for domesticity." He shook his head. "No. That's not true. He chose not to be competent at it. When my mom died, he was devastated, yes, but I have to admit it was also very inconvenient for him."

Jamie edged closer until their knees touched.

"But that's not you, is it?" she said. "The majority of Ben's day-to-day care falls on you. You're a hands-on parent."

"And I want it to stay that way. But when I have you here helping me, there's a part of me that really enjoys it – that wants to share the burden with you. That's the part I'm scared of. That it's my father in me, wanting to pass the buck."

"You're not your father, Tom. It's not natural to raise a child completely alone. It's normal to want to share the burdens, because then you share the joys, too. Do you really want Ben to have only one person in his life who cares for him?"

"I don't want to let my own selfish desires land him in a situation that will make him miserable."

"What desires?" Jamie asked in frustration. "What selfishness?"

"You!" he said. "You, okay? I've fallen in love with you. And it scares the hell out of me."

27

Jamie had always imagined that when a man said he loved her, it would be an iconic, softly lit moment, possibly with appropriate background music.

She never guessed he would be glaring at her over the head of a toddler, looking as if he hated her.

The silence stretched on.

"I don't know what to say," Jamie said at last. "It feels as if 'I'm sorry' might be most appropriate. I'm sorry for wantonly and with malice aforethought causing you to fall in love with me."

Tom grinned. "You should apologise, you black magic woman. Look what you've gone and done."

"You're not as pure as the driven snow yourself. I've fallen in love with you too, so the hex goes both ways. Now what are we going to do about it?"

Before Tom could answer, Ben jumped to his feet and tugged at his father's hand.

"Hungwy!" he said. "Supper."

Tom glanced at his watch and groaned. "It's nearly six o'clock. No wonder you're hungry, Bennie."

Jamie got to her feet as well. "Then let's get supper into gear."

"I was going to bake fish fingers and courgette pieces. Then I got distracted."

"I can scramble some eggs and cut up an apple in five minutes flat. How does that sound?"

"Perfect, thanks."

They went into the kitchen and Jamie got busy with a frying pan. She tried to involve Ben in the process to take his mind off his empty tummy. Tom stood watching them.

"I can hear you thinking from over here," Jamie said. "There's practically smoke coming out of your ears."

"Is that so? And what am I thinking?"

"That I'm helping you out here, which is great, but you should really being doing it all yourself and never accept any help from anyone ever, because being a good father equals being a lone warrior in the battlefield of parenthood."

Tom pulled a wry face. "It sounds silly when you say it like that."

"Something to think about."

———————

FROM JAMIE BURCHELL'S TWITTER FEED:

Jamie Burchell @jamieburchell
He loves me! He really loves me. He said so last night! #hotneighbourguy

Bronwyn Jones @redhighheels
@jamieburchell Oooh! *shiver* That is so delicious. I remember the first time my hubby said those words. You never forget it.

Jamie Burchell @jamieburchell
@redhighheels I know, right? Best feeling in the world. And I said it back! So it's all puppies and rainbows today.

Cyril Attlee @inthemiddlecyril
@jamieburchell Oh, really? He loves you, does he? Well, he's got a funny way of showing it. Trying to push you out of his life…

Jamie Burchell @jamieburchell
@inthemiddlecyril I know, I know. But it's understandable. He's trying to protect his son.

Nikki Levy @nixlevy
@jamieburchell Really happy for you, hun! So what's the situation now? Is he getting over his stress about letting you near the little boy?

Yaseen Mufar @Muslimah7
@jamieburchell @nixlevy That's exactly what I was wondering! Have you got your all-access pass to the cute kid now?

Jamie Burchell @jamieburchell
@Muslimah7 @nixlevy Ha! Don't get carried away, ladies. Cute kid is still sensitive territory. But hopefully we're making progress.

Cyril Attlee @inthemiddlecyril
@jamieburchell You can't have love without trust. If he doesn't trust you around his son, he doesn't really love you.

Jamie Burchell @jamieburchell
@inthemiddlecyril Always the little ray of sunshine, right Cyril? ☹

Cyril Attlee @inthemiddlecyril
@jamieburchell Just being realistic!

Jamie kept checking her Twitter feed as the morning wore on. As the hours passed with no sign of her stalker joining the conversation, she became more cheerful.

Maybe he was getting bored with her.

The morning shift at Delucia's was as hectic as ever. Pumla had a 9.30am appointment at the obstetrician, and had asked Jamie to stand in for her. She'd be getting the last of her blood tests back, and the doctor would do a long diagnostic scan to make sure both babies were developing properly.

Dumisani had insisted on driving Pumla there and being present for the whole thing. He'd had to take the morning off work to swing it. Apparently a 9.30am appointment at the obstetrician could mean being seen any time up until 9.30 the next morning. Baby doctors were notoriously at the mercy of labouring mothers and babies who decided to put in an appearance at inopportune times.

Jamie hoped she wouldn't have to take the lunch shift alone too. Okay, she wasn't really alone, strictly speaking. Nomsa could switch from pastry chef to front-of-house hostess in the blink of an eye, but she couldn't do both at the same time.

Normally, the pastries for the day were ready by now. But the weather had unexpectedly turned chilly. Sweltering summer days had given way to grey skies and a drizzly rain that was far more suited to Cape Town than Johannesburg. When people went through the working day shivering, their thoughts turned to doughnuts, Danishes, *pains au chocolat*, Florentines and custard slices, and a long coffee to go with their treat of choice.

There'd been a run on baked goods all morning, and it was showing no sign of abating. A frisky wind had joined the drizzle, and it was blowing customers into Delucia's warm, fragrant interior like autumn leaves.

"Listen," Jamie said to Nomsa as the breakfast crowd thinned out. "I can manage on my own out here. You go back and take over the baking. That last batch of lamingtons came out a little wonky. Not that the starving hordes seemed to notice. But you'd better go in and supervise."

Nomsa nodded and stripped off her front-of-house apron, tossing it onto a hook. She tied on her considerably less smart baking apron and strode into the kitchen where she could be heard telling some unseen person to stop being so stingy with the chocolate paste.

As more tables finished up, Jamie took advantage of the lull to log onto Pumla's Facebook page in the hope that she was updating from the waiting room. Pumla was a Facebook fan through and through. It was her social media Mecca – she didn't bother with any other platforms.

FROM PUMLA MASEKO'S FACEBOOK PAGE:

Fuck, I'm scared. I'm sitting here googling twin births and freaking myself out.

266

Apparently in some cases one of the twins gets "reabsorbed" and suddenly you have only one baby, not two. Or they don't separate properly and you end up with conjoined twins. Or the birth goes wrong and one of the babies doesn't make it. I've never been so scared in my life. I'm terrified the doctor's going to put that scanner on my tummy and tell me there's only one baby in there.

Nonna Mzambo But, babes. You were devastated when u heard u were havin 2. Wouldn't it be convenient for 1 to go away?

Victoria Mooki Nonna, you've obviously never been pregnant. Convenience has nothing to do with it. You fall in love with those babies you're carrying whether there's one or two or three of them.

Pumla Maseko Yes, exactly. And I know I'm going to be all, like, "What did I do wrong? What did I do to hurt my baby? Why am I such a bad mother?"

Sizwe Dhlomo Girl, you seriously need to calm down. First of all, it hasn't happened yet. And second of all, if anything does happen it's not your fault. Fate's a bitch and you can't blame yourself for the stuff that goes on.

Nala Ahmed As a twin mom myself, I know exactly how you feel. Twin pregnancies ARE more high risk than singleton pregnancies. I know I didn't relax ONCE in nearly 9 months. I just kept picturing the worst. But I also know all that worry didn't help the babies one bit, and I wish I'd let myself enjoy the pregnancy more.

Sizwe Dhlomo Nala hit the nail on the head. Relax and enjoy it.

Pumla Maseko I know you're both right. And I promise I'm going to try, as long as this scan is okay. I just can't shake the feeling something horrible is going to happen.

Jamie put down her phone and shivered. She kept seeing a pregnant doll with a knife plunged into its belly.

She checked the time of Pumla's last post – 10.37. It was 11.05 now.

So either Pumla had got bored with Facebooking or her appointment had finally been called. Maybe she was being scanned right now and finding out that everything was fine with both babies. Jamie hoped so with all her heart.

The man clucked his tongue.

It shouldn't be this easy to get into a private hospital. A single man on his own should really not be allowed to wonder about an obstetrician's waiting room unchallenged.

He picked up a leaflet on breastfeeding and stared at the picture on the front. It showed a young mother looking down at her feeding infant with a wistful smile on her face. The baby seemed to be asleep, its mouth grotesquely stuffed full of breast. He looked at it a bit longer, wondering if he would start to feel aroused.

No. That woman was too fat. Anyone who had a swollen, bulbous breast like that must be too fat. He liked women to be slender, like Jamie. Her breasts were neat and high and on the small side.

He glanced up and caught the eye of one of the receptionists. Her expression was merely curious, but he knew it could turn suspicious at any moment. Saliva gushed into his mouth and sweat soaked his armpits. He replaced the pamphlet on its rack, holding it with two hands so any shaking would be less noticeable.

Then he sat back down in one of the hard armchairs. The receptionist had already looked away, distracted by a patient handing her a urine sample in a bottle. This place was disgusting. It was impossible for him to feel at ease here. All these women with their distended bellies and waddling walks. Their thick wrists and fat ankles. It made him want to throw up.

How much longer could this possibly take?

The only reason he'd gone unnoticed until now was because there were two obstetricians sharing the same waiting room. Dr Patel and Dr Brown. They had two separate reception desks, which were both very busy. Dr Patel's staff thought he was waiting for Dr Brown, and Dr Brown's staff thought he was waiting for Dr Patel. Or rather, they thought he was waiting for his wife to emerge.

But it wouldn't take long for someone to notice that he wasn't waiting for anyone. He stood up and put his jacket back on. It made him sweat worse, but at least it covered the stains on his shirt.

He was just about to sit down again when Jamie's black friend came out of Dr Patel's rooms with her boyfriend, or whatever he was.

A slim Indian woman was showing them out. Probably a nurse or something.

"Please don't worry any more," the woman said. "Everything really is fine."

Jamie's black friend nodded tearfully, and her boyfriend said, "Thank you, Dr Patel. We'll see you next month."

The man's head spun. Dr Patel? That slender woman? What an unfeminine profession. Thank goodness Jamie didn't do anything so disgusting with her time. Serving food was a good decent occupation for a woman.

They went to the counter to pay and to make their next appointment. He watched them over the cover of a magazine. When they turned to leave, he put his magazine down and stood up. He gave them a ten-second head start and then followed them.

"What's wrong?" Pumla frowned at Dumisani as he looked over his shoulder for the third time. "What do you keep looking at?"

"I'm not sure."

"Well, stop it. It's annoying."

When he swung his head around for the fourth time, Pumla's blood started to sizzle. "Okay, now you're just trying to irritate me. Let's annoy pregnant woman today. What fun."

Dumisani gave her the patient look he used every time her hormones surged to the surface. It was accompanied by the raised right eyebrow that made him look like a headmaster.

Pumla rubbed her hand over the bulge in her tummy and seethed.

"Listen," said Dumisani. "Don't look now, but there's a white guy in a brown jacket who's been following us ever since we left Dr Patel's waiting room."

Pumla swung around to look.

Dumisani sighed. "I said, don't look now."

"Okay, I can see him," she said. "But so what? This is the way to the parking lot. Most people would walk this way."

"I know. I was just thinking, after what Jamie told you about her stalker..."

"Oh, please. Jemima Burchell is a fruitcake. With added nuts. Ooh, nuts! I could do with some nuts. Those salty mixed nuts from Woolies in the big tub. Can we stop at the shops on the way back?"

"You're not supposed to eat nuts, remember? It increases the babies' chances of developing allergies."

"Oh, yeah." Her face fell. "But I can have trail mix, can't I? A nice bag of salty trail mix."

"Trail mix is fine."

"Let's see..." Jamie stroked her chin. "She saunters in here just before midday, stuffing her face with trail mix. I'm going to go out on a limb and guess that everything was fine at the doctor's office."

Pumla grinned with her mouth full and nodded.

"Have you never heard of updating your Facebook status to let everyone know you're all right?"

Pumla chewed and swallowed. "Oh, don't fuss, Mom. Everything's fine. The blood tests were perfect. The nuchal layer looks good on both babies. She couldn't tell the sex yet, but maybe next month. The spines are fine. All the organs are where they should be and looking normal." She shot her fists up into the air like a boxer and grinned. "If I were allowed to drink, I'd crack open a bottle of that

Möet we've got in the back."

"Better not," said Jamie and Dumisani together.

"I know, I know. I'm not an idiot."

"You go and put your feet up with a cup of tea for fifteen minutes," Jamie said, steering her to the back office. "Nomsa and I can handle it a bit longer."

With Pumla out the way, Jamie turned to Dumisani. "Is everything really okay?"

He smiled. "It's fine. We found out that the babies are fraternal, not identical, so there's even a chance we might have one of each, which would be awesome. Pumla called her mom from the car. You could probably hear the screams of joy all the way over here. Then her aunts got on the line and I kind of tuned them out."

"That's great. I know how much it means to her to have made her mom and aunts so proud. But are you sure nobody accosted you? Nobody tried to talk to you?"

"No, nothing like that."

Dumisani paused, and Jamie pounced on his hesitation. "Something happened, didn't it? Tell me."

"It wasn't exactly something that happened. There was this guy sitting in the waiting room while we were there, and when we got up to go to the car, so did he. It was really nothing," he added when Jamie looked dubious.

"Was he kind of paunchy with blondish, receding hair?"

"Not really. I couldn't see his body because he was wearing a big, bulky jacket. But he had a full head of brown hair."

"And sweaty? Was he all sweaty and shiny-looking?"

"I didn't get close enough to see, sorry."

Jamie had to break off the conversation to deal with an influx of early lunchtime customers.

"I'll be back as soon as I can."

She ferried so many trays of drinks and platters of bread back and forth that she half expected Dumisani to be gone before she could take a breath again. The miniature loaves of bread were chilli and red pepper, sesame sourdough, and three-cheeses with parsley today. The sesame sourdough was a new recipe she'd developed herself, and judging by how fast it was disappearing, she had a new hit on her hands.

When she looked around for Dumisani, she saw that he had parked himself at one of the tables for two.

"It's lunchtime," he said as she came up with her notepad. "I might as well eat. And if you don't bring me a plate of that bread, I will break down and cry."

"With a Miller's?" she asked, knowing his taste in beer.

"Uh, better not. I'm trying not to drink around Pumla. It doesn't seem fair seeing as she's not allowed to. Just a Coke, thanks."

Jamie snapped her notepad shut and stared at him. "How did you get to be such a sweetie? And what did Pumla ever do to deserve you?"

He looked down at the table. "She doesn't even want me."

"She'll come round if she knows what's good for her."

Jamie left to put in his request for a Coke, and to pick up the first of her lunch orders. She saw that Pumla was back in the swing of things. She was behind the coffee counter, doing a brisk business in lunchtime takeaways. Today's special of a spiced chicken, feta and avo ciabatta with a fruit smoothie was moving briskly.

"I don't know what to think about your guy in the jacket," she told Dumisani as she brought him his Coke and bread. "It doesn't sound like the person I met in the Spar, but he's a bit of a chameleon. He makes small changes to his appearance."

"Could he be in here right now?"

Dumisani's question threw Jamie off balance. She scanned the room, looking at all the men of the right age and build. Anxiety forced its way up into her throat, and she swallowed it down. There was nothing he could do to her here, on her own turf, in front of a crowd of people. And there was nothing he could do to Pumla.

Then Jamie noticed a man at the takeaway counter holding his hand out to Pumla. She dropped the Coke she was pouring for

Dumisani and rushed across the room. Now the man was leaning across the counter, reaching for Pumla.

"What's going on here?"

Pumla and the man both jerked back at the snap in her tone. She saw he had a credit card in his outstretched hand.

The smile Pumla gave Jamie was laced with warning. "This gentleman is just paying for his order, Jamie. Do you need me for something?"

Jamie backed away. "No, nothing. Sorry to barge in like that. Enjoy your lunch, sir."

"What the heck was that?" Pumla asked when he'd left.

"Paranoia. For a second, I thought it was my stalker. "

Pumla shook her head. "Whatever grip you once had, you are losing it fast. You know that guy. He comes in here at least twice a month. I think he works in that insurance office around the corner."

Jamie winced. "I know, I know. I recognised him as soon as he turned around. But you aren't the one who found a pregnant doll tied to her gate. So pardon me for being a little twitchy."

28

Stocktaking this evening with **Pumla Maseko**. Officially my least favourite job in the world. Times like this, I wish I weren't a grown-up and didn't have to care how many bottles of red passata sauce we own, and whether our loss-and-breakages inventory record ties up with the actual number of wineglasses we have in the cupboard. (Hint – it never does.) And what's the deal with teaspoons? Do they go to the same secret hiding place as socks?

Clinton Smith OMG, I used to work in restaurants. The way people just help themselves to serviettes and salt shakers! This one woman once loaded her handbag so full that the strap snapped on the way out and all these ashtrays came bouncing out.

Zanele Motsoepeng LOL @ Clint! When I used to work as a waitress, my granny made me steal her packs of butter and sugar every night. One night I brought her home Flora and she was, like, "No, Zanele, I want real butter." That was three years ago and she still brings out the little packets of sugar whenever we visit. :)

Jamie Burchell Next time your granny comes to Delucia's I am totally frisking her on the way out! ;)

Ella Burchell How's it going with you and Hot Neighbour? Are you seeing him tonight?

Jamie Burchell Depends how long this takes. Pumla and I will probably grab something to eat here. There's nothing like stocktaking to sap your strength.

Amanda Stanislau Speaking of Hot Neighbour Guy. When is he ever going to join Facebook so we can get to know him?

Jamie Burchell Never. He doesn't really approve of social media.

This is cruelty to pregnant women. Stocktaking night. I've already been on my feet all day. I think **Jamie Burchell** should take pity on me and let me go home now. This can't be good for the babies.

Jamie Burchell Whine, whine, whine! I asked if you would trust anyone else to do the stocktake with me and you said NO!

Dumisani Keorepetse Don't go climbing on any chairs or stepladders, see? That really would be bad for the babies. Not to mention for you.

Pumla Maseko Don't worry, daddy. I've got this.

Dumisani Keorepetse We're not going to call each other "mommy" and "daddy" after the babies are born, are we? I have friends who do that and it makes me a little nauseous.

Pumla Maseko After the babies come, you'll be too busy with your sidechick to worry about me and the kids.

Jamie recorded the number of dinner forks on her tablet computer and immediately backed up. The thought of somehow losing the spreadsheet and having to start this process all over again was too hideous to contemplate.

"We need to order more dishwasher salt," Pumla called from the scullery.

"I thought we were going to start using that all-in-one dishwashing powder that comes with the rinse aid and salt already added," Jamie shouted back.

"We did, but I didn't like what it was doing to the glasses. They were coming out all streaky. So we went back to the old way."

Jamie swiped to the New Orders screen and added dishwasher salt. "Listen, I'm going to the front to count linens. Don't climb on any chairs while I'm gone. If you need something, you call me to come and get it for you, okay? I don't want Dumisani coming after me with a horsewhip."

Pumla made a grunting noise that may or may not have signified assent.

Jamie went through to the restaurant and knelt in front of the linen cupboard. It always amazed her how much stuff they had in there. White tablecloths, green overlays for summer, purple overlays for winter, green and purple striped napkins. Millions of dishcloths – many of which were so holey they should be retired. Aprons – both the smart kind for front-of-house work, and the more scruffy kind for kitchen work. Lint-free cloths for wiping glasses. General cloths for mopping spills and wiping up blood, both of which happened more frequently than people thought.

She stood up and stretched her arms over her head, yawning.

It was a lovely, quiet evening. In the wash of light from the other shops, Jamie saw the shift manager from the Spar roll down the metal blind over the double doors and lock up. He waved as he walked past, and she waved back. Then the freelance security guard who looked after cars in the little parking lot waved to Jamie too, indicating that he was knocking off for the day.

It was only ten past seven, but already almost dark. While it might still feel like high summer, Jamie knew the sun was in retreat, heading to the northern hemisphere to herald spring over there. But that didn't stop it from being a warm, close, late-February evening. Rather than run the aircon, Jamie and Pumla had the front door wide open and a window in the kitchen open too, to create a through-draft.

They were perfectly safe, Jamie reminded herself. The security gate was firmly locked, and all the windows had steel bars on them. Not to mention the panic buttons under the counter by the till and above the worktop in the kitchen. Those rang straight through to the private security company.

Jamie gazed across the road to where the Earl & Badger was clearly hopping, its parking lot comfortingly full. It was live-music night and she could hear faint strains of whatever easy-listening band the Nikolaides brothers had hired for the evening. Perhaps she should drop in there for a drink after stocktaking. She would talk to Pumla into it.

No, wait. Pumla wasn't drinking at the moment, and would probably just want to go home and put her feet up.

Well, maybe she could text Tom to meet her there and they could split a bottle of wine.

Then she remembered Ben. Tom could hardly swan out of the house for a drink, leaving his son sleeping alone upstairs.

For a moment, Jamie felt a pang for the carefree days of her early twenties when friends and boyfriends were always available for spontaneous nights out. Now they were doing grown-up things like having babies and raising toddlers.

Then she cheered up. She'd buy a bottle of red wine from their own supply here and take it over to Tom's with a tub of that chocolate mousse they'd been serving at lunch. They'd make their own romantic evening at his place. Grown-up didn't have to equal boring.

Smiling to herself, she turned back to the linen cupboard and pulled out all the citronella candles.

She didn't turn her head again until she heard the faint *snik* of the security gate clicking open.

"Hello, Jamie."

It was a man she didn't recognise. He was standing inside the doorway, closing the security gate and locking the front door behind him in an unhurried manner.

"Who are you?" Jamie asked. "How did you get in? This restaurant is closed."

He smiled at her. "I tampered with the slam-lock mechanism on your gate earlier. It appeared to close but would give way to a firm push. But don't worry, it's okay now. We're locked in tight as can be."

"Get out," she demanded. "This is private property."

Now he was going from window to window and lowering the blinds so that no one from the outside could see in. "I know you're closed. It's stocktaking night, isn't it? Nice of you to let your Facebook friends know that you girls would be alone here this evening."

Jamie's temporary paralysis left her, and she ran to the till where she fumbled for the panic button under the counter. Relief flooded her as she found it – round and reassuringly large. She stabbed at it several times, feeling the answering vibration in her fingertip that told her it was working properly. The security company would respond within minutes. Their headquarters were only a few blocks away.

"I do hope you're not wasting your time with the panic button," said that placid voice. "You sent an email to the security company earlier today letting them know that there would be a technician upgrading your system this evening, so they should ignore all alerts until tomorrow morning. Your password is 'pomegranate', isn't it? So appropriate for a restaurant owner. But you really shouldn't use the same password for everything. It makes keystroke logging almost ridiculously easy."

Jamie's head started to pound. What did he want? What was he going to do to them? He didn't look very strong. Perhaps they could overpower him.

No. It was better if Pumla just stayed out of sight.

"Jamie? Who are you talking to?"

Jamie shut her eyes in despair as Pumla emerged from the kitchen holding a notepad and a feather duster.

"Welcome, Pumla, welcome!" said the man, taking a handgun out of his pocket. "How wonderful for us all to be together like this."

Pumla gasped when she saw the gun. "Jamie...?"

The man waved her over to stand with Jamie. "There now. Isn't this nice?"

Jamie heard Pumla swallow. "Okay, you want the money, don't you? We don't keep much on the premises. It's basically just the day's

278

take and a small cash float. You can have it all. I'll open the safe for you. And then there's the computers and stuff. We'll show you where everything is. You can be in and out of here in five minutes."

Jamie couldn't help admiring her calm. From where she was standing, she could see Pumla's hand gripping the feather duster so hard her knuckles stood out like pearls, but otherwise her manner didn't change.

The man laughed, clearly delighted. "What a cool customer you are. No, no. I'm not here to rob you, although that cash float does sound rather good. We'll talk about that later. Hasn't Jamie told you about me? I've been following her on Facebook and Twitter for ages. And I'm ever such an avid reader of her blog. In fact, you might say I'm her biggest fan."

He stepped closer and Jamie caught his smell. The whiff of recent sweat made her stomach contract.

"You killed that old dog," she said. "That harmless old dog. That was an evil thing to do."

"Oh, please." The man rolled his eyes. "You eat meat, don't you? What's the difference between me killing that half-blind old mutt, and a butcher killing a young steer in the prime of its life so you can enjoy a steak? That's the one thing I've found irritating about you, Jamie. Your lack of internal consistency and a coherent life philosophy. Now shut up a moment while I think."

Jamie and Pumla glanced at each other as he paced up and down. Jamie thought she could just about hold it together as long as she kept her eyes off the gun he was carrying. The sight of it turned her legs to water. Then she saw Pumla touch her stomach – a brief stroke of the bump – and her knees began to shake again. There were four lives at stake here, not two.

The man stopped pacing and swung around to face them. "Here's what we're going to do. You two are going to finish pulling down all the blinds. You're going to lock all the windows. You're going to do it together, and I'm going to come with you. Then you are both going to update your Facebook statuses to say that the stocktaking is taking longer than anticipated. We don't want anyone bothering us, do we?"

He waved the gun at them and they went from window to window making sure every catch was locked and every blind down. He tested the kitchen door and found it locked and bolted.

"Right. Now pass me your phone." He tapped Pumla on the arm with the barrel of his gun in a way that made Jamie's heart lurch. "You first."

She handed him her phone and he opened her Facebook account. Then he cocked his head at her. "Let's see ... what's your narrative style?"

> Jeez, this is taking forEVER! We'll be another few hours at least. No texts or calls please, we want to get this stupid stocktake done asap.

The man pressed "post" and watched the update appear in Pumla's timeline. His mouth stretched into a smile. What an unexpected thrill. He had no idea how powerful it would make him feel to post on someone else's behalf. His smile broadened when the "new message" light came on.

"Responses already!" His eyes lit up. "I had no idea what a popular girl you were."

> **Michael Blackthorn** I can drop by with some coffee if you like. Oh wait, you're already working in a coffee shop. Forget I spoke! LOL.

> **Nonna Mzambo** When I realise I've typed a stupid comment, I usually delete before posting, Michael. ;)

> **Sizwe Dhlomo** Guys, let's get off Pumla's timeline. She's trying to work here.

The man slipped Pumla's phone into his pocket and almost skipped over to Jamie, holding his hand out. "Now you!"

She passed him her phone. "You'd better let me type it, you know.

My writing style is unique. You won't get it right, and someone will suspect something."

"Right!" He scoffed. "So you can tip off one of your little friends."

"You can watch me while I type. And you can be the one to press 'post'."

He narrowed his eyes, watching her face. "Why do you want to do this? Why would you want to help me not make a mistake? It's not logical."

Jamie hesitated. "I don't want any of my friends barging in here. You've got a gun, and someone might get hurt. I think the three of us should be left alone to sort this out."

He stared at her a moment longer, and then handed back the phone. "I will watch you while you type. Make one wrong move and I will shoot you dead. No…" A new idea struck him. "I will shoot your friend in the stomach. Her babies will die, and so will she."

Jamie's fingers shook, but she stiffened them and started to type.

Will this stocktake ever be over?? I don't think theirs a more boring job in the world. Still a few more hour's to go. See you on the flip side, guys.

The man studied this update for a long time. "What does 'see you on the flip side' mean?" he asked.

"It just means that you'll see someone later."

He googled the phrase and saw that it did indeed mean what Jamie said. Then he pressed "post". It wasn't quite as satisfying as having composed the update himself, but at least he knew it wouldn't raise any alarms.

Jamie's phone joined Pumla's in his pocket, and he rubbed his hands together. "Time for a little bite to eat, I think. Will you girls have anything?"

Jamie and Pumla both shook their heads.

"I'm not hungry," Jamie said. Just the thought of food was enough to make her throat close.

"Me neither," said Pumla.

"Good, good! More for me then." He helped himself to a pile of pastries from the takeaway counter and started to eat them.

"That's one of the things that first attracted me to you, Jamie," he explained through a mouthful of croissant. "Your indifference to food. I hate to see a greedy woman. It's so unfeminine. You're wonderfully slim, Jamie. There's not a spare ounce on you anywhere." He seemed to think he'd been rude, because he added. "You're slim too, Pumla, but we mustn't forget you're pregnant, so you won't be for long. Pregnancy makes women fat."

His eyes were very light, Jamie realised when he looked up and caught her watching him. They were a grey so pale they were almost the colour of water. No wonder he wore coloured contact lenses all the time. Aside from making him look different, they would give him some protection from the light.

None of the hairstyles she'd seen on him up until now had been real. He was in fact completely bald. Anything nature hadn't got rid of he'd shaved off himself. She'd been right about his height and build. About five foot nine, and slightly paunchy. His face was thinner than she remembered, suggesting he might have been wearing cheek pads before.

The fact that he was letting them see how he really looked was not comforting. It suggested they would never be in a position to describe him. Possibly because they would both be too dead to talk.

Watching the man carefully, Jamie leaned towards Pumla and whispered, "Don't worry."

He looked up, but kept eating, so Pumla whispered back, "What do you mean 'don't worry'?"

"Someone is going to come looking for us. I put a clue in my Facebook update."

"He said he was going to shoot me in the stomach if you did that, Jamie!"

"He didn't pick it up. I knew he wouldn't."

"What was the clue?"

"I made two grammar mistakes in my update. Real howlers."

"So?"

"So, people who know me know I don't make grammar mistakes. Especially not misplaced apostrophes. Someone is going to realise I posted that under duress."

"That's your grand plan? That's supposed to make me feel better?"

"It's foolproof. Didn't you ever read the Famous Five books?"

Pumla took her eyes off the man and gave Jamie an incredulous look. "Do I look white to you? Do I look like I spent my childhood reading Enid fucking Blyton?"

"Anyway," Jamie went on. "This one character, George, she's the tomboy, see? She gets captured by a bad guy and he makes her write a note to her friends to trap them. But she signs it Georgina, instead of George. And Julian knows something is wrong because George hates to be called Georgina. So he makes a plan to rescue her."

There was a long silence.

"Right." Pumla nodded. "And you think your grammar Nazi friends are going to be all, 'Oh, my. A misplaced apostrophe. Poor, dear Jamie must have been kidnapped. Let's notify the authorities at once.'"

"If you've got a better idea, I'm listening."

"I'm working on it."

29

Tom closed Ben's bedroom door inch by silent inch until it finally clicked shut. Nothing woke that child faster than the sound of a door closing.

He'd gone back to sleep again after waking up barely an hour after Tom had put him down in the first place. It seemed to be mosquitoes that were bothering him tonight. Unfortunately, he'd made the connection between the whining noise he heard circling his bed at night, and the itchy bumps he found all over his legs and arms in the morning.

Now the merest hint of a mosquito in his room was enough to set him off yelling. Tom longed to shut his son's window at night, but then he woke up because he was too hot. Early tomorrow morning – the second the shops opened, in fact – Tom planned to be first in line to buy a fan. One of the parenting websites he frequented suggested a fan as the best way to discourage mosquitoes while still keeping a child cool in summer.

His breath caught as he heard a slight moan coming from Ben's room. He stood dead still in the passage, one foot raised on tiptoe.

All was quiet.

Relieved, he crept down the stairs and put his ear to the baby monitor to confirm that it was working properly. And speaking of work, he should probably spend the evening taking notes from the new book on cyber-policing he'd downloaded. But he really didn't feel like it. He wished Jamie would come over. He knew he'd be able to settle down to work if she were only sitting next to him, tapping away at her laptop, preparing her blog post for the next morning, or browsing through one of her many social media accounts.

It was ridiculous how much he missed her when she wasn't there.

Ben missed her too. He kept asking for her when she wasn't around. They were both becoming too dependent on her. It was time to claw back some of their self-reliance.

Tom opened the book on cyber-policing on his iPad and started skimming through it, but his concentration was lousy. Because Jamie wasn't answering her texts, he'd checked her Facebook page, so he knew that stocktaking was going on longer than expected. She must be really preoccupied, because she usually answered a text within minutes.

Tom thought he might pour himself a whiskey and take his iPad up to bed with him.

———

"What do you want with us?"

The man smiled, enjoying the note of panic in Pumla's voice. "Now that depends. At the moment, all I want is to chat to you. I feel as though I've got to know you both so well over the last few months. We have lots to talk about. And there are always points of clarification."

"Look," said Jamie. "You haven't done anything wrong yet. You can still walk away from this with no charges against you, no police coming after you…"

She broke off when he burst out laughing. "What's so funny?"

"The thought of the police coming after me. This is South Africa, Jamie. People get away with murder every day. The police will pretend to investigate for a while. And when the media interest dies down, they will quietly let it go."

"You're forgetting how double standards work in this country," Pumla said. "You come into the suburbs and kill a white girl and a middle-class black girl, and the police will be breathing down your neck until the day you die."

His sniggers deepened into chuckles. "You let me worry about that."

"Is that what you're going to do with us?" Jamie asked. "You're going to kill us?"

"You know…" He smiled at them. "I wasn't sure I could. I'm still not completely sure. I've never killed a person before. But if I do, would you like to know how I'm going to do it?"

His eyes, Jamie thought. His eyes are like blank, shallow pools of water. Nothing behind them.

"If I hadn't killed those animals to scare you, Jamie, I might never have known what it's like to open an abdomen with your knife and feel the guts spill into your hands. They don't die immediately. It can take minutes, but eventually you see the eyes go dull and you know they're gone. It's an intimate moment to share with another creature. I saved the rat for you. I left it alive so you could share that special moment with it. How you screamed when you found it, Jamie. I thought I'd crack a rib laughing."

"Sicko," Pumla whispered in Jamie's ear.

Jamie didn't dare nod. Her vision had gone grey around the edges, and there was a whining noise in her ears. She stumbled backwards towards a chair.

"So let's talk then," Pumla said, giving Jamie a chance to pull herself together. "Shall I make you some coffee?"

He started to say yes, until he caught the flicker in Pumla's eyes. "I'll watch while you make it. If you try slipping something into it, you're really going to annoy me."

As Pumla and the man went to the coffee machine, Jamie put her head between her knees and took deep breaths. It was nearly an hour since she'd posted that Facebook update. Nobody had come, nobody had called. She had to face the fact that nobody was going to. They were on their own. This wasn't a movie. There would be no eleventh-hour rescue.

Pumla's idea of tampering with his coffee was a good one, but he'd seen through it. Still, they were in a working restaurant with access to all kinds of sharp implements. If he wanted to talk, they'd talk. As long as they were talking, he wasn't thinking about gutting them like fish.

"Why me?" Jamie asked when he came back, carrying a mug of

coffee. "Why did you choose me? We'd never even met before."

The man settled himself on a chair opposite Jamie. He waved his gun barrel at Pumla, indicating that she should also sit down opposite him. He took a sip of his coffee. "Well … I'll tell you. You weren't actually my first choice. I tried other women before you." He made a little *moue* of regret with his mouth, and gave Jamie's hand a quick squeeze. She forced herself not to shudder or pull away. "The trouble with those other women was that they all turned out to be older or fatter than their photographs. They looked gorgeous online, but when I saw them in real life, I was always disappointed."

"How did you find them in real life?" Pumla asked.

He laughed. "It was too easy. It was literally no challenge at all. I simply waited for them to check into a local restaurant, and then I went to see how they looked. You can triangulate someone's physical location very precisely on Facebook. I didn't waste my time with women living outside this basic area."

Jamie sat forward as though riveted. "Where did you see me for the first time?"

"Right here! Right here in Delucia's. Honestly, Jamie, not only were you the most truthful woman I'd ever seen in terms of your appearance, but you were also the easiest to follow. You tweet, blog or Facebook every moment of your day. A photo of your street address is on Instagram. This restaurant has its very own Pinterest board. In fact, that was the only thing I didn't enjoy. You made it almost too easy to track you."

"But it was worth it, wasn't it?" Jamie smiled into those shallow-pool eyes. "I was worth every second."

"You were! Oh yes, you were. Lovely, slender Jamie. So coltish and delicate. You're a thoroughbred, all right. And you take such good care of yourself. Always exercising. Never overindulging. I love the way your waist looks small enough to fit into my hands."

"You don't mind if I eat something now?" Jamie asked, standing up.

He looked disappointed. "Really? You want to eat now?"

"It's after nine o'clock."

"Well, okay."

Jamie turned and stared at Pumla – a long, steady look. Pumla glanced up at her and then looked away. When Jamie continued to stare, she looked up again with a question in her eyes.

"Aren't you hungry, Pumla?"

Pumla was about to say she was feeling too tense to eat anything when she realised what Jamie was up to.

"I could eat," she agreed. "Yes, of course I could eat."

The two of them went to the bakery counter and piled plates high with pastries.

"What exactly is the plan here?" Pumla whispered. "We annoy the unstable maniac by stuffing our faces?"

"Maybe if he stops seeing us as perfect skinny angels, he'll let us go."

"And maybe he'll just kill us quicker."

"If you've got a better idea, I'm waiting to hear it."

"If I could just get my hands on something sharp or heavy…"

"I know. I was thinking exactly the same thing."

"What are you whispering about?" he demanded.

They split away from each other and brought their plates back to the table. Jamie looked at the beautifully made pastries, glistening with sugar and butter, and felt her stomach lurch. Her appetite was fickle enough. Add being in fear for her life, and her throat felt as though it had slammed shut.

She breathed in deeply and started to eat.

———

An hour later, the situation was starting to unravel.

The man's attitude of amused superiority had disintegrated, leaving frustration, anger, and a kind of shrill indignation in its place. Pumla and Jamie were still eating, but at a much slower pace. They were both sweating slightly, and so nauseous they could barely hold it together.

"Stop it! Stop it!" he screeched. "You've had enough. Stop eating."

"I always eat when I'm stressed." Jamie shrugged. "I can't help it. It's the only thing that soothes me."

He was sweating profusely now. Wet stains were blooming all over his shirt and drops were running down his face. "It's disgusting. You must stop it. And you!" He turned to Pumla. "You must also stop. Think of the babies."

"I'm eating for three now," Pumla said through a mouthful of doughnut.

"You'll get diabetes. You'll make the babies fat. You have to stop it." He looked down at the gun that was dangling from his hand. The sight of it seemed to put heart into him. "Stop eating, or I'll shoot you. I swear to God I will shoot you."

Jamie stopped eating at once, but Pumla carried on. A flash of headlights against the blinds distracted all three of them. The man hurried over to the window.

"What was that?" he said. "Who's here? There's a car driving into the parking lot! What's happening?" His voice rose in panic as he waved the gun around.

"People often drive into this parking lot to turn around," Jamie said in her most soothing voice. "They use it to make a U-turn, especially at night when it's empty. I'm sure that's all it is."

And indeed, the sound of the engine was already fading. The man stayed where he was at the window, vibrating with nerves.

"He's really rattled," Pumla said softly. "I'm going to keep eating. You're right. It's thrown him completely off balance."

"And I was just thinking that you were right," Jamie whispered back. "He's far too unstable. I think we should stop eating and try to calm him down. And anyway, if I eat another thing, I'm going to throw up."

"You do what you like, but I'm going to keep eating. When he comes over to shout at me, you slip off to the kitchen and try to get your hands on a knife. He keeps turning his back on us. If we'd had a knife before now, we could have killed him half a dozen times."

"No. Pumla, it's too dangerous. You're pregnant. Our only priority is to get out of this alive. Look at him. He's right on the edge. One little push from us and he's going to turn dangerous."

Pumla's mouth was squeezed in a stubborn line. Before Jamie could say another word, the man was back. Sweat was running down his cheeks and dripping from the end of his chin. "You were right, it was just a car turning around."

Pumla launched herself at the petit fours with gusto, popping the rich little cubes into her mouth one after the other. "Oh, man! These are good." She spoke thickly through all the icing and marzipan in her mouth.

"No, no! You mustn't," he clucked. "How can you be so greedy and reckless? I thought you girls were different."

"There's no such thing as different," Pumla said. "We are all animals. We're no different to each other. We all eat and sleep and fart and shit. Nobody's pure. Nobody's special."

"Stop it! Stop it!" He held his hands up to block his ears, the gun swinging towards the ceiling at a crazy angle.

Pumla hiccupped. "Well, it's true."

With an effort, Jamie pulled her eyes away from the gun to look at her partner. "Are you all right?"

Pumla pressed a hand to her mouth and shook her head. She hiccupped again. Then, in one fluid move, she vomited the entire contents of her stomach onto the floor.

The man shrieked and jerked back as some of it splashed his shoes. "You bad girl! Now look what you've done. Oh, you bad, wicked, disgusting girl. Look at the mess you've made. I should kill you for that. I … I…"

As Jamie watched in horror, he raised his gun with shaking hands and pointed it at Pumla. Then he closed his eyes and pulled the trigger.

The noise was shockingly loud in the enclosed space. Jamie had never heard a gun fired in real life before. The sound almost deafened her at the same time as it flooded her muscles with adrenalin. She was on her feet in a second. She saw a splinter of wood fly as the bullet buried itself in a table leg.

He missed, she thought, almost weak with relief. He missed.

Then Pumla dropped to the floor, blood welling from her stomach.

So much blood, Jamie thought as she tore chunks off a roll of kitchen paper. So very much blood. As fast as she pressed the wads of paper onto Pumla's wound, they soaked through with blood and had to be discarded. The first-aid kit lying open next to her contained flimsy dressings more suited to a nicked finger than a bullet wound.

"This is no good," she muttered. "I need something else." Her eyes swivelled around the room and landed on the linen cupboard. She jumped to her feet and rushed to the linen cabinet to gather clean cloths and napkins. The man stood watching her, drinking deeply from a bottle of water he'd taken out of the fridge. His eyes were out of focus.

"Why won't it stop?" Jamie asked, pressing a wadded napkin as hard as she dared onto Pumla's abdomen. "Why won't the bleeding stop? Where is it coming from?"

Pumla's breathing was shallow and laboured. Her face was ashy and her eyes wide. "My back," she gasped. "It's wet. It's so wet."

Jamie tilted Pumla's body and saw crimson gouts of blood coming from a wound in her back. She realised what had happened. The bullet had entered Pumla's side from the front and exited at the back. She was bleeding from two separate places.

Jamie swallowed. "Okay. This is good. Now we know what we're dealing with." She forced a smile. "The good news is, you don't have a bullet in you. It went in at the front and out at the back." Trying to control the violent trembling of her hands, she fashioned another wad out of a napkin and pressed it to the exit wound.

Then she unwound and cut strips of surgical tape from the first-aid kit, and used them to secure the two dressings in place. It took two more napkins, and all the remaining tape, but at last the bleeding was under control.

"There we go." Jamie looked up at Pumla. Any relief she felt disappeared at the sight of her partner. Her colour was dreadful, and her eyelids were drooping. "My babies," she whispered. "My babies."

Jamie hung onto Pumla's hand. "Don't talk. Just breathe. Lie still and breathe."

But Pumla ignored her. "I was so stupid," she said. "So arrogant and stupid. I wanted to be pregnant for the status of it. I wanted to show my mom and my aunts that I could fall pregnant like all the other daughters and nieces. Nothing I ever achieved was good enough. No matter how successful I was, they just weren't interested unless it was baby news."

"I know, I know." Jamie kept one eye on the man. He was sitting at the till now, dangling his gun from one finger, apparently disengaged from them.

"There's nothing special about getting pregnant," Pumla said. "Any idiot can do it. And I showed them. I proved I could do it. But, oh Jamie, it *felt* special. It felt so special when it was me who was pregnant. I felt like the cleverest person in the world."

"Of course you did. And it is special."

"I used to dream about my babies, you know."

Pumla's voice was getting weaker.

"I spent all day dreaming about what a good mom I was going to be. How much I loved them. What a great future they were going to have. And now it's all over." Tears leaked out of the corner of her eyes.

"It's not over," said Jamie, tamping down her panic. "You're alive, and you're going to stay that way."

"Even if I live," Pumla slurred. "Even if he lets us both live, my babies are dying. They're dying inside me right now. Getting shot in the stomach tends to do that to you." The tears flowed faster and faster.

"We don't know that." Jamie wanted to promise Pumla that her babies were fine, but the lie would have choked her.

"Yes, we do. Dumisani will be so sad. He was so excited to be a dad. He's a good man, Jamie. He's a really good man."

"I know he is."

"I was almost done, you know. I was almost done testing him. I was starting to believe he wasn't like those other guys. Those baby-daddies who head for the hills as soon as the babies are born. I was starting to let myself fall in love with him."

"Yes." Jamie had seen it happening. The gradual mellowing of Pumla's scepticism towards Dumisani. The way her eyes lit up when he walked into a room.

Pumla shifted position and gasped with pain. "The first-aid kit..." she wheezed. "Is there a pair of scissors in there?"

Jamie held up the scissors she'd used to cut the surgical tape so that Pumla could see them. They were very sharp and pointed, but the blades were short.

"Stab him with the scissors," Pumla hissed. "Kill him. Kill the bastard."

Jamie thought the scissors would barely inflict a flesh wound, but she nodded. "I will. I will. Don't worry."

"Call him over here." Pumla's voice was weaker than before. "Tell him I want to apologise. Then kill him with the scissors. Do it!" she panted when Jamie hesitated.

"Um ... excuse me?" Jamie raised her voice.

The man's eyes snapped back into focus. "What?"

"Pumla wants to ... to apologise to you. She's very sorry for what she did."

The man stood up. "Well, I should hope so. That was very upsetting indeed. And look at this mess on the floor." He pointed at the blood and vomit staining the floorboards.

"I can clean it up if you like," Jamie suggested. "I mean, I didn't make the mess, but if it's bothering you..."

"It's bothering me very much. Go and fetch a mop and bucket at once. You can see your friend is in no condition to do it. I can't bear an unhygienic environment." He walked over to Pumla and looked down at her. "Now, what do you have to say for yourself?"

Jamie walked to the kitchen to fetch the mop. She located a plastic bucket and half-filled it with water and Handy Andy. Then she looked around. She reached into a cupboard and took out the biggest cast-iron pot Delucia's owned. It weighed over ten kilograms and was notoriously difficult to lift.

She could hear Pumla talking: "I know what I did was wrong, and I'm very sorry. I hope you can forgive me."

"... not that simple..." The man still sounded aggrieved.

"... call an ambulance...?"

"... absolutely not ... only yourself to blame..."

Jamie walked back into the restaurant with a mop in one hand and the cast-iron pot in the other. The man didn't turn around. He was explaining to Pumla that actions had consequences, and that she had to face up to her own choices.

Pumla's eyes flickered towards Jamie for a second. The man started to turn. Pumla gave a loud groan of agony, and he swung back towards her. "Just look at the state of you," he said. "All because of your own folly..."

Jamie gripped the pot by its handles and hefted it into the air. With a sinking heart, she realised she wasn't tall enough to bring it down on his head.

Then she gritted her teeth, swung the pot sideways, and crashed it into the side of his head with all her strength.

30

Jamie sat folded over in the chair with her elbows on her knees and her head in her hands.

The smell of hospital disinfectant stung her nostrils. She felt drunk with tiredness, but her heart was racing and her hands wouldn't stop trembling. She tried to block out the conversations going on around her – the muted sobbing and whispered reassurances – but it wasn't working.

Scenes from that evening ran through her head like a demented film reel.

The man buckling at the knees with a groan and sinking slowly to the floor. Blood seeping through the hair at the base of his skull. Jamie grabbing her cellphone from his pocket and trying to hold her hands steady long enough to dial for an ambulance. Her disbelief when headlights streaked across the windows just minutes later.

The ambulance already? How could it be?

It wasn't.

Opening the door to let Dumisani and Tom in – both of them open-mouthed with shock at the scene of that met their eyes. Dumisani's cry of horror when he saw Pumla. Apparently Tom had phoned Dumisani at eleven when Jamie still hadn't returned home and wasn't answering her phone. Dumisani had been about to get in his car to drive to the restaurant, equally worried about Pumla.

The arrival of the ambulance. The paramedics' insistence on attending to the man, despite Jamie's incoherent demands that they make Pumla their priority. The nightmare ride in the ambulance to the hospital, with Pumla drifting in and out of consciousness, and Dumisani clutching her hand.

Pumla and the man being whisked off to separate theatres the moment they arrived at the ER. Jamie phoning Pumla's mother to let her know that her daughter had been shot and was currently in surgery.

They were all here now – Pumla's mother and aunts. Normally a noisy and cheerful crew of women, they were eerily subdued. Pumla's mother was crying quietly into her hands, and her sisters were consoling her. Dumisani looked like a ghost, his face pale and drawn as he paced up and down the waiting area outside the surgical ward.

Jamie jumped up as she saw Tom approaching. At Dumisani's request, he had gone to see what he could find out.

"Sshh. It's okay. It's okay." He wrapped his arms around her.

"What happened? What did you find out? Is there any news of Pumla?"

Tom raised his voice so Dumisani and Pumla's mother could both hear. "They took a long time to stabilise her, apparently. She'd lost a lot of blood and they needed to transfuse her. The actual surgery only started just over an hour ago."

Dumisani stopped pacing for a moment to grip Tom's forearm hard. "But she's going to make it, right? She's going to be okay?

Tom hesitated, then shook his head. "I don't know. I honestly don't know."

Pumla's mother made a whimpering sound and rocked in her chair. Her sisters moved closer to pat and stroke, murmuring words of encouragement. Dumisani's face lost another shade of colour and he resumed his pacing.

Jamie could hear the prayer in her head start up again on a repeating loop. *Please, God. Please, God. Please, God. Let Pumla live. Let her be okay. I'll never fight with her again as long as I live. Please, God. Please God. Please, God. Just let her be all right. Oh, please God.*

The doors to the surgical ward swung open and a young doctor came out. She was still wearing her green surgical scrubs, with little booties covering her shoes. She walked straight up to Pumla's mother.

"Excuse me. Are you family of Pumla Maseko?"

Pumla's mom turned a tear-stained face up to hers and nodded. "I'm her mother."

Oh, this is not good, Jamie thought. This can't be good. Tom said they only just started operating. They can't possibly have finished already. This is not a good sign.

"Your daughter was very lucky," said the doctor. "The bullet entered a fold of skin at her waist and exited without doing too much damage. There is some trauma to muscles and ligaments, but none of her organs were touched. The main problem was the loss of blood, but she responded well to the transfusion. We've sewn her up as best we can. I have some plastic surgical training, and I did my best. She told me she would come and hunt me down next summer if she can't wear a bikini."

"She's ... she's awake? How can she be awake?" Pumla's mom stared in disbelief.

"We did the surgery under spinal block because of the baby. We can't give pregnant women general anaesthetics, you know."

Dumisani stared at the doctor with a sudden fierce hope in his eyes. "The baby? You mean one of them made it? One of them survived?"

"I'm sorry..." she said. "You are...?"

"The father. I'm the father."

"Then I'm pleased to tell you that she is still pregnant. But sadly one of the babies didn't make it. The smaller twin died some time ago. It doesn't appear to have been injured in any way. It may have died due to the stress and blood loss that Pumla suffered."

"Oh, God!" Tears rushed into Dumisani's eyes, and he turned away to cover his face with his hands.

Pumla's mother peppered the doctor with questions. Would the other baby live? How long would the dead baby have to stay in the womb? Were they boys or girls?

Jamie turned towards Tom and felt his arms come around her.

Oh my word, the food in this hospital is uber kak! What I wouldn't give for a chicken, feta and avo tramezzino from Delucia's right now…

Sizwe Dhlomo You narrowly escape death and you're bitching about the food?? Stop being such a drama queen, my love.

Pumla Maseko Hey, food is important to me. When you run a restaurant you get used to thinking about food.

Jamie Burchell I'm bringing you a wrap from Nando's as we speak. We're a little busy at Delucia's right now cleaning the blood and puke out of the floorboards with industrial strength detergents.

Pumla Maseko Does that mean you haven't been arrested, Jemima? When I phoned earlier, Tom said you were in your fourth hour of talking to the cops.

Jamie Burchell True story. I feel like my life has turned into an episode of *CSI Miami*. If the guy who tried to kill us ends up dying, I could be facing a murder charge.

Nonna Mzambo You have GOT to be kidding me. He shoots Pumla, threatens to kill both of you, holds you hostage for five hours, and YOU'RE the one facing a murder charge?

Jamie Burchell The Director of Public Prosecutions will probably decide not to prosecute, but obviously there has to be a thorough investigation. Anyway, he might not die. The last I heard they were picking bits of skull out of his brain from where I hit him.

Pumla Maseko As far as I'm concerned, he's a murderer. My baby would be alive right now if it weren't for him.

Sizwe Dhlomo ((((((hugs))))))) Pumla. Who is the guy? Does anyone know yet?

Jamie Burchell They're getting close to finding out. They found his car parked a couple of streets away from Delucia's, but it was unregistered. There was a cellphone in it, though, so they think they can trace him from that.

Pumla Maseko Blah, blah, blah. Get off Facebook and bring me my wrap.

Jamie Burchell Yes, ma'am. :P

FROM JAMIE BURCHELL'S EMAIL INBOX:

FROM: Amanda@bantamhouse.co.za
TO: Jamie Burchell
SUBJECT: Offer to Publish

Dear Jamie,

We've been following your blog for some time now and would very much like to make you an offer to publish a book based on your experience of being stalked, and culminating in the dramatic events of this week.

Please find an offer to publish attached. I believe you won't find it ungenerous. We offer a substantial advance as well as royalties.

We at Bantam House are very excited about working with you on this project. We believe that this book could be a real hit if properly marketed.

The offer of publication is valid for seven days from today. I hope to hear from you as soon as possible.

Kind regards,
Amanda Wheetling
Deputy Editor
Bantam House Books

FROM: editor@CapeBooks
TO: Jamie Burchell
SUBJECT: Your story

Dear Ms Burchell,

I see from your website that you are an aspirant writer. How would you feel about turning your recent stalking experience into a book?

We at Cape Books held an editors' meeting this morning and agreed that the story of your experience would do very well in book form. It has certainly captured the media's attention over the last few days. We believe there would be a strong market for a book.

If you don't feel confident about turning your experiences into a book, we can supply you with a good, and very discreet, ghost writer. Please see the offer to publish attached to this email.

Looking forward to hearing from you soon!

Warmest regards
Michael Epstein
Editor-in-chief
Cape Books

. . . .

FROM THE TWINLESS TWINS FORUM HOSTED BY MOMS IN NEED:
. . . .

From coping with Vanishing Twin syndrome to planning a funeral after a stillbirth, we will be with you every step of the way. This is a safe space for parents of twinless twins. No one will tell you to "get over it" or "just be grateful" for your one surviving child. This is a forum for you to vent, cry, grieve, ask questions, and be comforted even as you comfort others.

Welcome to Twinless Twins. Get comfortable and stay for as long as you need.

Poster #69384 Hi, everyone. My name is Pumla. I'm new here. My girl twin died in the womb at 5 months when I was attacked at my place of work. Her brother is still alive and the doctors say there's a good chance they can keep him that way until it is safe for him to be delivered. My boyfriend and I are really struggling with this and I feel like there's no one who understands what we are going through.

Admin Nikki: Hi Pumla and welcome…

Tom woke up from the nightmare gasping.

He lay still for a moment, listening to the silence over the pounding of his own heart. The echoes of Ben's crying in the dream still rang in his ears, and he strained to hear real cries, confused for a moment between dream and reality. But the light from the baby monitor glowed steadily. It really had just been a dream.

Tom stared at the ceiling, afraid to close his eyes and plunge straight back into the nightmare. Ben had been crying and crying for Jamie, his wails becoming more desperate and choked with sobs. Jamie was trying to get to Ben, but the stalker was holding her back. He was clutching her around the waist as she desperately tried to fight him off.

Jamie's arms were outstretched, every ounce of her being focused on getting away from the stalker and reaching Ben. Tom could feel the arms holding her around the waist as though it were his own waist, and his own frustration. It was getting darker and darker. Ben's cries were sounding further away but also somehow louder and more desperate.

The arms of the stalker tightened like snakes around Jamie until she couldn't move at all. She started hitting at his arms, begging him to release her so she could go to Ben.

Then suddenly it wasn't the stalker holding Jamie at all, but Tom.

He was the one stopping her from reaching Ben. The struggle of Jamie in his arms and the cries of his son were the last things he registered before he woke up.

Tom stood up and went to get a drink of water from the bathroom. If he didn't wake up properly, he would just fall straight back into the dream. Back in the bedroom, he looked down at the sleeping form of Jamie in his bed. He was no psychologist, but he knew when his subconscious was trying to tell him something. That dream had been anything but subtle.

It wasn't as though he hadn't been coming around to the same conclusion himself.

Now he needed to make sure that Jamie was on the same page. He sat down on the bed and shook her.

"Jamie! Jamie, wake up!"

"Whassrong?" She woke up immediately, if a little blearily. "Oh, right." She rubbed her eyes. "Time for me to go, huh?"

"No, no. You don't have to go. I don't want you to go."

"Hokay," she sighed, and sank back down under the duvet.

"Jamie, wake up. Seriously. I want to talk to you."

"Can't it wait until morning?"

"No, it can't. It needs to be now."

She sat up, yawning and stretching, and propped herself up against the pillows, glancing sideways at him in the dim light. Something about the look on his face had her coming fully awake.

"Uh oh. Something's wrong, isn't it? You'd better not be dumping me at..." she reached across to check her phone, "2am. That's something that could definitely have waited till morning."

The serious look was banished with a grin. "I'm not dumping you. I want what we have, Jamie. I want it for me and I want it for Ben. I've done everything I could to build a wall around us to keep you from getting too close, and I've failed. I don't want to do it anymore. Ben loves you and I love you. I'm ready to believe that you love us too. I want us to be a family, Jamie. I want to give Ben siblings, if that's what you want. I know life doesn't come with guarantees, but I'm

ready to take that leap with you. It feels right. And I need to know –
are you ready to jump with me?"

For a moment, shock kept Jamie silent. Her sleepy brain struggled
to process what he was saying. Then she reached her arms out to
Tom. Her big, American neighbour. Hot Running Guy. Father of the
toddler she adored. Her love.

"I am," she whispered into his neck. "I'm ready to jump with you."

The baby monitor shimmered into life as Ben began to cry in
sleepy, cross little wails. Jamie felt Tom's body stiffen and his head
come up. She stroked his back.

"Let me go," she said. "Let me go to him. This is something we
can share."

So Tom lay back in bed as Jamie went next door to scoop Ben out
of bed and cuddle him. The wails stopped at once. And a sense of
deep peace spread through Tom.

Epilogue

Waking up was like struggling out of a very deep well.

He'd lifted himself out of that well before, but never quite so completely. Where before there had been flashes of light and the murmur of voices, he could now form a clear impression of where he was. He was lying on a bed. Something was beeping next to him.

A hospital. He was in a hospital.

Was he hurt? Why couldn't he remember? He tried to move his head, but something was holding it still. The effort caused pain to shoot up to his left temple and down into his neck. It was better to lie still.

What about his hands? Yes, he could move them. He could flex his fingers. So why did his feet feel as if they didn't belong to him, as if they weren't really there? On a surge of panic, he tilted his head up. Then he let out a long breath when he saw the peaks of his feet tenting the hospital blanket.

There was a rustling noise, and he swivelled his eyes to the left. A policewoman in uniform sat in the chair next to his bed. He had a feeling they'd talked before, although he couldn't remember what she'd said.

She gave him a cold stare. "You're awake again."

"Yes." He attempted a smile. "Properly this time, I think. What happened to me?"

"Indriven skull fracture. You'll need therapy to get well."

"Oh."

"Well enough to stand trial for attempted murder." She nodded with satisfaction.

He turned his eyes to the ceiling again, trying to make sense of this. Why couldn't he think? Why couldn't he remember? As he clawed his scattered thoughts together, one name floated out of the chaos.

Jamie.

Jamie of the dark eyes and fair hair and long body. Yes, of course.

He had been following Jamie. He needed to get well again in order to keep following her. Whatever they did to him – wherever they put him – he would keep on following her.

Jamie would never be out of his reach. The only way she could escape would be to go offline. And she would never go offline. Not Jamie. She was a digital creature. She needed the cyber world like other women needed food and water. As long as she continued to inhabit virtual space, he would be waiting for her.

Like a spider for a fly.

Printed in the United States
By Bookmasters